WHEN STARS FALL

A HOLLYWOOD ROMANCE

WENDY MILLION

STOMILL BOOKS

Copyright © 2021 by Wendy Million

All rights reserved.

No portion of this book may be reproduced in any form without written permission from the publisher or author, except as permitted by U.S. copyright law.

This book is a work of fiction. The names, characters, and establishments are the product of the author's imagination or are used to provide authenticity and are used fictitiously. Any resemblance to any person, living or dead, is purely coincidental.

First published by Wattpad Books in eBook format: September 2021.

Paperback cover design: Najla Qamber Designs

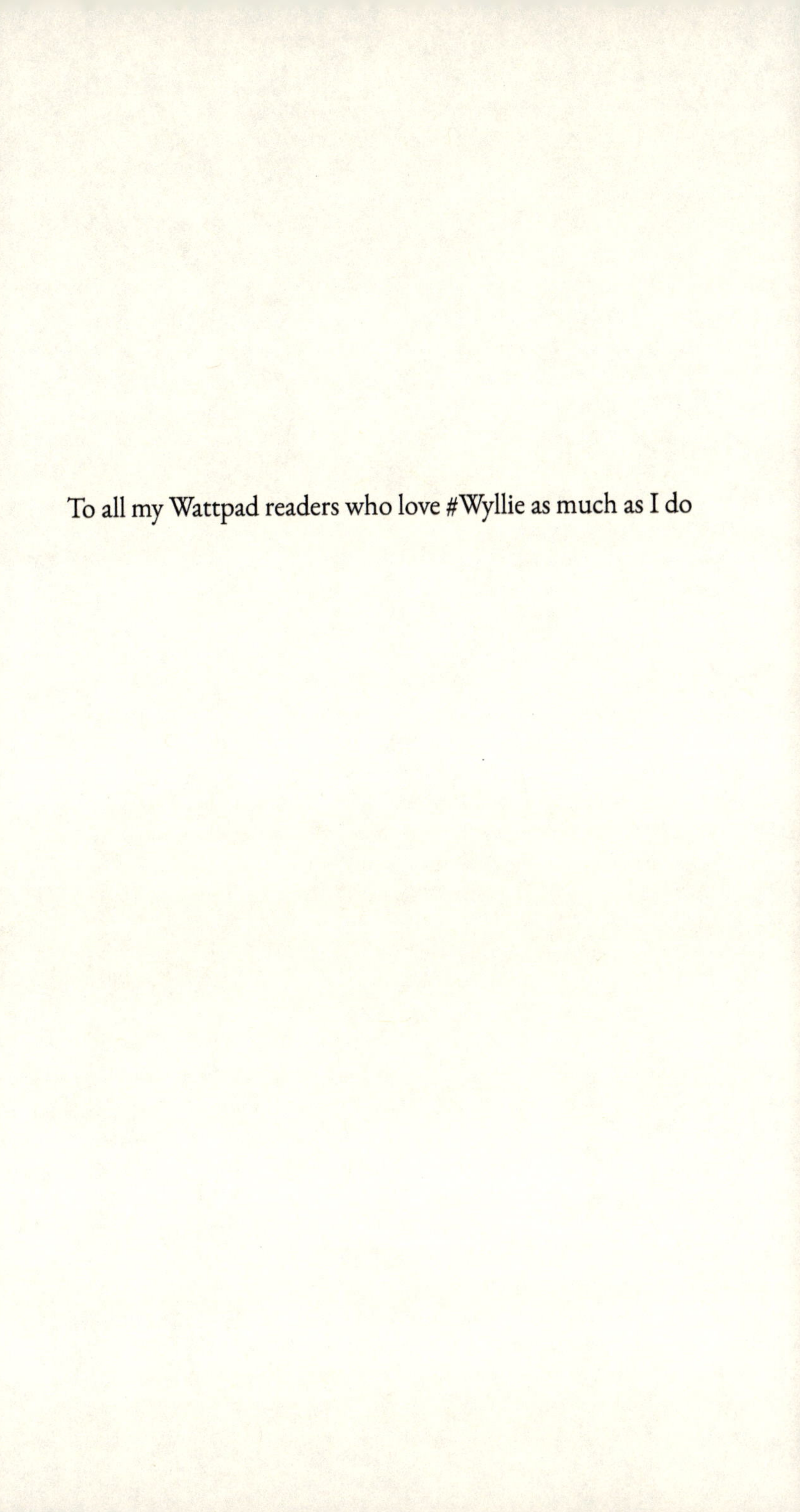

To all my Wattpad readers who love #Wyllie as much as I do

CONTENTS

WYATT

TEN YEARS AGO

As soon as the Rolls-Royce pulls into the driveway, I'm out the door of the rambling brick bungalow we share in Bel Air. I haven't seen her in weeks—since I was on location in Shanghai, and she flew home to visit her family.

Before Kyle can get to her door, I take Ellie's hand to draw her out of the back seat. "How'd your visit go?" I cradle her cheeks in my hands, scanning every peak and valley of her face. Something is off. She's hollowed out.

"Fine. Just tired." A weak smile rises, and she closes her eyes briefly.

"Grab her bags, will you, Kyle?" I sweep her up in my arms and carry her through the foyer into the huge open-concept living space. She could walk inside herself, but after so long without her, I'll seize any excuse to hold her close.

"Sure thing, sir," Kyle says.

"Have you eaten? I can make you something." She's lost weight, and she doesn't have a pound to spare. "Did some tabloid say something shitty about you again?"

"No, nothing like that."

When we get to the couch, I set her down. "Talk to me." I sit beside her and then shift to get a better vantage point. "Do you want a Perc to take the edge off?"

"I don't want anything." She twists her hands in her lap, a sure sign she's nervous. If she starts playing with her hair, there's definitely something wrong.

"What's going on?" I ask.

She doesn't say anything for a beat. "I've been thinking a lot lately. About us. Our relationship. About where we're headed."

There's a ring sitting in my underwear drawer. I dragged Isaac with me to choose one a week before he died. I haven't been able to face the diamond since, but I understand what I want.

She leaves the couch and goes over to where Kyle dropped her bags. From a side pocket, she takes out some pamphlets.

Maybe she discovered the ring and spent the week looking at wedding venues in Bermuda. She wouldn't want the chaos an LA wedding would bring. Wherever she wants to get married is fine by me. There's no need for her to be nervous. Not like I'll be mad about any of it.

"What's this?" I try to stifle my amusement.

She tries to pass me the pamphlets and flyers. My brain stalls, and it takes a moment for me to process the bold headlines claiming effective treatment for addictions. A chill streaks across my body. This has nothing to do with weddings and nothing to do with our future. I remove the bottle from my pocket and shake out a Vicodin, then throw it back. I'm not addressing what's written in these things. She's going to have to say it. I set the bottle on the coffee table between us.

After a deep breath, she says, "I think—I think if we want to have a future together, we should be doing that clean and sober."

"This is bullshit." I grab the pamphlets and toss them onto the table and they scatter everywhere. Some of them fall to the floor at her feet. My chest is tight with disbelief. She knows better than anyone what she's asking.

She tucks her hair behind her ears. *Shit, her hair.* She doesn't say anything.

An uncontrollable rage rises in me. "What the hell happened to you on that damned island? We've been together for three, almost four, years and you've *never* asked me to quit. You've never said my using was a problem. In fact, Ellie, you do it with me."

"I haven't touched anything since Isaac died."

"You're a liar. We've gone out lots of times." Even as I say those words, I can't remember the last time she accepted a pill or took a drink or did a line of coke. My younger sister, Anna, started calling Ellie a No-Fun Nellie. "Nah, I don't believe you. I would've noticed." She must be lying, otherwise my intake has been much higher than I realized.

She points at a pamphlet on the table. "My mother says this one is very good. The best."

"You think I don't know about rehab programs?" I scoff. "You think I don't have friends who've tried it? Rehab doesn't work. It won't work. I'm not going."

"We're getting older. Maybe we should be considering a family." She rubs her face. "Kids, possibly, someday . . . maybe."

She can't even make eye contact when she says that. She's not serious. Wherever these notions are coming from, she needs to send them packing back to Bermuda. A week ago, she and I were just fine, and now she's returned with a truckload of bullshit ideas.

"No, Ellie. No. You're twenty-four, not forty-four. Don't play the kids card. What the fuck do kids have to do with anything?"

She stares at me, indecision on her face, and then her expression cements into a stubborn mask. "You're out of control."

I take the pills off the table and shove an oxy in my mouth, this time to dull the memory of this conversation, which will hang over us like a cloud. Tomorrow, I won't want to remember she even suggested this. "The only person who gets to decide that is me."

"I want you to quit." She crosses her arms. "Deal with Isaac's death, deal with your parents being terrible. Whatever underlying issues make you want to do this, be like this."

"You knew who I was when you went home with me that first night. I've never lied to you," I say with a harsh half laugh.

"You haven't, but I'm asking you to be better. To want more for yourself—for us."

"Now that you've fucked your way into better jobs and higher paychecks, you think you can dictate some terms?" I shove the coffee table out of the way, and the metal legs shriek against the stone floor. "Come on, Ellie. Where would you be without me? Still pretty far down the call list." The second pill was a mistake. Words are tumbling out of my mouth and I can't stop them. Her tears fall faster than she can brush them away. "Sure, Ellie. Sure. Bust out the tears. They won't work. I'm not going to rehab; I'm not quitting any of it. We were fine until you went home to Bermuda. Who's been pumping you full of this shit? Your mom? Your sister, Nikki? One of your old high school buddies who saw something on TMZ?"

"*I* want you to go to rehab." Her voice is thick, garbled.

"You're the only one." I throw out my arms. It's incomprehensible that she'd ask this of me.

"I'm not." She shakes her head. "I'm not the only one."

"Your family doesn't count." Her mother has never liked me. Maybe her sister doesn't like me now either. Someone has been feeding her these lines. My Ellie is full of softness and understanding. She doesn't give ultimatums.

"Producers, directors, people who know you have been asking me to do something. To intervene. You're not coping."

A surge of anger courses through me, but not at her—at the people who put her in this position. "They have no idea what they're talking about."

"You'll lose jobs. People won't want to work with you anymore."

"Bullshit. I make people money. I've made you a lot of money over the last four years. Being tied to me is the best thing that ever happened to you."

"It could be," she says. "If you'll get help. You could be the best thing to ever happen to me."

"I don't need help, Ellie. I'm fine. *We're* fine. Screw the rest of them who don't understand."

"*I'm* one of those people. Me. I don't understand anymore either. You need help. I can't—I'm not capable of giving you the help you need."

My mind is muddled. She doesn't ask me to do impossible things. She'd never ask me to choose. We had a pact. "Who put you up to this?"

She takes a deep, shuddering breath. "No one. It's coming from my concern for you. I love you."

"I was clear from the start. If there's a choice, the choice is easy." If she loved me, she wouldn't be asking me to do this.

"Still? After we've been together almost four years?" Her voice catches on a sob.

My resolve wavers. I always let her win. She's not winning this one. Once she cools down, she'll realize I'm right. There's nothing wrong with us. "I told you never to ask."

She snatches a pamphlet off the floor, thrusting it at me again. "Try one of them. Any of them. Just go. Even for a little while. Doesn't matter which one. If you won't get help, I can't stay. I won't watch you spiral." Her rambling pleas are almost incoherent through her tears.

"There are plenty of others who will." I grab the pill bottle off the coffee table. "I'm going out. You have two choices. You can stay and accept that this is who I am, or be moved out by the morning. I'm not going to rehab, and we're *never* having this conversation again."

"Wyatt!" My name is a frantic call as she chases after me to the front entrance. "Wyatt. Stay. Please. We need to talk about this."

"We're done talking. If my not being clean and sober is suddenly a deal breaker for you, then we're broken. I'm serious. Forget about rehab or move out."

"You don't mean that." Her face is already puffy from crying. She's crying so hard I barely understand her words.

"I do. I really do." Before I can reconsider, I slam the door behind me.

She won't leave. Even if she wanted to, packing up and being gone in the next twenty-four hours is impossible. Our lives are too intertwined. Tomorrow, when I come back, we'll pretend like this conversation never happened. Maybe we'll even laugh about it. Ellie loves me. I know she does.

When I climb into the back of the car, my pills press against my leg through my pocket. I take out the bottle, pop off the lid, and stare into the container. Shaking out an Adderall, I throw it into my mouth. A little something to take the edge off, make me completely forget this conversation so I'm not so pissed at her tomorrow.

"Where to, sir?" Kyle asks from the front.

"Drive around for a while and then to a hotel. Doesn't matter which one."

Kyle glances at me in the rearview mirror. "Everything okay, sir?"

"It'll be fine." I glance out the window as we drive onto the street. "Ellie needs a little space."

WYATT

PRESENT DAY

I'm sweating. Profusely. It's disgusting. I tug at the collar of my freshly pressed shirt and loosen my tie. I'll tighten it before I go on set.

Leaning forward on the couch, I grab my water from the coffee table. Bottles of alcohol line the bar to the right. A sign encourages everyone to help themselves. There is nothing worse than wanting a drink, being surrounded by alcohol, and not being able to have any. I need to be sober for this interview. Ellie will see it.

I grab some candy off the table and pop it into my mouth, chewing slowly. The greenroom is a weird shade of lime. Whenever I'm in a green waiting area, I'm always disappointed. We're in a creative business—lime isn't creative; it's just hard on my eyes. Jackson Billows, the host of the late-night program, probably thinks the color is hilarious.

I wiggle my back along the too-stiff couch. Maybe I've been doing this whole scene too long. Few things in the entertainment business surprise me anymore. Of course, having this big a stage, a platform for my announcement, is helpful. Surprises may be few and far between for me personally, but I can still deliver a couple.

"You're on in five, Mr. Burgess." A dark-haired man pops his head into the room.

I nod. Say nothing. Check my phone again. The few people who understand my plan are reluctantly on board. A last-minute *Break a leg* text rolls in. I turn off my ringer, readjust my tie and collar. My suit jacket is stifling, but she used to like me suited and booted. Every advantage is necessary. I'm about to blow up her life.

For ten years, Ellie has been coordinating her projects and schedule to avoid me. We've developed an unspoken agreement to keep each other and Isaac, my best friend, out of the press. The weight of his death has remained ours to carry.

Jackson enters from the hidden side door. "You all right, buddy?" He perches on a chair across from me.

"Sweating like a pig."

"It's been ten years, man. This will be great television, don't get me wrong, but Ellie is going to eat your nuts for breakfast tomorrow."

"I picked you for a reason, Jack. Don't let me down." I drain the rest of my water and wish the liquid was something much stronger.

"We could have booked you both on the show. Left you here in the greenroom to sort out your issues in private." Jackson stands.

"She'd have canceled. Whenever she's gotten wind I'm in the area, her cavalry rides to the rescue. I even flew to Bermuda and not one person—not one," I say, holding up a finger, "would tell me where she lived."

"What makes you think she's going to take any notice of you this time?" he asks.

"She'll have no choice." Certainty washes over me, and I point to my phone. "Finally got her address. I'm headed to the airport as soon as we're done."

"Ten years and you're just going to show up on her doorstep? Do you need the public spectacle first?"

He has a point, but if I go without the spectacle, she'll slam the door in my face. "I'm trying to make it impossible for her to say no."

"I hope that doesn't make it hard for her to say yes later." Jack arches his eyebrows.

Truthfully, I haven't thought that far in advance. All I've done is organize Operation Get Her to Talk to Me. The rest will fall into place. A long time ago, I was her kryptonite. God knows she's always been mine.

The doors split as we walk toward the set. Jack heads to the stage and I stand in the wings, waiting to make my entrance.

By midnight tonight, she'll realize I'm done with our unspoken truce.

I'm coming for you, Ellie.

Jackson gives his rambling introduction, then I strut onto the set. The crowd goes wild, and I drop into my seat. I adjust my jacket and wave to the audience as the screams die down.

Jackson's right about one thing: Ellie will not take this well.

ELLIE
Present Day

My Google Alerts tell me Wyatt's on *The Jackson Billows Show* to promote his latest movie. Every time I try to convince myself it's normal to have an alert on for my former boyfriend from ten years ago, I realize I sound crazy. I avoid analyzing it. I don't follow him on social media, so the notifications are it. #Wyllie will never make a return.

While I fold laundry, I flip to the right station and dial my sister. She'll still be awake. As a real estate agent, she keeps the weirdest hours of anyone I know.

Nikki doesn't say hello like a normal person; instead, she says, "I hope you had a good flight. You're not watching *The Jackson Billows Show*. Please tell me you've turned off the TV."

"My flight was fine," I say. "It's idle curiosity." I tuck the phone between my ear and neck. Calling her was a bad idea.

"You call it curiosity, I call it obsession." Nikki's voice is tight with disapproval.

"Tomayto, tomahto. How's Haven?"

"She's sleeping. All okay. Want me to drop her off after school tomorrow?"

"Do you mind?" I finish the last piece of folding. Wyatt struts onto the stage, and I realize my screen needs to be bigger. So much bigger. "Oh," I breathe.

"I'll let you go." Nikki sighs.

Without comment, I hang up and circle the couch to get comfortable. In these moments, when I'm transfixed and hungry for the sight of him, a little voice in my head tells me something isn't quite right. Ten years and just a glimpse of him on a television is enough to scrape off the scab, leaving behind raw, tender skin. His effect on me is a burn that won't heal.

Since I left Wyatt ten years ago, acting is a job now, not a lifestyle. I've built a better, more stable life without him, and seeing him shouldn't cause nostalgia for what once was. We were bad for each other—or maybe he was bad for me . . . but in any event, we didn't work, couldn't work.

He takes his seat and I smother the urge to lean forward. I don't see his movies—I'm not interested in pretend-Wyatt—but I can *never* resist his interviews. If I still did drugs, he'd be crack.

They banter about Wyatt's race-car movie. When Wyatt turns on the charm, he is breathtaking. Jackson shuffles the cue cards on his desk after the brief movie clip plays. A nervous habit. I've been a guest on his show enough times to recognize the pattern. I narrow my eyes. He and Wyatt are genuine friends, so his nerves make no sense.

Wyatt appears sober, which is a delightful change. Sober Wyatt wasn't someone I saw very often, but he'd spent years balancing his moods with drugs before we met. Another ten years since to hone his skills to *appear* sober.

His suit fits him like a glove, and seeing him so together stirs long-buried desires. My eyes travel the length of his body, taking in his dark hair, broad shoulders, and narrow hips. When he gestures to Jackson, his biceps flex under the suit coat. He looks good—too good.

No. No. No. If I saw him in person, I'd run the other way. I've been turning away with military precision for ten years. Sober, witty Wyatt in a nice suit can't change the past, the choices we made.

Jackson squares his shoulders and grins. Wyatt tugs at the neck of his shirt. It's brief, but noticeable. I sit forward. Another nervous habit. There's a vibe between them that I've never seen before.

"Are you single right now?" Jackson's inquiry is a softball. "Anyone special in your life?"

The crowd goes wild, and I cringe. I hate that question—for him, for me.

"You know," Wyatt says, "I've been thinking a lot about old flames still flickering." He winks at the camera.

Jackson laughs. "Old flames. Give us a hint?"

Wyatt opens his jacket and leans against the couch, throwing an arm over the back. Confidence blasts from him like a siren's call. My ship longs to steer toward him.

"Have you got a photo, Jackson? Help a guy out?"

Jackson rotates in his chair and a familiar photograph of the two of us pops up behind him.

There's an explosion in the crowd. My heart threatens to gallop away.

What is he doing?

My phone on the coffee table jumps to life. Nikki's name flashes across the screen. I send her to voice mail. My attention sticks to the screen. When my phone buzzes again, I don't check who it is. I send them to voice mail. Bile rises in my throat, and I swallow it.

Shit. This can't be happening.

The crowd is alive with wolf whistles, catcalls, and screaming. An album of old photos of me and Wyatt flips across the screen.

The memories. Oh, my heart. The memories.

"Ellie Cooper." Wyatt draws out my name like he's licking an ice-cream cone, and his attention is glued to the last photo of us.

Ten years since I've heard my name leave his lips. The genuine animation in him, the love on his face when he stares at the picture, softens me, even as rage builds deep in my gut. He loved me so hard once.

"Have you and Ellie been in touch?" Jackson asks.

I will tear Jackson apart for agreeing to be part of this ridiculous spectacle. He'll never have me on his show again. He's dead to me. I'm half tempted to call my manager right now, but that would mean missing where this is going. Wyatt must realize the storm he's setting off. People still label us #couplegoals. The stories I could tell them . . .

"I'm hoping to be reacquainted with her soon." Wyatt laughs. "Anyone know how I can get in touch with her?" His hopeful bewilderment plays to the crowd. His brazenness is achingly familiar. He wasn't the only one who loved hard.

"Wyllie was huge when you two were together. I think people even wore T-shirts picking sides when you split. But in the ten years since, neither of you have spoken publicly about what happened."

"Ellie's a classy woman." He holds up a finger. "The best woman. I mean . . ." His expression softens. "That face." He points to another, more recent photo that's appeared behind Jackson. "Brains, beauty, the biggest heart. Our breakup was my fault—completely my fault. I couldn't give up the drugs." He takes a deep breath. "I didn't want to get off them."

"And where are you at now?"

Wyatt or his people approved these questions. Unbelievable. We've never spoken about each other. You ask, you're blacklisted from interviewing me. I assumed Wyatt had the same rule since he's never talked about me either. Our relationship is a void stuffed with public opinion and speculation.

A constant stream of buzzing comes from my phone as calls, texts, and social media notifications flood in. If I ever see Wyatt again, it'll be too soon. I'm ghosting the jackass harder than I've been the last ten years. It might not be possible to intensify our distance any more, considering we haven't shared a room since I left our house, but he's not getting anywhere near me now.

"I've been drug-free for two years now. I'd never tell anyone sobriety is easy, but I'm ready to put the past behind me."

Sure, Wyatt. All talk. He might be sober at *this* moment, but sober for two years? Impossible. His morning routine consisted of popping Vicodin, oxycodone, Percocet, or Adderall and drinking a coffee, often chased with a few shots of Jim Beam or a couple of beers. Lean smoothies of codeine, hard candy, and soda were a favorite snack.

Wyatt, even when he looked sober, was never without something in his system. His supply was endless and his taste eclectic.

His addictions weren't to be questioned or analyzed, just accepted. One taste. A little buzz to take the edge off. A sharpness that needed to be constantly dulled. For him to be on national television talking about his habits, he must be high.

"I'm sure people battling their demons find a lot of hope in your words." Jackson turns to the audience. "What would it be now? Ten years ago that Isaac Sharma died from an overdose while you and Ellie were with him?"

He's letting Jackson bring up Isaac's death? Talk about a shot to the heart.

"Yeah." Wyatt stares at his hands. "Almost eleven."

There's a deep sadness in Wyatt's voice. Whatever else is going on in this interview, the rawness of his loss remains the same.

"We all expected Isaac's death to be enough motivation for you to get sober."

"It should have been." Wyatt tips his head.

Sometimes I hate myself for watching these interviews. Hearing him talk about Isaac and about me will cause me to spiral into uncertainty for weeks. His movie must be turning into quite a lemon in postproduction if the studio convinced him to get on Jackson's show and talk about the more salacious bits of his life.

"Remind me again where you and Ellie met?" Jackson stares at Wyatt. He knows. Everyone knows. We had the biggest movie in the world the year it came out.

"On the set of *Love Letters from Spain*," Wyatt says. "There was something about Ellie. Right from the start." His eyes bore into the camera, coming through the screen, threatening to burrow into my soul. "I was a fool to let her go, but I'm not a fool anymore."

In a panic, I turn off the TV and stare at the blank screen. Then I flick it back on.

The crowd quiets, and Jackson laughs. "You're going to reignite #Wyllie fans."

He did *not* do that. Another great rush of humming comes from my phone, but I refuse to acknowledge the notifications. People can think what they want. I answer to no one. Besides, I'll have levitated off Bermuda and be landing in New York to commit Jackson's murder soon.

"Maybe they deserve to be reignited." A cocky, playful smile bursts onto his face.

This time when I switch off the TV, I do it with finality. We wouldn't have needed to be reignited if the jackass chose me instead of an 8 ball.

Emotions dash through me, hard to identify. Anger, for sure. Fear. But under those is one I don't want to consider because it feels a lot like hope. What could I hope for? He's lying. Wyatt lies. He's not sober. Drugs have been part of his life for as long as he can remember. His constant companions were his prescription pill bottle stuffed with whatever he could get his hands on and a water bottle of codeine, soda, and hard candy mixed together. Lean was his drink of choice.

One of the first memories he told me about was sitting beside his dad and being offered a glass of lean. Those first sips tipped Wyatt and his younger sister, Anna, into a spiral of addiction. Neither of them ever had any desire to climb out. They blamed their parents for their troubles, and I never doubted they were a huge factor in Wyatt and Anna's issues. According to Wyatt, his parents were always desperate for their next fix, and they didn't mind who paid for it or what it cost. But any suggestion of Wyatt or Anna seeking help was met with resistance. They were content to wallow in their dysfunctions. To think Wyatt ditched it all two years ago is impossible for me.

I pray my manager is mobilizing my PR staff, otherwise this stunt could spin out of control. It took years for the swirl surrounding our breakup to die enough for me to be able to spend time in Los Angeles. Any trips there were carefully coordinated to avoid paparazzi. Those damn team T-shirts were everywhere, breaking my heart, mocking my choice.

In a daze, I wander the narrow hall to my bedroom at the rear of my home. Although I can afford a lavish house, I have a small three-bedroom bungalow on an oceanfront lot. Nothing fancy, but it suits my needs. When I have to, I put on the glitz and glamor, but for the most part, I'm hidden away here in Hamilton, Bermuda. The frantic pace of Los Angeles is kept at bay by careful scheduling and an adherence to privacy above all else. The Hollywood pomp and circumstance were never for me; just the right place and people. Wyatt never understood that.

My security intercom buzzes, and I answer the nearest receiver. "Headed to bed, Freddie. What's up?"

"Uh, Ellie, there's a man here who wants to see you."

"It's late. I have jet lag. No one who knows me would come this late."

I've made sure my house is hard to find. Entrances and exits are concealed by overgrown bushes and shrubs. The property is gated and not listed on any documents that are easy to access. Cab drivers and sightseeing tours get a hefty donation at the end of their high season if they haven't used my name or property to advertise their businesses. Extreme privacy has been my companion since I left Wyatt and Los Angeles behind.

"It's Mr. Wyatt Burgess, and he says he isn't leaving until you agree to speak to him."

Ice freezes in my veins and then fire chases it out. Turns out I don't need to levitate off the island to commit murder tonight. "Oh, Freddie. I have a thing or two to say to Mr. Burgess. You can deliver him to the door."

"Yes, ma'am." A grin is evident in his voice. He must have watched *The Jackson Billows Show* too. With the show taped in the late morning, Wyatt had lots of opportunities to hop on a two-hour flight here. Never occurred to me he would.

I check my appearance in the kitchen mirror and then scold myself. I'll open the door only to tell him to go to hell. Using national television to declare his undying love after ten years and a series of bad choices and then expecting me to take him back?! I don't think so. Not happening.

At the side entrance where expected guests are delivered, I swing the door wide.

Immediately, I realize my mistake. He's taller than I remembered, which seems ridiculous. That's not all, though. His dark hair is a little darker, and his blue-green eyes more electric. Without the barrier of the screen, everything jumps at me at once.

My heart does one loud, crushing thump and falls to pieces.

Ten years, gone in a heartbeat.

ELLIE

THIRTEEN YEARS AGO

The *rat-a-tat-tat* on my trailer door stops me in my tracks, and I grin. Isaac knocks the same way every time. It's late, but filming just wrapped for the day. Isaac must have been in one of the final shots.

"Come in." No matter the time, I'd answer for him. I drop my phone into my purse and check the rest of the trailer for anything I'll need overnight.

When Isaac enters, he shoves his hands into his pockets. His grin splits his face. "Hey, Ellie. We're heading out to Club Cobra tonight. You in?" His almost-too-white teeth glow next to his brown skin.

One of the most notorious clubs in LA. I've never been, but if the tabloids can be believed, anyone who's even remotely famous parties there. From the studio, it'll take at least an hour to get to it. LA traffic is horrendous. "What's your call time tomorrow?"

"Six."

"At night?" I throw the last couple of things in my bag. A late night is a bad idea for me; I'm on set at eight in the morning.

"Nope. In the morning. You in, Short Stuff, or what?"

He was a child star and can ride on his name recognition. Isaac Sharma is beautiful and rich, and he has a wicked sense of humor. Everyone loves him.

This movie is my big break. Screwing up isn't an option. I bite the tip of a manicured nail.

"You're twenty-one, not sixty-one. Come out. I'll cover your ass if we're tired."

We're only two weeks into filming, and I've heard enough about my costars to realize there's a good chance they won't sleep tonight.

"Last week in Cali before we leave for Spain. Live a little," he says.

"Oh, fine." With a small shake of my head, I loop my arm through his and vow to keep my wits. Should be easy enough. In the two weeks that I've known Isaac, we've become good friends, and he won't lead me astray.

As we wander to where he requested a limo meet us, he maintains a running stream of inappropriate but hilarious jokes. Up ahead, a gaggle of models, extras, and crew stand at the edge of the lot.

"Where's everyone going?" I whisper into Isaac's ear.

"Oh, Ellie. We're going out. We're gonna make it rain money." He throws his hands up flamboyantly. I suspect he's already high on something.

The money from this movie pays my rent until I get another job. There is no guarantee for me that there will *be* another film role. I slow my pace beside him.

"Isaac!" Wyatt jogs up behind us, emerging from the darkness and into the streetlights like a myth come to life. "Man, I thought you were going to leave without me." He slaps Isaac on the shoulder.

"Would have, but I had to convince Ellie." Isaac steps to the side so Wyatt's view of me is clear.

Was I hiding from him? I think I was hiding. Heat fills my cheeks, and I let my long blond-brown hair swing forward to partially conceal my face. On a film set I can hold my own, but when the mask of a character is removed, I'm tongue-tied.

"Ellie Cooper is finally coming out?" Wyatt sweeps me into a giant hug.

My heart thuds at the warmth of his embrace. If Isaac is beautiful and classy, Wyatt is dark and dangerous. He's a storm thundering off over the ocean. Everything about him makes me anxious when we aren't acting together. He's too unpredictable when someone isn't directing him.

My laugh sounds nervous to my ears, and I ease away from him, shifting my purse higher on my arm. He was making me sound like a prude. *Finally coming out?*

Wyatt deftly rolls a joint, the paper crinkling in the surrounding stillness. He lights it, takes a deep drag, and then passes it to me. Without hesitating, I accept it, inhale for a full second, and grin at him before passing it to Isaac. *See? I'm fun.*

Isaac waves me off. "Nah, man, I got better stuff."

Wyatt's brow furrows, and he gives Isaac a dark look. "You keep that away from her."

"You're one to talk." Isaac laughs. "I bet you're loaded to the gills." Isaac howls, a wolf in sheep's clothing.

Wyatt takes the joint back. "We don't want her ruined on the first night out. They could still fire her ass." He peruses me, amusement dancing across his features. "And I like working with her."

Thank God it's nighttime and he can't see the full impact of his words. I'm like a schoolgirl desperate for a compliment from a cool kid. "Gee, thanks."

Wyatt tips his chin at me in challenge. "What have you done?"

"Like, acting?" I pluck the joint from him again and take a deep drag. Maybe this will help suffocate my nerves.

"No, like, drugs." His tone is mocking. I don't know why he always unnerves me so much. He must find me so ridiculously boring.

"Weed, that's it." No point in lying. My mother is a doctor specializing in addiction treatment, and so my parents would have murdered me when I was younger for even touching marijuana. Even when I was no longer living under their roof, I didn't stray far from their guidance.

Wyatt's eyebrows lift in silent communication with Isaac.

"Point taken." Isaac's expression turns rueful.

"Well, what have you two done, then? If you're both so hard?" I take another puff from the joint.

Isaac loops his arm around my neck and tugs me to him as smoke billows out of my mouth into the midnight sky. "Name anything and I bet we've tried it. Wyatt and I go way back to the *Petalateers* days."

"You weren't doing drugs when you were on a Daisy Network show." Adults wouldn't have allowed that to happen.

They both burst into laughter. "How do you think we survived Daisy?" Wyatt asks.

"What about your parents?" Someone had to be looking out for them.

My parents insisted I get an education—anything useful—before moving to Los Angeles. Massage therapy has proven to be a good choice. Until I landed the leading role in this drama, *Love Letters from Spain*, opposite Wyatt, I gathered massage clients in between auditions for movies, TV, and commercials, while taking some smaller parts in whatever I could get. Massage offered a flexible schedule and decent money. At the end of this film, I might have to rebuild my clientele, but this role and paycheck could be the start of something. My agent is convinced this will be my big break. Massage was always plan B.

"My parents tried, I think. Sooo long ago. Too many other people around me saying yes for their voices to matter much." Isaac waves a dismissive hand. "I'm fine."

A layer of dark stubble covers Wyatt's jawline, and the urge to run my hand along his cheek seizes me. He catches me staring at him and winks. Another blush rises in me. At this point, he's going to think my natural complexion is deep pink and that I'm a terrible actress, but embarrassment is a tough emotion to fight or fake.

"My parents tried to get me into rehab. I had myself emancipated. Wanted to take my younger sister with me, but that didn't work out." Wyatt raises his hand to the limo entering the lot.

"Oh." The ground vibrates under my feet. Loopy—I'm feeling loopy. Not quite right. I'm familiar with weed but I've never done so much of it. "Emancipation seems . . . excessive."

Wyatt glowers. "Drugs or my parents—choice seemed easy. One of those things was always there for me when I needed it." He ducks into the vehicle, followed by Isaac.

I hesitate at the door, scanning the others still waiting. The limo is big. "What about everyone else?"

"Cabs," Isaac says. "They don't have enough money for rain."

Something about that doesn't seem right to me, but I'm not in the frame of mind to argue. I give a self-conscious wave to everyone before the limo driver closes the door behind me. I think I might be an asshole for leaving them standing there.

"Is that normal?" We streak out of the parking lot.

"No." Wyatt fishes a small vial out of his pocket. "Normally we would have piled a bunch of those models in here too. Some hot extras. I resisted. You're welcome." He gives me a sideways glance as he opens the bottle. He taps out and divides the white powder. With a finger covering one nostril, he snorts a row and then Isaac does too. Isaac stares in silent question at Wyatt, but he shakes his head.

"Nah, man. Buzzed, not annihilated. I told you, I don't want Ellie getting fired." He shuts down Isaac's unspoken suggestion.

"Why would *you* doing drugs get *me* fired?" I clutch my purse in my lap. They seem to be fine. Maybe I would be too. I should try a line to shock them. Except I need this job. I'm not sure what'll happen to me if I try cocaine and my brain goes wrong. Isaac said he'd cover for me, but I'm not sure how much he's prepared to hide if I go off the rails.

Isaac laughs—a deep, hearty, drug-fueled sound. "Why would drugs get you fired? 'Cause Wyatt is a beast and comes up with all kinds of bad ideas when he's lit."

The intensity of Wyatt's blue-green eyes when they meet mine makes Isaac's comment ring true. He hasn't asked me to do anything, and I already think I'd do everything he asked. Those eyes. They make my dark brown ones seem dull and boring in comparison.

"They're real." Wyatt winks.

"They're such an odd color." Something in them tugs at me, yanks me under. I am so focused on figuring out his allure that I don't notice how much closer we've gotten. We haven't filmed any scenes together yet, only had table reads and walk-throughs.

His lips quirk up, and my gaze is drawn down. They're the perfect mix of firm and full. A little closer and I could touch mine to his. A taste.

Isaac clears his throat. "You two will be practicing your love scenes off camera before you know it." Another flash of bright-white teeth.

The bubble bursts, and I sit back. "You have to admit, his eyes are amazing."

"You should see his other body parts." Isaac puts on a falsetto voice. "He's simply to die for." From the cooler in the armrest, he removes a beer.

There's a cooler stocked with beer in the armrest. The opulence is astounding.

"Sexiest Man Alive last year. Who crowns a twenty-five-year-old the sexiest man? They must have been desperate," Isaac teases.

Wyatt swipes the beer from Isaac's hand and downs half of it. "Jealousy doesn't suit you."

Isaac digs out a second bottle without missing a beat. His dark brown eyes meet mine, and they sparkle with amusement. "The three of us are going to light this town on fire. You'll see, Ellie. You'll see." He passes me the opened beer.

I take it with an answering flare of delight. As long as we aren't literally lighting the town on fire, that sounds amazing. Pictures and gossip columns of their exploits, the people they've dated, the famous friends they have, float to the surface of my memory.

"A beer drinker?" Wyatt gives me an appreciative glance.

"Not too much I won't drink." I take a long gulp.

"Remember she said that." He points his bottle across the limo at Isaac.

"So you'll get me drunk but not high?" I ask.

"The shoot is months—*months*, Ellie. You gotta learn to pace yourself." Wyatt bumps his shoulder with mine, and this time his smile reaches his eyes.

My breath catches at the close contact and how handsome he is. He zeroes in on my mouth. In the space between us, electricity zips.

From across the limo, Isaac calls out in a singsong voice, "Pace yourself, Wyatt."

Without breaking eye contact with me, Wyatt jerks his beer bottle, sending a brief spray in Isaac's direction. We burst into laughter, and I chug the rest of my beer. A fire ignites inside me, warming me, threatening to rage out of control.

Being around them is going to be a lot of fun.

WYATT

PRESENT DAY

The door opens in a whoosh, and blondish-brown strands fly around, obscuring Ellie's expression. I'm ten years late, but I'm here. That's what matters.

She pushes her hair out of her face, and her brown eyes shoot daggers at me. Not the response I was hoping for, but expecting her to jump into my arms was likely too high of a bar.

"You saw *The Jackson Billows Show*?"

"You're a jackass. What the hell was that?" Her expression morphs from angry to sad in a heartbeat. "To let him talk about Isaac . . ."

"If Isaac was here, he'd wonder what took me so long." Discussing him isn't the first thing I expected her to call me out on, but it's high on the list.

"I stopped wondering that almost ten years ago. I hope you have your return flight booked for tomorrow morning."

"Excellent. I can spend the night here." I step toward the threshold.

"That is not what I meant, and you know it."

"Ellie." I use the tone designed to weaken her knees.

"Don't you dare. Don't you dare. You lost the right to say my name like that when you let me walk out of our house."

"I'm here to repair that mistake." I set my hand on the doorframe and lean closer.

She inches backward and doesn't open the door any wider. "Doing this so publicly seems like the way to make it right? I have a life now. One that has nothing to do with you. Nothing." Tension radiates off her.

I expected her reaction, sort of. Part of me had hoped a Herculean effort would have her falling back into my arms. Eight of our years apart are a blur of drugs and alcohol. Time has moved differently for her.

"You can't snap your fingers and expect me to come running." Her temple rests on the thick wooden door.

Her posture makes the breath in my throat catch. She looks like the girl I fell in love with, the one I followed around like a lost puppy. Until she up and left; then I was just lost.

"I'm clean now. Let's talk. If you have such a great life without me, it can't hurt to let me in."

Indecision floats across her face, and she steps away from the entrance. She leads me from the side door through the galley kitchen and into a large open room with high ceilings and exposed wooden beams. Everything is decorated in creams and grays. She wasn't such a fan of neutral shades when we lived together. Off to the right is a bar. Does she keep it stocked?

"Nice place." Suddenly, I'm not sure what to say. My plan worked, and I'm here, with her. Now I need to plead my case. Maybe I should have made a list or come up with concessions.

Ellie gestures to one of the couches, her posture stiff. I perch on the armrest, and she sits opposite me. Something buzzes, and I pat my pocket. I frown when I dig out my phone, but it's turned off. The buzzing isn't me.

She holds up her device, and her home screen streams with new messages. The stock exchange and her notifications are twins.

"Oh," I say. "That's . . ." How do I respond? I'm not sorry. The attention is what I wanted. She used to hate the madness, the insanity of people's curiosity, but I needed it for her to open the door.

"Yeah." She sets her phone facedown on the coffee table between us. It buzzes nonstop, and the glass amplifies the sound. She's put it there on purpose.

Watching her in person is surreal. I spent years devouring any image of her I could get my hands on: magazines, movies, interviews, commercials—the few things she endorsed, I bought. Any other woman who entered my life was always second best and ended up walking out on me. I let them all go. Ellie's the only one I've ever chased. I should have gone after her harder back then.

She stares at me, and I remember I'm supposed to be talking. I'm about to say something, anything, when an unfamiliar ringtone pierces the quiet of the living room.

Ellie crosses to the box on the wall and hits a button. "Yes, Freddie?"

"Calshae Simmons is here to see you."

Ellie bites her lip and glances at me.

"Calshae? You two still good friends?" Whenever we came to the island, Calshae, along with Ellie's younger sister, Nikki, were always part of the crew.

"Let her in," Ellie says.

An old, familiar pang niggles at my brain. I'm itching. The desire to take something to dull the edge of seeing Ellie again is strong. Mentally, I list the drugs I could swallow, snort, or inject to smooth out this conversation. I clutch my phone in my pocket. I'll have to make a call when I leave here to ensure I don't screw this up before I get started.

Ellie disappears to the side door, and when she comes back into the living room, a short, curvy Black woman trails behind her. Sometimes when I see people I haven't been around for a while, the years lie on my shoulders like bricks. A reminder of the blurred span after Ellie left. Calshae isn't a party girl anymore. Of course, she was never as wild as me or even Ellie.

"It's been a while," I say to her with a grin.

"Ten years," Calshae says. "What brings you to Bermuda?"

"About time I got my shit together. Go after the people who matter."

Ellie's jaw tightens. "Calshae and I have a girls' night planned. I can't break my plans just because you showed up at my door unexpectedly."

Her claim and their postures don't go together. There's a tension and a wariness between the two of them that didn't exist when we were younger.

"A girls' night at almost midnight?" I check my watch.

"Wyatt was on his way out when you got here." Ellie turns to Calshae.

"Was I?" I give a sly smile. "We haven't even had a chance to catch up."

"There won't be any catching up. What time is your flight tomorrow?" Ellie cocks her head.

"I cleared my schedule for a week or so. It's such a beautiful island." I ignore Calshae and assess Ellie's reaction. She swallows hard.

That's right, Ellie. You might push me out of your house tonight, but I'll be coming back for more.

"Don't let us hold you up from your vacation." Ellie shoves her hands into the pockets of her shorts. "Coming to my house was a mistake."

Old Wyatt would draw a line on the floor and dig in his heels. Ellie's tight posture seems to anticipate my reaction. But I'm here to show her I'm not the guy she walked out on. I can be reasonable.

"I won't keep you, but I'll see you tomorrow," I say. "Give us a chance to get reacquainted."

She hesitates and swivels to Calshae. "Can you give us a moment?"

Calshae's gaze ping-pongs between me and Ellie. "Sure, yeah. No problem. I'll go out on the balcony."

As soon as the glass door clicks closed, Ellie grabs my arm and drags me into the kitchen.

"Stop," she says, pointing a finger at me before getting a glass of water from the fridge.

"What?" I stare at her, wide-eyed.

"All of it. Just stop. This isn't a game. My life is not a publicity stunt. All of this—the visit, the interview, the rest of the press . . . Is this for your race-car film? Is it so bad the production company got desperate?" She sets her drink on the island and glares along the length of the counter. "Are you using me? Our history?"

"No," I say. "My visit has nothing to do with any movie. I'm here for you. I've wanted to see you for ten years."

"Guess what? I was here the whole time." Ellie thrusts her hands wide in exasperation.

"You seriously don't think I tried? You don't think I made phone calls, asked friends and acquaintances, phoned your manager, contacted former acting partners? I did all of that. All of it. Hell, I even flew here once. But the islanders acted like I was a disease. No one would tell me where you lived. I went to your parents' place but they wouldn't let me past the gates. I even booked one of those See Famous Houses tours, but as soon as they recognized me, they canceled the whole damned thing."

Ellie stares at her glass but remains silent.

"I tried," I say.

"For how long? It's been ten years. You tried that hard the whole time?"

"The first year, maybe two, I was angry at you." Before Ellie left, I was already spiraling out of control, but once she was gone, any brakes I'd applied to my behavior were cut. Rage and grief fueled my addiction. "Once I calmed down, I came looking."

I splay my hands on the island, shoulders up, mirroring her posture. Many, many days I was too out of it on drugs or alcohol to do much of anything. The acting jobs I took required a careful coordination of uppers and downers for me to pull off, and a lot of days, I didn't function at all. Neither of us needs a reminder of who I once was. The court appearances and the questions around insuring me on a film set aren't happening anymore.

She gathers her hair into a ponytail and lets it fall in a wave behind her back. "You were still using when you came. You must have still been using."

"I was, but I'm not anymore. Spend time with me over the next week while I'm here. I promise you, I'm not the man I was." She needs to believe me. I'm going to show her, but I need her to trust me.

"Ten years ago, I asked you to go to rehab, to choose me over your addiction. You couldn't do that. Your reliance on pills and alcohol, your grief over Isaac and his father, were tearing you apart right in front of me. I wanted to choose you then, but I needed you to get help. I can't choose you now. I'd be a fool to throw away the life I've built to relive old memories."

The reminders of how foggy I let my life get after Isaac's father, Kabir, died of a heart attack and then Isaac died make me feel like shit. I might have made a lot of poor choices, but I never stopped loving her. "We could make new memories."

"I moved on." Ellie sighs. "That first year after I left you, I thought you might come. Get better on your own. I hoped you would. *Maybe today will be the day*, I used to think. But every day, I woke up, and you never appeared."

I can't argue with her. She still knows me better than anyone. If I was determined to find her, I'd have left no stone unturned. Two years of intense therapy has led me back to her. This time, I pushed until someone caved. But the person who gave in is also the reason I'm sure I have a chance.

"I'm here. Maybe that doesn't count for much right now, but I came to show you things are different; I'm different," I say. "What are you doing tomorrow?"

"No. I won't blow up my life for you." She wags her finger and takes a drink of her water.

"I'm here for a week." Frustration seeps into my voice. "You kept me away for ten years. Should I have tried harder? Yeah, I should have. Did you make it damn hard for me to get to you? Yeah, you did. You canceled appearances, didn't come to awards shows, stayed away from LA. It felt like the moment you caught a whiff of me in the general vicinity, you ran. So if you're stringing me up for not coming, at least give me a chance now that I'm here."

Her eyes soften. She bites her lip and tucks a strand of hair behind her ear. Her stance relaxes, and she nods once. "Tomorrow. Only until three in the afternoon." She stares at me, searching.

"Who knows you're here? Will there be a flood of paps outside my door tomorrow?"

To her, the press scrutiny is invasive, frustrating. I love the attention—I like to be wanted. "Only my team. I didn't purposely lead anyone here. You have my word."

"I guess we'll find out whether that means anything anymore." She turns from the island and opens the side door. "What time are you coming?"

"Ten? You'll be jet-lagged, right?"

"Uh, yeah." Surprise flashes in her eyes. "Freddie will call you a cab."

"No limo service?" We spent a lot of time in the back seat of one. The memories are there with every glance. On my lap. Underneath me. Laughing over a shared joke. Leaving a funeral.

"Not the kind you're seeking, not in Bermuda," she says. "It's weird, but I don't miss any of that."

Her words slice into my heart. She meant them to. Can't blame her. There were a lot of mistakes, all of them mine. "Guess we'll see about that too." Before I leave, I loop my arm around her waist and whisper in her ear, "Tomorrow."

Goose bumps form on her arms, and they're not from the cold.

ELLIE

PRESENT DAY

I'm at my side door, pacing, waiting for Wyatt to appear. Calshae came to warn me last night about Wyatt's arrival on the island. A lawyer circulating with NDAs at her family's hotel coupled with Wyatt's interview made her think he'd be in Bermuda shortly. She was as surprised as me that he was already at my house. We might not be close anymore, but the island mentality of looking out for one another has been ingrained in each of us from birth. We're both from intergenerational Bermudian families, and she'll protect my secrets like they're her own even if she never agreed with them.

My sister wasn't impressed when I called her back to tell her I was spending the day with Wyatt. She reminded me of what was at stake. I argued that giving in a little now would mean I could manage him better later.

I lied.

He doesn't work that way and capitulating won't help me. Today's dilemma is why I've kept the emotional door shut and locked with any form of security available. Once he lodges in my heart, rooting him out is impossible. Leaving him crushed me. At a certain point, I wasn't sure I'd bounce back, be whole again.

But I survived. I'm capable of enduring enormous heartbreak and not crumbling. There's no need to learn that lesson again, and definitely not from him.

The security intercom buzzes, and my heart rate skyrockets. With my hand on my chest, I close my eyes to center myself. "Yeah, Jerome?"

"Mr. Wyatt Burgess is here?"

Right. I forgot to tell him. If he saw *The Jackson Billows Show* last night or checked any form of social media, Wyatt's appearance might not be a surprise. He's a tornado ripping through my life, but no one else has been sucked into the vortex yet.

"He can come through." Wyatt anywhere in Bermuda during broad daylight is a disaster waiting to happen. There are only sixty thousand people on the island, and we're all six degrees of separation away from each other. One person's aunt is another person's cousin. I've never worried about anyone selling us out because very few people have come looking, and Bermuda values loyalty over betrayal. They protect their own, and in return, my family is exceedingly generous with our time and money.

#Wyllie is trending. People have tagged me and Wyatt in stories, videos, GIFs, and memes. Anything with a touch of relevance has our old nickname. I can't check social media for more than a second. Too much, too soon. My burner phone has only vital contacts, and it's stemming the torrent.

I peek out the blinds as Wyatt rounds the hedges. My breath hitches in that old, familiar way. When he used to stride in my direction, eyes trained on me as though he could devour me, I wondered how I got so lucky.

Before I can talk myself out of letting him in, I open the door. My expression should be neutral, but my heart is running wild. I'm a good enough actor to fool him, right? He takes me in from head to foot, and a grin spreads, lassoing the out-of-control beast in my chest.

"You look amazing," he says.

"Thanks."

My fingers tingle. To have him this close and not touch him goes against every instinct in my body. We were always very affectionate, very connected. He had a lot of faults, but demonstrating his love to me and everyone else was never one of them.

Sitting across from him in the living room last night was a huge test of my willpower. When he came close enough for me to smell his cologne, I breathed him in. How can this connection be the same? Memories rushed through my barricades. Instead of fending them off, part of me welcomed them, wanted to drown in them.

I grab the two motorbike helmets off the kitchen island and pass him one. He eyes me. "You're still driving a bike?" he asks.

We fought about a few things, but we were both risk takers, thrill seekers. After I left LA, I *had* to change—but I have no idea what he's like now.

"You're not?" I open a side entrance to the garage and hit the button that lifts the door to reveal the private laneway.

Wyatt caresses the helmet. "No, not really. Got too dangerous with the number of paparazzi I had hunting me." He follows me into the garage.

"Ah, the life of a famous person. Must be exciting for you." A low blow since Wyatt's rides were one of his only outlets from his fame.

I catch myself staring at him but he's still focused on the helmet. When he glances up, he shrugs. "Turns out there were a few things in life you were right about."

I purse my lips. Externally, I won't give an inch. Internally, there's a riot brewing. "Who could have predicted?"

We're standing beside my favorite Honda motorcycle. Not the best or most expensive, but it attracts the least attention and is powerful enough to maneuver us up hills.

I lower my helmet and climb on. "You coming?"

"Which bike?" He takes in my collection.

"You don't have a license." I flip up my visor.

He raises his eyebrows in question, as though laws were meant to be broken.

"Yes, that matters," I say. "If we're caught—can you imagine? As it is, there are limited places we can go where people won't be uploading my life to social media without my consent."

"If we get pulled over, I'll snap a few photos or sign a few things. Problem solved." Wyatt searches my face. "We've done it before."

"Life was different." Part of me wants to soften. The massive weight I've carried on my shoulders for years has lifted at his proximity. A weight I've carried so long, I didn't realize the heaviness was a burden.

He came. Finally, he came.

He shoves the helmet on and swings his leg over the bike. Once his feet are on the pegs, he inches forward so his pelvis presses against my ass. My sharp intake of breath at his closeness is involuntary. He goes still behind me as tension rises between us, fills the garage. Wyatt has always been attuned to me physically. He secures his hands on my waist and then leans forward, the length of his chest pressing into my back. I close my eyes. I'm grateful he can't see my face. The brush of our bodies is intoxicating. Every inch of me has noted every inch of him, and my body is singing, as it once did, just for him.

I start the bike and rev it a few times. The roar is powerful. I can resist him. His brief visit doesn't have to become anything. With a surge of confidence, I peel out of the garage to the gate. Jerome gives me a salute as he opens the metal doors and then watches us cruise along the narrow path. Foliage conceals the route to my house, and anyone who has managed to get the address has trouble finding it if they aren't familiar with Bermuda.

When we were dating, Wyatt came with me to visit my family several times. The temptation to wander memory lane is more than I can resist, and I take him past things that have changed in the last ten years. Every time we hit a new landmark he recognizes, he brushes against me to speak into my ear. Delicious shivers of pleasure race up my spine. That's normal, right? The urge to draw him close, have our skin slide against each other, is a muscle memory. Means nothing.

He reacts to each reveal as I expect. Our favorite old hotel demolished to be replaced by a modern monstrosity—horrible. The restaurant where we got food poisoning turned into a cleaning company—hilarious. There are too many places that remind me of him, but for a long time, there weren't enough.

Our final stop is also recognizable. I drive into the deserted parking lot of my favorite beach at the tip of the island. It's the greatest distance from the airport and has no amenities. A parking lot, a rambling walk through brush, and then a wide, expansive beach with pink sand. It's rare to find other people here, and since it's low tourist season, even less of a risk today. This place brims with memories.

Wyatt gets off the bike first. I secure my helmet and extend my hand for his without checking his reaction. My sunglasses are inside the seat, and I slide them onto my face. He's here, in the flesh. Not a hallucination or my deepest wish sealed into a coin and tossed into a fountain.

"I'm glad this place hasn't changed." He scans the area and sucks in a deep breath of ocean air. "Man, it feels like yesterday we were here." His eyes, the color of the shallow sea, seek mine. "So many memories." His expression is wistful. I hope mine is not.

His implication is clear, but we can't go back. There is no future for us. The beach is to the right, and I let him trail behind me.

When the path widens, he falls into step beside me. "I'm sorry, Ellie."

"The attention will die if we don't do anything to attract the focus to us." There are a million things he could be sorry for, but I choose the easiest one, and when I let myself gaze at him, longing pours out of me, pools at my feet. I am a terrible actress today.

"I'm sorry about ten years ago too," he says. "For a long time, I've wanted to say that. Those words, to you, in person."

An unexpected lump forms in my throat. I have to close my eyes, and I'm glad for my sunglasses. His apology makes me weak in the knees. This conversation is too intimate, painful.

"Is this a twelve-step, making-amends thing? 'Cause if it is, we're fine. Well, we were until last night."

"Do not throw that shit in my face, Ellie." He growls in frustration. It's the first sign I've seen of the hot-tempered Wyatt of old. "You're better than that."

"Then what is this? Why now?" I flick off my sandals in irritation. They fly across the sand, and a weird satisfaction settles on me to see them land so far away.

"I've been clean for two years," he says. "I had to be sure sobriety would take this time." He shakes his head. "I wanted to be completely certain."

"Certain about what?" My heart must be in my eyes. There's nothing I want more than for this to be true. For him to be clean would be a gift, such a gift to me . . . to other people too.

"That I could be the man you deserved, the one you asked me to be. I wasn't ready then, but I'm ready now. The man you need—I can be him. I *am* that guy." Wyatt closes the distance in the warm sand so we're only a foot or two apart.

I've built a good life. A decent existence without him present. What choice did I have when he refused to get help? Letting him back in could set my world, my family's world, on fire, especially if he can't maintain his sobriety.

"You going to tell me that being around me hasn't stirred up any old feelings? 'Cause I gotta say, I don't believe you." He searches my face. There's a grain of truth I don't want him to find.

"Memories and nostalgia aren't a solid reason to renew a relationship that wasn't functional."

"You're boiling our problems down to the wrong pieces." Wyatt throws up his hands.

My phone buzzes in my pocket, and I take it out. It's Nikki, and part of me is relieved at the interruption. I hold up a finger and walk away from him.

"Hey, Nikki, what's up?" I try to keep my voice calm while my insides riot.

His proximity has disoriented me, and I can't get my feet on firm ground. The muscled expanse of his back shifts beneath his shirt as he skips shells and stones along the still surface of the shallow ocean water. His aura tugs on me, a tie I tried to sever with time and distance. But he's right. A thread is there, binding us, more than he knows.

"I'm at the hospital. The school called. Haven has a high fever. Probably nothing, but I thought I should tell you," Nikki says. "I wasn't sure I should interrupt, but I didn't want you to get mad at me later."

A cool sweat breaks out under my arms at Haven's hospitalization. "You were right to call. I have to drop Wyatt off somewhere and then I'll be there."

We say a hasty goodbye, and I tuck my phone into my pocket. "That was Nikki. She's at the hospital. I have to go."

"Is she okay?"

"She doesn't think it's anything, but I have to go." *Who's the liar now?*

"I'll come with you." He collects my discarded sandals.

After I take my shoes from him, I slip them on. I wish I could stay, try to sort out my complicated, overblown feelings, but the hospital is more important. "You can't. People will recognize you. We do not need to feed the gossip mills. I don't want paparazzi on my doorstep. It's why I live here. Privacy. Freedom. Neither of those exist in your world."

He sucks in a breath and shoves his hands in his pockets. "Ellie." He uses the voice that makes me melt in a puddle at his feet. This time, it's not intentional. The result is the same.

A desire to steady myself rises, but my only support is Wyatt. Leaning on him, emotionally or physically, is a terrible idea. At a deserted beach, we could slip into chartered, but rough, waters. Too easy to drown in him again. Haven's fever could be nothing, but I have to go.

"I'm sorry." I head toward the path, ignoring the clench in my gut trying to convince me to stay.

He hesitates for a beat and then follows. Younger Wyatt wouldn't have taken no for an answer. We'd be fighting. He'd be forcing me to tell him the truth. I'm not sure how I feel about the change.

As we walk through the brush, he's behind me. "You remember the MTV awards when we won best kiss?" he asks.

"Hard to forget."

If I closed my eyes, I could relive it. In true Wyatt fashion, he staged an elaborate scene to garner maximum attention. Our best kiss was a shower scene, and he had them bring a portable one onto the stage. When we stripped down to skimpy bathing suits, the crowd went wild. The minute we stepped into the shower, though, the whole stage and everyone in the Hollywood Palladium disappeared. The press of his firm body against mine, the warm water rushing down our bodies, and the innate chemistry we had right from the start made everything else fade away. We loved each other so hard, so well, until we didn't. Seeing the expressions on our faces after we kissed onstage sent cracks through my heart, and each new view of the YouTube video widened them into crevices. We were in awe, like we'd stolen the moon out of the night sky and slotted a piece of it into each other. Shiny. Lit up. Deliriously happy.

"Why." I take a deep breath to steady myself. "Why did you bring that up?"

"Had it on repeat when you first left me." He chuckles, but the sound is sad. "YouTube is horrible and wonderful sometimes. Nothing like torturing yourself with something you no longer have."

My steps falter. Wyatt sitting alone in our massive house reliving our relationship replaces my warmth with a colossal ache. A grief I remember. If I dig deep enough, my heartache burns—covered over, but never forgotten. Never quite healed.

When we arrive at the bike, I pop the seat and hand him a helmet. Before I put on mine, I take him in, memorizing, savoring. This might be the last time we're together. Tears prick at the back of my vision. He can't see them or he'll realize how conflicted I am. Here. Gone. I want him in both places and neither.

"Ellie." He holds the helmet between his hands, and he's focused on the plastic surface. "Tomorrow or any day for the rest of this week? It'll depend on your sister's health, of course . . ."

I shove my helmet on my head, hardening my resolve. He wasn't good for me ten years ago, and I'd be a fool to let him back in, to risk what I've built. The sight of his clear, beautiful eyes almost stops me short. Sober, charming Wyatt is so hard to resist.

I swing onto the bike. "I can't."

He opens his mouth to say something, thinks better of it, and then gives a curt nod. He climbs on behind me, and this time he judges the distance with precision. His pelvis connects with my butt. I fight the urge to lean into the contact, savor him. I rev the engine harder than necessary, then peel out of the parking lot to deliver Wyatt to his hotel.

Getting to Haven is all that matters. Wyatt can't be allowed anywhere near her.

ELLIE

THIRTEEN YEARS AGO

I'm flying, and I want to stretch out my arms in the limo to drift on the current of the wind. Whatever Isaac gave me is magic. I'm more relaxed than I've ever been.

He pats my leg and grins. "Bet your late call time tomorrow seems fantastic about now."

I'm drifting, floating, drifting. My hands. My fingers are so long. Who painted my nails this weird purple color?

Isaac turns to the limo driver and says something, but I can't focus enough to catch it. The rear door opens and lights flash. Wyatt climbs in, and he drags a leggy brunette behind him.

He's blurry, as though the lights from the cameras smeared him. Still beautiful, though. Bright eyes, dark hair, and so many glorious muscles.

Isaac's arm is around me, and I lean into him. Wyatt's brought some random woman for our night out. Guess he won't be expecting me to thank him this time.

"Blanca, the Spanish supermodel." Isaac gestures toward her and passes her a glass of white wine. "This is Ellie Cooper. Remember that name. She's incredible. Gonna set the world on fire."

I nod at her instead of offering my hand. Everything in the limo is hazy, softer. Wyatt's been pissing me off. Blowing hot and cold and every temperature in between when we're in a room together. Keeping track of his moods makes my brain hurt.

"What the fuck did you give her?" Wyatt leans forward and shakes my knee.

"Leave me alone, Wyatt." I burrow deeper into Isaac's side and slap Wyatt's hand away.

"Seriously, Isaac." Anger clouds his face. A storm is brewing, though they never seem to fight . . .

"Why do you care?" I stare at Blanca, who is sipping her wine, amusement teasing the edges of her mouth. Maybe she doesn't speak English.

Wyatt cracks the tequila bottle and pours three shots. He passes one to Isaac, one to Blanca, and keeps one for himself.

"Hey." I manage to sit forward in annoyance.

"Not happening." Wyatt gives me a pointed, pissed-off look. "What did you take? Pill, powder, or liquid?"

I shrug. A drink of some sort. Tasted like candy. Isaac wouldn't give me something bad.

"You didn't tell her?" Disbelief is clear in his voice. His brow furrows with disappointment.

"It was a glass of lean. Calm down," Isaac says.

I swipe Isaac's shot before he can drink it, and I down the liquid in a gulp. "You're a hypocrite." My words slur.

Isaac pours another, handing it to me. Wyatt settles into his seat with his jaw clenched. Blanca drapes herself over him. *Gross.*

His sea-colored eyes are trained on me as I chat nonsense with Isaac. When we step out of the limo at the club, the camera flashes are rapid and blinding. I stumble, and Isaac drags me tighter to his side to keep me from falling. We navigate the crush of people with club security as a wall around us until we reach the front entrance.

Strange that we're arriving this way. We rarely go in the front entrance because of the paparazzi. Wyatt and Isaac enjoy the attention, but I've learned they like it best on their own terms.

Inside the bar, Blanca leads the way to a VIP room at the back. At least this part is normal, even if I don't feel normal in any way. There are others in the VIP area, and Isaac glues himself to my side so I don't feel out of place. He always knows everyone. For what seems like hours, he takes me around from person to person, introducing me and speaking a weird mix of Spanish and English that I couldn't follow sober. Isaac speaks Hindi too. Right now, I can barely speak at all.

"What's Wyatt's problem?" I ask when we slide into a booth without him.

One side of Isaac's mouth tilts up, and he turns to examine me. "Oh, Ellie. How much time have you got?"

"Isaac!" The crowd in front of us parts, and a striking dark-haired white woman appears. She's tall and reed thin, and the closer she gets, the more recognition dawns in my addled brain. Wyatt's younger sister.

Isaac scoots over to give Anna room to squeeze into the booth with us. She's on the other side of him, and he throws his arm around her narrow shoulders. "Anna, have you met Ellie? She's starring opposite Wyatt in the movie we're shooting." He shifts to me. "Ellie, this is Wyatt's baby sister. Kinda like my baby sister too." He kisses her temple. "The Sharmas unofficially adopted the Burgess kids."

Anna takes me in with eyes that are an unusual blue-green shade, just like Wyatt's. Her allure is remarkable, and her modeling career makes a lot of sense. She's the same age as me, but there's a toughness to her I don't possess.

"You the flavor of the month? How long are you going to last?" Anna asks, and she sips her drink while watching for my response.

"Be nice," Isaac says.

Anna rolls her eyes and then focuses on Isaac. "Have you got anything?"

"What're you after?" He digs into his pocket.

"You got any benzos?" She peers into his pill bottle.

While they sort through Isaac's stash, I look over to see Wyatt brush Blanca off his lap and leave his bar stool. With a swagger, he comes over to where Isaac, Anna, and I are sitting, and he holds out his hand. "They're playing our song. You gotta come dance with me." He tips his head toward the dance floor.

"Did he just say 'our song'?" Anna asks Isaac in an overly loud voice. "Wyatt, stay and do a line with us. Don't be lame."

"Not now, Anna," he says, and he doesn't break eye contact with me.

I listen and catch a few bars of the chorus. It's the Alicia Keys song he asked to have played the other day during our love scene.

"Come on, Ellie," he says.

Longing is written on his face, and I cave. When I rise, I stagger, and Wyatt lifts me out of the booth as though I weigh nothing to carry me to the dance floor. He sets me in front of him and then ever so slowly draws me into his arms.

While we dance, he holds me close and sings along at a level only I can hear. The lyrics to "If I Ain't Got You" flow out of him, smooth and deep. We sway to the music with his lips next to my ear. I relax into him, letting him lead me around the dance floor, wishing the song would go on forever. He's a good singer. The Daisy Network days benefitted him in at least one way.

When the song comes to an end, Wyatt brings the back of my hand to his mouth and places a soft kiss across my knuckles. My body vibrates, anticipates. The tension that's sprung up between us is one I recognize.

There's an unasked question in the depths of his eyes. My answer now, and probably for the rest of my life, is yes. I can't imagine saying no.

I want this. I want him, and I close the little space between us in a silent plea for something, anything. He tugs me toward him and buries a hand in my hair. He gives me a last desperate glance before his lips rush to meet mine. I clutch onto him, rising on my toes to deepen the kiss. Throwing my arms around his neck, I press myself closer, and I lose any sense of where we are as heat rises through my body. If I could stay in his arms, I'd never want the night to end.

"Come home with me," I say between kisses.

"Ellie." There's so much need in his voice that my knees almost collapse. He shifts to create space between us, and I'm sure he'll tell me no. Blanca is here, and one kiss between costars on the dance floor means nothing. But I want so much more than a kiss. *Say yes to me, Wyatt.*

"I can't." He kisses me again as though he can't help himself.

"We're young. This doesn't have to be some great love affair." He's cracked a window between us, and I'm not letting the opportunity pass. Whatever Isaac gave me hours ago is wearing off. I'm buzzed enough to ignore Anna's rudeness, but not so out of my head I don't understand what I'm suggesting.

"I can't make any promises." He dips into my neck and his lips trail kisses along the sensitive skin.

"Don't need them." I dig my fingers into his biceps. My knees won't hold me up, and my blood has rushed to my core in anticipation.

"I wish you weren't high right now. What if you don't re-member?" he murmurs.

"Doesn't that mean we get to do it again?" I run my hands through his dark hair.

He groans and returns to my lips, kissing me deeply, cradling my face in his hands. This time when we break apart, he sweeps me up off the dance floor and carries me through the crowd toward the side door.

"Why'd we come in the front earlier?" I loop my arms around his neck and tuck my cheek under his chin, away from prying eyes.

"Blanca wanted to be seen with me," he says.

"You do that sort of thing?" I try to covertly scan the crowd for anyone watching us. There are a few curious stares but nothing out of the ordinary.

"Trade favors? Sure, why not? Her agent called my agent. None of it matters." He strides up to the exit with determination. "It's a game, Ellie. You'll see."

At the door, he sets me down and takes his phone out of his pocket as we head outside.

"What about your sister or Isaac or . . . Blanca?" Her name tastes sour on my tongue.

"You don't need to worry about them." Wyatt tugs me toward him, and his lips find mine again. He backs me against a pillar, running his hands along my sides. "I've thought about doing this with you for real a thousand times."

Only a thousand? A glance from him across a crowded set was enough to make me think about dark rooms, beds, the brush of his skin against mine. Every place he touches lights up, glows, explodes with sensation. His hands and lips offer a special kind of magic.

"One other thing." He kisses me again, and then he gives me a hard stare. "No more accepting shit from Isaac, okay?"

"It was one drink. Made me feel good." I try to reach for him, but he maintains space between us.

"I'm serious. If you want to try something, ask me, and I'll get it for you. But Isaac takes stupid risks and mixes shit he shouldn't. He thinks he's invincible."

"You and Isaac are friends." They both pop pills, drink alcohol, and manage drug combinations like they're working a second job.

"He's my best friend. There isn't a friend in the world like Isaac. That's the truth. He's my brother—his whole family is more mine than my own." He pauses and runs a hand through his hair in frustration. "Doesn't mean what I said isn't true too."

"Are you on something right now?" He seems together. Coherent. His eyes are clear, focused.

"I'm always on something. Sometimes I hide it better than others. If we're doing this," he takes a breath and then continues, "whatever this becomes, my habits aren't up for discussion."

"You're fine. Why would we talk about them?" Other than his oscillating moods toward me, he's professional and focused on set. He's a phenomenal kisser, and a lot of fun on nights out. "What if I did bring it up, so what?"

"I'd pick the drugs." He doesn't hesitate, and a shiver cascades down my body. "Now you know the answer, so you never have to ask the question." The limo arrives, and Wyatt examines me for a long beat. "Still time to back out. Things will stay as they are. I won't treat you any differently on set if you say no."

I drag him to me for another kiss. Change my mind? Not likely. He occupies all my thoughts. Whatever happens after tonight I can't control. But for now he's mine, just mine. My hand is linked with his as we climb into the limo.

In the back seat, I straddle him and frame his face with my hands. Confidence oozes out of me. He stares at me with such contentment that my heart swells. I can't imagine ever asking him to be anything other than who he is right now.

WYATT

PRESENT DAY

An hour after Ellie drops me off at the hotel, I'm in my room, pacing. I called my addiction coach, and we had a long chat about Ellie as a trigger for my addictions. Camila doesn't think I should be here. Some bullshit about not being able to recapture the past.

Camila wasn't there to see the way Ellie looked at me today. The connection between us isn't dead, it's just buried under years of neglect.

I take out my phone and search the location of the hospital. My suitcase is open on the bed, and I rifle through the items I brought. Baseball cap and sunglasses. Lamest disguise ever. Best I can do.

I tug the Yankees cap low on my forehead and grab my sunglasses. At four inches over six feet, I draw people's attention due to my height, disguised or not. Normally, I don't mind. If I'm spotted at the hospital, Ellie will murder me. At least I'll be in the right place for resuscitation.

In the doorway of my hotel room, I second-guess my lack of a plan. Impulsiveness and my addiction go hand in hand. Some knee-jerk reactions I need to curb. Nikki will be there, even if she's sick. When I was using, I'd needed someone to blame for Ellie's abandonment. She spent a week at home with her family and decided my addictions weren't acceptable anymore. That notion had to come from someone, because Ellie was fine with my behavior until then. Nikki and her mother bore the brunt of my anger, but I don't know if that was justified. I'd hoped sobriety might bring clarity around how or why we broke up, but it hasn't. We were good . . . and then we weren't. Snap of the fingers. Blink of an eye. In my bed. Out of my life.

I take the stairs instead of waiting for the elevator. At the concierge desk, I join the line. The high, open ceilings lead out to the beach, and the paintings on the wall depict scenes from the island. Even the tiles on the ground are vibrant blues and greens. I've missed Bermuda with its bright buildings. LA has always been my home, but there's something to be said for the tight-knit community that exists here. I take a deep, cleansing breath. Ten years was too long.

As soon as the concierge sees me, he motions me to the side. "Mr. Burgess, what can we help you with?"

"I need to get to the hospital."

"Are you ill?" The concierge's expression turns concerned, and he keeps his voice low.

"No." I hesitate. "A friend is there."

"Is it an emergency, sir? We can have a staff member drive you there themselves. Very discreet."

"Yeah, that would be excellent." A sigh of relief escapes me. The fewer people who are aware, the better. I squeeze my phone in my pocket. The itch is back, my constant companion, a restlessness that plagues me.

Christ, maybe my sponsor is right. Maybe Ellie is a trigger. At this point, life in general might be a trigger. If she was the reason I used, I'd have quit the bullshit the minute she packed up and moved out. I wouldn't have been so into it when she met me. She put up with my nonsense during the three years we were together, every bit of it, and she never complained. In the end, she just left.

"Do you happen to have any stress balls?" My coping mechanisms to handle the itch are varied. When one doesn't work, I try another, and another, and so on until the itch stops. Anything to keep me from reaching for a bottle of pills or contacting an old friend for one hit.

The concierge passes me one from behind his desk. The hotel name is emblazoned on it. "You get a lot of stressed people?" I ask, amused.

"Just me, sir." He grins.

Calshae approaches with a set of keys dangling from her hand. "I hear you need a ride."

"What are you doing here?" I ask.

She nods at the concierge and leads me toward the exit. "My family bought this hotel a few years ago. I run it."

The humid air hits me in the chest the minute we step out of the main building and coats me in a thin mist. Calshae takes me to a tiny car, and I stare at it before I open the door to wedge myself into the passenger seat like a human pretzel. Maybe I should have risked a cab. My knees are glued to my chest.

"Sorry. The hospital's not too far." She scans my cramped position. The car chugs to life, and I pray I'll make it there in one piece before Ellie leaves.

While we drive, Calshae taps her fingers on the steering wheel. The tension in the car swells. Small talk. I need small talk before she starts asking questions I don't want to answer. Engage first. Control the conversation. Basic strategy, but I'm not in the mood to charm Ellie's friend, to convince her I should be here.

"Your family own many hotels on the island now?" I clutch onto the holy-shit handle each time she takes a corner. She's mistaken this car for a Formula 1 masterpiece. Impressive this death trap can take a corner at full speed.

"A few."

I shift in my seat and suppress a groan at how tight my body is. She'll have to pry me out. Maybe I can take my mind off my stiffening muscles by inching into a conversation about Ellie. "You and Ellie are still good friends?"

She gives me a sideways glance. "Ellie's good to everyone on the island with her time and money."

Not a yes, and not a surprise given the tension between them last night. "You're not really friends anymore? Why were you at her house last night?"

"I was worried about her, so I went to see her."

"Worried about her?"

"I thought what you said on Jackson Billows' show was brave." She fiddles with the radio.

"Which part?" I ask. "The part where I declared my undying love for Ellie or the part where I admitted that I'd tried to commit suicide after she left me?" When she opened the door to me last night, I expected her to ask about or at least acknowledge that piece of the interview. Again today, I was sure she'd bring it up. Still nothing. Head in the sand approach? Maybe she doesn't care. Too long ago.

"Both, Wyatt. Both." Calshae's expression is sympathetic when she glances at me. "Somewhere, someone watching will be grateful for your vulnerability, even if it doesn't end up being Ellie."

Telling the world instead of telling Ellie might not have been the best strategy. Camila says I need to work on my communication skills.

"We're here. Where do you want to be dropped?"

"Oh." I take in the massive white stucco structure. "Uh." I hate when I don't plan far enough ahead. Happens to me all the time. You'd think I'd learn.

"Would you like me to go in and find out what room?" she suggests.

"Yes!" I point my finger at her with a stupid amount of enthusiasm. "Ellie won't be happy if people realize I'm here."

"I'll be right back." She disappears into the hospital, and she isn't gone long before she returns. "Side entrance. Room 237." She starts the car, checks over her shoulder, and steers us onto the road. "You realize who you're visiting, right?" A frown creases her brow.

"Yeah. I mean, I know who's in the room. I'm going so I can talk to Ellie."

When she draws parallel to the curb, she searches my face before passing me a slip of paper. "For the door. It's coded. The girl on reception is a family friend and I told her what I needed."

"Oh." The small-town mentality across a whole island is unsettling sometimes. None of this would be happening if I was in LA. Well, maybe having a driver, but I would've had to throw around celebrity weight to get the rest. Even then, not a guarantee. "Thank you." I open the door and ease out a leg. My muscles groan in response. When did I get old?

"Would you like me to wait?"

I focus on the entrance to the hospital. Ellie might chase me out with some sort of cutting instrument. "Nah, that's okay. I'll convince Ellie to give me a ride to the hotel." Or maybe to her house. You never know.

"I'm sure you convince a lot of women to do a lot of things."

"No comment." I chuckle and climb out of the car.

"Let me give you my number in case you need that ride after all," she says through the car window, and she holds out her hand for my phone before inputting her number. When she passes it back to me, her black eyes scan my face again. "Good luck in there."

Once I'm in the side door, the nearest set of stairs is to the left, and I head for room 237. The door is ajar, and Nikki and Ellie are on either side of a hospital bed. I jerk away, unsure. She told me Nikki was in the hospital. If she isn't sick, who is?

I'm here now, and I'm sure as hell not lurking in the hallway. *Flowers*. I scan the area for anywhere obvious to purchase something. Poor planning. Again. Except I now realize I have no idea who I'd be giving them to.

I rap my knuckles on the door and walk in without waiting for a response. Nikki turns toward me, and her gasp of surprise is audible. That's the kind of reaction I wanted from Ellie last night. At least I'm capable of surprising someone.

"Wyatt." She rounds the hospital bed with a pointed glare at Ellie. Both Nikki and Ellie are a combination of their parents' physical traits. Nikki got their father's darker, wavier hair coupled with their mother's blue eyes. Whereas Ellie got the brown eyes and hair that, whether through highlights or the sun, is streaked with blond.

If Nikki is greeting me, then who is in the bed? The room is large but sterile and without personality in the way most hospital rooms are, and as I stride forward, more of the sleeping figure becomes visible. Ellie turns, and her complexion is pale, stunned.

In the bed is a young girl who is maybe eight. She's flushed and unconscious. Ellie tries to block my view of her with her body. The child's identity is obvious. Why is she hiding her?

"This your little girl, Nikki?" I approach the hospital bed.

"Wyatt." Nikki's focus zips from me to her daughter. "What are you doing here?"

"Why didn't you tell me it was Nikki's daughter who was sick? I thought it was Nikki." With her eyes closed, she resembles her grandmother. Evelyn as an eight-year-old. Strong gene pool.

"What are you doing here?" Nikki brushes shoulders with Ellie, helping her block my view of the bed.

"What's your daughter's name?" I ask.

"Haven. Haven's her name." Ellie is flushed.

She doesn't seem angry, which is surprising. The emotion stretching across her face isn't one I can place. I thought I recognized all Ellie's expressions, but this is new.

"It's funny how much she looks like your mother." Her sharp intake of breath draws my attention. "You don't see it? First thing I noticed."

"No, I . . ." Ellie stutters and trails off.

"How do you know about Haven?" Nikki cocks her head to the side.

She's not happy to see me. If I'd had to bet on a family member liking me, it would have been Nikki. But then I spent years confident Nikki and Evelyn were the ones who'd convinced Ellie my lifestyle was no longer acceptable. I second-guessed myself, but her tense posture now makes me wonder if I was right.

Since I got sober, I've been using TMZ as my own personal version of Facebook to keep track of my ex-girlfriend and her family. Ellie is rarely spotted anywhere off Bermuda. My fixation is weird and unhealthy. Camila told me as much.

"Uh, I think I saw Haven in a few set photos or out with you and Ellie? Maybe? I'm not sure." I toy with the brim of my hat to disguise my lie. "The website said she was yours, Nikki." The pictures I saw were taken through a long, grainy lens, showing

Haven coming in or out of a trailer holding hands with Nikki or Ellie. I couldn't quite recall . . .

"Right." Nikki shoots Ellie a glance loaded with a meaning I can't grasp. "That makes sense."

They're both being so stilted and strange. Is Haven sicker than they thought? Or maybe they think I'm a stalker with my comments about Nikki's daughter. Whatever it is, I'm not going to figure it out, so I focus on Ellie.

"Look, I'm sorry I came. You asked me not to. But if you're only giving me one day, I don't want to let it slip through my fingers."

Haven stirs in the bed and opens her eyes. They are a brilliant blue, a shade or two lighter than her grandmother's. Haven sees me, and her eyes go round. She looks to Ellie first and then to Nikki.

Ellie is mute and if it's possible, she's gotten paler. She fiddles with the sheet and takes Haven's hand in hers.

Well, if no one else is going to speak, I'll break the ice. "I'm Wyatt."

"I know who you are." Her eyes are glassy with fever, and her skin is as white as the sheets covering her slight frame.

Nikki looks as though she might throw up, and she says to Ellie, "Why don't you and Wyatt go get a coffee, and I'll stay with Haven?"

Ellie gives Haven's hand a squeeze before reluctantly letting go. "I'll return soon." She smooths Haven's hair and kisses her forehead, lingering for a beat.

"Is he coming back?" Haven stares at me.

"I don't know." Ellie holds up a thin blanket from the bottom of Haven's bed, but Haven shakes her head. The air-conditioning has made it cool in the room.

"If you want me to, I will," I say. She appears so tiny lying there in the bed, and something in my chest constricts. She's hooked up to an IV, and there's a machine that beeps periodically. Haven's vulnerability tugs at my protective instincts. *Tell me what to slay, kid, and I'll do it.*

She nods, and the worry vanishes.

"Okay, we'll see what we can round up for you while we're gone. Ice cream?" I ask. Her face lights up. "Is it okay, Nikki? If we can find some?"

"I'm not sure you should be in the room. Family only." Nikki shifts in her chair and takes Haven's hand.

"I'll buy the ice cream," Ellie says.

"Are you sure that's a good idea, Ellie? Maybe we should check with her doctor to ask if ice cream is appropriate."

"All right." I purse my lips, trying to figure out how to defuse the tension. "No ice cream. How about a teddy bear or a balloon? There'll be a gift shop somewhere."

Nikki and Ellie are locked in a silent battle I don't understand. Siblings. My younger sister and I have gotten into lots of battles of will. Anna's stubbornness drives me nuts, but I don't remember Nikki being quite so resistant to Ellie before. Maybe it's the stress of the situation.

"A balloon," Haven says from the bed. "I want him to come back. I want to talk." She glances from Ellie to Nikki and lands on Ellie.

Ellie doesn't say anything but leads me into the hall. Her behavior is odd. The tension between her and Nikki as we leave the room is unreal—worse than anything I've ever had with my sister, and that's saying something.

Once we're outside the door, I decide to tackle the situation head-on. "Are you okay, Ellie? Will Haven be okay?"

"She's—" She breaks off, and her voice catches. "It's a virus. Sometimes kids catch something that flares up and fades away. They're keeping her overnight to make sure it's not more serious. Her fever is very high, and her energy level is low."

We start down the hallway together. Having her niece so ill has thrown her. It would do the same to me. I understand that kind of responsibility because my nephew, Jamal, lives with me. But I'm surprised she's not worried about people seeing us together. We reach the end of the hallway and rather than taking us to the gift shop, Ellie stares out the large window with a view across narrow streets, palm trees, and brightly colored houses. It's a view I would normally find relaxing and peaceful, but Ellie is brimming with anxiety and sadness.

I give her space, watching her grapple with Haven's sickness. Then I approach her from behind, not touching her, but close enough she probably senses me, the same way I always sensed her. Seeing Nikki's child in the hospital bed did strange things to my insides too.

"She looks so much like your mom, and so there's this resemblance to you. A reminder of what my life could have been if I had made a different choice. Made me a little sad."

"Wyatt," Ellie says. "Please don't. Don't." Her breath hitches on a sob.

I turn her in my arms and hold her close. The number of times Ellie cried when we were together can be counted on one hand.

"She's going to be okay, right?" I rub her back in slow circles as she clutches me. I draw her closer, fitting us together. She rises on her toes and throws her arms around my neck, and I lean down to let her bury her face under my ear. I close my eyes while the scent of vanilla and flowers surrounds me. The emptiness that's plagued me isn't quite so vast with her pressed against me. We still match perfectly, like two puzzle pieces. "Ellie?" I don't want to break whatever spell has let her lean on me for support. "Are you okay?"

She nods, easing away and wiping her cheeks. "Sorry. It's just . . . the last couple of days—you, Haven, it's a lot."

"My reappearance came out of nowhere for you. But I've been trying to find my way back for years."

She shakes her head and can't quite look at me. "I find that hard to believe," she says, bitterness tingeing her voice. "I read TMZ too."

There's no defense for anything she read or saw. She left such a massive void, and I tried to fill it with more drugs, relationships, even death. Nothing worked.

"Ellie." I reach for her again.

She backs away and raises a hand to ward me off. "No, Wyatt. Just—no." She turns on her heel and yanks open the door to the stairs. "Let's get the damn balloon you promised Haven."

ELLIE

PRESENT DAY

I wait for the explosion. Tick, tick, tick. The time bomb of my life is about to detonate.

Haven eats the ice cream I bought and chats to Wyatt like they've been friends for years. The balloon he got her is tied loosely to her wrist. Wyatt hasn't asked her how old she is. Usually it seems to be the first or second question people ask. She's petite and looks younger than she is. Maybe he thinks he knows. Nikki's daughter. We didn't even have to say anything.

His baseball cap is turned backward. His posture, his mannerisms, and the jokes he tells remind me of when we met. He's so light and carefree with Haven. This moment is everything I've ever dreamed of having but haven't let myself hope for. Sober Wyatt. Here. It's mind-boggling.

She's asked him about movies, and actors and actresses he's worked with. A few questions about me too. She stumbled over calling me Ellie, but she's used my name enough in public that

I'm not sure Wyatt noticed. Why would he question it? To him, she's Nikki's.

Before answering Haven's questions about us, he glanced at me, and my heart shattered. The love in his eyes took my breath away. It's been ten years, and he still looks at me like I'm the only woman in the room.

Of course, love was never the problem.

While he stared at me, he said, "Ellie is the best woman I've ever known. You're lucky you get to spend time with her."

The truth is so much more complicated, for all of us.

There's a tightness across my chest at the sight of them together. He's patient and kind with her. Bittersweet has a new meaning.

When it starts to get late and the room shades over, one of the nurses pokes her head in. "You both staying here tonight?" She eyes Wyatt, another question on her lips.

"Ellie and I will be staying." Nikki jumps in before any other assumptions can be made.

The nurse nods. "I'll get a cot wheeled in here."

Wyatt sighs and stands. He grins at Haven. "I should probably get to my hotel. If you're still here tomorrow, would you like me to stop by?"

An objection rises to the tip of my tongue, and I hold it in. I can't deny either of them their time.

"Yes!" Haven says. "Even if I'm home, you can come over." She turns her bright eyes and flushed face to me for approval.

Nikki intervenes before Haven gets carried away. "We'll see what tomorrow brings, Haven."

"Spoken like a true mother." He stares at me, as though he's memorizing me for later. "Can I have a quick chat with you in the hall before I take off?"

"Sure," I say.

"Ellie." There's a hint of warning in Nikki's voice.

"It's fine." There's nothing Wyatt can say in the hall that'll change my life. I have Haven and a career I love. He's ten years too late to wheedle himself back in.

I follow him out of the room with my hands in the pockets of my shorts. When we're alone, I lift my eyebrows in silent question.

"Dinner tomorrow? If Haven is better?" Wyatt leans his shoulder against the wall in the hallway.

"Wyatt." Impatience seeps into my voice. "I already told you I can't."

"Sounds like won't." He scans my face, seeking something I don't want him to recognize. "Look," Wyatt says. "You can either agree to eat dinner with me or I can track you down. I've done it before."

I shake my head, more from embarrassment than annoyance. Charm seeps out of him. Part of me is dying to react to the memories he's stirred to the surface. We did have some good moments.

He crashed my date after we finished filming *Love Letters from Spain*. The memory of that night is vivid, visceral. Without a doubt, it's the moment he swept me off my feet. He disappeared overseas to do another project. I thought we were only a set romance, so I agreed to a date with a friend of a massage client. Somehow, Wyatt found out where we were eating. He turned up, pulled up a third chair to our two-person table, and ordered a meal.

The guy I was with, I don't even remember his name now, took the intrusion well. Wyatt was Wyatt, after all—enthralling when it suited him. He charmed the pants off my date, and he charmed me out of mine later. When our movie blew up, my date had a great story for parties—his dinner with Wyatt Burgess.

"Dinner," I agree against my better judgment. Maybe I owe him this chance. "But it has to be at my house, and you have to cook."

"You still don't cook?" The corners of his mouth quirk up.

"I can cook," I say. "But I'm not sure I'll ever be able to cook like you."

He rubs his hands together. "This is gonna be good, Ellie. I can sense it. The salmon?"

I close my eyes and almost moan. I snap them back open. *Shit.* Why does he keep bringing up these freaking fantastic memories? His salmon dish used to be like sex on a cedar plank.

His grin chips away at the ice around my heart. Crying in his arms earlier might have made the chipping a little easier. My senses flood with the memory of having him so close, and my eyelashes flutter.

"What time should I come over?"

"You cannot go grocery shopping." I twist the ring on my middle finger. Give an inch, and he takes a mile. "Where's your phone?"

He fishes it out of his pocket and unlocks it before passing it to me.

I click on his contacts, and I pause for a minute to question my sanity. This is for Haven. I plug my burner number into his phone. Agreeing to spend time together is wrong and right. My mind is in turmoil over the door I'm cracking open.

He's triumphant when I return his phone.

"Text me what you need. I'll buy it and come pick you up. Five o'clock?"

"Sounds perfect."

"This is conditional on Haven being out of the hospital."

"I know, Ellie. You're a good aunt."

I can't make eye contact when I give him a curt nod. *A good aunt.*

He steps closer to me and places his hands on either side of my waist. He kisses my cheek, and I breathe him in. Can't help myself. *He's here.*

"I'll see you tomorrow." He turns his baseball cap around and slips his sunglasses onto his face before heading for the stairs.

"Wyatt!" I call after him. "How are you getting back?"

"Calshae said the hotel can send a car," Wyatt says. "Go be with your family." He disappears down the stairs with a final wave.

On the threshold of Haven's room, I pause. Her storm of questions awaits me. Taking a deep breath, I enter.

Haven's raised her bed to an upright position, and as soon as she sees me, she says, "Is he gone?"

"Yes," I say.

"Mom, you have to tell him," Haven says. "He's so nice. And he's my dad. He should know he's my dad. He came, right?"

"Haven, honey. We've talked about this before." My heart squeezes at the joy and confusion on her face. I sigh and drag my chair close to the side of her bed.

"I know." Haven releases a heavy sigh. But the defeat doesn't last long. Her resolve roars back. "I want to know him. I'm old enough to get a choice." She reminds me so much of Wyatt—impulsive and bullheaded. Scares me to think where it could lead.

"You're nine. You're not twenty-nine," I say.

"If he comes tomorrow, I could tell him. Or I could slip and call you Mom in front of him."

Her attitude is partly the fever. I told her if Wyatt ever came looking, and he wasn't sick anymore, we'd tell him about her. We only recently started discussing the realities of her father's sickness. Wyatt is right about YouTube. Wonderful and horrible when your daughter is curious about her famous father.

"I'll consider it. He's here for the week. If you want to spend time with him, you can. But whether we're going to reveal you're his daughter . . . As long as you're living under my roof, it's my choice."

Haven huffs out a breath and stares at Nikki. "I spend a lot of time under your roof too. Can I tell him at your house instead?"

Shit. Her teenage years will be fun.

"Speaking of which," I say, and I glance at Nikki, "I might need a favor."

"What'd Wyatt get you to agree to outside in the hall?" Nikki's eyes narrow.

"Dinner tomorrow night."

"I'm coming!" Haven says.

"No, Haven," Nikki says. She gives me a pointed look across the bed. "If you want your mother to tell Wyatt he's your dad, then she needs to be sure he'll be good for you."

I nod, as though that's what I would have said. Our daughter as a buffer, a reminder, might be nice. Whether or not Haven could go a whole night without calling me Mom is questionable. Whenever she visits movie sets with Nikki, she calls us both Mom. People have assumed it's a cute affectation. Bermudian citizens have protected our privacy from any prying eyes, and Nikki jumped in to help me with Haven the minute I faltered and has been by my side ever since.

The nurse comes back with the bed and rolls it in. She clicks the wheels into place. "Evelyn is on rounds tonight. Hospital is buzzing that Wyatt Burgess visited." She grimaces. "You're going to tell your mother that he was here, right?"

"Yeah, I'll speak to my mom before she hears it from someone else." Since she's the doctor on call tonight, I might even get a chance to speak to her in person. Best to warn her before the hospital gossip mill gets to her. I take my phone out of my pocket and notice Wyatt's already sent me his grocery list. I type out a message to my mom and then open Wyatt's. A long list of ingredients, some I have, others I'll have to buy. As I'm reading the list, another message from him appears.

Did you watch the whole interview the other night?

"If I turned off the interview the other night, the one Wyatt gave, would I have missed anything important?" I stare at the text. Doom drops like a stone into my stomach.

Nikki's complexion loses its color. "You didn't watch the entire thing? I thought you watched all of it."

"No." I flush and glance at Haven, who is following this conversation. "When he started talking about certain people and things, I switched it off."

"Before you see him tomorrow, you should watch it. I'm not sure how you'll react." She picks at the blanket on Haven's bed.

"Was it—did he talk more about Isaac?" My sister will understand that's not something I can watch.

"No. It was about you and him. Mostly about him. But you should watch it. Really. People will assume you know."

"Can I watch it?" Haven asks when the room grows quiet.

"No," Nikki and I say in unison.

Her YouTube searches will need some heavy restrictions with the two of us thrown into the public eye again.

"Tomorrow," I say. "I'll watch it tomorrow before I pick him up."

I don't answer Wyatt's question. We're spending time together so I can determine if he is capable of being involved with his daughter. We aren't getting back together. To encourage any more closeness would be wrong.

WYATT

THIRTEEN YEARS AGO

From the set of *Love Letters from Spain*, I flew to England to prep for my chef biopic about Gordon Lampton. He's a cool guy, but learning to cook and mastering a British accent was time-consuming. After arriving from London last night, I'm enjoying some time with two of my favorite people. Anna is coming for dinner later, assuming Isaac and Ellie have found me a suitable cooking challenge to show off my abilities. They've been scheming at the computer for a while now, and I have no idea what they've picked.

Isaac snatches the paper off the printer and brings it to me at the island, where I'm working on my knife skills with a slew of vegetables strewn around me.

"I'm not even sure I like haggis," he says.

"Not exactly your mom's curry." I scan the ingredients over his shoulder.

As first-generation immigrants, Isaac's parents moved to America as kids. Other than passing on their love of Indian cuisine, speaking Hindi at extended family gatherings, and sharing with him their incomprehensible obsession with cricket, they haven't encouraged their son to delve too deeply into his Indian heritage. A strange dichotomy for him, to be American and to have other people often treat him as *other*. Bugs the shit out of me to see it, and I'm not the one it's happening to.

"The day you can cook better than my mom is the day I marry you," Isaac says.

"Generally, I don't swing that way. Unless you're paying me. Then I can swing any way you want." I grab my phone and text my driver, Kyle, the shopping list. Then I message Gordon a plea for discreet help. Haggis can't be that hard. Ellie and Isaac won't get the best of me with their menu request.

"Beer?" I get one out of the fridge and tilt the bottle toward him. Sober cooking isn't much fun.

"Nah, I took an oxy. It'll kick in soon."

"Ellie!" I yell. Sometimes my huge house isn't so great. She peers at me over the couch. "Beer?"

"Yes, please!" she calls.

"Did she just say please?" Isaac slides his phone onto the island.

"She did indeed." I grab her a beer, pop off the top, and walk it over. When I pass it to her, I kiss her forehead. A swell of protectiveness rushes over me. Nothing I wouldn't do for her.

When I return to the kitchen, Isaac says, "I can't believe she thanked you for getting her drunk."

"I kinda like it." One of the best things about Ellie is her easy-going nature. She's the opposite of my sister, who blows into the house like a thundercloud. Not that I blame her. She was stuck with my parents longer than me. Thinking of her reminds me of the low-level tension vibrating off Isaac since he arrived this afternoon. "What's up, man? You've been kinda weird today. How'd the pilot go the other week? You never texted me back."

"It was whatever. My agent said they're not sure how well I'll test with audiences."

"Say the word, and I'll make some calls. If we form our own production company, we can do whatever the fuck we want. I'm starting to think that's the way to go if these fuckwits won't let you in the door anymore."

"We're twenty-five, and we're both disorganized as shit. Who's going to run it? My parents?"

We'd pay people to do the parts we didn't want to do, which would be almost everything. I've been making money hand over fist the last few years, but Isaac has struggled to land bigger projects since we branched out into more adult content. Casting agents still throw him into the mix as the dopey sidekick teenager, but he's never the lead. Even TV has been proving harder to penetrate than either of us expected. Isaac believes his skin color is the barrier, and I'm starting to think he's right. We left the Daisy Network with the same level of fame and ability, but I eclipsed him within a year.

He's not in the mood to hear my production company idea right now. The TV pilot must have been a disaster for him to be in such a foul mood. His problem is one I'm convinced we could fix if I threw enough money at it. Prove he's bankable. Not sure how much I'd make in return at first, but that's an accounting issue.

Isaac works his jaw. "Did Ellie tell you she had an audition yesterday?"

Last night is a blur. We didn't talk much. Too busy making up for lost time. She goes to auditions all the time without telling me. Despite *Love Letters from Spain* being set to blow up her career, and our frequent tabloid appearances together, she wants to make a name for herself without my being involved.

"Her manager arranged for her to take a meeting with Phil Leeman at his house." Isaac removes a bottle from his pocket. He pries it open and takes two pills. I hold out my hand, and he drops a Percocet into it.

"No woman takes a meeting with Phil Leeman at his house. He's a class-A perv." My heart does funny things in my chest. If he hurt her, he'll find out there is nowhere in Hollywood he can hide from me. I'll ruin him.

"Ellie called me in a flood of tears yesterday afternoon after Leeman tried to force himself on her. She wasn't sure who else to call. You weren't home yet. She didn't have a ride, and she'd run out of his house." Isaac keeps his voice lowered as he speaks.

Rage rises in me, unchecked. I shouldn't have taken the Perc because a plan is forming, and I'm already not sober enough to figure out if it's a good one. No one touches Ellie without her consent and gets away with it.

"I thought about going in and kicking his ass. But Phil's got clout."

I grab my phone and call my manager to get Leeman's contact information. Phil has substantial influence, even if he shouldn't. With the trajectory my career is on, I'm not worried. He'll be a small fish in my big pond.

Ellie wanders over from the living room. She wraps her arms around me from the side, squeezing me. "Everything okay?"

Her sweet, open face resting against my chest undoes me. I'll rip Leeman to shreds. Her crying and afraid is enough to make me contemplate murder.

"Yeah, fine," I say.

She glares at Isaac, but he won't make eye contact.

My phone rings, and I pick it up. I extract myself from Ellie to grab a pen and a piece of paper from the kitchen counter. I jot down Leeman's location at the Los Angeles Country Club and hang up before my manager can ask any other questions. He wouldn't be happy with what I'm about to do. But he's well paid. He can deal with the PR and legal fallout. Ellie peers around my shoulder to see what I've written.

"You don't play golf. Why are you going there?" When I don't answer, she glances at Isaac again. His expression must give him away because she says, "Wyatt, it's fine. Really. I'm fine. Nothing really bad happened, he just—I just . . . I left. It's fine."

"It's not *fine*, Ellie. It's the opposite of *fine*," I say through gritted teeth. "You're getting a new manager. That's bullshit they set that up." I grab the piece of paper off the counter and head for the door.

She begs Isaac to intervene. *Good luck, Ellie.*

When I open the front door, she rushes to my side and tugs on my arm, trying to drag me back. "Wyatt, I don't want you to go to jail or get sued or anything. Don't do something stupid."

I wrap my arm around her waist and gently back her up against the wall at the front entrance. I smooth the hair that's fallen into her eyes. "Did he scare you, Ellie?"

She searches my face, looking torn. "Yes, but—"

I kiss her to stop her from rationalizing Leeman's behavior or her reaction. She bends into me, tugging me closer, moaning into my mouth. Taking her back to my room is so tempting. But the idea of that smug asshole seeing her at a party later, thinking he almost took something from her she didn't want to give, fuels my rage. Her body isn't his to take. It isn't anyone's.

I pull back, give her a quick peck on the forehead, and disappear out the door before she can convince me to stay. Kyle arrives through the gates right on time. What I'm about to do requires a getaway driver. My hands shake, and my head is cloudy with rage. I pass Kyle the address and climb into the back.

During the ride to the country club, I drum my fingers on the armrest. Every time I think about what could have happened to Ellie—how her day might have gone yesterday—I want to beat something bloody. If anyone put my younger sister, Anna, in a similar situation, I'd go for the jugular. When I left home, I couldn't protect her, but I do everything I can to watch out for her now that she's out of my parents' house. The predators in the industry hide in corners, but if I have to drag every one of them into the light to shield the people I love, I'll do it.

At the country club, I signal for Kyle to get out of the Rolls-Royce and follow me. He does so without question. "If I get out of hand, pull me off him, okay?" Someone needs to have a level head 'cause it sure as hell won't be me.

I storm into the dining area at the club, and a few staff try to waylay me until they recognize who I am. At the other end of the restaurant are huge bay windows. The warm California sun streams in with a view of the greens. The gold-and-brown decor is not to my taste, but I'm not in the market for a country club. Most of the patrons are wealthy, stuck-up assholes. I spot the biggest one in the far corner, talking to a woman. I hope it's his wife. "Phil Leeman!"

He turns in his seat, surprise rising to the surface. My interest in him won't make his life better, though he probably got a hard-on at the sight of me. We've never had a reason to speak before. He rises and leaves his table with his hand extended. Fat fucking chance I'll take it. I flex my fingers, draw back, and land a right hook to his face. His head jerks, and he lands on his ass. Satisfaction floods through me. Man, that felt good.

"Sir." Kyle reminds me before I can climb on top of Phil and finish the job.

"I got it, Kyle." Not dead, just warned. I shake out my hand. Been a year since that boxing movie, and I'm a little rusty.

"What the hell!" Phil rubs his cheek. A giant bruise blooms under his eye.

"Yesterday you met with Ellie Cooper at your house," I say. "You so much as look at her and I will get you blackballed. Do you understand me? Tell your pervy friends that Ellie Cooper is off limits."

He climbs to his feet awkwardly as I start to stride out. "I'm going to sue your ass, Wyatt!" he calls.

I turn and throw out my hands. "Do your worst, Phil. I have more money than God." I storm back, fist cocked. "You know what? If you're going to sue me, I might as well make the court case worth it." This time, I hit him with my left. He lands on the ground with an *oof*. Much better technique. I don't have to shake my hand at all. Or maybe the Percocet kicked in.

"Ah, sir?" Kyle strides along beside me.

I glance at him, too caught up in my own thoughts. Leeman's not gonna sue me. His dirty laundry would get aired.

"You split your knuckles." Kyle points to my hands.

Shit. Gratification swells in me. He hit the ground so hard, so shocked, each time. I flex my hands in wonder. That Percocet came in handy after all. Just the way I like it; I didn't feel a thing.

WYATT

PRESENT DAY

I'm at the front entrance of the hotel waiting for Ellie. Sweat trickles down my back. The humidity is brutal.

Earlier, I saw Haven. I took her a small tub of ice cream and stayed for a chat. She reminds me of Ellie, or maybe I want to see Ellie in her. My heart squeezed in my chest over and over again as Haven and I talked. They must spend a lot of time together. Nikki was the only one there, and I dusted off my most charming material. Ellie's sister barely cracked a smile.

Just before I left, the doctor came around and confirmed Haven's fever was gone, and the virus had likely run its course. Hearing the news was a load off my mind, and Nikki breathed an audible sigh of relief.

Ellie approaches the circular entrance of the hotel on her bike and when she stops in front of me, she takes off her helmet. Her posture is stiff, and her eyes are blazing. Something's changed, and not in the good way I expected with Haven's release from the hospital.

She throws her second helmet at me but doesn't say a word. I examine her with the helmet in my hands. This is how I expected her to react when she found out about my suicide attempt.

"Well," I say. "Are you going to tell me what I did, or should I guess?" That'd be a short game.

"I am unbelievably angry with you." Her hands shake as they rest on the handlebars.

"You didn't watch the whole interview the other night?" I climb on behind her.

She shifts forward so we aren't touching. At least this reaction makes more sense. She roars out of the hotel lot, and we make it back to her house in record time. The gates are already open when we arrive. One of her security guards must listen for her coming. She drives into the garage, takes off her helmet, and drops it on a rack. She doesn't wait for me.

I place my helmet beside hers and trail behind her with my hands in the pockets of my shorts. My approach to this conversation might set the tone for where we go from here, but I'm not sure what to say.

In the living room, she's pacing, and there's a wildness to the movement I've never seen from Ellie before. "When?" She stares at me with pained eyes. "I watched that interview a million times today, trying to put it together. When did you do it?"

"Right after you left. Within a week of you being gone." No point in lying. Most of it is common knowledge if you call the right people. Now that it's out, the tabloids have been trying to reach every person in my circle, if my social media notifications are to be believed.

"When you were admitted to the hospital for exhaustion? It wasn't exhaustion? Your stay was because of attempted suicide?" She perches on the edge of the couch and then stands again. She vibrates with restless energy, like me when I'm itching.

"Come on, Ellie. We played those games before. How many people are actually admitted for exhaustion?" I give her a wry smile. "It's rarely just that."

In many ways, we're discussing a different person. Sometimes I pretend I can't remember why I took way too many pills. Better if I don't think about my reasoning too hard. Even after years and a lot of therapy, I'm not sure if I overdosed on purpose or if I just let it happen. The result would have been the same. So I've worked to own that episode, privately until recently, and very publicly now.

"I just—I imagined you went on a bender, maybe weren't sleeping." She keeps pacing and takes a deep breath while running her hands through her hair. "Katrina Wexler. That woman who moved into our house within a month of us breaking up . . . She was some sort of suicide counselor?" Her voice brims with confusion.

"Yeah." I spread my hands wide. "The media storm about us was all bullshit."

"Those shirts," she says in disbelief. "All the team stuff. Team Ellie, Team Katrina. People were sure you cheated on me."

"What did you think?" I paid a lot of money to keep my suicide attempt quiet, and my lawyer had everyone and their uncle sign an ironclad NDA.

"That you were an asshole." She collapses onto the couch, and agony coats her face. "But I never believed you cheated on me." She shakes her head. "I would have . . . if I'd known, I . . ." She trails off, closing her eyes and swallowing. "Who found you?"

"Isaac's mom stopped by to bring me soup." That admission will make this much worse for Ellie. She loved Isaac's mom. Tanvi treated us like her kids. "She understood how torn up I was about you leaving, and coming on the heels of Isaac's death, she was worried about me. Had a right to be worried about me. I was . . ." Part of me thought I was beyond saving, not worth her time. Tanvi saw those feelings, even if she couldn't convince me to do anything productive about them. "I was out of control."

"Wyatt, you almost died." When Ellie glances up, there are tears in her eyes. "And I didn't know. I . . . If you'd died, I—I'm not sure I would have ever been okay again." Her shoulders slump, and tears trickle down her cheeks. "But you know what makes me so angry?"

I squeeze the stress ball in my pocket. The couches are between us, a barrier, giving me room to flee. But I'm not going anywhere. She needs space to process this, not me. I've had years. She's only had days and with this new bit, mere hours. "That almost dying didn't make me quit?" I rest my hands on the back of the nearest couch.

"Yes!" She bursts out. "I don't understand. Almost dying wasn't enough?"

I shake my head. "Told myself what happened wasn't because of the drugs. You were the problem. Get you out of my system, and I'd be fine. Back to normal." I rub my neck and shrug. "If there's one thing I've learned, it's that an addict can come up with all kinds of reasons for things that wouldn't make sense to anyone else."

Ellie sits on the couch, stunned. "I need time to digest all of this, I think." She glances at me. "It's so unbelievable, but it makes so much sense." She rests her head in her hands, her shoulders slumped. "Wyatt, if I'd known . . ."

"I didn't want you to know. Didn't want anyone to know. Having you come back out of sympathy or obligation . . . or even anger wasn't what I wanted." I focus on the ceiling to keep my emotions in check. "It seemed easier to let people believe I was a lying cheat than to let them realize I was a desperate fool."

She stands up and rounds the couch to stop in front of me, just out of reach. Tentatively, she slides closer and wraps her arms around my neck, drawing me into a hug. Squeezing her tight, I breathe her in. I wish I could close my eyes, take us back ten years, and tell her I'd do anything to keep her. That's the truth. I want her, and once I've got her, I'll do anything to keep her.

"I'm so glad you're still here," she whispers into my ear. "And I'm so sorry you felt so broken. I didn't realize. I had no idea."

She's pressed against me, and our bodies fit together like a key in a lock. Perfection. We stand for a long time, neither of us moving. We soak each other up. How did I let years pass without experiencing this rightness in my soul? Such a fool to think there was anything, *anything*, better than being with her.

As she starts to pull away, I say, "Did you get my groceries?"

"You still want to cook for me?" Her chuckle is a little broken, and she wipes her eyes. "We can order in or . . . I don't know." The air thickens around us, but it's not from grief or confusion this time. The urge to kiss her is a physical ache. If I didn't think she'd slap me or kick me out, I'd risk it. My hands linger on her waist.

"I want to cook for you." My voice is rough with desire.

"Wyatt."

My name is a caress from her lips, soft, pliable. No one else makes my name sound quite as good as she does.

She rises on her toes, puts her hands on the sides of my face, and kisses my cheek. "You'll never understand how glad I am," she says, "that you made it out alive."

Before I can coax her into a real kiss, she steps back and heads for the kitchen.

I follow her, and there's a surprising lightness in me now that she knows my worst secret. To hear her admit she cares, that I matter to her, validates me coming here. Time might have dulled the connection between us, but with a little polish, it'll shine again.

I lean on the kitchen island while she removes the ingredients from the fridge and various cupboards. She checks the list on her phone. The silence is companionable, despite everything we said to each other in the living room. The secrets are coming out. We're starting fresh.

When she finishes, she turns to me with her arms out. "Ta-da!"

I raise my eyebrows at the stack of spices, cooking utensils, and food items in front of me.

"No idea how to cook any of it. Gathering the ingredients, pots and pans, cutting board, and measuring things is my contribution."

"Who cooks for you normally?" I round the island and our shoulders brush as I survey everything. The recipe is one I've memorized. When we lived together, I cooked it regularly. One of our favorites.

"Anyone I want at the press of a button." She wags her phone. "I *can* cook, as you're aware. Just never elevated much past the basic heat, stir, serve." She gives me an amused look. "I'll have to go through my scripts to see if any hotshot chef wants me to play them, and then I can learn to cook like you."

A few tendrils of her hair shift over her eyebrow, and I long to brush them away. There are so many things I long to do. "I learned a lot."

"Geez. That's an understatement. You attended Gordon Lampton Chef School for his biopic and became a professional. The transformation was incredible. Isaac and I used to search for the craziest recipes we could find to see how good you were."

"I never let you down," I say with a touch of pride.

She scans my face. Her good humor fades, and she looks away.

"Apron?" I search the kitchen. Maybe the food I cooked didn't let her down, but I didn't keep my promises either.

From a drawer nearby, she takes out random things until she comes to an apron. She holds it up. Emblazoned across it are the words I don't know what I'm doing.

I burst out laughing and snatch it from her. "Who bought you this?"

She shrugs, and I put it on. Must have been an ex-boyfriend. There have been a couple from here who she took to the odd movie premiere or event. For the most part, she's kept her life locked away, out of the spotlight.

Good job, Wyatt. Way to remind her of someone else.

I shift the ingredients around and organize the kitchen tools into a pile. She takes a seat at the island, watching me. Occasionally, I glance at her.

"Like old times." I cut up the sweet potatoes.

"It's weird having you here." She stares at me with an expression I don't recognize and then she focuses on tracing the pattern of the granite with her fingertip.

I don't regret coming. Each minute I spend with her, I am that much more certain that I made the right choice to seek her out. Whoever else she's been with, she's been settling. A love like we experienced is a once-in-a-lifetime event.

I fly around the kitchen getting everything started. When I have a break in my duties, I splay my hands on the island and try to decipher the emotion behind her words. "Do you wish I hadn't come?"

"I don't know yet."

I stand straighter. Not a clear answer. Time. I just need time. There's not a doubt in my mind I can bring her around. Her quietness is unnerving, so I take out my phone. "Music?"

On the wall is a Bluetooth Connect button, and she hits it to pair it with my phone. I scroll through my playlists until I come to my favorite one. A little melancholy, but the songs fit how I'm feeling. Sad, but underneath that, hopeful. The door isn't closed on us. Get a crowbar and pry it wide open.

As the music plays, I sing along and cook. She watches me with a mixture of amusement and sadness. Even ten years later, her moods shift around me, creating the climate in the room. One of the reasons our split wrecked me so much was because I didn't see it coming. I thought I recognized her moods better than my own. I was wrong. I still don't—not well enough.

I finish everything and plate our meals as the first bars to our song start playing. Alicia Keys saving my ass again.

"It's fate." I grin.

She laughs, a real laugh, and shakes her head. "It's not fate when it's on your playlist."

"Life's about timing. The timing here is impeccable. While the food rests, you can humor me."

She eyes me. "And how would I do that?"

I hold out my hand. "It's our song."

"Wyatt." She looks from my hand to my face. "That's not a good idea."

"There's no one here to know but you and me. One dance."

She hesitates for another breath and then takes my hand. I secure her in my arms. Her cheek is on my chest, and her ear is pressed to my heart. A sigh. *She sighed.*

"Who knew that night was the start of this?" We sway to the music and I run my hand along her spine.

"Not me." There's happiness in her voice. "I had no idea what was coming. The high highs and the low lows."

"Do you ever wish you'd backed out that first night at the club? Decided I wasn't worth it?"

"Never, Wyatt. Never." The song comes to an end and she draws back, still not making eye contact.

"Ellie," I say. "If that's really true . . ." What I want to say is on the tip of my tongue, but I'm not sure she'll stick around if I voice what I'm thinking.

We can have it again. Better this time.

She takes her plate and heads for the kitchen table out by the living room. I follow her with my own plate and take a seat across from her.

Ellie focuses on her salmon for a moment. "It is true. I don't regret what we had in the past. A lot of those memories, I cherish them. We had so much fun. You, me, and Isaac. We did set the town on fire for a while. But that lifestyle wasn't sustainable. The drugs. The alcohol. The parties. The endless need to feed the paparazzi." She gestures around her. "Look at how I live. Could you live like this? On the island, away from the glitz and glamor? Could you turn away from the constant attention?"

I pinch the bridge of my nose because I haven't gotten to the nitty-gritty of what we'd do if we tried again. I want her. There isn't too much I won't give up to get her.

"Oh, Wyatt," she says with a sigh. "You haven't even considered it?" She picks up her fork and stabs her food. The salmon doesn't deserve that. "You're here, asking me to turn my back on everything I've built the last ten years, and you haven't even thought of how we'd work? None of the practicalities?"

"I want you, Ellie," I say. "How our relationship functions isn't a deal breaker. I'll do anything to make us work. The guy sitting across from you isn't the jackass who was high on drugs and dug in his heels. Told you to accept him as he was or leave." Whenever I remember the day Ellie came home with those rehab pamphlets and started talking about the benefits of getting clean and sober, I want to punch some sense into myself. Caught off guard, I'd raged out of control.

God, that fight. I never believed she'd leave. How could she leave me? She loved me so much. *God knows I loved her too much.*

"And I'm not the same person," she says.

"I'm not asking you to regress to who we were. I want us to build something new." I take a mouthful of my food and sit back in my chair, crossing my arms. "Tell me any of your other relationships have set your heart on fire the way ours did."

"Not everything has to be big and bright to be real."

"All the best things are."

"That's not true." She points her fork at me. "That's not true. Love always burns bright at first, but at some point, it doesn't have the same intensity."

The thought of her being in love with anyone else bothers me. I'm a hypocrite. After Ellie, I told a couple women I dated that I loved them. Never loved anyone with the power with which I loved her. None of the other relationships burned big enough, hot enough, bright enough to match our connection.

"We were together for three years. Are you telling me you didn't love me as much at the end as you did at the beginning?" I know the answer. Even if she left me, even if I don't understand why she changed so much so quickly, I *know* the answer.

"You're being ridiculous."

"Answer the question."

She sits back and crosses her arms.

Why won't she admit that what we had was special? I want to grab her, sweep away the plates, and show her love doesn't have to burn out. Sometimes it just burns for years, even when there's nothing to stoke the fire.

We're not over, have never truly been over. The embers are still there, and this week, I'll prove it.

ELLIE

PRESENT DAY

Every fiber of my being wants to go over, straddle him, and pretend ten years haven't passed. Long-dormant parts of me flutter to life, beating their wings, begging to be let out. My body aches in remembrance of how good we were together. But I can't. Haven is my priority, not Wyatt or my aching body.

"There's nothing wrong with stable." I toy with my food, pushing pieces of salmon around my plate. If I'm honest with myself, I would have never left Wyatt if I hadn't gotten pregnant. I'd be over in his arms right now. I'd be living in LA in our house.

Or I'd be dead. Or he'd be dead.

"There'll be no drama with us this time." His elbows are on the table, and his sincerity kills me.

"You enjoy the chaos that surrounds our industry. We're not a good fit."

"Compromise. Not new to you, I'm sure." He's being a smug bastard. I compromised all the time when we were together. He glances at his plate and his practically untouched food. "I can't prove to you I'm worth the risk if you won't see me."

"You've been gone for ten years. *Ten years*. You've been here for forty-eight hours. Did you expect me to drop everything? Pick up where we left off? Even if I had, you haven't considered how a relationship would work between us." I sigh and pick up my plate, no longer hungry.

In the kitchen, I tuck away ingredients and wipe the counters. Collapsing in a flood of tears on my bed is appealing. I want to be sure of Wyatt's state of mind. Last time we were together, I let myself get sucked into a lifestyle I almost couldn't handle. If Isaac hadn't overdosed, I have no idea how much further I would have slid in a bid to please Wyatt. Back then if I loved him, I had to love his addictions too. They were so intertwined I had no choice. He says he's clean, but it's been two days. What if he's not? So many of his old habits are bad for me and very bad for Haven.

Wyatt doesn't follow me, which is surprising. I bang around the kitchen, washing and putting things away. When he wanders in, his plate is empty. I can't believe he ate everything. Men are a mystery.

He's silent while he puts his plate in the dishwasher and picks up a dish towel to dry the remaining dishes. When they're done, he slings the damp cloth over his shoulder. He crosses his arms and gives me one of his intense stares. He's about to go on the offensive.

Brace yourself.

"Five more days. I want all of them."

"You can do anything you want on the island for five days."

"Perfect." His lips quirk up, but it's not quite a smile. "What time should I come over tomorrow?"

"Anything but me."

"Look, at the end of this week, if you want to write me off, I won't stop you. I'll pretend, at least in public, that you don't exist."

There's a media circus swirling around us, and I'm ignoring it. The earthquake he set off will have aftershocks in my life long after this week. My manager and PR person are earning their money. Sealing up cracks and checking for leaks. My lawyer has his ear to the ground for any rumblings about Haven. We haven't had this much scrutiny since I left Wyatt and dropped off the famous radar. When I returned to work, I took smaller projects, and I maintained a low profile. Ignoring #Wyllie again is going to take years—probably his plan when he booked Jackson's show.

I open my mouth to deny him, and Wyatt holds up his hand.

"We can spend the time here at your house or wherever you want. Doesn't have to be public. I won't"—his jaw works and determination stretches across his face—"I won't ever tell anyone what happens these next few days." He swallows. "Even if it doesn't work out. It'll stay between you and me."

I try to speak again, but he must realize he hasn't won me over yet.

"You can work me in around anything else—other commitments, people, anything. Anything, Ellie. I'll take five minutes on the balcony of my hotel room if that's all you've got."

Sounds so easy. He has no idea how high the stakes are. I'm slipping, inching closer to the person I was ten years ago.

"You don't have to answer me right now." Wyatt takes the dish towel off his shoulder and wrings it between his hands. "I'll do anything to make it work."

He tosses the towel on the island and thrusts his hands into his pockets. One of them is making a fist and then releasing something. He's bothered. He leans against the counter, his palms pressing into the cool granite. He won't keep pushing. This is my last chance to decide our path.

Wyatt is Haven's father, and she wants to know him. I owe it to her to see whether he's better now. If he can be trusted, then I have to let him in, at least for her sake. "Okay," I say. "Okay."

He nods his head. "Thanks, Ellie. I won't let you down this time."

Something in his tone causes a cascade of cracks across my heart. "I hope not," I say. He won't want to hurt me, but there's no way to gauge whether he can keep that promise. "I'll take you to your hotel."

At Nikki's house, I sit outside on my bike. Haven will be asleep since she was discharged earlier this morning when her fever broke. I'm the worst mother. No way to be sure whether giving Wyatt a chance is right or wrong. Once something happens to make me sure, it'll be too late to shield Haven. Sighing, I use my key to open my sister's door.

Nikki comes out of the kitchen with a glass of water. "Haven's already sleeping. You staying here tonight?"

I nod and walk over to her couch, collapsing into it.

She takes in my appearance while she sips her water and then sits down in one of the armchairs. "Are you okay? How'd it go with Wyatt?"

I shake my head, unable to formulate a coherent sentence. "It's dumb to even consider a second chance with him, right?"

Her sharp intake of breath is audible in the quiet room. "Wow. Already?" She sets her glass on the coffee table in front of her.

"I don't know. I don't know. I don't know." I gather my hair into a ponytail and let it fall, over and over. "It makes no sense. I don't know him anymore. In typical Wyatt fashion, he has no idea how we'd make it work with our different lifestyles. No plan, none," I say. "It's been ten years. *Ten years*. How can anyone still be in love with someone when they haven't shared a room in ten years?"

"I realized you still had feelings." Nikki moves to sit beside me on the couch. "You organized your life to avoid him, so it was clear there was something to avoid. But I started viewing the distance as more for Haven's sake than because you couldn't handle seeing him."

"If it makes you feel any better, I convinced myself it was because of Haven too." Out of the corner of my eye, I see her thoughtful frown matches mine.

"He's still the same charming guy he was before. But that's not all he was before. Remember that."

I close my eyes and press the heels of my hands into my forehead.

"There are very real reasons why he isn't parenting Haven."

Behind my eyes, a headache builds. "What if he's clean?"

"What if he's not? How do you know? You've spent ten years getting him out of your system, raising your daughter, trying to keep her away from his lifestyle, those risks. If you're not certain, you're undoing everything for nothing."

"He seems different. More grounded, less Hollywood."

"Seemed pretty Hollywood at the hospital today."

"Yeah, well, he can't help turning on the charm when someone doesn't like him. It's an instinct."

"Haven likes him just fine."

I give her the side-eye.

"Oh, you mean me. I'm not that obvious."

"You are. You really are." I sigh.

For almost my entire relationship with Wyatt, he and my sister got along very well. Now I'm not sure she dislikes him so much as she doesn't trust him and his poor decisions. We've watched the YouTube videos and the interviews that went sideways, knocked over by one stimulant too many. When I was with him, his issues seemed subtle, hard to see. Once I left, every time I caught a glimpse of him on TV or the internet, all I saw were the ravings of an addict.

"What are you going to do?" Nikki picks up her drink.

"Spend time with him for the next five days?" It's a terrible plan, cracking open a Pandora's box. But sending him away without knowing whether he's telling the truth is vindictive. My goal has been to protect Haven, not to punish Wyatt.

She nods. "Yeah, that seems like a *great* way to get him out of your system. A *great* idea."

"He's Haven's dad. She wants to know him." The more I say it, perhaps the more likely I am to believe she's the only reason I want him to stay. "If he knew about her . . ." My voice thickens, and I suck in a deep, unsteady breath. "He'd want to spend time with her too."

Nikki rubs my leg. "You haven't told him for a reason. You want reasons? Go on YouTube. There are more reasons to keep him away than to let him get close. Charming and good-looking and rich and famous don't make someone a good father."

"Once I tell him, I can't ever take it back."

Of course, he might never forgive me for not telling him in the first place or not confessing the truth as soon as he arrived at my house or when he showed up at the hospital or any other time since he reappeared. "If he relapses, the reasons I didn't tell him for ten years are validated, but Haven's protection goes up in smoke."

"Are you going to talk to Mom and Dad?"

"No," I say. "They'll call me nuts for even considering it. Like you. I don't need more of that."

Nikki sips her water for a few minutes. "Does he remember you went to see him when Haven was a baby?"

"No. I didn't expect him to. Maybe I hoped he would, but I didn't expect it." I rub my forehead. "Deep down, I knew he'd come if he remembered. He was very high and very drunk. The exact opposite of what I needed in my life, in her life." I'd done what I set out to do and told him we had a daughter. The fact I said it has always made me, at least inside, more self-righteous in my choice. If he wasn't so out of it, he would have known.

"She's your daughter, but for ten years I've functioned as her other parent. When you're on a film set or doing promotion, I've been the parent. Telling Wyatt might be your choice, but I feel like I should get a say. I've been doing his job for ten years."

I stare at the blank TV screen, absorbing her words. "I'm sorry I've put you in that position."

"I volunteered. Did I really understand what I was suggesting back then? No." She lets out a disbelieving chuckle. "Not a clue. But I don't regret being Haven's other parent, being your support system. She's a joy, Ellie. I don't want to see that joy dimmed by a man who can't keep himself together."

My sister has sacrificed relationships and freedoms she would have had if she hadn't agreed to our parenthood ruse. Even here at home, there are probably people who aren't completely sure whether Haven is Nikki's daughter or mine. When I returned from seeing Wyatt and reached out for help, my sister answered in a big way. She does deserve some input into Haven's life. She's earned it.

"I understand the risks Wyatt poses if he's still using. I lived it. Those memories are easy to access. What I don't understand is whether he's truly better, whether he'd want to be her father if I gave him a chance."

"Maybe *this* Wyatt deserves to be a dad. Maybe. That doesn't mean you and Wyatt should be together or even need to be together."

I steeple my hands over my nose, taking deep breaths. "The only way for me to be certain he should have a chance with Haven is by spending time with him. Otherwise, I'm throwing her to the wolves. I'm not doing that. I'll gladly put my own heart on the line if it spares hers. I'm capable of walking away from him if he's lying."

"You're sure? It's been ten years and I swear after two days you're already half in love with him again."

"Half in love or fully in love, Haven comes first. She did back then and she does now too. That's not going to change no matter what pretty words he sings in my ear."

"This situation screams 'potential disaster' to me." Nikki's worry and disapproval sit between us palpably. "Do you need me to get Haven to school before I head to my open house?"

"No. I'll take her. It's something I miss." I take a deep breath. "Then I'll text Wyatt."

I leave Nikki in the living room and head up the stairs to the bedroom beside Haven's. All of Haven's life, my younger sister has maintained the stability I couldn't give her once I started working again. People said I turned down jobs after Wyatt and I split because of my heartbreak. That I hid from the spotlight out of embarrassment because Wyatt appeared to move on so quickly. For more than a year, there wasn't a single paparazzi shot of me. The island was my cocoon. Even if I hadn't been pregnant, I would have refused to feed the "poor me" narrative.

When I returned to acting, the roles were smaller and in independent films. The projects had to be short. Once Haven started school, and Nikki agreed to keep her routine, I took bigger jobs, longer shoots, but never the big budget project to skyrocket me into the megafamous stratosphere again.

To the outside world, we were a close family. Keep a low enough profile and no one cares enough to come looking.

Haven is in the backseat of Nikki's car as I drive her to school. I haven't texted Wyatt yet, and he's being surprisingly patient. At one time, he'd have emailed, sent a text message, and called by now. He likes to know where he stands.

"I'm so glad you're driving me today." Haven stares out the window.

"Oh yeah?"

"Yeah, it's been forever since you drove me."

A pang of guilt strikes my heart. "You enjoy spending time with Aunt Nikki, though, right?"

"Yes, Mom." She uses that voice only a child can perfect, as though I'm the one being ridiculous. "What are you doing today? Interview? Phone call? Reading scripts?" Haven pauses and meets my eyes in the rearview mirror. "Seeing my dad?"

Her face is alight with mischief, but the emphasis on the last word is joyous. After hearing about him, she can label him hers. The novelty of having him visit might never wear off.

"Yes, I'm seeing Wyatt today for a bit." I turn into the school parking lot and pull up to the kiss-and-go curb.

She undoes her seatbelt. "I want to see him too."

I take a breath, not wanting to deny her. She doesn't understand the risk. "We'll see how today goes, okay?"

I'm not even sure what I'm going to do with Wyatt today. If he sees Haven's room, he'll be able to put the pieces together. The house is sparsely decorated except for our bedrooms, which are both filled with a flood of photos. It'll be obvious she isn't my niece. Maybe I could keep the doors to that part of the house closed.

I climb out of the car to give her a quick kiss and hug. She greets her friends as she enters the school. Watching her, I'm sure I've done the right thing in shielding her. She's happy, she's healthy, and she hasn't had to suffer most of the chaos of my lifestyle.

That chaos is waiting for me in his hotel room, and I don't know if Nikki is right and I should keep him away. When I left him, I felt like I had no choice, but I'm faced with the reality of that decision now.

I went back once to try to tell him about Haven, and when he was too out of it to understand what I was saying, I left, and I sealed the door to him behind me. Addict Wyatt wasn't an option. I couldn't build a family or any kind of life with him as he was.

Part of me, despite what I implied to Haven over the years, never expected him to be well enough to re-enter our lives. Now that he is, I'm paralyzed with indecision. At what point is it safe to trust him, if ever?

ELLIE

Eleven Years Ago

My favorite time with Wyatt is any day when we're not rushing out of the house to meet a manager, to take a meeting about an upcoming production, to discuss clothing for scheduled appearances, or to catch a flight to our next movie set.

Tomorrow I leave for a gymnastics movie I'm starring in that's shooting in Vancouver, Canada, and Wyatt begins production mid-week on a thriller filming at Alcatraz. But today we get to pretend we're normal people. A lazy morning in bed, followed by a trip to the gym, a table read for Wyatt at the studio, and then Sunday dinner. A rarity, lately.

Wyatt's phone vibrates on the bedside table, and he rolls over to grab it. He squints at the screen before writing back.

"Who's that?" I ask.

"Tommy. Reminding me I have an interview with *Faces* magazine tomorrow in Malibu for *Right of Passage*."

"What do you think they're going to ask you about?" Sometimes we play a game where we list the most ridiculous interview questions we've ever received.

He sets down his phone and stretches his arm across my middle, tugging me close to him. "Probably bring up my relationship with my parents. Ties into the movie, and everyone's always looking for the emancipation details."

His emancipation and his family dynamics are murky waters to wade into when he hasn't self-medicated. Any time I try to gently prod, he usually shuts me down. Tells me they aren't memories worth reliving.

"Are you going to discuss it?"

"It's not a great story." He traces the curve of my hip. "My hairdresser-to-the-stars mother and my boom-operator father had kids as a way to stop working and get high all the time. From the time I was a baby, I was in commercials. Same with Anna. We were a means to an end. Not kids to raise."

My upbringing is on the opposite end of the spectrum. My parents doted on me and my sister, and we're all very close. Wyatt's already told me that I'll never meet his parents, and he's not even sure they're still alive. He says he doesn't care, but I find that incomprehensible.

"At six, I was pouring Baileys over my ice cream. At nine, my sister and I were being dragged into nightclubs with my parents. They were always after the next high—whatever that might be. By sixteen, I'd had enough. Isaac's family was proof my parents were no good. They're probably the only reason I'm not dead. Hired a lawyer, and I got the hell out of there."

"No one tried to help you?"

"Child services came once in a while, but our parents convinced us we'd be worse off with a stranger in foster care. So we lied. Maybe we would have been treated worse in care. No way to be sure."

"Why didn't Anna leave too?" We've never delved so deeply into his family history before. A comment here or there, but an entire conversation has been impossible.

"She wouldn't leave." He strokes my hair and kisses my forehead. "I think they guilt-tripped her into staying. Either way, she feels I abandoned her. Left her to fend for herself in that house."

"Sometimes the best thing you can do is save yourself." I run my fingers along his cheek. Lately, I've been worried about Anna. Wyatt doesn't see it, but she's become more erratic. Can't keep any of her modeling jobs. The last time she came to our house high, she flew into a rage at Wyatt and left scratches on his face. Isaac had to pull her off and then he held her as she cried.

We lie in silence, and Wyatt buries his face in my neck. "I've never loved anyone the way I love you."

I squeeze him tight, and I hope my next comment lands in the spirit I intend. "You and Anna went through a lot as kids. It seems like she's been struggling lately. Maybe she should talk to someone?"

He releases a deep sigh and flips off the covers. "I'm grabbing a Perc. You want anything?"

"No." The days we see Tanvi and Kabir, I don't indulge. I'm not as good at managing my ups and downs, and I hate feeling out of control.

Wyatt leans against the doorway to the en suite, a glass of water in his hand. "When I left, I let her down. I'm not doing that again."

I sit up in bed to face him and hug my knees to my chest. The distance he's kept is deliberate, and I realize I need to tread carefully. We'll never see eye to eye on his sister, but I don't know how to watch her get worse and say nothing.

"You and Anna are just really different people," he says. "We should get to the gym."

His misjudgment where she's concerned isn't new, but his version of protecting her is more like coddling. I throw back the blankets, and I pad after him into the walk-in closet.

Isaac and I take the Rolls-Royce to Tanvi and Kabir's house in West Hollywood, while Wyatt jets off on the motorcycle to pick up Anna from her latest crisis at a photoshoot.

Since the night I met Anna at the club, she's been trying to poke holes in my relationship with Wyatt. From snide comments to introducing him to a bevy of models to inventing any kind of predicament that needs his immediate attention, she's happy to drive a wedge between us however she can. She hates how much he dotes on me, and I hate how much he indulges her bad behavior.

At the house, I help Tanvi set the table while Isaac and his dad sit in the living room discussing the latest cricket scores.

"I'm so glad we could all have dinner together tonight," Tanvi says. "It's been months since everyone was in LA. You and Wyatt have been out of the country, and Anna has been modeling. Isaac has been so busy too."

Isaac has been in the city the whole time auditioning, but he avoids Sunday dinners unless the rest of us can come too. I'm pretty sure he lies to his parents about his availability. He drops in on them, but he never stays for long. As soon as he turned eighteen, he moved into Wyatt's mansion, and he's never looked back.

Lately, Isaac's work situation has been dicey. Endorsements and commercials are his bread and butter, along with some tech investments. Sometimes I think he'd be happier if he got out of the Hollywood scene. Whenever I try to discuss his employment situation, he shoves a Xanax in his mouth and tells me I don't need to worry about him.

Wyatt and Anna burst through the door. Anna is laughing with a lit cigarette in her hand. When she waves it around, Wyatt snatches it from her fingers, steals a drag, and then takes it to the sink to stub it out. As the smoke drifts toward us in the dining room, I realize it wasn't tobacco they were smoking.

Kabir and Isaac emerge from the living room, and Kabir envelops Wyatt in a hug, then Anna. "So nice to see my Burgess children," he says with a wink.

As soon as we're seated and passing the dishes Tanvi would have spent all day making, Kabir begins his familiar round of questioning.

"Isaac, when are you going to bring a girlfriend to dinner?" At the head of the table, he heaps his plate with more rice.

Isaac rubs the back of his neck, and Wyatt jumps in. "Didn't you say she was in Shanghai filming a movie?"

"Yeah," Isaac says. "She's out of the country. Next time."

"It's always next time. I'm starting to think you're ashamed of your family," Kabir says.

The only times I've met her have been in big groups at clubs or places where paparazzi lurk. None of the women he dates last very long, and his parents aren't the only ones who never get to know them.

"I just want grandbabies," Tanvi says with a wide smile. "If Isaac is not going to give them to me, I'll have to count on Wyatt and Ellie."

Wyatt chokes on his sip of his water.

"Kids?" Anna scoffs. "Yeah, right." Her eyes are glassy and bloodshot. She gives me a wicked grin. "No one at this table will be having kids. Recipe for dysfunction."

Wyatt squeezes my knee under the table. "Kids aren't really in the cards for us."

We've never talked about it, but his answer doesn't surprise me. Family, in any capacity, is a tender spot. Doesn't stop my heart from sinking a notch. While I might not want them soon, I can't imagine *never* having them. The life we live right now isn't child-friendly. Anna isn't wrong in that regard.

Tanvi taps her spoon on her plate to dislodge a piece of chicken. "You'll change your mind. Children are a gift. You are all my gifts." She takes Anna's hand and squeezes it.

Tears spring to Anna's eyes, and she covers her face for a beat. Whatever has caused her glassy eyes has also put a chink in her tough exterior. She's more prone to rages, and tears are often from regret.

"No crying at the dinner table," Isaac says, but he's on the other side of Anna, and he throws his arm around her in a consoling gesture. He whispers something in her ear, and it makes her laugh. She bumps his shoulder and picks up her fork.

"When do you start shooting the TV show?" Kabir asks Isaac.

"That was a bust." Isaac releases Anna. "Didn't test well with audiences, so they recast me. But Wyatt got me an audition for the villain in his new thriller, and I nailed it."

That's not *quite* what happened. Wyatt tied Isaac to him when the studio came calling. If they wanted Wyatt, they had to find a part for Isaac.

"You get to work with Wyatt again?" Kabir grabs a piece of naan from the center of the table. "Should be a good movie. Lots of promotion behind it. Very bankable. Maybe you can ride this opportunity to some success."

"Maybe." Isaac's tone is tinged with annoyance.

Later when we go to leave, Kabir draws Wyatt into another hug and whispers something in his ear. At the Rolls-Royce, after some cajoling from Isaac, Anna agrees to ride with him so I can go on the motorcycle with Wyatt. When they leave the house with Kyle driving, I can't contain my curiosity.

"What did Kabir say to you?" I ask.

A hint of a grin tugs at the corners of Wyatt's mouth. "Told me he was proud of me, and he thanked me for watching out for Isaac." He passes me a helmet. "About the kids thing—"

"It's okay," I say. "You don't need to explain. I understand."

He kisses my temple before putting on his helmet. "You always do."

WYATT

PRESENT DAY

I called Camila an hour ago to check in. Everything is fine at home with my sister and her son. Thank God. I don't want to cut my time short with Ellie for anything or anyone. But if my sister needed me, I'd return to LA. When we were kids, I couldn't protect her from our high-functioning drug-addicted parents, couldn't even protect myself. I'm doing my best to be there for her now. To be there for Jamal.

On my balcony, I wait for Ellie to text me. I can't be in my room. The minibar is there, calling to me. The devil in a tiny bottle. I haven't touched a drop of alcohol since I arrived, but it's getting harder and harder to resist. I should gather the bottles and take them to the front desk—remove my temptation. I stride into the room, intent on getting rid of them, when there's a knock on my door. To be safe, I check the peephole. Since I used a pseudonym, the only people who realize I'm here are staff and Ellie's family.

A sigh of relief escapes me at the glimpse of Ellie. I yank open the door, and the suddenness startles her. When the surprise dissipates, sadness settles over her features. Not the expression I want to inspire.

"You ready?" she asks.

"For anything." I tip my chin at her. "You okay?"

"Having you here is a lot to process." She shrugs, and uncertainty coats her like a blanket. "Nikki and I had a long talk."

"Let me guess. She's not happy."

"She gave me some things to think about, that's all," she says. "We don't have to go back to my place, but we shouldn't go anywhere too public either." She sticks her hands into the pockets of her shorts.

There are two places on the island that are special to me. The deserted beach and the hotel ruins. When the two of us were together and insanely famous, those places were a refuge from the craziness of our lives. I cock an eyebrow at her. "The hotel?" She didn't take us past that one the other day, so I'm hoping it's still derelict and uninhabited.

She nods and turns on her heel. The defeated slant of her shoulders causes my protectiveness to spike. Whatever she's thinking about, whatever Nikki said, makes her feel like shit. There's a thing or two I'd love to say to Nikki right now.

We pass Calshae in the hotel foyer, and I call out a hello. She waves at me as Ellie and I exit the building. Ellie tosses out a hi laced with a sheepish dip of her head.

"You two aren't close anymore?" I ask as we walk to Ellie's bike.

"We lost touch."

We climb onto the bike. This time, she doesn't move away from me when I press myself close, but she doesn't respond in typical Ellie fashion either. Nikki's words, whatever they were, must still be buzzing in her ear.

We cruise to the hotel, another out-of-the-way spot on the island. The location thrived once, long before I ever came to visit. We nicknamed it the Mermaid Mansion years ago, after its cement pool built into the ocean with mermaids perched in various positions around the ocean side, guarding swimmers from going too deep.

The hotel stands four or so stories high. The pale-pink paint is fading and chipped. There are places where the cement blocks are visible. The outline of grandeur is still there. Deserted. Private. Exactly what we need.

Ellie slides on her sunglasses, which I know are armor from me more than from the sun. We stand at the edge of the tide pool. The waves lap over the sides of the cement. Ellie sighs before she sits. I take a seat beside her, giving her a minute before I say anything. I don't want to spook her. There's a fragility that's new and old. The young girl is still there underneath.

"What are you thinking about?" I pick fragments of shells out of the surrounding sand.

"How am I supposed to understand the right thing to do with you? It's impossible." She faces the ocean, her glasses concealing her eyes.

"Follow your heart." I give her a sideways glance. Might be terrible advice, but I hope her heart leads her to me. Our connection is still there. The air between us hums with old feelings brought back to life.

She shakes her head, picking up a fistful of sand and letting it run through her fingers over and over before she speaks again. "When I left ten years ago, it was the right thing to do. You weren't good for me anymore. You wouldn't get help. I had to leave."

"Why then?" I say. "Why did you decide to leave me then? I'm not saying you were wrong. Looking back, I was out of control. My sober self can see that now. Couldn't admit it at the time." I try to slot a piece that's never fit into the puzzle. My trip here is as much about seeking answers as it is about rebuilding what we shouldn't have lost.

"Our breakup had been coming for a long time."

She's a good actress, but not good enough to make me believe something that far from the truth. Unless I was so out of it I missed all the signs, she's lying.

"Didn't feel that way."

"I'm surprised you could feel anything. Percs, oxy, Adderall, bennies. I could probably list about ten more that were in rotation. After Isaac died, your consumption went through the roof, and mine went to zero. That whole 'scared straight' thing was real for me. I didn't want to die, and I didn't want you to die either. Sober Ellie wasn't good at coping with addict Wyatt."

Maybe *that's* true. Or partially true. She's on the defensive, which isn't like her. My grief, which fueled my worst habits, would have been hard to be around, but what I don't believe is that she went home for a week and got tired of my issues and then left after barely *one* conversation. The suddenness of her departure is what throws me every time I think I'm close to cracking her true reason open.

"You lied to me about your habits all the time. You could still be on something now. How would I know?" Ellie asks.

On movie sets, during interviews, at family dinners, I could fake sobriety as long as I managed my drug combinations. An upper here, a downer there. When I wanted to be, I was a master at it.

That's all behind me now, but I can't change her opinion of me, of who I used to be, if she won't get to know me again. We're both quiet for a long time as we watch the ocean ebb and flow through the decaying cement pool.

"Did you bring a suit?" Avoidance is the best I've got right now.

She pulls her shirt away from her body. "Looks like." Her amused expression is tinged with sadness. "You're not going to touch my last question?"

"The answer is trust, Ellie. I gotta earn that. It's not going to happen in five days. It just isn't. The real question is whether you even want to take a chance. Am I worth the risk? Are we?"

"Oh, is that all?" She chuckles, a sound that is almost bitter.

"I've got the drugs under control. All I'm asking for is a chance to prove that to you." I stand and offer her my hand.

She stares at me for a moment before taking it. When I pull her up, her chest is inches from mine. Her breath catches. I grin. She gives me a gentle shove, so I'm forced to take a step back, and a laugh escapes me.

"You did that on purpose."

"I need all the advantage I can get." I wink.

"Me wanting to sleep with you isn't the same as me wanting to be with you." She takes off her shirt and shorts, and she tosses her sunglasses in her heap of clothes.

The ability to think coherently vanishes at the sight of her. Her bikini is a swirl of sea colors and fits her in the right places. She always understood how to dress for her body type. My dick twitches at the memories, the reality of her here, with me.

She raises an eyebrow.

I'm not the only one doing devious things on purpose.

I take off my shirt, slow stripper fashion, and she laughs. With a flick of my wrist, I toss my shirt right at her.

She catches it and pretends to be overwhelmed. "Oh, my gosh, Wyatt Burgess threw his shirt at me." She fans herself and tugs the shirt over her own head. "I'm *never* taking it off."

"Oh, I can think of a few ways I could get that off you." I close the distance between us, and my smile is wicked. "Looks good on you, but it'd be even better laid out on the sand."

She tries to run from me, but I grab her around the waist. Her back connects with my chest. I turn her around, keeping her as close as possible. She meets my eyes in challenge. Now *this* Ellie, I recognize. Never one to back down. I grip the bottom of my shirt and slide my hands up her body, taking the shirt with me. As the fabric comes over her head, her hair cascades around her shoulders and down her back. The things I want to do to her right now are limitless.

She gives me the once-over, and a hint of a smirk crosses her face. "Last one to the mermaids has to buy lunch." Shoving me, she sprints for the water.

I kick up the sand as I chase her. In the shallow water, I catch her. As soon as we're at swimming depth, she overtakes me. She grew up around the ocean, and she's an excellent swimmer. I survive. Barely.

We swim around the cement pool instead of through it. My eyes are open, even though the salt stings them. The fish dart underneath me as I thrash around. Ellie videotaped me swimming once. I was convinced I couldn't be that bad. At the time, I thought I did everything well. My swimming was not a pretty sight.

When I get to the closest mermaid, Ellie is already sitting on the edge of the pool. Her feet dangle in the water. I hoist myself out to sit next to her. Water streams down my chest back into the ocean, and its sticky remains coat my body. I'm more of a lounge-by-the-pool swimmer.

"Never thought to take any swimming lessons?"

"Too busy learning other skills," I say. "Unless I'm being paid to learn it, it doesn't happen."

"Favorite skill you've picked up over the years?"

We're shoulder to shoulder, and for the first time since I showed up on her doorstep a couple days ago, the rapport between us is easy. Almost like old times.

"Playing Gordon Lampton. The cooking and the accent were definitely highlights. Recently? I finished a superhero movie."

"Yeah, I knew about that." She gives me a sideways glance.

"You heard?" Did she keep tabs on me?

"I took a few calls about the love interest, but it was too high profile. Then as soon as you were locked in, that cemented my choice." She splashes the water with her fingers.

"You stopped doing big budget films. How come?"

She leans back, her palms resting on the edge of the pool. "I like my quiet life here."

I let the crush of the press get too extreme when we were younger. I lived for the attention, and the intense need to be wanted didn't fade. There was no threshold that was high enough for me. Camila has helped me delve into why I sought acceptance and love in public opinion instead of finding it in myself or in my personal relationships. No surprise to find those negatives are rooted in my parental issues.

The media machine could treat me any way they wanted as long as they fed my need to be seen, but I hated how our fame impacted Ellie. The crotch shots. The insults hurled at her. How insecure she sometimes felt. Got in more than one fight with aggressive cameramen. I was fair game, but they weren't supposed to touch her. Never quite worked like that.

"You didn't even come to the Oscars the year we were both nominated," I say.

"You mean the year you won?"

"Oh, is that what happened?"

Ellie bumps my shoulder. The waves hit the reef further out and settle as they come closer to shore. We sink into a comfortable silence. There's peace in sitting beside someone and not having to say anything.

"I watched the show on television. Not my year to win. Jen had the award locked in—her performance was head and shoulders above the rest of us." She stares at the breaking waves and then continues, "I sobbed my heart out during your speech when you raised your Oscar and said you hoped that wherever Isaac had gone, he was proud of you." She rubs a hand along my back, the way she once did years ago. "You taking Tanvi as your date slayed me. Heartbreakingly perfect." Her head falls on my shoulder.

With my arm around her, I kiss the top of her head. "Wish I'd known you were watching. I was so sure you'd be there—I got so lit up that night because I was frustrated and angry. And disappointed. Won an Oscar and didn't care. Didn't care at all. I would have given back the golden man for five minutes in a room with you."

A heavy silence rests between us. The number of times I braced myself for an encounter with her that never happened were too numerous to count. The Oscars stung more than the others. She'd been so driven to succeed when we were together, seeking out character-driven pieces and directors who would hone her skills. That nomination would have meant something to her, but not as much as avoiding me.

She eases away, but I sense her reluctance. "Ready to head back to shore? It's probably almost lunch. What do you fancy?" She slips into a British accent.

"I watched that film of yours. Was quite good." I use my best British in response.

"Ten years." She puts a hand on my unshaven face.

"Weird, isn't it?" Some things don't change. Ellie is as beautiful to me at thirty-four as she was during the three years we dated.

"You've been everywhere and nowhere." She gives me one last glance before slipping off the edge of the pool.

Everywhere and nowhere.

I don't plan on being nowhere anymore.

ELLIE

PRESENT DAY

We eat at a food truck that sells locally caught fish on a bun. Sitting on top of a picnic table on the side of the road, we have an ocean view. Being with him is normal and surreal. Ten years stretch between us, but each year is a snippet of time, not a sequence of days. Those years should matter, make it hard for us to connect, to understand, to feel close, but they've fallen away as though they didn't happen. Without Haven as evidence of their passing, I might believe we could pick up where we left off without missing a beat. Every time I glance at him, my heart aches or races, sometimes both. I can't get my bearings.

"What are you doing after this week?" I take a bite of my sandwich.

He dusts off his hands, having eaten his much faster than me. "I have a couple things to check on and take care of in LA, then I start a promotional tour for *Sixty Seconds to Live*."

His elbows rest on his knees, and he plays with his sandwich wrapper, bouncing it between his hands.

The promo material for *Sixty Seconds to Live*, his race-car movie, has been everywhere. Like many of the movies he does, it's a big, splashy production with a hefty budget. I check my watch, conscious of school ending soon.

"What do you have at three?"

"I'm picking up Haven from school." I hope I sound like a wonderful aunt and not a concerned mother.

"Nikki seems like she's doing a good job with her. Haven has a great sense of humor."

Before I can talk myself out of it, I say, "She's been asking about you. Did you want to stay and have dinner with us?"

"Yeah. I'd love that." Wyatt's eyebrows go up and then a slow smile is in bloom. He flexes his hand around the empty wrapper. "You taking her to Nikki after dinner?"

"No." The truth. Now what? "She'll stay at mine tonight."

He nods. "Being a single parent can't be easy."

My lies of omission are as bad as confirming his ideas, but I can't bring myself to lie outright. Single parenting is hard, and Nikki does bear the brunt of that when I'm on a movie set.

"Where's the father?"

"Not in the picture." A normal question to ask, but my stomach rolls.

"That's too bad." Wyatt juggles the wrapper from one hand to the other. "I can't imagine having a kid and not wanting to be involved."

When we were together, kids were an abstract thing for me and us—something for someday. The day I peed on that stick and saw the positive test result, I had a mini-panic attack. In shock, I booked myself on a flight home to have my mother confirm I was pregnant. A long chat with Nikki and my parents about my options ensued. Remembering those days causes a spike of anxiety. I was so lost and unsure. When the lines on the stick appeared, my heart understood I wouldn't be able to keep Wyatt and the baby. At that time, the two didn't go together.

"You think you'd be a good dad?" His relationship with his mother and father was fraught with animosity. In the three years we were together, I never met them, but I heard a lot, nothing good, from him and Anna.

"I'd sure as hell try, Ellie. My parents were such a disaster that I don't have good role models. But Isaac's parents were great. What happened to Isaac wasn't from a lack of love and care."

"Did you ever tell Tanvi what Isaac told us?" I keep my voice low in case anyone around us is trying to listen in.

"No. What would be the point? She can't change the past. It was too late. I felt guilty for a long time."

"About what happened to him as a kid or about his relationship with his father?" I try to make eye contact. After Isaac died, we were both so raw, in so much pain, and we never talked about Isaac's revelations. We carried the weight, and soldiering on undid both of us in different ways.

"That the abuse didn't happen to me. Stupid, I guess. I don't know. Or that I didn't somehow protect him. But he never told me. All those times we were getting wasted together and he *never* said a word."

"You were both kids." Some secrets are impossible to reveal. Haven's face flashes before me. The waves roll onto shore. "You can only ever know what people are willing to tell you. Isaac didn't want any of us to recognize his pain. I'm not sure why he told us that night, but it must have been such a heavy weight." The club was chaos. A blur. Tears prick at the back of my eyes.

"I sometimes wonder if his drug use didn't spiral even more out of control once his dad died. He got so reckless after that—mixing shit that shouldn't be mixed, hanging around people who were even worse than me," Wyatt says.

They both got deeper into prescription drugs, their Jim Beam, and their lean concoctions after Kabir died. Maybe we all did. They led and I followed. "I think about it too. If there was something I could have said that might have turned things around. But we were out of our heads. I'm not sure if I remember what happened correctly. His death doesn't feel real when I think about it too much."

"I know exactly what you mean."

Reluctantly, I check my watch again. "We should go. I have to zip home to get the car before going to Haven's school." Before she sees him, I need to lay the ground rules. "Do you mind waiting at the house while I get her?"

"You're letting me spend more time with you. I get to know your niece. I'd stand on my head if you asked me to."

"Maybe later—I'd kinda like to see that."

Wyatt's eyes darken as they meet mine. While we dated, I played a gymnast in a movie. The costume came home a few times.

"Wyatt." A glance from him can dredge up so many memories.

"I can't help where my mind goes. It was three years, Ellie. But sometimes the memories are infinite." Wyatt hops off the picnic table and throws out our garbage.

My time with him wasn't sustainable, but it sure was fun. Three of the best years of my life. The backbone of who I've become, but I won't say that out loud. Instead, I lead us to the bike.

From the back seat, Haven shifts to stare out the windshield. "He's at the house?" Her voice is an octave higher than usual.

"Yes," I say, again.

"We're eating dinner as a family?" She squeals.

"I'm still not sure if I'm going to tell him." I sigh. "It's complicated. I need you to be on your best behavior. Movie set behavior. Do you understand?"

"Sure, Ellie. Whatever you say."

I let out a frustrated groan. Sometimes her ability to flip from a nine-year-old to a teenage brat is astounding. The stakes are too high to correct her. If she wanted to, she could blow the secret up, tell Wyatt the truth. We drive the rest of the way in silence, both of us staring out windows.

The gates to the property open as we approach, and I wave to Jerome in the small security hut. Sometimes having him and Freddie, my other full-time security guard, seems excessive, but then I remember the few times someone unwanted or unexpected has turned up, and I'm grateful to have them as the first line of defense.

"Can I show Wyatt my room?" Haven asks as we enter the garage.

"No."

"Why not?" She crosses her arms and gives me a defiant pout.

"It's too risky." I put the vehicle in park. "And you're eight, if he asks your age." Guilt eats holes clean through me. I'm a bad mother. Who asks their kid to lie for them? Ugh.

She has a framed photo of me and Wyatt on her nightstand. When she was old enough to understand what happened, she insisted on a photo of both her parents. The picture of us is one Isaac took at the MTV awards, at the podium—the night of that kiss. I'm focused on Wyatt, love oozing out of me. He's looking at the crowd with his arm draped around me. We're happy and natural, unlike in the posed photos Haven finds on the internet. The moment is all us—we're not movie stars, we're two people in love.

Haven grabs her backpack from the seat beside her and follows me into the house. The most delicious smell greets me. It's like we've walked into an Italian restaurant. Wyatt isn't in the kitchen, but the oven is on with something cooking inside.

A frisson of fear snakes through me. Would he have snooped around the house? I wasn't gone that long, and he's prepared dinner.

Haven takes a few deep breaths. "He can cook? Like, more than 'heat, stir, serve'?"

The panic in my chest is threatening to take over my common sense. Wyatt wouldn't snoop. No reason to. I laugh a little while taking her backpack to try to ease the tension in me. "Yes. Remember that chef movie you asked to watch, and I said you couldn't because it had too many adult words?"

"Oh, wow." She takes another deep breath. "I don't know what he's cooking, but I'll eat it even if I don't like it."

I shake my head in amusement, following her into the living room. Wyatt is sprawled out on one of the couches, the TV remote in his hand. When he sees us come in, he sits up and gives Haven a little wave.

"What's up, Short Stuff?" Wyatt grins at Haven and pats the seat beside him.

The nickname takes me back. Isaac called me "Short Stuff" sometimes whenever he got impatient with me. His voice echoes in my head.

Haven circles the couch and plops beside Wyatt. "What're you watching?" She eyes the remote. Her afterschool routine does not involve television. In general, her access to electronics is limited.

"You don't get many stations. I was just flipping." Wyatt slouches beside her. "What do you normally do after school?"

She hesitates. "Here? I usually play outside in the pool, swim in the ocean, or read. Uh, Ellie doesn't like the TV on too much."

"Would explain the lack of good TV." Wyatt holds up the remote.

"Yeah, it's almost never on. What are you cooking?" Haven perks up as the smell wafts into the living room.

"I figured most kids like pasta, right?" He's probably wondering why I'm frozen to the spot outside the kitchen instead of joining them. "I made a version of this pasta bake I've done many times before. Your aunt didn't have much to work with in the house."

"Yeah, Aunt Ellie's not much of a cook." She gives me a conspiratorial smirk and then focuses on Wyatt again. "Is that a bathing suit? Do you want to come swim with me?"

"You coming too?" Wyatt peers at me over the back of the couch.

"Sure." I shove my hands in my pockets. "What about the oven?"

"I programmed it to send me an alert when it's almost done." He holds up his phone.

"You what?"

He laughs, a deep, full sound that I haven't heard in a long time. "It's a smart oven—you can do all kinds of things with the app enabled." He comes toward me with his phone outstretched. "You had no idea?"

"I sent Freddie to buy it—said I wanted the best. That's what he came back with." I shrug. "My other one conked out on me when I was actually attempting to cook." I shift my feet and meet his eyes. "You and Isaac were the techies. I rode on your coattails."

"I actually can't believe how good it is to talk about him again."

"You don't see Tanvi anymore? Or Anna?"

"Ah, no, I see Tanvi a lot, actually. But she never knew Isaac the way we did."

Haven's disappeared to put on her bathing suit, and the two of us are standing far too close. Neither of us makes a move to put distance between us.

"I haven't talked about him in a long time either. I've thought about him a lot. So many times. I didn't know him as long as you did, so I imagine it's even harder for you."

Haven comes bouncing into the room clad in her bathing suit, with a towel clutched in her hand. "Are you guys ready?"

"You bet," he says, and he takes a reluctant step back from me. "I need a towel. If you tell me where they are, I can grab one."

"No." He can't go down that hall. "That's okay. I'll grab them and be out in a minute."

He doesn't argue and follows Haven into the backyard, where the pool has an edgeless design, making it seem like someone could walk off the cliff and right into the ocean. When Haven was little, the design made me nervous, but we both adapted. Now I love the vastness of the view. I also like the short, narrow, rocky walk down the cliff to the private beach.

The spacious hall is full of family photos. From the linen closet, I take out two towels. I often host people in the living room and kitchen for functions, fundraisers, and the occasional interview. Those spaces are devoid of anything personal. Beyond that, the walls become a shrine to the people who matter to me most. Front and center is always Haven.

When I open the sliding door to the deck, she's showing off her swimming skills, and he's watching in awe. "She's incredible, Ellie." He smiles as she surfaces. "She said you taught her?"

"It was a family effort, I think. But yeah, we spend a lot of time together in this pool."

"She says she can kayak, canoe, snorkel, and she's been diving?" His expression turns skeptical. "Is this kid really sixteen or something?"

"She understands physical things quickly." I try to ignore the hollow pit in my stomach. "She's very sporty." Wyatt picked up many skills on movie sets. He has always been a quick study too.

He nods, and his brow creases in thought.

"Watch this." Haven pushes off the far side of the pool.

"It's a shame about her dad. She said she's only met him a couple times."

"You asked her about her dad?" A balloon of panic forms in my stomach.

"Yeah, sorry. We were chatting. She said she got her sportiness from her dad." He shrugs as though Haven's revelations are normal, natural.

Every once in a while, Haven's quickness and ease with lying makes me concerned about her teenage years. She didn't lie to Wyatt, but she misled him. I'm grateful and horrified.

"Right." I take off my clothes while I think of something to say.

Haven pops up beside Wyatt and looks between us. "What are you talking about?"

"I don't think Ellie's pleased I asked about your dad."

Haven nods as though his assumption makes sense. I brace myself. "Well, Auntie Ellie, it's true, though. I do wish I knew my dad better." She gives me a pointed look. "I wish there was some way that could happen." She grins and drops under the surface. I can't blow up at her with Wyatt here, and she knows it. If the stakes weren't so high, her behavior might even be amusing.

I slip into the water and do a few laps to clear my mind. Haven challenges Wyatt to a swimming race. He creates so many waves I worry I'll need to refill the pool. His strategy seems to be to drown Haven with his thrashing, but she's adept at swimming in open water and overtakes him.

"Let's go again." Wyatt huffs at the edge of the pool. "But I need a head start."

Haven puts her hands on her hips and shakes her head. "You're the adult. You don't get a head start."

Wyatt gestures to his heaving chest. "I almost drowned."

Haven giggles. "You almost drowned yourself. Who taught you how to swim?"

"No one, Short Stuff. My parents stuck around for the money and the drugs, not for me."

"Wyatt!" I exclaim. Why is he talking about drugs with our daughter? I'm at the opposite end of the pool, but I hear him loud and clear.

"Uggs—the money for the Uggs." His expression turns helpless. "They loved those expensive boots."

"I heard *drugs*," Haven says in a singsong voice.

"Okay." Wyatt points his finger at her. "I said drugs. But if you only remember one thing I tell you, remember this. Drugs ruin families. They don't bring them closer together."

Haven's smile fades. I wade through the pool to stand beside her. "How much longer for the food?" I throw my arm around Haven's petite shoulders.

Wyatt checks his phone, which he'd propped up by the towel. "Five minutes. I'll get out and get it ready. You ladies hungry?" He hoists himself out.

The muscles across his back and shoulders ripple. Why does he have to be in such good shape? I'm certainly hungry for something.

"Sorry—I shouldn't have . . . that was dumb." Wyatt dries off, and he nods at Haven, who has swum away.

I shrug. Haven will have something to say about his words later, I am sure, but not for the reasons he thinks. "You didn't mean anything by it."

He gives a slight nod before he disappears into the house.

WYATT

TEN YEARS AGO

Before today, I'd never thought about the heaviness of a casket, the weight of a body once the soul was gone. But it keeps running through my head as I hoist Kabir's coffin onto my shoulder. It's heavy and light, which makes no sense. I mixed too many pills before the ceremony. Since I was eating oxy and Adderall like candy, I didn't care.

My knees are wobbly, and I'm trying not to stumble out the door to the hearse. There are so many cameras and photographers, I wish I'd put one of the pills back in the bottle. Just one.

Ellie clutches Isaac's hand. He looks vacant, checked out. My mirrored expression will probably be splashed across the gossip rags tomorrow. We slide the casket into the rear of the hearse. Other people are talking around me, but I can't focus on anything or anyone.

Ellie moves beside me. Her hand starts on my lower back and travels to my shoulder. I close my eyes. Without her, I'd be lost. She's earthquake-proof and nothing shakes her. I turn, scooping her to me, and I bury my face in her neck while she squeezes me tight.

"Isaac and Tanvi are coming in our limo to the graveside service, right?" she asks into my ear. "I can't find Anna."

I shrug. My brain is fuzzy. My memory's checked out for the day.

"I think so. Tanvi said something about it." She leaves me to go to Isaac's mother. Ellie's phone is in her hand, and she's texting someone. When she glances up, her expression brims with concern. *God, I love her face.* I could sit and watch her age minute by minute and never get bored.

Kyle appears at my shoulder. "Sir, Ellie requested I get you to the car. She's escorting Tanvi and Isaac."

Of course she did. I yank at my shirt collar, which is always too tight. As we walk to the car, Kyle is silent. That's not unusual. We've known each other for years, and the silence is often comfortable.

My mind drifts to Kabir. Massive heart attacks shouldn't be a thing. Fifty-year-old men who act more like my father than my father shouldn't die out of the blue. When I've thought about that over the last few days, I've reached for a glass of lean or one of my pills more than usual. My life could be half over right now and I'd never know.

Cameras follow us and click as we walk. I glance at Kyle and then I stop in my tracks. "Where's Ellie?" My heart pumps in my chest. She's been swarmed before. When I went into the crowd to get her, I threw punches at anyone who blocked my path. There was a court date for that one.

"Ellie organized for Tim and David from the security firm to come today, and she's with them. She thought it might be a zoo." Kyle glances at me out of the corner of his eye. "She was worried about you and Isaac, sir." He motions with his hand for us to continue walking to the vehicle.

We get to the limo first, and I slide in. Kyle has the divide down between us. "Ellie's always looking after me."

"She looks after all of you," Kyle says.

The back door opens and Isaac stumbles in, followed by Tanvi, and finally Ellie slides in beside me. She squeezes my leg, and I loop her arm through mine, lacing our fingers together.

"Anna is still out there," Tanvi says, and she peers out the window. "We need to wait."

"Isaac." With my free hand, I shake his knee. "You in there, man?"

Tanvi glances at him. She's been a rock, like Ellie. Isaac, Anna, and I are eroding from the inside out.

"I'm fine," Isaac mumbles. His mother grabs his hand, and he squeezes hers without taking his focus from the window.

The rear door of the limo pops open, and Anna falls in, almost landing on Tanvi's lap. Tanvi scooches closer to Isaac to make room for Anna, who tugs on the hem of her dress.

"You were going to leave without me?" Anna glares at Ellie and then me. "Abandoning your sister?"

If I wasn't so fucking high, that comment would sting. When my parents lost my acting income, they threw her into modeling. We don't talk about what happened to her from twelve to eighteen, but I can imagine, and it's all toxic.

"No," Ellie says. "That's why we're still here. You know Wyatt wouldn't do that."

We don't mention our drugs or alcohol around Tanvi, but Anna's still got powder on her nose, and I kick her foot. When she turns toward me, I pinch my nose. She runs the back of her hand across hers and then stares out the window.

The silence in the limo is oppressive as we follow the hearse to the grave site. Kabir's brother is doing a speech, and Ellie agreed to read a poem. The rest of us couldn't face the performance. Did Tanvi experience this aching hollowness in her chest when her own parents died? Whenever the pills wear off, my brain is sucked into a black hole. That's Ellie's term, not mine. She calls it the black hole of doom.

On those days, I've wandered the house raging about parents. One way or another, parents devastate their kids, either by being shitty like mine or dying like Kabir. The world is tilted, and I'm not sure it'll ever level out again. This is a depth of heartbreak I never realized existed.

"Are you okay?" Ellie asks in a low voice.

I shake my head. Examining her hand, I lift it and press her palm to my lips. She leans her head against my side and sighs. "I can't imagine a worse day," I say.

The ceremony passes in a blur of other people's tears and the bottom of a pill bottle. When my brain checks in, I'm standing in the middle of my living room alone. I'm not sure how we got back to my place.

"Ellie? Isaac?" I call out.

"Why are you standing there?" Ellie emerges from the hallway with her brow creased.

"No idea." I shrug.

"Wyatt, man, why aren't you changed?" Isaac enters the living room from the opposite side of the house.

I stare at Ellie while I try to get my bearings. I glance down, and the pieces of my suit seem to be in the wrong order.

"We should stay home." Ellie crosses to me and wraps her arms around my waist.

"Short Stuff, don't let him wimp out on me." Isaac narrows his eyes. "Pull your shit together, Wyatt. He was *my* dad."

"I never really had a dad," I whisper.

"Yeah, mine was a good one." There's an edge in his voice that yanks me into the moment.

"What's that mean?" I take a step toward him. "He *was* good. He was a hell of a lot better than mine. You were lucky."

Isaac's dark eyes are glossy. He sniffs and shakes his head. "Get your shit together. We're going out."

"I'm not sure," Ellie says, but Isaac shoots her a glare that would get him punched if I was even close to sober.

"Short Stuff, my dad died. I watched my dad be put in the ground. I'm never gonna see him again." Annoyance spills out of him. "You can tag along to babysit Wyatt if you want, but we're doing this."

I stagger into our room, and Ellie follows on my heels.

"I'm not sure about this." She plays with her hair. She's already changed into a dress fit for the club. Stripping off my suit, I leave it on the floor. "Wyatt, did you hear me?"

"Yeah, I heard you," I snap. "He wants me to go, so I'm going."

"The two of you have been out of it all day. I'm worried, and your sister is going to be there, and she . . . She makes things worse."

"What are you trying to say?" With one leg in my jeans, I stop to stare at her.

"We're all sad, but I'm worried that one of you might go overboard."

"Get whoever it is to the hospital, have our stomach pumped or whatever they do to fix it. Tell my PR guy to label it 'exhaustion' and litter the place with NDAs. Voila. Problem solved." I slide my second leg into my pants and do them up. "It wouldn't be the first time we've had to cover up some bullshit."

She drums her fingers on the doorframe as I continue getting ready. She wants to say more, but she doesn't dare.

"Look, Ellie. I'll slow down if that'll make you happy, okay?"

She nods but doesn't make eye contact.

The shirt she loves that matches my eyes is in my hand, and I slip it over my head. I cross the room to stand in front of her. "You don't understand what this feels like."

"Do you?" She searches my face. "You and Isaac have popped so many Xanax and oxy and who knows what else the last couple of days. You're chugging lean smoothies for breakfast. I'm not sure how you feel anything."

"Thanks for everything you did today. What would I do without you?" I sigh and loop my arms around her waist, tugging her close.

Ellie frames my face. "I don't want to lose you. I love you. You're scaring me."

"I'm scaring you?" Normally, I'd brush off her concern, but she's making no effort to hide her true feelings.

"I've never seen you like this. You're losing time—gaps in your memory. You're not *you* when we're together."

"I don't want to accept this loss."

"Take all of it down one notch. I'm not saying stop; I would never ask you to stop."

I give a curt nod. Slowing down is easy. No issue.

"I'm worried about Isaac too. There's something wrong with him."

He lost his dad. He found his dad dead on their kitchen floor. She's overreacting. I leave her to get my wallet out of the front pocket of my suit pants.

"You should talk to him."

We talk all the time, and if something was really wrong, Isaac would tell me. Neither of us is any good at keeping secrets. I grab my pill bottle out of my other pocket, and I shake it. *Empty.* "Did you have any of these?"

She stares at me for a beat before shaking her head.

Going to the en suite, I count the pills out loud as I collect some from the various prescription bottles in the medicine cabinet. Variety is the spice of life. Then I add a few more. Tomorrow, I'll slow down.

"I'm not policing you," Ellie says when I come back into the bedroom. "I'm worried. It's a real thing."

"I don't usually count pills. Maybe you can start keeping track for me."

"How would I ever do that?"

"I counted them out for you just now."

"That's bullshit. You probably added pills after you stopped counting." Ellie turns to the doorway.

I grab her arm. "I love you. I'll slow down, okay? I'll slow down."

"You two lovebirds done fighting?" Isaac appears at the bedroom door. He pushes his phone into his pocket.

"Who are we going out with besides Anna?" I tug Ellie close so I can kiss the top of her head. She can never stay mad at me long.

"Jimmy Walker, Bryson McCoy, and Aman Paul."

Those names don't mean anything to Ellie, but I recognize them. "Since when?"

"What?" Isaac laughs. "I'm expanding my social circle."

"They're the same dickheads who got Anna in so much trouble the last time. I had to send Kyle to bail her out of fucking jail for disorderly conduct."

"Nothing like keeping it in the family." Isaac chuckles. "I'm the brown brother." He takes out a pack of cigarettes. "Come on, Wyatt. It's bygones."

"I'll come out 'cause you asked me to. But I'm not talking to those jackasses, and I'm keeping Anna the fuck away."

"You take things too personally. Pop another Perc. I see a sharp edge poking through." He backs up toward the front of the house. "I'll meet you in the car."

I grab my keys off the table.

"Who are those people?" Ellie's hand is grasped in mine.

"Bad news," I say. "Nothing good comes from hanging out with them."

WYATT

PRESENT DAY

Haven keeps a running commentary during dinner. Who knew a young girl could be so chatty with strangers?

"What do you think, Wyatt?" Haven takes another heaping spoonful of pasta.

The amount of food she's eating is surprising. She's a tiny slip of a thing. I've tuned out the conversation, and I glance at Ellie for help, but she offers none.

"Sorry, I think my mind wandered," I admit. "What were you wondering?"

"Kayaking and snorkeling tomorrow after school. There's a cool reef not far out. Do you want to go with me and, uh, my aunt?" she asks.

"If you want to come, you're welcome to." Ellie shrugs.

"Sounds like fun." I nudge Haven's arm.

Haven gives Ellie a triumphant look. A curious exchange. Having me back tomorrow is a victory? Nice to have someone in my corner. My support club is pretty thin on this island. Ellie shakes her head at Haven, love for her niece shining out of every pore.

Pushing back my chair, I clear my plate and grab Haven's. She thanks me, and I wink. Ellie trails behind me to the kitchen.

"I have to help Haven with her schoolwork." She puts her plate straight into the dishwasher.

"That's fine," I say over my shoulder. "I'll clean up here."

"I'll have to take you to the hotel before Haven goes to bed."

She's beside me, her shoulder almost, but not quite, brushing mine. As the sink fills, I focus on Ellie. Do women keep the same perfume for this many years? She smells like vanilla and flowers—exactly like I remember. The small space between us vibrates, two magnets struggling to stay apart. She adjusts the plug for the drain, and her arm brushes mine. She snatches her hand back like I've shocked her. It's too humid here for static electricity. I know what she feels; I feel it too.

"Calshae said she'd pick me up if it's too hard for you to get me to the hotel." The more time I get with Ellie, the better my chances will be at the end of the week.

"Is that so?" She chuckles, leaning her hip against the counter to face me. "Trust you to get the hotel owner's daughter to volunteer to be your personal driver while you're here."

"She's very concerned with customer service," I tease Ellie as I sink my hands into the soapy water.

"I bet she is." She pushes off the counter and puts away the leftovers before disappearing to help Haven.

Not wanting to disturb Haven's homework routine with my presence, I take my time cleaning. I'm wiping down the counters when Haven comes in and throws herself at me, enveloping me around the middle. With a chuckle, I drop the cloth to pick her up. Her weightlessness amazes me. Her eyes are a striking blue, and she scans my face in return, grinning.

"No one ever picks me up anymore unless they're carrying me to bed," Haven says.

"You're pretty light." I bounce her in my arms to prove my point. She's slight like her grandmother and aunt. There's almost nothing to her.

She shrugs. "I guess." She loops her arms around my neck. "I'm done my schoolwork, so I have to go to bed."

"Already?" I check the clock. Later than I thought.

"Yeah." Her eyes connect with mine and she says, "You have pretty eyes."

"I get that a lot."

"I do too," she whispers.

"You must get the color from your grandmother and your mother," I say. "They both have blue eyes too."

Ellie appears in the doorway. "You ready?" she asks Haven.

Haven hesitates for a beat longer, as though there is more she wants to say, something I'm not getting. She stares at Ellie in a silent exchange.

"Let's go." Ellie motions with her hand for Haven to follow.

"Want me to carry you to the room you're sleeping in?"

Haven hesitates, and Ellie half turns. Haven shakes her head, and I set her down. While I stand in the kitchen entry, they disappear behind the opaque door that conceals the hallway and bedrooms.

On the back patio, I grab a seat in one of the recliners. The ocean waves lap against the towering cliff edge, and the tree frogs serenade me. Life is good here, in this house. I unlock my phone to find a host of social media alerts and Throwback Thursdays dedicated to me and Ellie. Ah, yes. The media storm is still swirling far away from us. I scroll through the posts with my fake accounts, liking some, reposting others. The temptation to write something, anything, almost gets a foothold in me. But if I fan the flames more and bring the press to her doorstep, I'll be dead in the water. No one knows I'm here. She loves her privacy as much as I love the publicity. #Wyllie is still trending across several platforms.

I click on my email. My manager has a note to call him. The costar in my next film dropped out, which is going to delay production. Camila sent me an update on Anna and Jamal. Everything seems well with them. I breathe a sigh of relief. Anna is a loose cannon, but I pay Camila well to provide stability when I'm not there to do it.

Ellie comes out the doors and flops down beside me. "Success," she says.

"She's sleeping?" I close my phone and stuff it into my pocket. I don't want to remind Ellie about the world out there waiting for us to emerge.

"Yep." She crosses her hands and lays them on her stomach, kicking off her sandals. "I love sitting out here at night."

The silence is companionable before Ellie takes a deep breath. "So if you're better," she says, "how do you maintain it?"

"Willpower?" I squint. At its most basic level, that's the secret. She doesn't want the simple answer. That answer never worked for me before.

"I'm serious."

With a sigh, I stare up at the starry night, letting the cool ocean breeze blow over me. "I have Camila. She keeps me on the straight and narrow."

"And Camila would be?"

"I call her my sponsor whenever anyone asks. The easy explanation. Everyone knows what a sponsor is. But I pay her a lot of money to do more than talk me out of the bottom of a pill bottle or a line of coke or a glass of lean." Ellie's face isn't giving anything away. "She's an addiction specialist."

Ellie sinks deeper into her seat. "She's not here, so what's stopping you now?"

"Camila's not usually with me anymore. A few years ago, when I first tried to get a handle on my addiction, I took a year off from everything. I'd been doing back-to-back roles for a while. People were tired of me. I was tired of me. I cleared my schedule and focused on being better."

"Any relapses?"

"At first, yeah. A lot. I almost gave up. Being clean is hard. It's still hard. Stress balls and chewing gum live in my pockets. I work out. Run. Channel those urges into other things. I don't even take aspirin for a headache anymore."

"Alcohol?"

"What about it?" I still drink, but it's too early to admit that to Ellie. We're starting to get somewhere. There's no mixing of prescription drugs or codeine cough syrup with it anymore. The danger she'd see doesn't exist.

"You used to carry around water bottles full of Jim Beam or lean or both."

"I don't do that anymore." At least that part is true. "I'm committed to this change."

She sits forward in the lounger, bringing her knees up and encircling them with her arms. She rests her cheek on her knees and looks at me. "I want to believe that."

"I will prove it to you. It's going to take more than a week. I realize that. At the end of this week, though, you'll have to decide if you're willing to take the risk." I drop my feet off the side of the lounger, resting my forearms on my knees. The breeze carries a whiff of her familiar perfume. *The memories.* I close my eyes.

"My reluctance is the drugs and alcohol," she whispers. "But it's not just that. I don't enjoy the spectacle you crave. When we were younger, some of the attention was fun, until it wasn't. Twitter, Instagram, Facebook, Snapchat, TikTok, and who knows what else—I can't keep up, but you do. Most of it didn't even exist when we were a couple. That kind of exposure isn't good for me and for—well, I don't want it." Her face is lit by the soft interior lights flooding through the doors and windows. Her hair catches on the breeze, lifting and swirling. She brushes it behind her ears.

"I'll quit all of it. I'll scale it back. Whatever. I don't care about that noise. It's fun, and it doesn't bother me. But if you hate it, I'll stop."

From my pocket, I take out the stress ball. I squeeze it and toss it from hand to hand, waiting for Ellie to come up with another obstacle to jump. Whatever blockade she erects, I'm scaling it, smashing it, removing it.

She snatches the ball from me in midair. "I don't want to live in LA again, ever."

Shit. Compromise on this point is going to be tricky. Anna and Jamal are in LA, not to mention Tanvi, who only has me left. "We could split our time."

"No." She tosses the ball back.

I catch it. "Come on, Ellie. You gotta be reasonable." I reach for her hand, but she scoots over to the far side of the lounger and stands.

"You should probably call Calshae for that ride." Ellie heads into the house without a backward glance.

I race after her and catch her arm in the living room. "You're being irrational."

She rounds on me in a burst of anger. "I'm being irrational? You showed up here ten years too late. You expect me to flip my life, to start over again with you. My house and family are here, not in LA."

I close the space between us, and she doesn't back away. I lace her fingers with mine. She deflates, the anger going out of her. She was always this way, quick to ignite, quick to burn out. Yet another reason I thought she'd come back to me. But she never did.

"Are you happy?" I ask.

"You want me to say I'm happy?"

I release one of her hands and put my arm around her waist, tugging her close. "I want you to *be* happy."

She stares at our joined hands and makes no move to step away. "I'm content."

"That's not the same thing."

"I know. But being happy with someone means they can make me sad too." Tension crackles between us. We're so close my breath stirs her hair.

A buzzing noise interrupts the silence. I curse the vibration in my pocket. *Ignore it.*

She steps back as though she's come out of a trance. "It's getting late," she says. "You should call for that ride."

I remove my phone from my pocket and see my home number. "Sorry," I say to Ellie. "I'll be a minute. I need to take this." With a grimace, I head into the kitchen and press Talk.

ELLIE

Present Day

While Wyatt is in the kitchen, I turn on my regular phone. I ignore the messages, voice mails, and other nonsense I'll be forced to deal with eventually. My PR can handle the bulk of the storm.

I scroll through my contacts, searching for Calshae's number. There she is. I send a text asking her to collect Wyatt if she's available.

Slouched into the couch, I wait for her reply. My skin hums from standing so close to Wyatt, from touching him. Any time I come near something similar with anyone else, I cut the relationship short. Tell myself I no longer crave the intensity. But that isn't it. I fear the kind of love Wyatt inspires. Once you realize its power, you either seek the sensation like an addict or run like hell whenever that emotion appears. I'm a runner; Wyatt is a seeker.

Calshae sends a thumbs-up emoji, and I sigh with relief. He needs to leave before I cave in an epic manner. Haven does not need to wake up tomorrow morning to find her father slept over. If he kissed me, he could ask for anything, and I'd give it.

I wander into the kitchen to tell Wyatt Calshae is on her way.

"I pay people to do those things," Wyatt says. "Have someone do it. If it's too hard for you to manage with Jamal, ask Camila to take over."

I stand in the doorway and frown. Jamal? He sees me and looks flustered.

"Look, I gotta go. You understand where I am." He listens for a moment and then sighs. "I know, I know. It's fine. It's fine. I'll see you in a few days, okay?"

He hangs up and slips the phone into his pocket.

"I texted Calshae. She's on her way."

He leans against the island and watches me, not bothering to explain his conversation. While he doesn't owe me the information, I want the details, even if I don't deserve them. His stare means he's calculating something. "What's up for tomorrow?"

"If we can't agree on how a relationship will work, it's best if we let whatever this once was go." Last time I compromised about everything, but I'm not a young, naive girl in love anymore.

"There might be movement on my end about where we live. I have something I'll need to check, but location isn't a deal breaker for me."

"You're willing to say anything. Anything to get me to say yes."

"So?" He shrugs.

"Once I say yes, I'm worried you'll change the playing field. Suddenly LA needs to be a compromise. Your social media accounts are for fun, maybe a drink or two socially . . ." I picture the younger Wyatt, who had no boundaries. The security intercom buzzer goes, and I walk over and press it. "Yeah, Freddie?"

"Calshae Simmons says she's here to get Wyatt?"

Thank God the island is small. "He'll be out in a minute," I say. "Tell her I said thanks for coming."

"Tomorrow, Ellie," he reminds me.

"It's a busy day." Only a partial lie. I could rearrange most of my commitments, but I haven't yet. I open the side door.

He stands so close the heat radiating off his body warms me. I shouldn't make eye contact. Avoid the charm. *Keep your head down, Ellie.*

When I glance up, his light eyes are filled with sincerity, not the desire or teasing I expected. Whatever he's going to say next, he'll mean it.

"You can be happy with me. I won't be the one making you sad anymore."

"My mom and I are having breakfast. I'm running a drama program in the afternoon for kids at a local high school." He lights up. "You can't come," I say. "Teenagers and their phones. You'd be spread across the internet."

"Kids love me." Wyatt waggles his eyebrows. He must be able to sense I'm close to giving in.

"Most people seem to—color me surprised." A short laugh escapes me.

"You wound me, Ellie." He takes my hand and places it in the center of his chest.

My breath catches, and my heart kicks into gear. A simple touch from him electrifies my body. Deeply unfair for this intensity to still exist between us.

"Dinner? That's it. Haven wanted to do that kayaking and snorkeling thing." He's pressing his advantage. His instincts are good.

I mull it over for a moment and nod. Dinner is harmless, right? He smooths my hair and kisses my forehead before disappearing out the door.

My eyes are closed to savor the contact, and the cool ocean breeze blows around me. Haven's the only reason I'm not following him out the door to drag him back. I must keep my head level. I can't be swept away again.

My mother pours another cup of tea from the tea set on her kitchen table and tips her chin in expectation. We've discussed everything but Wyatt. People talk, and the hospital is a gossip hive.

"What do you want to know?" I sigh.

"It should be obvious." She throws out the hand that isn't holding her cup of tea. "Are you going to tell him about Haven?"

"I'm not sure." I wiggle in my seat. The big question, the one looming over every interaction.

"How long did he say he's been clean and sober?"

"About two years." Not long, but I don't know how long it needs to be.

My mother works with addiction cases as a doctor. The first time I brought Wyatt home, she told me he seemed like a nice guy, but it was a shame about the drug habit. Those words would come to haunt me later.

"Are you happy he's here?" She's getting to the other heart of the matter.

I take a deep breath and decide on honesty. "Yes."

"Mm-hmm."

"What does that mean?"

"Do you remember about a year ago, when you were dating Matt, I asked if you would ever get married?"

That conversation is burned into my brain. At that point, marrying Matt hadn't occurred to me. We broke up not long after. Even though the relationship was good, I couldn't make myself feel what Matt clearly felt.

"I realized then Wyatt was the one holding you back. Whether you want to admit it or not, you've had one foot in a relationship with him for ten years. That's the truth. You never let anyone else get close enough. The men you dated after him were dependable, reasonable, logical. Wonderful for some, but not right for you."

I take my empty cup to the sink. My mother has always been insightful. In the ten years since I left him, she's never confronted me about my residual feelings. "Why didn't you say anything?" I turn around so I'm leaning against the counter to face her.

"Because if he was still an addict, love or not, he wasn't right for you and Haven. He wasn't. He couldn't be."

"You always seemed to like my other boyfriends . . ."

"There's nothing not to like. Steady, dependable. They treated you well. You seemed to like them."

"You make it sound so dry."

"Seems like a good word."

I've never thought of my mother as being on Wyatt's side, and maybe that's not what this is either. Maybe she's digging at the same point as Wyatt. There is a difference between happy and content. But I'm terrified of what Wyatt and I will have to wade through to have any chance at happiness again. "Should I tell him about Haven?"

"I can't decide that for you." She consults her teacup, as though it has all the answers. "If it was me, I'd wait a day or two. The risk, of course, is twofold. Someone else could expose you—so many people on the island are aware she's his. And the second problem is that the longer you wait, the more likely he is to be Wyatt-level angry."

Wyatt-level angry. Been a while since I've had to consider that.

"But it's not my fault. I tried to talk to him before leaving, and he wouldn't listen. Mom, the things he said to me that day." I shake my head. "After Haven was born, I went back to try to talk. He wasn't capable of being a good father or partner. When he didn't remember, I decided he couldn't know. Inviting that version of him into my life was a bad idea."

Her expression softens. "I'm aware of the choices you made, honey. I'm warning you Wyatt might not process it through your eyes. He's missed almost ten years with her. It's a lot. He's her father, and you've tried twice in ten years to tell him."

"Mom!" Anxiety creeps across my chest. "You're not helping."

"This is preparation for how he's going to view it. I don't disagree with how you've handled your situation. Given the lifestyle Wyatt was leading, you did your best to protect Haven and keep her safe." My mother's blue eyes are filled with sympathy. "I realize how hard it was for you to give him up."

My secret shame is how much I resented Haven for the first few months. If she didn't exist, I would have been with Wyatt. But I made the choice to keep her, knowing what it might mean. Deep down, I was sure Wyatt would cave. He'd seek me out. He'd get help. I didn't expect it to take him ten years. The way he loved me—I didn't believe there was anything bigger, more intense than that. I was wrong.

"I want you to understand that if you do tell him, it might not be sunshine and roses with a happily-ever-after." She drains the last of her tea and crosses to put it in the sink beside me.

"He's decided she's Nikki's daughter with a deadbeat guy."

"Yes, Nikki told me. That's what you've wanted the rest of the world to believe. Why wouldn't he?"

"I guess I thought that once he saw her, he might recognize the parts of himself in her that I see so clearly."

"Oh, honey. You have to *know* to look. That's doubly true if you're a man." She gives me a wink.

"What does Dad think?"

"Oh, in your father's eyes, you and Nikki can do no wrong. He'd walk through fire for you both."

We've always had a strong father-daughter relationship. "Haven should have a chance to experience that relationship with Wyatt."

My mother doesn't say anything; she just looks at me with her wise eyes.

"If he seems okay today and tomorrow, I'll tell him."

She pats me on the arm. "Good girl."

ELLIE

TEN YEARS AGO

Wyatt and Isaac are passed out in lounge chairs on the other side of my parents' pool. We went out last night and partied a little too hard. Par for the course lately. The two of them seem to be in a battle to see who can be more wasted. Calshae and Nikki found their outlandish behavior hilarious, but I can't help feeling as though we're on a collision course.

Beside me, my mother flicks through a magazine. We're here for a long weekend. Wyatt's idea. He wanted to get Isaac away from LA for a while. His father's death and the dried-up acting roles have finally led Isaac to agree to a production company. The only problem is that neither of them are in the proper headspace to build the company with good people. Instead, I'm the one trying to do the hiring, and I don't have a freaking clue what I'm doing.

"When you first brought him home," my mother says as she flips a page, "I could see what he was. I've seen it before. But

I wasn't worried about you because I thought you were smart enough to stay out of it."

I'm glad for my sunglasses when she stops turning pages to stare at me. The sheer number of tabloid stories about Wyatt and Isaac meant their exploits were bound to get back to my mother. She doesn't follow gossip, but Bermuda is small, and lots of other people would be happy to fill her in on her eldest daughter's colorful, celebrity-filled party life.

"You'd tell me if you weren't okay, wouldn't you? No matter what you get yourself into, I would always help you get out."

"I'm fine." Despite the life Wyatt, Isaac, and Anna lead, the only thing I have ever craved is Wyatt—his company, his attention, his touch.

"But *they* aren't. And if you truly are fine, then you're lucky." She tips her chin at Wyatt and Isaac. "The path they are on doesn't lead anywhere good. You understand that."

If she'd witnessed the depths Wyatt and Isaac had sunk to over the last few months, she'd lock me up in a rehab center as a precaution. Isaac had a friend of a friend hook him up with all kinds of drugs the minute we arrived on the island. Their addictions don't take vacations.

When Wyatt suggested coming here, I tried to talk him out of it. There was never any doubt my mother would recognize what was happening, but I'm surprised it took her almost twenty-four hours to say something. Of course, Wyatt has been glued to me since we arrived. Just as strong as his raging addiction seems to be this overwhelming need to keep me close, as though he's afraid to lose anyone else.

"It's just because Isaac's dad died," I say.

"They weren't like this before?"

"Not like this," I say. Sometimes uncontrolled, but never this sustained. "Wyatt says he can pull himself out."

"Ah, yes. The promises of an addict." She sets the magazine on the table between our lounge chairs. "I know you love him very much. But there is a difference between being a partner and being a caretaker. To me, it seems as though the balance has shifted."

I adjust my sunglasses and cross my arms. "This is temporary. Once he and Isaac get beyond Kabir's death, they'll be back to normal."

"What is normal?"

I huff out a breath.

My mother releases a sigh. "You've never had to face the death of someone close. My mother died when you were very young, but here's what I'll tell you about that kind of grief—it might fade, but it never, ever goes away. What those boys are carrying now, they'll be carrying thirty years from now. How they carry it is their choice, but it'll always be there. Right now they're trying to bury their grief under a mountain of substances. The bad news is that once they try to level out again, they'll realize the grief they haven't dealt with is still there. Just as powerful and present as it was before."

"I'm not leaving him," I say.

"I'm not asking you to, though I can't say I'd be upset if you did."

Wyatt and Isaac stir on the loungers, and the front door opens. Nikki and Calshae tease my dad for being inside on a beautiful day, and their flip-flops slap against the tile floor as they make their way to the open patio doors.

"Don't get dragged into those deep depths with him." Her stare is penetrating. "When you can't get someone back, the temptation is to get lost with them."

On Front Street, Isaac slings his arm over my shoulders and passes me his cigarette. "Your momma is scary as fuck."

I choke on the smoke and cough my laughter. "She's not scary."

"She is. I grew up with 'don't ask, don't tell' parents. They never ask why I might seem out of my head sometimes, and I don't mention the drugs. Every time I talk to your mom, I feel like she's going to crawl into my brain and discover all my secrets."

"Evelyn's not that bad," Wyatt says, and he flicks the ash off his cigarette. "She sure as shit doesn't think I'm good enough for her daughter. Cannot blame her for that."

I leave Isaac to wrap both my arms around Wyatt's middle, and Isaac turns to talk to Calshae and some of my other friends from high school while we wander toward the Hamilton Princess for drinks on the terrace. "I love you, and so she'll love you." Eventually. At some point she'll have to love him because I plan on being with him forever.

Isaac takes a tin out of his pocket, and he lights a blunt. He motions to Wyatt after he inhales deeply. I try to grab it on the way past, but Wyatt blocks me and takes his own puff before raising his eyebrows.

"Get Ellie a regular one," he says to Isaac before taking another drag.

The one he has must be laced with something, and when he releases a deep sigh and his shoulders loosen, I figure it's heroin. When I'm home, I keep my consumption of harder drugs to a minimum. My mother doesn't know what she's talking about. Wyatt understands me, looks after me.

Isaac lights a joint and passes it to me. We've reached the entrance for the Hamilton Princess, but instead of going in, we stand outside the arched entrance smoking. Wyatt and Isaac keep their blunt to themselves, but I pass the joint to any of my friends who want it.

Inside, we order rum swizzles from the bar closest to the terrace entrance. We aren't there long before Wyatt passes me his glass, and he disappears to the bathroom with Isaac.

Calshae appears at my side, stirring her drink with her straw. "I'm not sure my liver can take another night with them."

"It's a whole new level of partying," I say. After three years, I've experienced it all.

Wyatt returns, and he takes his drink from my hand before turning to Calshae and asking about her future aspirations.

Since he's been working in the industry forever, he loves asking other people about what they want to do with their lives.

As the night wears on, we lose track of each other in the crowd. People are snapping photos of him and asking for autographs. Since I grew up here, I'm less in demand, and Isaac might as well be Wyatt's groupie for all the attention people seem to be paying him.

Last call has gone out when I go in search of Wyatt. He and Isaac have disappeared to the bathroom several times in the last half hour, which means they're likely hopped up on a wicked drug combination. I strut around the terrace, weaving between groups of people. This panic gripping my chest could be paranoia or it may be justified. Hard to tell after the amount I've had to drink.

Rather than asking people if they've seen him, I head toward the water. Though Wyatt is a terrible swimmer, he has a strange fascination with water when he's high. In the distance, outside the well-lit area, I catch sight of a figure tightrope-walking along the waist-high ledge that borders the water to the left of the marina. The top of the wall is flat and wide, but Wyatt is weaving.

"Wyatt?" I call when I get close enough. A commotion breaks out behind me on the terrace, but I'm laser-focused on him. One wrong step, and he's tumbling into the dark ocean below fully dressed. It's not a long drop, but at night, with his poor swimming . . . I can't catch a full breath.

He glances up, and a grin splits his face. He seems to forget he's on the ledge because he tries to walk toward me at a normal speed, and he topples off the side, toward the ocean.

I let out a cry, and I rush over to the edge. Down below, Wyatt is thrashing in the water, but rather than swimming to the boat dock or back toward the wall, he's headed out into the darkness.

I kick off my shoes, and I launch myself into the surf. When I hit it, the coolness sends a shot of adrenaline through me. Wyatt is easy to catch, but he's already barely keeping his head above water. I latch onto him, and he scrambles for me, pushing me down with his weight. Before I go under, I manage to snatch a breath.

When I resurface, Wyatt's face is barely visible against the gentle waves. He's going to drown. A cry of agony escapes my lips, and I plunge back over to him. I manage to grab the neck of his T-shirt, and I drag him through the water behind me toward the dock. At the edge of the concrete pier, I swing him around, and Wyatt grips the ladder.

"You're stronger than you look." His voice brims with amusement, and I want to slap him.

The adrenaline and the shock of the situation has washed away any of my drunkenness. We could have died. He could have died. I hold onto the ladder with one hand while I grip his chin with the other. "Are you okay?"

"If you wanted a swim, you should have told me." He runs a hand down his face, wiping away the residual water, and he grins.

Once we're at the top of the ladder, he slings his arm around my shoulders while rivers of water run off us. The terrace has been cleared out, and the staff eye us as we walk past.

"Are you okay?" one of the bartenders calls to us as he cleans up his station.

"Went for a swim," Wyatt calls back. "Water is refreshing."

The guy chuckles, and I shake my head.

Outside the hotel, Calshae, Nikki, and Isaac are bent over laughing about something while the rest of my friends are trying to coax them toward Front Street so we can walk home.

"What's going on?" I ask.

"Isaac climbed the moon gate and got banned from the hotel for life. They took a copy of his license and everything." Nikki blinks and cocks her head. "Are you wet?"

"I went for a swim, and Ellie came too," Wyatt says.

Isaac claps Wyatt on the back and launches into the story of when they were high and jumped off a roof into a shallow pool. As they walk, water forms rivers on the ground from Wyatt's soaked clothing. I shiver as a breeze sweeps across Front Street.

While I peer into the starless sky, Nikki recounts Isaac's moon gate escapades, and I wonder whether my mother is right—that the depths will keep dragging us down until one of us drowns.

WYATT

PRESENT DAY

I toss another pebble into the water, and it skips across the surface. A day and a half left. Annoyance floats above me like a cloud. Ellie could have cleared her schedule. She could have breakfast with her mother any day.

"That was a good one," Calshae says from her seat on the blanket.

"There are no good rocks on this beach."

"We pay a lot of money for there to be *no* rocks on this beach. Every time you find a pebble, I consider firing our beach maintenance people."

"Not worth it. Not high tourist season." I bend down to grab another tiny pebble and rub it between my fingers. "Thanks for coming out here with me. I'm not good at being alone."

"Sometimes being alone is good for you." She sifts sand with her hands. "Any progress with Ellie?"

"No idea. She's hard to read. Something is holding her back."

"Probably the addiction thing." Calshae doesn't miss a beat.

I turn on her, and I'm sure my frustration spews out of me. Of course that's a factor, but during every conversation, there's an undercurrent I can't quite ride to its logical conclusion. There's something else.

She holds up her hands. "Come on. You can't pretend that's not a big deal. We hung out when you and Ellie were together, and I've seen the YouTube videos."

"Made bad choices the first year or so after she left me," I admit. "A cease and desist went out on as many of those as I could wrangle." Most of those videos are a black hole. I want to crush the pebble in my hand. "That's not representative of who I am. Hell, I was never like that with Ellie when we were together. I went insane for a while." Which reminds me of something I haven't gotten around to asking. "Why aren't you two friends anymore?"

"I wouldn't say we aren't friends. It's complicated. People drift apart for lots of reasons." Calshae smiles, and her white teeth are striking against her dark face.

Sort of what Ellie said too, but again there was an under-current to the conversation. Most of the time I drift from people when they start treating me like the bank of fame and fortune instead of a friend. Can't imagine that was the issue between Calshae and Ellie, since they are both from prominent and wealthy families on the island. Whatever happened to their friendship, Ellie hasn't minded me spending time with Calshae, and I liked her company then and now. She's a straight shooter.

"You leave the island not tomorrow but the morning after that, right?" she asks. "Want me to drive you?"

I squint out at the ocean. "I'm kinda hoping Ellie might want to take me."

"If that doesn't work out, I'm around that morning anyway."

I search for more rocks, wandering down the beach. There's a restlessness in me today that I don't like. Whatever is preventing Ellie from diving back in with me is niggling at my brain, prompting my addictive tendencies. Whenever there's a chance something in life is going to be painful or hurtful, my instinct is to reach for old habits to soften the blow.

"Hey, Calshae." I walk back toward her.

She raises her head in question.

"Where's the school Ellie is helping out at today?"

"That's not a good idea."

"I gotta keep occupied or I'll do something stupid." I fish the stress ball out of my pocket and squeeze it over and over for emphasis.

"What would you be doing if you were at home?"

I flex the stress ball a few more times. "Running around after a three-year-old."

She frowns and looks confused. "You have a kid? Does Ellie know?"

"He's not mine. My sister lives with me in LA. Very few people are aware. She doesn't enjoy the attention anymore, but she needs my help."

"Have you told Ellie? I'd think that would be kinda an important detail."

"Ellie hasn't really asked about Anna." She brought her up the other day, but I sidestepped the question. "It's a long story, but she lives with me now and so does Jamal." I crash down beside Calshae on the blanket. "Ellie and Anna didn't get along."

"Yeah, I remember how tense their relationship was. She was a model for a while, right?"

"She was. Like me, she spiraled out of control once Isaac died. Couldn't hold down a job. We even lost touch for a while when we were both at our worst."

"You haven't told Ellie about Anna and Jamal?"

I shrug. There are only so many things I can spring on Ellie while I'm extending my pleas for a reunion. Pretty sure my sister is a deal breaker.

"You're being stupid." Calshae shakes her head. "You want her back, but you're not laying it all out there. I mean, she has a life here. Did you expect her to pick up and move to LA?"

"You sound like Ellie."

"Well, it's true." She dusts sand off her legs. "It's a big deal. Concealing that from Ellie isn't going to make her trust you again."

"I don't want to talk about it anymore." I lean on my elbows, staring up at the cloudless sky.

"She's got her work cut out for her with you."

"What's that mean?"

"You're still so stubborn."

"I hold a grudge like you would not believe."

"That why it took you ten years to get here?" She gives me a sideways glance.

"Maybe. Who knows? Sometimes I have no idea why it took me so long. I did try a few times. I kept waiting for Ellie to cave. There was also that small drug habit I had going on. Kept me pretty distracted from reality for a long time. Between back-to-back movie roles and feeding my addictions, I didn't let myself dwell on why I felt so shitty."

"Why are you here now?"

"My sister." I purse my lips. "We've been doing counseling, trying to get to the bottom of our mutual issues. Ellie kept coming up over and over in sessions. How much I loved her, how sad I was that I fucked it up. Anna asked me at what point I was going to go after what I wanted. Funny coming from her, but something clicked. I started making phone calls, trying to connect with Ellie, get someone to talk to me." I trace patterns in the sand.

"I remember I had a message about a year ago from your personal assistant. Ignored it."

"You and a bunch of others. Some things don't change. No one wanted me back in Ellie's life."

"Someone finally talked?" Calshae stretches out her legs in the sand.

"You don't get all my secrets, Calshae." I lie back on the blanket. "I think I should go to the school. They'll like seeing me, right? Who doesn't want to hang out with Wyatt Burgess?" I cock an eyebrow, and she grins a little. "Ellie's doing some kind of drama thing?"

"You're not going to the school."

"I'm going to do something stupid if I sit around all day." I throw an arm across my face to block out the sun.

"Going to the school would be stupid."

"I get that." Sort of. I'm sure the students would like to see me. Even Ellie wouldn't be mad for that long once I turned on the charm.

Seeing Ellie has fanned the flickering flame, creating an inferno that is threatening to consume me. I can't get her out of my head. Leaving her behind when I have to return to LA is going to gut me. If she won't give me another chance, I'm worried about my ability to cope.

"What do you normally do when you feel like this?" Calshae asks. "You can't always be playing with your nephew."

"When I'm on location or on set, I run a lot or work out. But I've done both of those this morning."

"Swim?"

"I'm a terrible swimmer."

"Want me to teach you?"

Removing my arm from across my face, I glance at her. "I'm not always the most patient person when I can't catch onto something."

"I remember you on a golf course. Then again, I think you'd been drinking that morning. Consider me warned." Calshae gestures for me to get organized. "Come on. You want to do something? I can teach you to swim. What are you doing with Ellie after Haven's done school?"

"How'd you know we were doing something with Haven too?"

Calshae stands and brushes off her legs. She takes her time before saying, "They spend a lot of time together."

"Haven wants me to kayak and snorkel with her tonight." I rise and flick the sand off my shorts. Once we're both off the blanket, I refold it into a neat square. "I would prefer it if she didn't have to save me from drowning."

"She's a great little swimmer. She's always making the local paper for her swimming competitions."

"Really?" There's a twinge of unexpected pride.

"You've been totally clean for two years?" She searches my face.

"Since I was never a boy scout, I'll swear on the Daisy Network's honor. I'll let you decide what that means." I put my hand on my chest. My drug habit started even before I was on my Daisy show. Ellie is one of the few people who realizes that. There wasn't much I kept from her.

She shakes her head and turns to walk up the path. "Come on. We'll start in the pool before we tackle the big, bad ocean," she says over her shoulder.

I stare after her. Sometimes, she says or does something that reminds me of Ellie. They used to be such great friends. Strange they've grown so far apart.

ELLIE

Present Day

Haven's laughter floats through the house as I drop my keys and purse on the island. Nikki, under protest, picked up Wyatt and Haven so they could do their kayaking and snorkeling right after school. She could also be a little more flexible in her stance toward Wyatt. She sees the risk in letting them get to know each other, and I'm starting to witness the reward.

I walk out to the back patio, which overlooks the black, rocky cliff and the route to the water. I can't see any of them, so I wander the narrow path, careful not to slip on the wet stones. Someone's walked this route a few times already. As soon as I emerge onto the beach and outcrop of rocks, Nikki, Wyatt, and Haven are visible in their snorkel gear. They're treading water by the coral with their masks propped on their foreheads.

I put my hands on my hips. Wyatt is treading water. That's a new skill. They haven't noticed me yet. "Honey, I'm home. What's for dinner?"

Wyatt catches sight of me first, and his grin causes my heart to drum in my chest. He always used to look at me that way—as though I was the only person in the universe worth noticing.

"We're pressing buttons," Nikki yells back.

Our shorthand for ordering takeout. I check my watch. My session with the drama club students at the high school ran over. If kids have questions, I stay until they're answered. Usually they're about acting terms, ways to break in, or experiences I've had on movie sets. A lot of the curiosity centered on Wyatt today: his addictions, our film together, whether he's truly better now . . . Exhausting and awkward. I don't enjoy lying, but I'm protective of my privacy when secrets can be sold. None of them knew Wyatt was on the island, so Calshae and the hotel have done a good job there.

Haven's bedtime is approaching. Someone needs to order dinner and that might as well be me. Before I can start up the hill again, Wyatt waves.

"Ellie!" His enthusiasm reminds me of Haven. "Watch!" He swims toward me in a ragged but improved front crawl. Treading water and now swimming better. What'd he do? Spend the day watching YouTube clips and teaching himself?

When he's close enough to shore to get his feet under him, he stands, and the water rushes down his toned chest. I have a hard time making eye contact with the rest of the view on display.

When I land on his face, he's grinning. "Impressive?" His eyes, almost the color of the shallow water, sparkle.

Impressive on so many levels. "What did you do today?"

"I learned to swim." He puffs out his chest.

"You taught yourself?"

He chuckles. "Nope. I tried to convince Calshae to take me to your school. She stopped me from doing something stupid by teaching me to swim."

"Calshae, huh?" My heart squeezes at the picture he's painted. "She must be a hell of a teacher."

"I'm that good?" His pleased grin widens, and he gestures over his shoulder. "Haven couldn't get over how much better I was. And this eggbeater thing for treading water—man, so hard."

Another soft laugh escapes me. The emotions running through me are jumbled together. "Calshae taught you eggbeater?"

"No, Haven did. I was sure I was going to die. But once you get the motion, it's not so bad. Still stupidly hard, but better than drowning."

The bitter and the sweet mix in me. We could have been a family for ten years if he'd gotten help. Haven would have had this relationship.

But he's here now. He's here.

Tears prick the backs of my eyes, and I focus on the distant houses while I collect myself. I shouldn't be crying over Haven teaching him the eggbeater or over one of my ex–best friends coming to my rescue.

Wyatt is now in front of me, and water trickles from his hair and along his body. "Ellie?" His voice is soft, curious. "Hey." He rubs my arm.

Somehow, he's come closer while I've been lost in thought. "Hey, Ellie. Are you okay? Did you have a rough day? Were those little shits at the high school mean to you?"

I choke out a laugh. A tear falls, and I wipe it away. "No, no. I'm okay. It was a good day."

"You sure? I'll go to that high school tomorrow and kick ass." His voice is deep and brimming with the old caring I remember so well. "If someone's hurt you, Ellie . . ."

We loved each other once, so much. Something on my face makes his brow furrow more. I take a deep, shuddering breath and shove my feelings down. We can't go back, so we have to find a way forward.

"I'm okay, Wyatt." This time there's firmness behind my words. "I'll order food, change, and come for a quick swim."

His snorkel and mask are still clutched in one hand when I slip past him and along the walkway.

I take another bite of my curry and listen to Wyatt and Haven talk around me. I ordered Indian food in honor of Tanvi. If Wyatt still spends time with her, he probably gets to eat this all the time. But I love the reminder of Isaac, of Tanvi, of what once was.

"What do you think, Ellie?" Wyatt prods, drawing me into the conversation.

"Sorry." I glance around the table. "I tuned out."

Haven shakes her head. "M—" Her eyes widen at her almost-slip. "Man," she says. "I'd get in trouble for that."

She's so comfortable around Wyatt now that I'm surprised she hasn't slipped yet. Maybe she has and Wyatt didn't realize it wasn't a flub but a tell. I take one last bite of food and my chair scrapes against the tile when I stand up. I go into the kitchen without another word.

My plate is in the sink and I stare into the drain. Energy shifts in the room when Wyatt enters. His presence whispers to my soul.

"What's going on?" Wyatt comes around me to set his plate on top of mine. "You haven't been yourself since you got home tonight."

Home. He used to be my home, and having him here in the home I built with our daughter is disorienting. I close my eyes. "I have a lot on my mind."

"Did something happen today?" He rests his side against the counter beside me.

"The kids asked a lot of questions about you. It was just . . . hard, I guess."

"About me?"

"Yeah, that's what happens when Wyatt Burgess goes on television and declares his undying love for someone. It blows up social media, tells people they should care. My life, my private life is worth caring about."

I leave out the awkwardness of discussing suicide with teenagers. Also, drugs. Too many of those kids have watched YouTube videos of Wyatt in states no one would describe as sober. Nikki and I need to keep Haven off the computer, iPad, everything electronic for a while. It's not just our relationship that's trending.

"Ellie."

"Can you leave me alone for a second? I need a minute."

He sighs, but he sidles out of the kitchen without protest. I'm not alone for long. The soft patter of Nikki's feet makes me turn. "What?" I ask sharply.

"Wyatt said you might need to talk to someone." She holds up her hands.

"It was a shitty afternoon of answering questions about Wyatt's more questionable choices. What am I doing even considering what I'm considering?"

Nikki steps closer and lowers her voice. "You mean Haven?"

"Yeah," I say in a clipped tone. "What kind of role model is he?"

"She already knows. She's known for a long time." Nikki sighs. "Stopping her from seeing him isn't going to change what's done. At least if he's around, she's not trying to find him in other ways. I don't necessarily disagree with him being part of her life. But you getting sucked back in? That terrifies me."

"He seems different. A little more together."

"Back then, I didn't have a clue what was going on with you two. Except for what happened to Isaac, you kept things to yourself. When you left Wyatt and he started to become a social media whore, the scope of the drugs was unbelievable. There's a difference between loving someone and taking care of them. Mom was right. If you'd stayed, you would have died."

"I never worried about myself. Once Isaac died, I got off the drug and alcohol train. Haven is the reason I left, but I would've been fine."

"You can't be sure."

"And neither can you." I cross my arms. "You weren't there. You don't have any idea what our life was like. We loved each other. It wasn't what you've seen. He wasn't—he wasn't exactly that person when we were together."

"You were afraid to raise a kid in his environment. You left him. That says a lot."

"And it's still Haven I'm worried about. It's not me. I'll be fine. Whatever happens, I'll be fine."

"Haven is too aware to let this go. She'll badger you for eternity to know him, to see him. You need to figure out how to allow that to happen without dragging yourself under. If he goes sideways, you need to be able to get yourself and her out." Nikki stares out the window over the sink. "If it was our dad, how would you feel about Mom if she kept him from you?"

"I'd hate her." There's no hesitation in my response. "As a kid, I would have hated her. But as an adult, I would understand. A few days ago you were against me telling him at all."

"I've had some conversations with Haven that made me realize my stance was naive. She is determined to know him." Nikki rubs her forehead. "If you wait too long, it'll be too late. He's here. She knows. You never wanted her to wonder about her father, so you've been honest. That seemed like a good plan, but it complicates things."

She has a point about trying to keep my feelings for Wyatt in check. It's possible for him to have a relationship with Haven and for me not to be part of the equation. At least she'll get her dad, and I'll maintain the perspective I'll need if he relapses.

"If you don't tell him, you'll lose Haven's respect." Nikki puts the lids back on some of the takeout containers on the counter. "She's a dog with a bone when she gets an idea in her head. I'm surprised she hasn't told him herself."

Gathering my hair into a ponytail, I secure it with the elastic around my wrist. "I'll figure it out."

"I love you, Ellie. So much." She turns to draw me into a hug.

"Can Haven stay with you tonight?"

"Are you going to tell him?" Nikki freezes for a beat before stepping back.

"I don't know. Maybe. I have a couple more questions before I'm sure that now is the best time. You're right, though. I need to do it."

She leaves me to go into the living room, and I take a few deep breaths before following her. This feels like a plan. Tell him, but make sure he understands he can't have me too. Assuming he even still wants me. There's a chance he'll never forgive me for keeping Haven a secret.

I enter the open dining and living room area and take in Wyatt and Haven playing cards at the kitchen table. "You're not teaching her how to cheat at cards, are you?"

"Uh, that would be wrong, right?" Wyatt gives me a sheepish grin.

"Watch," Haven says and then motions for Wyatt to pass her the cards. Haven does a complicated shuffle that shouldn't be possible for a nine-year-old. Wyatt's watching her with something that looks like pride. She deals the cards and then stares at Wyatt.

He's teaching her how to play poker. *Wonderful.*

"Okay." I make a throat-slitting gesture behind Haven's back, directed at Wyatt. "That's it for tonight."

"We need to get going, Haven," Nikki says.

Haven throws her cards into the center of the table and runs to hug me. I sweep her into an embrace and whisper the details in her ear. When she steps back, there's protest written on her face. Nikki must cue her over my shoulder because, other than a frown, Haven doesn't say anything.

Spinning on her heel, she races to Wyatt and throws herself at him. He catches her without missing a beat, as though they've been doing the move for years. He hoists her up in his arms and grins at her.

"Will I see you tomorrow, Short Stuff?" he asks.

"I don't know." Haven stays focused on him.

"W-e-e-e-l-l . . ." Wyatt drags out the word. "If not, I'll miss you. But I'm happy I got a chance to meet you."

"I hope I see you again really soon." She puts her hand on the side of his face and stares at him.

"Me too, Short Stuff. Me too." He sets her down, and she runs around the house collecting her things from after school. Wyatt watches her with amusement. "She's a tiny tornado," he says.

"That's an excellent description." Nikki's smile is strained.

Haven hands Nikki her backpack and then tackles Wyatt one more time. He gives her another hug and then sets her on her feet. At the side entrance, I give my sister one last squeeze, a wordless thank you. Once they're in the car, I close the door and lean against it, reluctant to venture into the living room to face Wyatt.

He wanders into the kitchen with the rest of the plates and dishes, but I can't tear my focus from the floor. Without saying a word, he loads the dishwasher and begins tidying up.

"You don't have any help?" Wyatt sticks the last dish in and closes it.

"No. Well, sometimes. If I'm having a party or function, I'll get the place cleaned by someone else." Dread is pooling in my stomach at the thought of what I'm about to do.

"You planning on staying here tonight?"

"Where else would I go?"

He tips his chin at the door I'm leaning against. "You seem pretty attached to the exit. I thought maybe you were considering an escape plan."

With my hands, I push off and stand behind the island, keeping it between us. "Sorry."

"What's going on?"

"Have you been completely honest with me?" There was the phone conversation the other day. If I'm going to tell him, I need to be certain about everything.

"Did someone tell you I hadn't been?"

Evasive. There must be something. My phone pings. When I take it out of my pocket, there's a text from my ex-boyfriend Matt. Whatever he needs, I can't deal with it now, and I switch off my phone.

"What aren't you telling me, Wyatt? There's something."

"Do you want to sit in the living room?"

I follow him with my hands shoved into my pockets. With a ball of anxiety lodged in my stomach, I brace myself for the worst. He sits on the couch, and I choose the couch opposite him.

Wyatt takes a deep breath. "It's about my sister, Anna."

My immediate reaction is to roll my eyes, but I stifle it. If there was trouble anywhere, Anna found it. She was a constant thorn in my side during my relationship with Wyatt, but he treated her with kid gloves. Part of me understood, given their terrible childhood, but no one ever gave Anna any boundaries or limits. Whatever she wanted, Wyatt gave her.

"Three years ago, she turned up at one of the drug addiction workshops Tanvi runs. She had a baby. Jamal."

Jamal. That was the name on the phone the other night.

"Anna and I lost touch when I moved out of the house we shared. Too many memories for me to stay there. Anna was constantly pawning her stuff to get money, and I guess the phone I messaged her on she didn't have access to anymore. The point is, we weren't in contact for a few years."

That tells me a lot about how out of control their addictions got. The two of them were thick as thieves when I lived with

Wyatt. A constant source of tension between me and him. For them to lose touch, they both had to be spiraling badly.

He runs his hand down his face. "When she showed up at the workshop, she told Tanvi she wanted to get clean, to raise her son in a better environment than the one we grew up with."

Tanvi has a soft spot for Wyatt and his sister. She used to have one for me too. "Okay," I say. "Does she live with Tanvi?"

"She lives with me." Wyatt grimaces. "She and Jamal share the house in LA with me."

"With you?"

"Which is why I wanted to spend at least some time in LA. Anna isn't overly stable. Sometimes for long stretches while she dries out, I take Jamal. Give him as much consistency as I can."

I try to process the new information and what's becoming clear. "You've been clean for two years?"

"Yes."

"For Jamal?" My mind goes to Haven. "How old is he?"

"He's three. Anna couldn't keep it together. She tried. She tries. Sobriety is too much sometimes."

"Where's the father?" My body is caught in waves of hot and cold. This conversation is surreal.

"Anna isn't sure who his father is. She was too high to remember. But she was hanging around a lot with Aman and that crew." He twists his hands in his lap and then takes out the stress ball.

I absorb this information. Wyatt's been preoccupied with Haven's lack of a father because he's been a father figure for Jamal. He understands the parental connection on a deeper level. I stare at my hands. If I'd told him about Haven years ago, would he have gotten clean then too? I search his face. He's brimming with sincerity. This story is true.

"One of us had to be stable. She couldn't do it, so I did."

The pieces of my heart that have been shattered for years start to slot themselves into place. I can trust him. I'm sure of it. If he got clean for Anna's child, what would he do to keep his own? "Wyatt," I say, "there's something—"

His phone rings, and he removes it from his pocket. "It's Anna. Shit. Sorry. Hold that thought. I've got to take this. Sorry. I'm so sorry." Before I can say another word, he stands and walks toward the kitchen.

ELLIE

TEN YEARS AGO

When we get to the VIP area of Club Cobra, I'm sober enough to experience a twinge of nostalgia. We haven't been here in a while, but this was the first club I went to with Wyatt and Isaac. Squeezing Wyatt's hand, I can't believe we've been together for three years. He grins and then draws my hand to his lips. Darkness sits on us like a cloak. The lack of lights is one of the things I remember Isaac saying he loved about the club. Someone could trip over a friend and never be sure who it was.

"Do you see Isaac?" My high heels bring me close enough to his ear that I don't have to shout.

"Not yet. He was coming with those assholes, though, so who knows?"

Bryson, Jimmy, and Aman. They came to the house a few times until Wyatt said he didn't like them around me when he wasn't home. The assessing gazes of Bryson and Jimmy made tiny spiders crawl over my skin. They surrounded me once when

Wyatt and Isaac weren't in the room. I tried to talk to Isaac about how they intimidated me, but he brushed me off, said Wyatt babied me. I needed a tougher skin. Then he took another oxy.

Kissing my temple, Wyatt says, "Drink?"

I nod, and he lets go of my hand to wander to the smaller VIP bar. Someone on the waitstaff could have taken our orders, but Wyatt's not good at waiting. A hand slides around my waist from behind, and I catch a whiff of familiar spicy cologne. *Isaac.*

He holds a little vial close to my face. "You in?"

I check where Wyatt is. Still at the bar. I bite my lip.

"Come on. It's not like he isn't going to hit me up as soon as he gets over here. You never get high with us anymore." His white teeth catch on the black lights, which are a club favorite.

Never is a stretch. For the last four months since Isaac's dad died, someone has needed to keep their head, and the urge to get high doesn't burn through me the way it does with them. I like the drugs and the alcohol because I feel connected to Wyatt when we do them together. In the last month, Wyatt seems to have turned a corner, and while he's still not back to normal, he's closer than he's been in a long time.

Instead of trying to explain this to Isaac, I follow him to a table crowded with other people—some I recognize, some I don't. Aman, Bryson, and Jimmy are already there. Everyone looks wasted. Glancing over my shoulder, I search for Wyatt. He's in conversation with a guy at the bar. He'll talk to anyone.

Bracing myself, I slide into the seat beside Isaac, careful to avoid Bryson and Jimmy in the process.

Isaac taps out the coke and divides it. Each person does a line in rapid succession, the usual routine. Before I do mine, I'm distracted by Isaac's gaunt profile. He hasn't been sleeping. He's in the living room at all hours of the night doing who knows what. I've tried talking to him, but he sidesteps my questions. He's a car accident in slow motion. Isaac's dad's death caused him to swerve. Now I'm waiting for the sound of the crash.

"You all right?" Isaac asks in my ear.

Snapping to attention after being lost in thought, I realize everyone is staring at me, expecting me to do my line. Without checking for Wyatt, I do it. Isaac wants to see a tougher skin, someone who is more fun, and I can pretend.

Wyatt appears now and slides my beer across the table to me. When I glance up, the coke hits me hard. He makes no effort to disguise the pissed off expression on his face. He hates when I get high without him. Sipping his beer, he scans the crowd.

Isaac chuckles beside me. "I find the two of you highly amusing."

"Why's that?" I ask.

"'Cause he loves you so damned much. It's a beautiful thing to see."

Isaac leans in, and his eyes are dilated. I giggle, even though I'm not sure what's funny.

"I'm glad I like you. For years, I worried. I didn't like any of the women he dated before you. Not one." He bumps my shoulder and grabs my beer, taking a sip. "But you're this tiny little flower. How could anyone not like you?"

"I'm a flower?" Another giggle escapes me. I close my eyes and rest my head against the back of the booth.

"The most beautiful flower in the whole world." Wyatt slides in beside me, and he tips his chin at Isaac. "Hit me."

Isaac divides more of the coke after giving me a knowing look. Both do a line and then Wyatt pulls me across his body so I'm straddling him, pinned between the table and his chest. He can never stay mad at me for long.

He fluffs my hair. Whenever I curl it, he can't keep his hands out of it. I bury my face in the crook of his neck. As he plays with my hair, my brain jumps from one thing to the next, never quite landing anywhere. I shiver, and Wyatt grips my ass, drawing me tighter, stroking my back as he chats to people at the table.

The coolness to my right draws my face out of Wyatt's neck. Time is passing in a strange pattern of fast and slow. "Where'd Isaac go?" I search the club, but it's useless with the black lights and my fuzzy brain.

"Off with Aman." His tone is annoyed. He tilts his beer to his lips around the side of me.

I climb off him and rub my head, disoriented. "I wanna talk to him."

He shrugs and stands. With his beer in one hand, he links our fingers together. Before we leave the table, he takes out a Vicodin for each of us and passes one to me. He leads me through the crowd. We wander for a few minutes without any luck. I squeeze his hand a little tighter. Unease dogs me, but I don't know if it's the drugs or something else. As we take the stairs to the second floor two at a time, Wyatt practically carries me. We go around the corner at the top, and there's a small room to the right I'd forgotten about. Wyatt and Isaac disappeared in there the very first time we came here, but I never saw either of them go back. "What's in here?" I ask as we walk through the door.

He hesitates, and then says, "Highly addictive and lethal shit. Heroin, shooting coke directly into the vein, morphine, fentanyl . . . We agreed not to go in here anymore when you were with us." This room isn't any better lit, and Wyatt narrows his eyes, searching the darkness. Tension radiates off him as he spots two people in the far corner. We're almost upon them when I realize it's Aman and Isaac, fighting in hushed voices.

"What the fuck are you doing in here?" Wyatt asks as we approach.

Isaac shoots Aman a warning glare and turns to Wyatt with a wide smile. "Taking in the view." Even in the darkness, there's something wild in Isaac's glittering eyes.

"That's bullshit. There's no fucking view here," Wyatt says. "What's up with you lately?"

My hand clutches his, but I'm focused on Aman, who is staring at Isaac. "Is something going on between you two?" The fuzziness clears as my brain ticks through their body language. Close talking, Isaac's fingers brushing Aman's hand, the way they sat next to each other in the booth earlier, sparks jumping in the dark.

Aman stiffens and shakes his head. "I'm out, man."

"Two brown brothers can't hang out without you thinking it's something shady?" Isaac directs his question at me, but he's still watching Aman leave the room.

"Not shady." I search for the right word, and I settle on one. "Intimate. You—you looked couple-ish."

When I glance at Wyatt, he doesn't seem surprised.

"It's nothing. Nothing." Isaac takes out his pills and pops two benzos into his mouth.

Isaac has dated women, at least publicly—at nightclubs and other events, when the paparazzi were present. None of them have stayed at our house.

"Brown brother's got a thing for brown brothers." Isaac pops another pill, but I can't tell what it is. He mixes all the time, but this is a lot, even for him. "A brown gay guy? One more reason for people in this business to shun me."

"I never told Ellie," Wyatt says. "Wasn't my place."

His sexual orientation is a deeply personal thing, but I've been around him for three years now. I'm not sure why Isaac would think I'd care about his sexuality or that I wouldn't keep it a secret if that's what he needed. The point of these mythical relationships when Wyatt knew the truth is beyond me.

"Ellie was never one of the people I was hiding from," Isaac says. "The *person* I was hiding from."

Then it clicks and I press a hand to my forehead. "Your dad." Kabir made many veiled comments about gay people in Los Angeles and in the film industry. His homophobia surprised me.

"Ding, ding, ding." Isaac points at me. "Ellie Cooper for the win. You've got a winner there, Wyatt. You're gonna need to hold on tight. She sees through our bullshit."

"That's what this shit's been about the last couple of weeks?" Wyatt gathers me closer to his side. "You're with Aman, and you'll never get to tell your dad the truth?"

Isaac stares at his feet and then takes his pill bottle out of his pocket again. He toys with the container, moving it from hand to hand. He narrows his eyes at Wyatt, calculating, and then he turns to me and says, "I should have gone after Phil Leeman when he tried to assault you. I'm sorry I only picked you up and didn't do anything about it."

"Oh, Isaac." Such a long time ago now, and Wyatt's split knuckles made sure no one ever tried anything again.

"No, I should have, Ellie." He holds up his hand. "I should have. That's always been my problem. I don't understand how to speak up for myself."

Wyatt glances at me, and my own confusion is mirrored in his face.

Isaac pops open his bottle and shoves another pill in his mouth. An oxy, maybe. I step forward. He's taking too many. I can't count, but that has to be too many. My brain isn't working right.

"All those years we were kids. I never stood up for myself," Isaac says.

"What are you talking about? With who?" Wyatt's grip on my hip tightens.

Isaac paces at the back of the small room. There are other people sprawled around, but they're half asleep or too busy shooting up to notice we're here.

"I bet it never happened to you. I've wondered so many times. But you're Wyatt Burgess, right? Someone hits you, you hit back twice as hard." Isaac releases an unsteady chuckle.

"Someone hit you?" Wyatt's confusion deepens.

"I don't—I don't think he means *hit*." Through the haze, ideas form in my head. I rub my forehead, trying to find clarity.

"Your girl, man. Short Stuff, you're on fire." Isaac points at me, and his grin is crooked, as though the muscles aren't working. "I didn't think they'd have tried anything with you." He grabs the back of his neck and stops pacing for a moment. "Why did I let them? I was old enough to realize what they were doing was wrong. I knew it. I did. But I . . . every time it happened, I froze. I just—I couldn't move."

Wyatt's expression is a mixture of frustration and confusion. He can't put the pieces together. Isaac's Phil Leeman happened a long time ago.

I move to stand in front of Isaac, and I take his face in my hands. "You were a kid. Whatever happened wasn't your fault," I say. "Even though you understood what they were doing was wrong, you were *just a kid*."

"I've never told anyone. Never." Isaac's eyes are locked with mine. "Who would I tell? I wanted to get into this business. I begged my parents to take me to auditions. They gave up their jobs to follow me around. But the fame wasn't enough for what they took." Anguish is written large across his expressive face. "This town. This business. It's not meant for a kid."

"It's not your fault," I say again.

"Isaac, someone . . ." Wyatt's voice trails off, and he rubs my back. "Molested you?"

"Not even once?" Isaac seeks out Wyatt. "No one tried it even once?"

"I had no idea," he says. "If I'd known . . ."

Scoffing, Isaac breaks free from me and paces again. "What would you have done? Huh? What, did I have some sign on me? Is there something about me that says people can do those things and I won't say anything? I'll just take it?" He points at himself and then pounds a fist into his chest.

My head swims from Isaac's revelations. The right words are somewhere, and I need to find them.

"I've hated that I like men touching me. My desire was disgusting. *I* was disgusting. My dad would think I was disgusting." Tears litter Isaac's face.

"I don't." My brain isn't functioning. "No, Isaac. It's not you—"

"You're my brother, man. I love you. You shoulda told me. I would have protected you." Wyatt's voice is raspy, like he's on the verge of crying. "I woulda stopped it. Whatever I had to do. I would have done something."

"How could I tell you that? Then you'd know." Isaac stops pacing and stares at him. "Then you'd realize I was weak."

Wyatt shakes his head, and I grab his hand to squeeze it. Whatever is going on with Isaac, his words are starting to slur.

That's not unusual, but he popped so many benzos and Oxy-Contin while we were talking. I can't calculate how much is too much.

"What happened to you wasn't weakness," Wyatt says. "You were a kid. They were adults, and they took advantage of you. Used their power and status against you. We were *kids*."

"But it didn't happen to *you*," Isaac says. "It happened to me. For years." Shaking his head, Isaac uses both hands to wipe his cheeks. He sniffs. "Why am I telling you this? I'm so fucked up right now. I gotta go. I gotta get out of here."

Wyatt tries to grab his arm, but Isaac shoves past us. We stampede down the stairs, with Wyatt calling Isaac's name—pleading at first, and then pissed off. Isaac moves much faster than we can. Dread fills my stomach, and acid bubbles into my throat.

Once we're outside the club, Wyatt grabs Isaac's arm and drags him to a stop. A small crowd gathers around us, and unease builds in me again. We shouldn't be doing this here. "Isaac," I say. "Let's go back inside. Drink some water. Get off this high."

"I don't feel well." In the lights from the street, a sheen of sweat glistens, and his lips don't really move when he says the words.

"What'd did you take in that room?" Wyatt scans Isaac, concern etched into his features.

On top of the pills we watched him inhale, he did coke with me and Wyatt, and he might have done something else in that room with Aman before we arrived. My heart contracts at the implication. "Let's get some water and food," I say.

Isaac chuckles and then it's as though he's a marionette whose strings have been cut. He collapses onto the ground in a puddle. The crowd gasps, and I rush to Isaac's side. As soon as I reach him, the convulsions start, his body jerking and contorting in ways a person shouldn't move.

There are so many people gathered around us, a sea of faces. Everyone is talking, or calling out to us, and there are people who are already crying. Why the fuck are they crying? They need to do something.

"Call 9-1-1!" Wyatt hollers into the crowd, grasping Isaac's head, trying to keep it cradled in his lap.

I fumble in my pocket for my phone. My fingers are too fat and useless to type in the numbers, and I have to erase them and start again.

"Stay with me, man," Wyatt says when Isaac's eyes roll back in his head.

While I try to work my phone, I scan the crowd for anyone. "Is there a doctor here?" My mom would know what to do, how to help. We just need someone to help.

A man approaches from the side. His shirt is emblazoned with Club Cobra. "I have 9-1-1 on the phone. What's the problem?"

"Overdose," Wyatt says through clenched teeth. "Cocaine, heroin, prescription pills." He's so focused on Isaac, I'm surprised he even knows to answer.

A guy comes close with his camera held out, clearly taking a photo or video, but I'm too dazed to say anything. When we don't wave off the first person, others gather closer, and the scrutiny is claustrophobia-inducing. The thumping techno music streams out the front door of the club to the crowd waiting to get in, those passing us to go home, and those who followed us out, eager for a celebrity encounter.

The seizure goes on forever, with Wyatt trying to keep Isaac's head from banging against the concrete sidewalk. Finally, he stills. I stare at the crowd, thick with strangers, and I wonder why no one has stepped forward to help. There must be *someone* who can help. "Is there a doctor?" I cry.

"He doesn't have a pulse." Panic vibrates off Wyatt. "Ellie, Ellie. Can you find a pulse?"

On my knees, I fumble at his neck and then his wrist, but it doesn't matter how hard I press, I can't feel anything. The crowd around us seems to gather closer, but none of them are helping.

Sirens build in the distance. People in the crowd are praying and crying. Their cries of terror echo the sensation building in me.

"Someone help us," I whisper.

There has to be a pulse somewhere, and I search again. People have a pulse, otherwise they're . . . His lips take on a blueish tinge. *No, no, no, no, no.*

Wyatt shifts to Isaac's chest and starts compressions. "You need to breathe into his mouth, Ellie." He doesn't break his frantic pace.

There are so many people around us that it's suffocating. Phones are out, cameras are snapping, and I dread what they're recording, what will be plastered across the news tomorrow.

When Wyatt pauses, I breathe into Isaac's mouth and his chest rises. "Come on, Isaac," he says. "Stay with us. Come on." He pushes hard and fast, and I wonder where he learned CPR.

The sirens are on top of us now, but we keep going. Someone is yelling, trying to organize the crowd, but it's thick with resistance. Everyone wants their piece.

When the paramedics appear through the crush of bodies, they push Wyatt off Isaac's chest to make him to stop. Wyatt wobbles as he tries to stand, and people in the crowd stumble with him, trying to move out of the way, but there's so many of them it's impossible. The paramedics fire questions at him about the possible drug combinations while they take vitals and confirm he's in cardiac arrest, load him onto the gurney, and rush him into the ambulance.

Kyle pushes through the crowd, and he's aided by Club Cobra bouncers who help guide us to the waiting car. Wyatt slides in, but he avoids eye contact. He stares out the window. "He's going to be fine," he says as we drive to the hospital. "He's tough. He'll pull through. He won't die."

My heart beats hard in my chest, and Wyatt's mantra is almost drowned out. If Isaac dies . . . He can't die. He's invincible. He's taken a lot more drugs than he did tonight. My memory flashes with the oxy and benzos Isaac took as we talked. So many.

We arrive at the hospital and rush through the emergency doors. At the threshold, we're greeted by a doctor who takes us to a curtained room. Behind the curtain there needs to be a smiling Isaac. I'll tell him he has to start taking better care of himself. I'll tell him I love him. I'll tell him he doesn't have to abuse drugs anymore. He can be saved. We'll save him.

"I'm sorry." The doctor stands in front of the curtain. "He went into cardiac arrest due to the drug combinations in his system. We won't have the toxicology report for a few weeks, but based on what we know, opioids, stimulants, and alcohol played major factors. We did everything we could, but we couldn't get him back."

Wyatt's legs buckle, but he manages to stay upright. He closes his eyes. "Can I see him?"

"We're calling his next of kin," the doctor says while he finds the opening in the curtain.

"Tanvi." Wyatt breathes her name like a prayer. His eyes, when they focus on me, are hollow, his face gaunt. "Tanvi."

"I know." First her husband, and now her only son.

Seeing Isaac lying on the hospital bed is surreal. He should wake up. But at the same time, I'm struck by the difference in a person once their heart no longer beats. He's Isaac, but he's not.

"I can't." His voice catches on a sob. "I don't—" He tries to speak again. Then a sob rises out of him so gut-wrenching the sound will haunt me for the rest of my life. Pure heartbreak. His shoulders collapse and rise again like the waves in a stormy sea hitting the shore.

I wrap my arms around him, hugging him from the back. He clutches Isaac's hand, and for the last time, the three of us are united.

WYATT

PRESENT DAY

I storm into the kitchen. I was on the brink of something with Ellie. But I can't ignore a call from Anna. Sometimes I'm the only thing keeping her from fleeing and taking Jamal with her.

"Anna?"

"Sorry, Wyatt, it's me," Camila says.

"What's up?" With Camila calling instead of Anna, this conversation could go two ways, but I'm certain it'll end up nowhere I'll like.

"Anna's gone. Kyle called when she hadn't returned after a few hours. Her phone is here, obviously, so I'm not sure when or how she'll get in touch with you."

I groan and plant my back against the kitchen wall, sinking to the floor. "What else have you got going on? I'm only here for another day and a half. Then I'm back and I can take him." She knows what's coming. This isn't the first time Anna has run off while I've been away. Camila flew with Jamal to Tokyo once. She wasn't so happy at the end of that flight. Jamal is not a traveler. Good thing I pay her well.

"Wyatt." There's warning in her voice.

"Camila, you understand how important my time here is."

"And you realize you and your sister aren't my only clients. Yes, you pay me for my services, but other people do too."

"Give me half an hour and I'll call you back." I hang up and dial Tanvi's number. She treats Jamal like a grandchild and might be willing to take him for a day or two.

"Wyatt?" Tanvi answers the phone, surprise in her voice.

"Hey, Tanvi, sorry to call out of the blue. Anna's taken off." I wince. "Any chance you could take Jamal for a bit?"

There's a long pause. "This happens a lot."

"Yeah." I close my eyes and take my stress ball out of my pocket to squeeze it.

"Maybe you should think about making more permanent arrangements?"

We've talked about this solution before. But I'm not going after custody of Anna's kid. Whether or not she's a good mom, she'd never forgive me.

"Can you take him for a couple of days? I should be back in a day or two."

"Where are you this time?" Tanvi asks.

"Ellie." She'll understand. She called me after she watched Jackson's show, but I didn't tell her what I was doing then. No point in getting her hopes up.

"Ellie!" Her voice is delighted. "Finally. Finally." Tanvi laughs. "I'll pick up Jamal. But if Anna comes to my house again looking . . ."

"Don't let her in. Call Kyle. Hopefully I'll be home by then."

Tanvi wishes me good luck with Ellie. When I hang up the phone, I'm lighter, more hopeful. I text Camila and Kyle the arrangements and then shove my phone into my pocket just as Ellie comes into the kitchen.

"Is everything okay?"

"Anna's run out on Jamal. I had to find someone to watch him for a couple of days." I scan Ellie from her ponytail to her smooth, tan legs.

"Who took him?" She runs her hand along the counter.

"Tanvi." I grimace. "I hope Anna doesn't go to her house this time before I get home."

"Anna still gets violent?" Ellie crosses her arms over her chest.

"It's gotten worse as she's gotten older. She's aggressive when she's been using, when Jamal isn't where she thinks he should be. If Kyle and I aren't around, she's not allowed in the main house until she dries out."

"Where does she go to dry out?"

"I have a guest house on the property. It's not much, but it's enough for the few days she always needs to get back on the right track."

"How . . . I mean—?" Ellie's expression is unreadable. She sighs. "I don't want to be around that, Wyatt. How can you be around that and not relapse?"

There have been many nights in my bathroom, staring at the drugs Anna brought home, contemplating how bad one hit or one oxy would be. So far, I've always flushed them or thrown them out or gotten someone to take them from me. But I understand Ellie's concern. "I'm committed to being better," I say. "I don't want to lie to you. There have been days where it's hard to stay clean. Exceptionally hard. But I don't want that life. I'm not going back."

"And Anna?" She pinches the bridge of her nose. "You're committed to helping her too? No matter what?"

The direction of this conversation isn't good, but I've let my sister down too many times in this life already. I won't do it again. "I can't turn my back on my sister, Ellie. Definitely can't turn my back on Jamal."

"Right." She reaches up and yanks her ponytail tighter. "I guess I need to consider that too."

"What does that mean?"

"Anna and I didn't get along. I—I can't put . . . I don't want to be in a situation where someone might get hurt."

"There's not a snowball's chance in hell I'd let her hurt you, Ellie."

"You're not always there! Has Anna hurt Tanvi? Hurt Kyle? Or you? Obviously you can't control Anna. I'm not blaming you, but it's not realistic to say she wouldn't hurt someone else—me . . . or anyone."

When Anna is using heavily, she's difficult to control, and she's unpredictable. I've never asked Anna how she treated Jamal before he came to live with me, but I've done everything

I can to maintain distance between them when she's using. "You keep tossing up roadblocks, Ellie. If it's not one thing, it's another."

She throws up her hands. "These are real concerns. My safety," she hesitates before continuing, "and the safety of anyone else in that house is compromised by Anna being there."

"You want me to kick my sister and her son out on the street? Turn my back on them? Come on, Ellie. Years ago, you would have been proud of me for helping her." She won't look at me. "Even if she wasn't my sister, there's a child involved. I have to help her. I have to."

Ellie starts to say something and then snaps her mouth shut. "It's just another thing I have to consider. I mean, where do you see this going? You and me? What's the five-year or ten-year plan?"

"I want you. To live with you, marry you, start a family with you. Us. The way I always wish we'd ended up."

Tears pool in her eyes, and she shakes her head.

"What?" I step closer. "That's surprising?"

"I'm not sure what to do. This is so impossibly complicated."

"Say yes, and we can work everything else out. Nothing here is so complicated we can't fix it together." I'm standing in front of her now. *Look up, Ellie. Look up.*

She shakes her head again and refuses to meet my eyes. "I should take you back to the hotel."

"Ellie."

"I just need some space," she blurts out.

"I'm only here for another day. After tomorrow, you get all the space you ever wanted."

"God, Wyatt. I never wanted any space. I didn't. I wanted you to come for me. I wanted you to get help. I wanted the house and the kids and the life. I wanted all of it." She closes her eyes and presses her hands to her face. Tears spill unchecked, but she still won't look at me.

"I'm sorry," I whisper, drawing her close and wrapping my arms around her. "I'm so damned sorry."

"And then you show up here with no plan, no idea how we'll work. You don't tell me about Anna and Jamal. It makes me wonder what else you're keeping from me." She draws back and her dark eyes are accusing. "What else aren't you telling me?"

"Why do you think there's something else?" Now I'm the one avoiding eye contact.

"Probably because I wasn't told about the first thing you were hiding." She laughs, but it holds no humor. "We're not doing this anymore. I can't. It's exhausting. I need a break." She doesn't wait for my answer. Snatching her keys off the island, she goes through the door and to the garage.

I follow her, head spinning. Something isn't adding up. Younger Ellie would have been pissed at me, but not like this. Nothing like this. She opens her car door, and I grab her arm. "What aren't *you* telling me, Ellie? Something is holding *you* back. I don't think it's the drugs, the fame—not even Anna. It's something else. I can't figure out what it is."

She swallows. Over her shoulder, she says, "That doesn't seem like enough to you? All of those are a problem. Every single one.

Combined, they seem like a sign to me." Shrugging off my hand, she slides into the car and starts it without another word.

Reluctantly, I go to the passenger side and duck in. The drive to my hotel is silent. I stare out into the darkness, sure I'm missing something. I replay conversation after conversation, but I can't crack the mystery.

"What time tomorrow?" I ask when I can't take the silence anymore. I'm going to need a new stress ball at this rate. Possibly a whole case. She doesn't respond. That's fine. I'll wait her out. When we pull up to the hotel entrance, I don't get out of the car. "Time?" I repeat.

"We're done, Wyatt." Her jaw tightens.

"We're not done, Ellie."

She turns her body toward me, anger written across her face. "You don't get to decide that."

"You're right. I don't. But you know what I've figured out over the last couple of days? You still have feelings for me. Whatever they are, they're there. When we make eye contact, when we brush against each other, when we're in the same room—we're alive. So if it makes you feel better, you can tell me we're done. We both realize that's not true." I climb out of the car and slam the door.

I storm up to my room, taking the stairs two and three at a time. Once I'm there, I grab the first bottle out of the minibar. I snap the top off and pour it down the drain. I toss the empty bottle into the garbage can and grab the next one.

Ellie's not getting rid of me. I'm getting my last day with her even if I have to go to her house and stand at the gates until she lets me in. Last time, I wasn't persistent enough. This time, I'm not walking away.

There's something going on that I don't understand. And I'm gonna crack that too. I twist the cap off the bottle in my hand and stare at myself in the mirror.

ELLIE
Present Day

I curl up in my bed, and I wish Haven was home. Nights like these, when I can't sleep, I crawl into bed with her. Something about the steady rhythm of her breathing always lulls me to sleep. Nothing is working tonight.

Frustrated, I climb out of bed and pad to the kitchen for a drink of water. My normal phone is charged on the counter, and I turn it on. There's nothing else to do this late at night, so I might as well see what's going on in the world.

My mind flicks to my ex-boyfriend's earlier text on my private phone. I didn't even look at his message before I turned it off. We haven't spoken in months. Whatever he has to say can wait for another day. Not right now.

Out of habit, I've navigated to Wyatt's Twitter feed. An hour ago, he tweeted: *Listening to Alicia Keys' "If I Ain't Got You" on repeat. Thinking, wishing, wondering.* Wyatt's alone in his hotel room, just as lost as me.

I was so close to telling him earlier. So close. He's not using anymore. I'm almost positive. Anna, though. She and her son are complications I didn't see coming. If she's worse than she used to be, putting Haven in that household is wrong. Irresponsible. Her behavior is exactly what I've been trying to avoid for the last nine years. Haven could have her father's addictive personality. Living with, being around someone who is an active user is extremely risky.

Isaac spiraled and hit bottom, never to emerge again. Wyatt spent years telling me his problem wasn't a problem at all. Anna's decline makes her one more person who's lost themselves to drugs. If Haven goes down their path, I'll scrutinize this moment and my wrong decision forever. My choice might be the difference between a healthy life for her or picking up the pieces if she becomes an addict. Once Wyatt knows she's his, there's no backtracking.

My brain isn't going to quiet.I pick up my phone and dial Nikki's number. When Nikki answers, I don't waste any time. She sounds wide awake anyway. "Can I come over?"

"Are you listening to Alicia Keys on repeat too?"

"I'm not the only one Twitter-stalking Wyatt?" My voice is light, but my insides are heavy. I dig my nail under a piece of paint on the counter. One of Haven's art projects left a little behind. Life is rarely neat and tidy.

"You didn't tell him?"

"He told me some things, and now the situation seems more complicated. Maybe dangerous."

Once she agrees to let me crash at hers, I throw a change of clothes into a bag and hustle out of the house to my car. When I arrive at Nikki's, the door is unlocked.

I drop my bag in the entryway, round the couch, and collapse next to her. It's three in the morning, but Nikki looks like she never went to bed.

"Did Matt get ahold of you?" Nikki scrolls through Wyatt's Twitter feed.

Pictures, articles, and other reminders of the past fly by. He certainly stirred up a shitstorm with that interview. He's also retweeting the nonsense. Stoking the fire. And he says he'd have no problem quitting.

"Earth to Ellie." Nikki waves her hand in front of my face.

"What?" I blink at her.

"Matt. He called me to get in touch with you. He said you weren't answering your phone. I tried to call you. No answer."

My phone is off because Wyatt and I were talking earlier, and I didn't want any distractions. I rummage around in my purse until I find my second phone and wait for the home screen to load. At the flood of notifications, my heart starts to race. I have a lot of voice mails. Holding up a finger to Nikki, I take a seat at her kitchen table so I can concentrate.

"Ellie—it's Matt. I had a phone call from one of those shitty tabloids snooping into your life. I think, well . . . I think Wyatt has created a problem. Call me."

I delete the message. Tabloids cold call people acquainted with me. They offer a lot of money to entice someone to say something, anything they can spin into a story. Of course they're going to contact Matt and anyone else who might talk now that Wyatt has made a spectacle of my life. The next message starts to play.

"Ellie—it's Calshae. There are reporters at the hotel. I—I . . . things are blowing up." There's a long pause. "The one at the concierge desk asked about Haven. We're locking things down here, but I thought you'd want to know."

My heart booms in my chest. Sweat breaks out under my armpits. Nikki is staring at me, but I can't look at her. Why did I turn off my phone? How do I stop this? I delete her message and start the next one, pressing a hand over my heart. I'm about to have a heart attack at thirty-four.

"Ellie—it's Vincent. I'm fielding calls left and right about Wyatt, about Haven, about you. There are fires, and I'm putting them out. We're bleeding money. I've reminded people about NDAs. But I've got to warn you, I'm not sure I can contain the truth. I'm trying. One of the reporters from TMZ said they had a birth certificate naming Wyatt as the father. Please call me back and tell me you weren't that dumb nine years ago. Call me. Anytime. Whenever you get this, okay?" No point in deleting his message. The word *dumb* bangs around my skull. *Yes, Vincent, I* was *that dumb.* But my mother made sure her birth certificate was sealed. Very few people could have leaked this. I close my eyes and drop my head onto the table.

Nikki gets up and comes over to give my back a rub. "What's up?" she asks softly.

"I'm screwed. I'm so, so screwed. Matt tried to contact me because reporters called him. Reporters were at Wyatt's hotel tonight. Calshae tried to get in touch with me. Vincent, my manager, left a message. TMZ has Haven's birth certificate."

That last sentence reverberates in my mind. The worst outcome.

"Oh, shit," Nikki breathes. "Mom sealed that."

"Unsealed now." Bile rises into my throat. "Why did I put Wyatt's name on it? Why? How could I be so stupid?"

"Because you didn't want to hide the truth from Haven." Nikki's expression is pained.

"But I haven't told him yet. If this breaks, he'll—what will he do?"

My phone pings. I check the incoming message, and I suck in a sharp breath.

"What?" Nikki peers over my shoulder.

"Wyatt." The blood leaves my head in a rush. Black spots appear at the edges of my vision. I'm going to faint. A heart attack might not be so bad.

"What's it say?"

"*Call me, now.*" I stare at Nikki. My body is weightless, but the hot and cold flashes won't stop coming.

"If your people were calling you . . ."

"Someone might have called him or one of his reps for comment. That's where you're going, right?" I can't sit here. I rise, but I'm dizzy. The room swirls, and I grip the back of the kitchen chair.

"You can't tell him via text message. And you can't tell him over the phone. If the first question he's going to ask is if it's true, you need to be there."

"He's going to be so angry with me."

"Maybe. Maybe. He might be reasonable. You said he's different, right?"

"Yeah. And I didn't tell him."

"Why didn't you tell him tonight?"

"I was going to. I was so close. Then his addiction person called and said Anna had disappeared."

"His sister?"

"Yeah. His sister and her son live with Wyatt. I had no idea. I think—well, you know how I feel about Anna. Wyatt was hiding her from me. She's still an addict, unstable, sometimes violent. I—I can't put Haven in that environment. I left him because I didn't want her in that environment."

"Wyatt won't turn his back on his sister and her son."

"I can't blame him for that."

My phone pings again. Another text from Wyatt. He knows. The phone rings, shrill in the silence of the room. It's him.

"Go," Nikki says. "Just go. See him in person."

"Don't take her to school today, okay? It'll be a circus."

"We'll stay around the house. Do you want us to go to yours instead? We can wake her and take her now."

I shake my head, and I grab my bag off the floor. At the moment, I have no idea where I'll be. Protecting Haven from the fallout is the most important aspect of all this.

"Stay here," I say. "They'll have to work to find your house. Go to Mom and Dad's if you have to, okay? At least the gates and security there will keep them away, and I can handle the chaos at mine." I open the front door. "If it gets intense or scary, call me. I'll have Freddie or Jerome come here—both, if needed."

Nikki nods, and worry overflows between us.

I get to the hotel in record time, but as I drive up to the spacious entrance, I realize I've dropped the ball in a big way. There are reporters everywhere. I slip into a side lot and drive around to the rear of the building. No one seems to be hovering around here yet. Reluctantly, I dial Calshae's number. She answers on the fourth ring. "Sorry to wake you," I say. "I'm at the back of the hotel. The front is flooded with reporters."

"Oh, Ellie," she breathes. "I'm so sorry. You haven't told him yet? He didn't know?"

"No, he didn't." My voice is thick with tears, and I close my eyes. When I found out I was pregnant, Calshae was adamant I tell Wyatt. Like my sister, she didn't understand all the ins and outs of the life Wyatt and I led in LA. She thought love would be enough for Wyatt to overcome his addictions. I'm not sure what she thinks now or whether anything's changed in the years that have passed in between. We stopped talking.

She whistles. "We disagreed about whether he should know, but I never wanted the truth to come out like this. Never. Never said a word this week."

"I know. The time he spent with you didn't bother me. I—I should have told him already, probably." She's moving around, doing something on her end. The back door swings open and she's standing at the entrance, peering out into the darkness, looking for me. "I see you," I say. In a rush, I exit my vehicle and squeeze into the hallway. "Didn't realize you'd be here."

"When the reporters started showing up late tonight, I came to help field questions. Then I stayed. I was worried. Just a bad feeling, and I tried to call you, but I couldn't get you. I was sure *something* was coming. Hoped it wasn't this, though."

"What room is Wyatt in?" My legs wobble, and I brace a hand against the wall.

"Top floor. Number 56. Are you going to be okay? Should I have security on standby? I've heard he sometimes has a temper."

"You might need a cleanup crew, but I doubt it," I say with more confidence than I have. Wyatt's reaction is an unknown. "He'd never hurt me. Never. No matter how mad he is." She scans my face, but I don't waver. "Stairs?" I glance down the hall.

Calshae points to the left. "Good luck."

I hurry up the stairs. My choice is gone, just like my mother had warned. I have to talk about Haven. Tomorrow, the truth will be all over the news. Hell, Haven's parentage might already be on TMZ's newsfeed. If that's how Wyatt found out, I'm in even more trouble. At the door to his room, I wipe my hands on my shorts and take a deep breath. My heart beats erratically. With one hand pressed to my chest to contain it, I knock on the door.

Almost immediately, the door flies open. Wyatt's expression is beaten, bewildered. He searches my face. I can't look away, even though he'll recognize what I haven't said in words.

"So it's true." He rocks back as though I've hit him. "Haven's mine?" His voice cracks.

"Yes," I whisper and close my eyes. "Yes."

He leaves the door ajar and heads into the room. The balcony doors that face the ocean are open. The reporters don't appear to be on this side of the hotel. But mere eyesight can be deceptive. Powerful camera lenses can get impossible shots.

"Can you shut the curtains or the door?" There's only a bedside lamp on. The TV is switched to *TMZ*. I swallow. *Shit. TMZ.*

"Why? Why does it even matter? The whole fucking world knows I'm Haven's father. TMZ knew before me. Christ, I've been sitting here thinking about the things people have said over the last few days, and I'm a complete idiot. She looks so much like your mother, Ellie, so much. But you know what's not you? Her eyes. That blue comes from my family, doesn't it? Now that I see it, I don't understand how I didn't see the truth before."

I'm silent, clutching my middle, watching him pace around the room. There's nothing I can possibly say. Sorry isn't enough. It'll never be enough.

"Does Haven know? She does, doesn't she? Some of the things she said to me . . ." He chuckles, humorless, and shakes his head. "Even she knew. A *nine-year-old*." His expression is filled with disgust. He's never leveled that in my direction before. "Were you going to tell me?" He stops pacing to stare at me.

I can't make eye contact. The expression I glimpsed on his face is enough. He hates me. But I've never thought of myself as a coward, and I'm not going to start tonight—one of the most important moments in my life.

"While you were here? I'm not sure." I flinch at the anger in his eyes. "I was going to tonight until you mentioned your drug-addicted, violent sister lives with you."

He winces. "That's a low blow, Ellie. I'm not the one who lied to you for ten years."

"I told you back then."

"When?" He puts his hands on his hips. The word is an accusation.

I scoff. "Why do you think I flew home out of the blue ten years ago? Why do you think I came back to you with the information on rehab? Why do you think I pushed so damn hard? Wyatt, why do you think I left?"

"But you didn't tell me. You didn't." Wyatt steps toward me. "When I asked you where the rehab shit was coming from, you never said anything about being pregnant. Not one word about a baby."

"Would it have mattered?" My voice is quiet, barely louder than a whisper. This question has haunted me. Before he talked about Jamal, I was confident of the answer. Ten years ago, the last thing Wyatt wanted was a kid. He was too consumed by his grief and guilt over Isaac.

"Are you fucking kidding me? Of course my daughter would have mattered to me."

"If I'd told you, you can tell me with one hundred percent certainty you'd have gone to rehab? You would have totally changed your lifestyle—given up the publicity, created stability, been completely sober? You can say that?" If he's going to make me the devil, I'm going to earn that title.

"How can I answer that?" He runs both hands through his hair in frustration. "You didn't give me a choice."

"You're right. I asked the question I thought needed answering, and you said no. I asked you to get sober. You chose the drugs. Maybe you didn't completely understand the choice, but if you were going to continue to live that life, I didn't want our child anywhere near it." I take in his haggard appearance. "How can you say you'd want a kid around that lifestyle? You grew up with that. You hated how your parents raised you and Anna."

"Which is why I would never do it. Anna showed up with a kid who wasn't even mine, and I got my shit together."

I debate how honest to be with him. We've gotten this far. No point in holding back. "I *did* tell you. I came back to our house three months after Haven was born."

Wyatt frowns, and he searches my face. He probably thinks I'm lying. "What?"

"I thought you were living with Katrina, but when I showed up, Blanca answered the door. She let me in. I went to the bedroom and tried to talk to you. You woke up, but you couldn't carry on a coherent conversation. I left." The breeze from the open window hits me. I shiver. "But I went to tell you. I wanted you to know."

Emotions flicker across his face in rapid succession. None of them are there long enough to identify. "You told me?"

"You were really high, Wyatt." I purse my lips, and more tears flood my eyes.

"And that was it. I got two chances to know my daughter, to see her grow up." His voice is soft, but there's steel underneath.

He doesn't believe I did enough. Maybe I didn't. But I couldn't worry about his feelings anymore once I saw how bad he was; I had to protect her. Back then, he didn't want to save himself, had no interest in getting better. He loved me so much, and he wouldn't get help for me. I couldn't take the chance that he wouldn't be sober for our daughter either. Faced with him now, and the weight of my decision, my guilt rests heavy on my shoulders. Maybe I should have done more. I don't even know anymore. But I didn't, and here we are.

WYATT

PRESENT DAY

My accusation sits between us, and rage simmers below the surface. Underneath the anger are emotions I'm not touching. Guilt. Remorse. Love. Anger is my friend, not that other shit. She should have told me when I was capable of understanding.

"Did you ever try again, Ellie? Twice in ten years? You made it impossible for me to see you or contact you. *Impossible.* You had my daughter, my—" I close my eyes and grit my teeth. "Daughter." The desire to punch something, break something, beat something bloody strains my muscles. All these pent-up frustrations with nowhere to go. Images of Haven from the last few days play over and over in my head.

"I couldn't risk her well-being," she says, as though the decision to hide my daughter from me was simple.

"Did you ever check up on me? What if I'd sobered up eight years ago, five years ago?"

"Oh, Wyatt." Her laugh is heavy. "I kept tabs on you. Google, YouTube, your wide-open social media accounts. I searched constantly for signs you were better." Her jaw hardens. "Then I stopped hoping."

For the first time, there isn't a glimmer of the Ellie I used to know. She was never vindictive. That was my game, not hers. "You've spent ten years punishing me for not saying yes right away."

"I spent ten years *protecting* Haven from an alcoholic and a drug addict who didn't always make good choices. Ten years *protecting* Haven from endless media scrutiny. Ten years keeping our kid away from YouTube searches."

"That's harsh."

"I'm being *honest*."

Anger rises in me. She doesn't get to be frustrated with me. We stare each other down. For ten years, she kept my daughter from me. Lied to everyone.

"How'd you find out?" She closes the balcony door and the curtains.

We should have done that earlier. She was right. Our arguing, drifting out the door and landing on the people below, wouldn't be good for any of us. But the room needed airing out.

"Tommy, my manager, called me. He caught wind of something. Wondered if I came to the island to meet *my daughter*." I mock myself. "I tried to set him straight. Laughed him off. Haven's not mine, she's Nikki's. Ellie wouldn't lie to me, not about something so big. Then he said TMZ called with the details from a birth certificate. Within the hour, the proof was on their website, livestreaming on their news program for the whole world."

"I just found out the story was breaking." Ellie's voice is quiet. "I turned off my phone. If I'd known it was going to come out earlier—"

"You would have enjoyed the last few hours of my ignorance?"

"Now who's aiming low?" Her expression is rock solid when she meets mine, the softness gone. "No. I would have come to tell you myself. I never wanted you to find out this way."

"Putting my name on the birth certificate is a stellar idea to keep the truth a secret."

"I thought you'd come for us. I wanted her to know, and I never expected it to take ten years."

"I fucking came, Ellie," I burst out, throwing out an arm. "Years ago, I came. You wouldn't see me."

"No one told me."

"Well, your parents were aware. Your mother met me at the gate. She took one look at me and walked all the way back down the path to the house. Didn't say a single word to me."

"You were still using."

"Of course I was," I snap. "I had no *reason* to quit."

"You needed a reason after what we had together? *I* should have been the reason. I asked you to. There's your reason."

"Yeah, you did. But you didn't tell me *why*, Ellie. And that would have made the difference."

"We're going in circles." Impatience sparks off Ellie, directed at me. "I didn't try to make you aware again, and I should have." She presses her fingers into her forehead. "I don't know anymore. But I didn't. I can't take it back."

"Just go—leave." Ten years of Haven's life are lost to me. All the firsts. How do we recover from a lie that big? "I can't stand the sight of you right now."

Ellie's eyes fill with tears. Something deep inside of me shifts on a dime, an instinct so ingrained I can't help myself, and I step toward her. With only one exception, Ellie's tears have always been my undoing. If only they'd undone me that time too.

"I shouldn't have said that," I admit.

Her bottom lip trembles. A tear falls, and she uses a finger to scoop it. Her shoulders shrug, almost imperceptibly. "Maybe I deserve it."

"I'm really angry. I'm frustrated. I can't—I don't know how to handle this."

"You think I do?"

"You've had years to prepare for this possibility. I didn't even realize it existed."

"Do you want me to go?" Tears slide down her cheeks. She brushes them away, but they don't stop falling.

My anger is a pit, bottomless. But every time a tear trickles out, I long to reach for her, to tug her close, to ease her pain. I want to beat the shit out of whoever made her cry. Not so simple this time. I wish it was.

"I want you to go," I say. "But I'm coming to your house later today. I'm spending time with my daughter. I don't care if I bring the storm to your doorstep."

"Okay."

"You should have told me, Ellie. *You* should have told me."

She closes her eyes, and more tears slide down her cheeks. "I'll go." She steps past me to head for the door.

My arms ache with the effort not to grab her. Seeing her so sad crushes me, but every time Haven crosses my mind, I can't get my anger under control either. I love her, but I hate what she's done.

Ten years.

The door clicks closed behind her. I stride over to slide the locks in place, but when I reach the door, her muffled crying comes through the thin wood. She must be leaning on the door because it rattles with each sob. My hands and forehead are pressed against the surface, seeking the connection. I want to go out, drag her into my arms, tell her I can fix everything.

I'm not sure we can be fixed.

The itch hits me in a rush, as strong as it did the first week I quit. I leave the door to grab my bag, and I tear through the nooks and crannies, searching for anything left behind. Whatever I find will be expired, but I don't care. Anything to take the edge off. In the bathroom I stare at the empty alcohol bottles in the garbage. An impulsive prick. I want another one of those bottles so badly.

My hands are splayed on the bathroom counter, and I stare at my reflection in the mirror. My wild look peers back.

I'm not going to screw up my life. Not this time. Not any time. Not anymore. I roll my shoulders and take out my phone. My manager, Tommy, answers on the second ring.

"It's true? What the hell is this?" His TV booms in the background. He's a compulsive TMZ consumer. Good for his business, I suppose.

"What I've been missing out on for ten years."

"This is why she avoided you for all this time? Canceled meetings, missed movie premieres, not coming to the Oscars?"

"Yes. Yeah, Haven's the reason." I pinch the bridge of my nose. "I need the number for the best family attorney on the island. Can you get me that?"

There's a long pause on the phone. "You just found out. Isn't it a little quick to be going for the jugular?"

"Get me the information. I don't need a lecture."

"Should I be calling Camila?"

"No. No. I'm fine. But Ellie's not keeping my kid away from me anymore either. I want to understand what rights I have. And if she doesn't play nice, I want the path to custody."

"Wyatt."

"Precaution. That's all."

"You went there to get Ellie back. Don't blow your life to shit when you could have what you've wanted for years."

"You're right. I should have had this years ago." There's a knock on my door, and I purse my lips in annoyance. "I've got to go. It's going to be a fucking gong show here today."

"Do you want me to send people to help you manage the crisis?"

"No, I leave in the morning. Anna's run off again. I've got to get back to Jamal." I take a deep breath when I realize how complicated my life has gotten with one revelation. "No idea what I'm going to do."

Tommy chuckles. "Well, the studio'd be pretty happy if you got Ellie on board with your next project. Kathleen Kirkton backed out."

"We're not quite there yet," I say. "I'm having a hard time looking at her. Not sure I'm that good of an actor."

"You are. So is she. If you want me to ask about a switch, give me a call."

"Sure, Tommy." Sarcasm drips from my voice. "Top of my list right now. Get me that lawyer's name." I hang up the phone without waiting for his reply and stride to the door. Whoever is there, they're persistent.

Calshae is framed in the view from the peephole. Stepping back, I stare at the door for a minute. She knew. I'm sure of it. I open the door, but I don't speak. On my way to a chair, I gather my thoughts for the millionth time since TMZ made me a father. After I sink into one, I stare at her blankly.

Her steps are cautious, and she peers around the room as though she expected a hurricane. Her breath leaves in a whoosh, and her shoulders fall. "I was worried about having to clean this place up."

My disgust at her, at Ellie, at every other fucking person who was aware of my daughter's parentage before me rises to the surface. "You knew, didn't you?"

Calshae freezes. "I did."

"For how long? Does every person on this damned island know?"

Her lips quirk up, but her expression isn't a happy one. "A lot of people do. The island is tight. We're good secret keepers. Were. Not so much anymore. Though if whoever spilled the secret gets found out by Ellie's parents, they'll regret doing it. Everyone and their aunt signed an NDA when Haven was born. Her mom sealed the birth certificate."

"I'm sure whoever leaked it is rich now and won't care." I drag my stress ball out of my pocket and examine it for a minute. "How do I get the minibar restocked?"

"Why?" Her eyes widen.

"I poured the bottles into the drain last night in a fit of rage. Now my rage wants to drink." I shrug.

"Don't see how getting drunk would be helpful."

"Don't see how waiting ten years to tell me I'm a father is helpful, but it happened." Every time I remember what she did, I want to explode or take a pill to dull the edge. I don't want to *feel* this way. Been a long time since I've felt something I couldn't face.

"I can imagine the news is a lot to process." Calshae perches on the chair opposite me.

"Do you think?" I ask and then stand. "I need to get out of here."

"It's a madhouse out there."

"It's, like, four in the morning. How bad can it be?" Which is a stupid question because I've been in enough media scrums to understand exactly how bad it could be. But we're in Bermuda, far from most media outlets.

"It's bad. I've never seen this many news outlets on the island. I have no idea how they got here. Private planes, maybe."

"They realize I'm here?" The TMZ reporter on the screen is at the front entrance of the hotel shooting live footage. "I guess so." I cross my arms. "When did you say you knew?"

"When Ellie was six months pregnant."

Her words are a punch to the gut.

"It's a well-guarded secret on the island." Calshae's voice is quiet. "I tried to talk her into telling you. You deserved to know. Ellie finally got tired of hearing me say what she didn't want to hear and stopped calling me to hang out, stopped responding to the messages I sent her. I let our friendship go. Friendships don't always blow up, sometimes they fade away."

"How old would Haven have been?" I squint.

"Only a few months old. Years later, I wondered if I should have tried harder. Maybe our rift wasn't about you."

Ellie came to see me when Haven was only a few months old. The friendship split and Ellie visiting LA are probably connected. Maybe she finally took Calshae's advice and seeing me didn't lead to the outcome she'd wanted. So many things I don't understand. "This is hurting my brain." I run my hands through my hair in frustration. "The gym. I need to beat the shit out of something."

"I'll come with you."

"I don't need a babysitter."

"We pass the bar to get there. I'll come with you."

"I'll be fine."

"You already asked about alcohol. Doesn't seem like your brain is in a great place at the moment. Why do you suppose she didn't tell you all those years ago?" Calshae raises an eyebrow.

"Not just all those years ago—*any* of the years." I scoff. "Any of them. She had ten years to tell me."

"Okay, so why didn't she?"

I sigh, frustrated with her, with Ellie, with myself. "Because I was an addict who made bad choices. Took a lot of risks when I was high. Did stupid stuff a lot of the time. I understand the reasons. Doesn't mean I'm not pissed off at the choice she made."

"Let me tag along with you today to make sure you don't do something impulsive and stupid to ruin this chance. 'Cause you still have one. You'll have a chance to spend time with your daughter, and I'm sure Haven would love that too."

I swallow a lump in my throat as Haven's hints about her father flick through my mind like a photo album. "I want that." My voice is a rasp.

"I know. I know. Let's hit the gym. Beat the shit out of some stuff with your fists . . . instead of reporters with the bottom of a Jim Beam bottle." She gets up and motions for me to do the same.

"You watched that video on YouTube?" I stand too, wearily.

"A few times. It was actually one of the funnier ones."

"Jesus, what must my kid think of me?" There are so many things on the internet I'm not proud of, so many poor decisions that I made when I was too out of it to realize I was being filmed.

Calshae's dark eyes search my face. She pats my back. "Ellie's a good mom. I'm sure Haven has a high opinion of you. She'd never want your daughter to think badly of you."

I grab some workout clothes from the suitcase, and before I disappear into the bathroom I say, "I guess we'll see."

I hit the bag in the gym over and over. Calshae runs on the treadmill, avoiding me. I beat the bag like I should have beaten myself ten years ago. My mind wanders between being amazed Ellie and I have a child together to being furious at myself, at her, to wanting to kill someone, anyone.

Calshae checks her phone and glances at me. She frowns, and I sigh.

"What?" I hit the bag harder and harder. The sound almost blocks out her reply.

"Text from the front desk. Evelyn is here, Ellie's—"

"I remember who Evelyn is," I say through gritted teeth.

Calshae yanks the emergency cord on the treadmill and stands still. "She wants to see you."

"Sure, let's add to the party. Let's invite *all* the people who knew I was a dad before I did." I throw out my hands and then slam another left hook into the bag. "At this point, it'd be the whole frigging island."

"I'll tell her to come back later."

"No, no. Tell her she can come in and explain shit to me." I whip off the boxing gloves and toss them to the side. Flexing my hands, I wait for Evelyn to walk in.

Normally the gym is bright with natural light. But today the windows are covered by blinds and anything else the hotel staff could find to block the paparazzi's view. The cameras and crews have descended on the hotel. For maybe only the second or third time in my life, I don't want the attention.

Evelyn breezes into the gym. She stands by the entrance, squinting in the dim lighting. I wouldn't let Calshae turn on any lights, so it's like dusk in here.

"Wyatt?" She scans the room.

Her petite stature reminds me of Ellie. Their hair is almost the same color too, so from a distance, they could be mistaken for each other. Those details soften me to Evelyn, even when I don't want to be softened. Like today—I don't want any softness today. "Evelyn," I say. "Or should I call you Grandma?"

"I was a grandmother even when you believed Haven was Nikki's."

"I should go." Calshae steps off the treadmill and tucks her phone in her pocket. "I'll come check on you in a bit."

"Like I said, I don't need a babysitter."

"How many times have you considered using?" Evelyn asks. "Searched any bags? The nooks and crannies? Maybe a pill was left behind? Considered calling any old friends?"

So fucking smug. Like she has any idea how I feel. Right now, I hate her. I clench my hands and release them, and don't answer.

"I'll come find you when I leave," Evelyn says to Calshae, who is standing at the door before she ducks out. The door clicks closed.

"You have to keep it together," Evelyn says quietly, clasping her hands in front of her.

"I'm aware." I push the words out, my anger barely in check. "Why do you suppose I'm here in the gym instead of at the bar?"

"A whiff of anything and I'll be counseling Ellie to stay away."

"Yeah, well, you won't have much of a leg to stand on when I tell her that you're the reason I'm here in the first place."

"I'm still Ellie's mother." Evelyn's expression tightens.

"And I'm the father of her child. That puts us at an impasse."

"You're angry. But having Tommy calling family attorneys on the island, asking questions about custody, visitation? Is that how you want this to go between you and my daughter?"

My hands are laced behind my head, and I release them. Pisses me off that she already knows about that. "My rights, since they've been denied to me for the last nine years, are important."

"Ellie isn't going to stop you from seeing Haven."

"I want to be sure she can't." I'm trying to work out why she agreed to give me Ellie's address. She knew what Ellie was hiding. "What did you expect would happen?"

She crosses to the bench that houses weights on one end. Slowly, she lowers herself to sit on the edge. "I hoped you'd come here clean and sober. Ellie would realize what I have known for years, and the three of you could work at being a family. Instead, you created this incredible public spectacle." She tosses her hand toward the windows for emphasis. "You found out in exactly the wrong way."

When I remember my conversation with Tommy, seeing the birth certificate on TMZ, I clench and unclench my hands. "How was I supposed to guess Ellie had a real reason for staying away from me?"

"I should have made the terms of our agreement a little firmer."

"Six months of meetups, breathalyzers, and random drug testing on my movie set weren't enough?"

"You agreed to that."

"And thank goodness I did. Right? Or else I still wouldn't know I had a daughter."

"Haven would have sought you out at some point. Ellie never lied to her about you."

"Small comfort, Evelyn. I've missed nine years. When I realize everything I haven't been here for—what the hell am I supposed to do? How do we overcome that?"

"You need to take a hard look at yourself. Ellie came to see you when Haven was only a few months old."

"I'm aware of that, *now*."

She watches me for a few minutes as I pace around the gym. The memory, if one ever existed, of Ellie coming to see me is gone. I can't locate it or verify its existence. They can tell me it happened, but it doesn't feel as though it did. When I glance in Evelyn's direction, there's a crease in her brow.

"What would you have done if she'd told you she was preg-nant?"

"That's a shitty question. I can't answer that. How can I answer that?"

"I suspect you can, you just don't enjoy the response springing to mind."

Fury tinges the sides of my vision, even though she's right. The truth, the horrible truth, is that I would have told Ellie we weren't ready to be parents. If Ellie had stayed, I'm not sure there'd be a Haven. I would have talked her out of keeping the baby. Guilt wells in my throat. Haven wouldn't exist.

"She understood you better than anyone. When she came to us, sobbing her heart out, she realized she had to make a choice between keeping her baby or keeping you." She gives me a hard look. "She loves Haven. Having a child is like watching your heart running around outside your body—how do you protect it? How do you keep it safe? You'll get to experience that. The most beautiful and terrifying feeling."

Those feelings should have been mine a long time ago. "You're just making me angrier."

"What I'm trying to say is when Haven was more of an idea than a person, Ellie struggled. She did. She loved you so much. Her devotion to you scared me as a parent, to see my child attached to someone who could destroy her."

"I didn't destroy her." My voice is tight. I'm sure of that, at least. I protected Ellie.

"After Isaac died, you were out of control. A loose cannon. Consumed by fame, drugs, drinking—anything bad for you was fair game. You were at your worst when Ellie found out she was pregnant." Something in her expression shifts and she gives me a rueful smile. "I was glad when she chose to keep Haven. I was worried you were going to get my daughter killed."

"There's nothing I wouldn't have done for Ellie back then."

Something on my face must tell Evelyn she doesn't need to correct me because she checks her watch. Then she stands up and crosses toward the door. "Remember that feeling you just had, that realization *you* let her down, when you talk to those lawyers. She needs you to make the right choice this time." Evelyn opens the door and disappears without another word.

Once in a while, I see where Ellie gets her dramatic flair.

From the ground, I scoop up my boxing gloves and pound on the bag again, trying to block out Evelyn's words. I don't want to feel sorry for Ellie. I don't want to be ashamed that she came to talk to me and I don't remember it. I want to be angry.

"Wyatt?" Calshae calls from the doorway.

"Go away." I hit the bag with more force. "I don't need another person on Ellie's side."

Calshae sighs, her hip cocked, and one hand braced on her waist. She's changed into some sort of summery island dress. The vibrant colors in it are in stark contrast to her dark skin. "You're insufferable."

"No, I'm not." I screw my face up in annoyance.

"Security's moving the reporters. It's still a bit early, but I can get you to Ellie's in about half an hour if you want."

The clock on the wall has just passed nine in the morning. This day is both speeding by and dragging along.

"Come on. Go shower. I'll get us breakfast to go. The reporters will be gone and then I'll take you over to Ellie's place."

I yank off the gloves and squint at her. There's still so much anger coursing through me, I'm not sure how I can be around Ellie without letting my rage show.

"You don't want to hear this, but she was really unhappy years ago—I think she's been unhappy for a long time. If Ellie has a chance to be happy, I want that." Calshae smiles again. "Besides, I kinda like your grumpy ass. Seeing you happy might be nice too."

I throw a glove at her, and she ducks.

"See? Grumpy."

Despite my sour mood, I chuckle and shake my head. "A half hour? Also, what's with the women on this island not knowing how to cook?"

"If a man can cook, he shouldn't complain. It makes him look more attractive to those of us that can't."

Ellie used to get so turned on every time I cooked. Never complained about that outcome. "Can you make sure no one cleans my room?" She gives me a quizzical look. "When the press swarm, people will take and sell anything that's been in the room as a trophy."

"Yeah. Of course," she says. "I'll make sure no one goes in."

Seeing Haven again is going to be weird. I can't quite process that she's known the truth for years, and I've only just found out. My chest tightens at the reality of becoming an instant parent. I don't have a fucking clue how to be a father, and I've got no idea where to start when I see her again.

My daughter.

WYATT

Ten years ago

My head throbs. I open one eye, wondering where I've ended up this time. In the semidarkness, I make out an alarm clock and a framed photo. Careful not to move anything else, I drag the frame toward me. Isaac and I are at a club, laughing, and someone—was it Ellie?—snapped a picture. I've looked at this photo a thousand times in the last few months. If I return home, I often end up in Isaac's room to sleep off my hangover. With a groan, I ease myself to a sitting position, rubbing my forehead. My clothes are missing. I must have shed them as I came in here. My legs are wobbly when I stand, and I fumble my way out the door.

In the living room, my pants are in the middle of the floor. I check the pockets for my phone. Did I call Ellie last night like I promised? Squinting at the screen, I try three times to punch in my passcode before being locked out. I hurl the phone across the room, satisfaction piercing my gut as it smashes on the tile and skids to a stop, pieces scattering everywhere.

From my other pocket, I take out my pills and shake the bottle. *Empty*. Can't stay that way. I turn toward my room to go refill it, and my foot catches on the Persian rug Ellie and I bought in Turkey. The snag tips me forward, but I catch myself just before my face connects with the hard ground. My skull barely contains my bouncing brain, and my eyeballs throb with each beat of my heart. I close my eyes to block out the pain, and Isaac is there, collapsed on the ground, thrashing on the dirty sidewalk.

Rage at my incompetence floods me, drowning out everything else. When I rise, I grab a fistful of the carpet, yanking it over and over until the furniture releases the fabric.

A fire. I want to burn it all down.

Striding to the massive fireplace, I shove the grate out of the way. I'm about to find out whether this fireplace even works. There's lighter fluid in the kitchen, and I grab that before returning.

I stare at the black pit for a minute in indecision. *Fuck it.* If I have a fireplace, I should use it. I douse the ornamental logs in fluid and remove a box of matches out of my discarded pants' pocket. When the match is lit, I toss it into the pit. The logs and fluid catch with a whoosh. Quick and ferocious. I step backward, laughing. Something else has to go in there. I stare at the carpet. Too big.

With the flames roaring, I enter Isaac's room and gather anything I can carry. I rip the sheets off the bed; I grab the photo from the bedside table and any other photos I can find. Back in the living room, I toss them into the fire. The sheet trails along the ground, and I grab the last corner, stuffing it into the fireplace. When flames lick at my hand, I shake it, chuckling. *Fuckin' hot.*

"Wyatt?"

My heart races at the sound of her voice. Ellie's by the kitchen island, a bag at her feet. The exact day and time is fuzzy, but I think she's home early. There's no way to be sure. I've gotten terrible at keeping track of anything.

"You're here." My back is to the flames.

"What are you doing?"

I hate when she treats me like a delinquent child. "I'm cleaning up." We don't need any of this stuff. He's gone.

"You're burning sheets?"

If my heartbeat wasn't so fierce and irregular, my head might not pound in sync to it anymore.

"Is there someone else here?" she whispers.

"No." I glance around the room, and my voice echoes in the emptiness. "Should there be?"

"Why are you burning sheets?" When she gets closer, her expression changes from uncertainty to one of realization. She sighs, and her shoulders drop. "They're Isaac's."

"Yeah." I scrunch up my face. "Why would I burn our sheets?"

She's wearing the silver bracelet I gave her for our first Christmas together. She rotates it, and stays focused there instead of on me. "Do you remember calling me last night? I took a red-eye to get here. I'm supposed to be on set today."

"Why aren't you?" Sweat trickles down my back. Turning, I realize the fire has tentacles peeking out of the cavern, shooting up the mantle.

Ellie's eyes widen, and she strides to the kitchen and throws open a door by the stove. She grabs the fire extinguisher and hurries to my side.

"No." I rest my hand on top of her arm. "Just a sec." I leave her to search Isaac's room. With the drawers open, I remove anything I can find that reminds me of him. My arms are over-flowing when I re-enter the living room.

"Wyatt." Ellie shakes her head. "No, don't do that. You'll regret doing it."

"Like hell I will." I toss everything into the fire. "He's gone, Ellie. He left us. Don't need his shit lying around anymore." The photos on top of the pile curl and smoke.

"Wyatt." She sets the fire extinguisher beside her feet. A thin sheen of sweat coats her face when she drags me into a hug. "Wyatt," she murmurs against my ear. "I want you to come to my set with me."

She's overreacting and worrying more than she should. I'm fine here, and she's only a plane ride away whenever I want to see her.

"You need to come to set with me. I know you're supposed to start shooting in a couple weeks here in LA, but I can't keep flying home on the spur of the moment. Chris is being kind to me because he knows you, he likes you, and he understands about Isaac. But I can't keep doing this. I'm costing people money. I can't—no one will hire me if I keep running to you."

"Then stop. Stay here with me. Quit the movie. I can look after you." I tug her closer. "We can spend all our time together."

"Do you remember calling me last night?"

"I got locked out of my phone." I gesture to the ground behind her. When I rub my forehead, my hand dampens with sweat.

"You pulled up the carpet?" She searches beyond where our Turkish memento had lain to the smashed phone. "And you broke your phone."

"Doesn't matter. I'll buy a new one."

She steps away from me and picks up the fire extinguisher. In one fluid movement, Ellie sweeps the spray across the fireplace, dousing the flames.

"I wish you wouldn't do that." My brain stalls while she smothers my blazing creation. "I wasn't done." The smoke gets to me, and I cough.

"Have you gone to see Tanvi?" she shouts over the noise of the fire extinguisher.

"Not lately, no." I grit my teeth.

"I bet you've had lots of time for Anna, though, right?" She tosses the fire extinguisher onto the couch. The fireplace is a mess behind her, but the flames are gone.

Watching her almost makes me laugh. She's so tiny and angry that I want to wrap her in my arms and carry her away. "She's my sister." I shrug. "She understands how I feel right now."

"She does, does she?" Ellie's dark eyes blaze. "She knows what it's like to watch her best friend overdose? I wonder why that is? What does that say about her?"

"You mean what does that say about *me*?" My anger rises. Her judgmental tone grates on me. She's silent, with her arms crossed. "That's bullshit. How could you say that to me?"

Her expression collapses from angry to pained. She clasps a hand over her mouth, muffling a sob, and a few tears slide down her face.

"Ellie." My anger is gone in an instant. Her tears are always my undoing. "Don't cry. Ellie, come on. I'm sorry, okay? I don't remember calling you. Don't have a clue what I said. My head . . . it's like I have a train in there. I need to take something and then I'll be back to myself."

"I don't know who you are anymore," Ellie whispers into my chest.

"You don't mean that." I smooth her hair. Panic toys at the edge of my sanity. "You don't mean that."

There's a hitch in her breathing before she says, "Maybe you should talk to someone."

I let go of her to grab the fire extinguisher. The flames are starting again. Fire can be so persistent. The last thing I need is for the house to burn. Pointing the extinguisher at the fire, I smother the new flames. "I talk to people all the time."

"You're not talking, not really. Not about anything that matters. You're stuffing it down, covering whatever you're feeling with more and more drugs."

Her words wash over me in a haze. The pounding in my head is winning out. I leave her and go to the master en suite bathroom to search the cabinets. Nothing left. Not a single pill in any bottle. I stride out past her to Isaac's en suite and check in the bathroom drawer where he used to keep his stash. *Success.* An old container of pills. I toss the bottle from hand to hand before popping the top off and taking a Xanax. Clutching the last of my sanity in my hand, I return to Ellie.

She faces the charred remnants of Isaac's memory, arms crossed against her middle. She doesn't look in my direction and tears are streaming down her face. The fire is out, so there's no need for her to be crying.

Standing in front of her, I run my free hand along the side of her face. With a deep breath, I say, "What do you want me to say? I'll tell you whatever you want to hear."

"I want your truth." More tears slip down her cheeks. "I want your hurt, your anger, your sadness—I want all of it. I want you. I don't have *you* anymore." She gestures to the pill bottle. "That has you. Anna has you. Who knows who or what else has had you."

"I would *never* cheat on you. You're it for me. I don't want anyone else. I'm never going to want anyone else."

"I don't understand how to do this."

"I'm having a hard time right now." Panic seizes my chest. "But I'll bounce back. I always bounce back." I lace our fingers together and tug her closer, wrapping our linked arms around her back. "You're not . . ." I search her face, dread building in me. "You're not going to leave me, are you, Ellie?"

"I just want you." She strokes my face and sighs. Tears pool in her eyes and spill over. "I want you back."

"I'll come to set with you. That's what you want?" A rush of relief hits me. She won't leave if I give her what she wants.

"I want to be sure you're okay. At least if you're there, I'll know if you're okay." She leans her head on my chest.

I toss the bottle of pills onto the couch. They'll be fine there until I get them later. With my hands under her legs, I lift her up so her face is flush with mine. "I'm going to be fine, Ellie. I've got you looking after me." One of my hands slides under her ass so I can draw her head closer with the other one. I kiss her long and deep. She relaxes into me, her tongue slipping along mine. I'd do anything to keep her. "Let me look after you," I murmur, deepening the kiss.

She loops her arms around my neck, pressing her breasts against my chest. "I love you, Wyatt," she whispers into my ear, kissing my neck. "I love you so much."

With her in my arms, I walk us back to our bedroom and lay her on the bed. She peels off her clothes. Her breathing is heavy, and her eyes are already darkening with desire. She drags me on top of her, my underwear falling to the floor.

"It's you and me. Forever. That's never going to change." I'll never let her leave me without a fight. Whatever she asks, I'll do, if it means she'll stay with me.

ELLIE

PRESENT DAY

I wake with a start, my heart pounding like I've been running. I sit up in bed, disoriented, and I rub my forehead. This is my room. My heart is racing, and I must have been dreaming about something. Then I remember.

Wyatt knows. He's coming here today. I snatch my phone off my nightstand to see if I've missed a call from him. It's ten in the morning. Three hours of sleep isn't much, but it'll have to do.

After I sobbed my heart out in the parking lot of Wyatt's hotel, I collected Nikki and Haven from Nikki's house and brought them here. But I didn't have the energy or the right words to explain what was happening to Haven.

Before Wyatt arrives, I have to tell her he learned the truth. I don't want her caught off guard by anything he might say. I swing my legs over the side of the bed and let my head rest in my hands for a beat. He's so angry with me.

My mind churns with the various ways today could go. It's going to suck for me. This has been what Haven has wanted for years, and I don't want to ruin the experience. I shove my anguish down and vow to keep a lid on my feelings. I'm going to earn an Oscar for this performance.

Once I'm showered and dressed in fresh clothes, I'm confident I can face him. I text Wyatt to see what time he's coming. In the living room, Nikki and Haven are playing a board game.

"Coffee should still be warm if you need it like I did," Nikki says when she sees me.

In the kitchen, I grab a mug and pour liquid gold into it. I'm drinking it black. The tangy taste should kick me into gear.

When I emerge, Nikki makes eye contact. "Mom called. We should have a quick chat."

"Outside?" I gesture to the back patio.

She ruffles Haven's hair as she stands and then follows me out. "Are you okay?" she asks. "You looked rough last night."

"I had terrible dreams. He's so angry. What if he never forgives me?" I slide into a lounger.

"I might not think he's good for you, but he loves you. His emotions are written all over him every time he looks at you. He's mad. He should be mad. But he shouldn't be mad at just you. He needs to point some of that anger at himself."

"That won't be the first place he points his anger, and we both know it."

"Robert Morris, the attorney, called Mom this morning to say Wyatt's manager was sniffing around looking for the best family lawyer on the island."

"And there's the anger." I'm not sure what emotion I should feel at the realization Wyatt's exploring his legal options, but all

I can muster is numbness. "Is he going to try to take her from me?"

"He's not that dumb." Nikki huffs out a breath.

My phone pings in my pocket, and I take it out. Wyatt's at the gate. My day is rushing at me full tilt, and I can't get my bearings. "He's here, and I haven't told Haven."

"She already knows. Let him tell her. Maybe letting him see her joy will ease the sting a bit. She's going to be so happy he knows." Nikki opens the patio door. "I'll let him in. Give you two a buffer."

I sit on the lounge chair for a beat, gathering myself for the hard day ahead. Whatever he says or does, I have to keep the right attitude, for Haven's sake.

When I step into the house, Wyatt is in the kitchen doorway, with Nikki in the lead. Haven is still seated at the table in the living room, the board game laid out. Wyatt's jaw tenses, and he gives me a penetrating stare before glancing away, but he hangs back in the kitchen, and I go to him. I swallow the anxiety bubbling into my throat.

Nikki returns to the board game with Haven with an enthusiasm I know she doesn't feel, chattering to keep Haven distracted. She keeps glancing at me and Wyatt.

Wyatt removes a stress ball from his pocket. This one is a different color than the one he had the other day. Probably wore the first one out. He's so silent. Nervous energy dances along the surface of my skin. I expected him to march in here and declare himself her father. Give me his rage over the silent treatment any day. Give me his overconfidence instead of this strange uncertainty I sense.

"I take it you haven't told her?" he mutters, his focus glued to Haven.

"She's going to be over the moon." I keep my voice pitched low.

"You know who should have been over the moon? Me. Nine years ago when she was born."

The ice in his eyes makes me flinch. As angry as he is, something is holding him back from going to her. "Haven, honey, can you come over here for a minute?" I say. Nikki has done an amazing job containing her this long. The tension in the room must be palpable. I'll have to work on concealing that for her sake.

Haven gets off her chair and rushes over to where Wyatt and I are standing. Wyatt crouches. He understands a cue better than anyone. His Adam's apple bobs, and a twinge of anxiety pierces my heart. "You're already aware of this, but I only found out last night . . ."

Haven's eyes widen, but she doesn't say anything. She glances at me, and I wipe away a few stray tears before nodding.

"Dad!" Haven flings her arms around his neck, burying her face in the hollow. "You're my dad."

"I am. I am your dad." His voice is hoarse, but he manages to get the confirmation out.

Haven squeals and laughs. She steps back from him, looks him over, and then tackles him again. Wyatt lifts her into his arms and smooths back her long hair off her cheek. The tenderness is overwhelming.

"I want to see your room. I want to know everything." He scans her face. "I want to know you. I'm so sorry I already missed so much."

"But you came." She puts her small hands on either side of his face and grins. "I was sure you'd come. I knew it." Haven's smile is triumphant. "We knew it, didn't we, Mom?"

Looking at them through my tears, my heart is full, on the cusp of overflowing. All I've ever wanted is right in front of me.

Wyatt doesn't glance my way before Haven takes him back to her room. She natters away like they're already the best of friends. Tears slide down my face. When I look at Nikki, she's crying too.

WYATT

Present Day

When I walk down the hall to Haven's bedroom, Ellie's insistence I not come back here makes more sense. The walls are covered in pictures of her and Haven through the years. I want to stop and stare at them—examine each one in minute detail. Tear apart the memories and slot myself in. If only rectifying the mistakes in your past was that easy. Instead of dwelling on what I can't have, I carry Haven until she tells me to turn into a doorway.

The room is a monstrosity of pink. I set her down, awed and horrified at the explosion of color. She beelines to a photo on her dresser. Me and Ellie at the MTV awards. I take it from her. Isaac took this picture. Pain shoots through my heart, and a familiar ache spirals out. The agony of missing him still takes me by surprise; it just flares a bit less often than it did at the start.

"That was a great night." I hand the frame back. "Your mom and I were really happy."

"Mom says I am the product of a lot of love—almost too much love." She sets it in its place with almost exaggerated care.

"She does, does she?" I examine her artwork, pictures, mementos of places she's traveled, things she's done with Ellie and her family. A life she's lived without me.

"Do you think that too?" Haven asks. "Did you love my mom like that?"

I turn and consider Haven's question. Rage at Ellie simmers inside me, but underneath my anger is an emotion that's been my constant companion for years. Dulled by the drugs for too long, but always present nonetheless. "I will love your mother until the day I die. I'll probably love her even after that, wherever that is."

"I'm not sure you can love someone after you die?"

"Someday I'll explain that idea better."

Haven grabs artwork and a few of her other treasures to show me. I sit on her bed, clutching the newest piece she's shoved into my hands.

"You like art?" That doesn't come from me or anyone in my family.

"No, I like sports better. They're all pretty easy for me. Mom says I'm like you that way."

"Did your mom talk about me a lot?" I don't know my daughter, but she believes she knows me. Such a strange imbalance to grapple with on top of everything else.

"If I asked, yeah. Oh!" She goes to her bookshelf and removes a thick scrapbook. "We used to go through this when I was younger and I asked about you. Do you want to see?"

"Sure." I set the book on my lap. On the cover is the same photo of me and Ellie from the MTV awards.

Haven perches on the bed beside me and helps me keep the large pages open. My heart pounds when I realize what Ellie has done. The scrapbook starts with snapshots from *Love Letters from Spain*, and then each page progresses from there. She mapped our relationship.

Haven is talking, but I'm having a hard time concentrating. She's retelling the story of me and Ellie. She's animated, completely into the tale, knows that period of my life almost better than me.

My heart cracks into a million pieces. What has Ellie done? Why would she do this? Her telling me earlier this week I was everywhere and nowhere makes a new kind of sense. Snippets of Haven's stories penetrate my brain. The memories. So many recollections she saved for our daughter.

"Dad?" She stops mid-sentence. "Why are you crying?"

I touch my face and realize she's right. I brush the tears away self-consciously. Not that I don't cry. Hell, I can cry on cue. But this is different. I've never cried and not known I was crying. The piercing pain in my chest needs to go away. This ache needs to be softened. A little something to dull the pain. So many options. My tongue remembers the sensation of a Percocet rolling around, being flipped to the back of my throat. One pill would make this ache go away.

Get a grip, Wyatt. I am *not* going there.

"Happy tears." Not sure I sound convincing. Not much of an actor at the moment. Out of the corner of my eye, I realize

Ellie is standing in the doorway. I stiffen at her scrutiny. "We're fine, Ellie. You don't need to watch over us."

She runs her hands down her face and brushes a few tears away, but she doesn't say anything.

"Why is everyone crying? We get to be a family now, right?" Haven looks between me and Ellie.

"That's a complicated question," Ellie whispers.

"Why?" Haven asks.

"There are grown-up things your dad and I have to sort out." Ellie's shoulders rise and fall almost imperceptibly.

Dad. So weird. I pat Haven's leg. "No matter what goes on between your mom and me, I'm in your life forever. You're not getting rid of me."

She flings herself at me, hugging me tightly. I stare at Ellie over Haven's shoulder, and I set my jaw. She's not locking me out of any more moments with my daughter.

Ellie vanishes from the doorway. The urge to follow her is instinctual. I release Haven and half rise from the edge of the bed, but Haven drags me back. "You didn't finish looking at the book." She flips through the pages in rapid succession.

"Sorry." I examine her as she sorts through the story of my life. At her hairline is the tiniest scar. Hesitantly, I brush her hair aside. She freezes and her expression turns quizzical. "What happened here?" I ask.

Haven runs her index finger over the mark. She looks thoughtful for a moment and then grins. "Australia. I banged my head on a reef when Mom and I tried to learn to surf."

"When was that?" She hurt herself enough to leave a scar, and I wasn't there.

"Last year. I kept begging Mom to let me try. We don't get waves like that here. She finally let me and then I hurt myself. She was pretty upset."

"I bet." I can't imagine how I'd react to seeing my daughter with a head injury. It's been bad enough watching my nephew hurt himself. The instinct I've always had with Ellie—to protect, to save—is already magnified when I look at Haven. "You were okay, though? Just this tiny scar?"

"Yeah, just that." She flips another page in the book.

Every entry I see is another notch in my aching sadness. After another flip, one of the photos catches my eye. I stall her hand before she can zip past.

"Are you looking at Uncle Isaac?" Haven glances from me back to the photo.

"Yeah." So many of Isaac's things I burned in a drug-fueled rage after he died. So stupid. Getting rid of the remembrances didn't make me miss him any less.

"Does talking about him make you happy-sad like it does my mom?"

"That's what your mom calls it?"

"Yeah, she says the memories are happy, but it makes her sad she doesn't get to make any new ones. Talking about you used to make her happy-sad too."

I pinch the bridge of my nose, willing myself not to cry again. "That sounds about right." The words squeeze out of my tight throat. "I might call mine sad-happy. Sad I missed so much, and happy I won't ever miss any more." I tug at the neck of my shirt. It's hot in here. Shifting the book off my lap, I stand. "I need some air." I glance around her room for a door or window I can open.

"The air conditioning is on. But there's a balcony off my mom's room." Haven jumps off the bed and leads the way through to the rear of the house.

When we enter Ellie's bedroom, the space is wrong and right at the same time. It smells like her in here—a weird mixture of flowers and vanilla. The scent stops me in my tracks. The decor is neutral like the rest of the house, and the photos on the wall tell the story of her life with Haven, here in Bermuda. I'm nowhere to be found. Of course I'm not, but the ache in my chest spreads like a virus.

Haven opens one of the French doors and turns to me. "There are a couple chairs out there. I'm getting a drink. Do you want one?"

I shake my head and step outside. With a deep breath, I take my gum out of my pocket. I pop two pieces out of the foil and stuff them into my mouth. The motion of putting them on my tongue is comforting. Better gum than the alternative.

"Back in a minute," Haven says, retreating into the house.

The ocean is calm again today. Haven is right, there isn't much of a surf on this side of the island. The humid air penetrates my lungs when I breathe in and out, stilling the chaos inside me. Outside is good. My brain clicks back to a photo I saw in Ellie's room. On the dresser as we walked through was a photo in a frame. Something pinches my consciousness. Why did it jump out at me? I step into the room and cross to take a closer look.

Ellie, Haven, and some other guy. One big, happy family.

Another surge of anger roils through me. I'm tempted to throw the picture, to smash it on the floor or to drop it from Ellie's balcony and watch it shatter below. In my pocket, I squeeze my stress ball while staring at the photo.

"What are you doing?" Ellie's voice comes from the doorway.

I hold up the photo to her without saying a word.

"I dated him for a couple of years. We broke up six months ago. I just haven't gotten around to putting a new picture in the frame. It's been ten years. Did you really think I wouldn't have dated anyone else?"

"That's not the problem." I bite down hard on the gum, chewing with force. "The problem is him in the photo looking as though he's Haven's dad."

"He was good to her." She takes the photo from my hand, tension radiating off her. She opens a drawer and lays it in, facedown.

"I should have had a chance to be good to her."

"You have a chance now."

"Yeah, thanks to TMZ. I can't even believe *TMZ* made me a father."

"I'm sorry." There's more steel in her voice than there was last time. "I never wanted you to find out that way." She's reached the end of her apology rope. Too bad. She needs to make amends for the last ten years. One or two conversations aren't going to heal those wounds.

"I've been here for days. I'm not convinced you were ever planning to tell me about Haven while I was capable of understanding what it meant."

"I wanted to make sure you were clean and sober," she says. "Haven can't be thrown into our old life."

"My old life hasn't existed for a couple of years."

"Yeah, I'm sure with Anna around there're no drugs or violence or shady people."

"That's not *me. I'm* not doing those things."

"You're a party to them. You're playing with fire. And honestly, I'm not comfortable with Haven being in a house with Anna when she's doped up and unpredictable."

"You know how I feel about my sister." My anger rushes out of me like water through a crumbling dam. I don't even want that lifestyle for my nephew, but there isn't much I can do other than be there.

"You love her. Consider yourself responsible. I understand. But you have a daughter now. You have to protect her. Even when that means you're protecting her from Anna."

"Who's Anna?" Haven is in the doorway, sipping from her cup.

"I'm sorry, honey." Ellie flushes when she realizes Haven heard her. "I shouldn't be talking to your dad about this stuff right now."

"Who is she, Dad?" She cocks her head.

"Anna's my sister." Watching her try to best her mother is a little amusing. Ellie shakes her head and gives me an annoyed look. "She was going to find out at some point. I think there have probably been enough secrets, don't you?"

"Anna has the same sickness as your dad."

"Except worse," I chime in.

"Wyatt," she hisses a warning. "She's nine. She doesn't need all the honest details."

"I get to make some of those decisions now, right?"

Ellie's eyes widen, and there's a chance she might start levitating. Haven recognizes her mood.

"I'm going to talk to Aunt Nikki for a minute. When you're done fighting, Dad, do you want to go swimming?"

"Sure." Her careless use of the word *Dad* echoes in the room. My anger has subsided for now, and I'm sort of enjoying winding Ellie up.

"No. No swimming." Ellie slashes her hand through the air. "There will be people taking photos."

"Let them take photos. They might as well use their lenses and get shots from far away than pursue us when we try to leave."

"It's never an either-or situation. It'll be both."

Haven is gone from the doorway. She got Ellie's sense of what's appropriate. I would have stayed for this conversation as a kid. My parents' verbal fireworks made them seem as though they cared about something.

Parents. We're her parents. I'm the one Haven is looking at and wondering about.

"This isn't going to work. We need to present a united front on things." Ellie sighs.

"I won't cave to whatever you think is best. I get a say now." She won't railroad me into towing an invisible, arbitrary line she's created. "You can't pretend I don't."

"A say is fine." She searches my face, frustration and sadness mingling. "But she's impressionable. She's looking at us to make good choices and decisions. What's easy isn't always what's best."

"Sometimes they're the same. Why do you think hiding out is what's best? The storm is at the door. It's out there. We control the spin. This is PR 101. Haven and I go swimming. Hell, you can come too, if you want. We appear to be a happy, functional unit. If there doesn't appear to be drama, there's less drama. They get their photos and their made-up stories."

She crosses her arms.

"She won't even know they're taking the photos. We understand what the crush of the press is like." Even though I'm pissed at her, my unwavering desire to shield her from anything bad keeps my anger in check. Sadness coats her, and I want to figure out how to fix it, even if she caused her own misery.

"I never wanted this level of attention for her. It's why we live here."

"Come outside with Haven and me. Let them get their photos. Maybe they'll think their scoop isn't a scoop at all. Maybe they'll think they were the ones who were duped for ten years."

"Wyatt, I'm—"

"Get changed, Ellie. Let's go put on a show. We need to protect our daughter, and this is the best way I know how."

ELLIE

NINE YEARS AGO

Staring down at my three-month-old daughter, I wish her awake. I like her best when her eyes are open, when I find hints of Wyatt in her features. The swell, the rush of love people say happens when you first lay eyes on your child, hasn't happened.

Numb. That's what I feel. And exhausted. So exhausted.

This absence of emotional connection is my punishment for keeping Wyatt out of her life. He can't connect with her and neither can I. A good mother loves her baby.

There's a gentle knock on the doorframe, and Calshae is in the entryway to Haven's bedroom, concerned etched on her face. "Ellie, are you okay?"

I turn back to Haven's sleeping form.

"You're crying again." She scans me up and down, assessing. "You've lost more weight too."

"I'm fine. I still have lots of baby weight to lose." I brush past her to exit the room. If Haven doesn't get her nap, she'll cry. No more wailing. I can't take the noise. "You just let yourself in?"

"I knocked and called your name. I was worried."

Her help isn't needed today or any day. She's been a broken record since she found out I was pregnant, urging me to tell Wyatt the truth.

"Do you want me to stay and you can get some rest?" Calshae's tone is even, like I'm the problem, like I'm being difficult.

"No, I'm fine. I'm fine."

"There's no shame in needing help."

"Women raise babies all the time. I'll figure it out." I enter the galley kitchen with her following behind. Buying this house is one of the few things I've done right since coming back to Bermuda. The place suits me. Ocean views. Not too much house to look after for one person. Privacy.

Calshae takes a deep breath and jams her hands into the pockets of her miniskirt. "Is how you're behaving about Wyatt? You can go see him. You can tell him. Whether he's with that other girl or not."

"Katrina. You mean Katrina." Her name is bitter on my tongue. Didn't take him long to move someone else into the house, into his bed.

"From what I've seen, he doesn't look at her like he looked at you."

"How would I even know if he was in LA?" I grab a mug from the cupboard and fill it with old, bitter coffee. "I don't know his schedule anymore."

"No one in his circle would tell you?"

"I left him because he wouldn't get sober."

"You're miserable. How much worse could being with him be?"

I stare at her, turning over her words. Maybe being with Wyatt would help. She's right that I'm not sure I could feel worse. I'm watching myself spin, spin, spin away into nothing.

"Maybe Wyatt would be able to help you. Maybe he'd want to help you." Calshae gives me a hopeful look.

I brush away more tears, and I sip my coffee, but the tears keep coming. Sometimes I don't even know I'm crying. "I'll think about it." I gulp the bitter coffee, and I pour myself another one, even though it's cold and sharp at the back of my throat.

"He deserves to know."

"Oh, I'm aware of what you think. Trust me. I'm sure lots of people think they know better than me. But they don't get to decide. I do. I decide. You cannot comprehend what he's like when he's using. Until you've seen him in person, until you're the one trying to explain his behavior to someone else, you don't get a say."

"I'm gonna go." She walks around the island to the side entrance. "Call me if you need help, someone to talk to, whatever."

The click of the door echoes through the kitchen, and I make it to my room before I collapse on the bed, sobbing. Something is wrong with me. Maybe that *is* Wyatt or Wyatt's absence from my life. If I tell him, maybe I can snap out of this freefall.

Before I can change my mind, I dial the number for Yasmeen, Wyatt's travel agent, from memory. She confirms Wyatt is in LA, and she offers to book me a flight, but I decline. The idea of seeing him has my heart racing, swirling its way into my throat.

Once I hang up, I sit and cradle the phone in my hands. Haven can't come. I dial Nikki's number. "Can you watch Haven?" I don't bother with a hello.

"Uh," Nikki says. "I guess? You getting groceries or something?"

"Or something. When can you get here?"

"I'll be over soon." There's a beat of hesitation before she continues. "Are you okay? You sound weird."

"Fine." I grab a duffel bag out of my closet and throw clothes in it. I hang up and call the

airport for the next direct flight. There's a coach seat left on a plane leaving in four hours. That's good enough for me. By the time Nikki arrives, I've packed my bag but done little else.

"Where are you going?" Nikki eyes my overnight bag.

She scans the messy house and frowns. There are toys, blankets, empty bottles, diapers, wipes, and dishes littering every room. It's hard to believe a baby can create such chaos. The thought of picking up even one thing makes my head spin.

"I think you might need some help. This place is a disaster," Nikki says.

"No, I'm fine. Quick trip to LA." I wave off her concern.

"Audition?" Nikki plops onto the couch. "I didn't know you were going back to work. What'll you do with Haven?"

"Not work," I say, impatient. "Wyatt."

"He called you?" She turns wide eyes to me.

"No, no. I just . . ." I shake my head.

"You're going to *tell* him? That's a bad idea. Such a bad idea. He can't help you. He can't even help himself lately. Have you been paying attention to anything?" She narrows her eyes.

"You don't get a say."

"You're going to shower, right?" Nikki sighs, and she scans my face.

"I'll be staying at a hotel, so I'll glam myself up before I go over." I pick up my bag and give her a dirty look.

"If people see you . . ."

"I used to live there. Getting in and out without being seen is easy. I'll be fine." My idea is good. She should stop trying to drag me down.

"How long?" Nikki stands and goes to the kitchen. The fridge door opens. "Did you leave bottles? Breastmilk? Formula? Whatever else I need to look after a baby?"

"Call Mom if you need help."

"Is that what you've been doing?" Nikki stares at me around the door of the fridge.

"I'm fine!" I shout. "Why does everyone think I'm not fine? Everything is fine. Once I get Wyatt back, once I tell him, everything will be more than fine."

"He's sober? Clean? Doesn't seem like he's anywhere close, from what I've seen."

"I don't care anymore." I open the side door to exit the house. "I don't want to feel like this anymore."

"Ellie." Nikki follows me to the door. "I think you might need some help."

"I'm going," I say. "I'm going to tell him, to get him back."

She leans against the island. "I start my real estate course in three days. You need to be home by then."

"Of course, of course." I give her a little wave as I close the door behind me.

The next morning, I text Kyle when I get to the side entrance of Wyatt's property. Kyle appears within minutes, and he grins, unlocking the gate and swinging it wide. "You coming back?" He scans me from head to toe. "Wyatt's been a mess."

I ignore his comment and try to keep focused on why I'm here. "I wanted to talk to him for a minute. I'm guessing he's home?" He was never a morning person, and I doubt that's changed in the last year. More of a mid- to late-afternoon kind of guy.

"Yeah." Kyle's enthusiasm fades. "Are you okay? You look tired. Don't seem like yourself."

"I'm fine." I give a slight laugh. "Long flight."

"Uh." Kyle sucks in a breath as we walk to the main door. He scratches the back of his head. "Wyatt's been having some parties and . . ."

"I got it." His warning could mean so many things. But I don't want to discuss Wyatt with Kyle. Seeing Wyatt, talking to him, that's my priority.

"Okay, I didn't want you going in there unaware."

I don't want to ask, to speak her name, but if he's still living with someone else, I need to brace myself. "Katrina . . ."

"Is gone. She moved out a few months ago."

"Oh." Some of my anxiety eases.

"It was never what people thought anyway." Kyle glances at me before we part ways. "My gut tells me it'll always be you, El-lie. I probably shouldn't say that. I don't know what happened between you two."

I wish I didn't know either. Talking to Kyle again, thinking about Wyatt, makes me want a different outcome. "It's okay," I say to Kyle. "I'll come say goodbye whenever I leave." Maybe I won't leave. Maybe I'll stay.

He nods and wanders to the security hut at the main entrance where he often goes when Wyatt needs or wants more privacy in the house.

At the door, I contemplate walking in unannounced. If I got this far, it'll be unlocked. But I don't live here anymore. I ring the doorbell.

When the door swings back, I'm surprised. The willowy, dark-haired Italian beauty I once despised in the back of a limo stands poised in the entrance. She's wearing a shirt I bought Wyatt.

"Blanca." The name drips from me.

"Ellie Cooper." She takes me in. "What brings the fallen star back to her former home?"

"I'm here to see Wyatt."

"Hmm . . ." She puts a manicured finger to her lips. "I suppose he isn't busy anymore."

I move past her into the house. "Where is he?"

"His room." She eyes me slyly. "Rough night."

I hate her. Part of me hates myself for coming. My life is coming apart at the seams, and he's whoring around.

"Put on a few pounds, huh?" Blanca calls out.

The living room is riddled with empty pill containers and alcohol bottles from beer to wine to spirits, at varying levels of fullness. A white powder is smeared across the coffee table. I hope Wyatt is alive.

With my fingertips, I push open the door to Wyatt's room. The stench of stale alcohol hits me in the face. His sleeping form is sprawled on the bed. His steady breathing brings on a rush of relief, and I release the breath I was holding. So many times I crawled into and out of this very spot. So many memories. Deep within me, sadness stirs.

"Wyatt." I perch on the edge of the bed, and I rock his shoulder.

"Go away." Wyatt groans and turns away from me.

"Wyatt." My voice is even. "It's Ellie."

"Ellie's gone," he says. "There is no Ellie."

"Wyatt," I try again. "It's me. Look at me." I want to grab his face and force him to see me.

He rolls onto his back and squints. He laughs, but the sound isn't normal. "You look like Ellie." When he sits up, he pushes my hair away from my face to examine me. "But you're not her. She's gone."

"Wyatt. It's me. Really, it's me. I need to talk to you. There's something I need to tell you."

He stares at me like he's never seen me before. He reaches for the pills beside his bed and pops another one. "I like this combination." He tries to read the label and shrugs. "If I get to see you, even a fake you, that's pretty fucking good."

The reality of who he is hits me in the chest. My racing heart slows to a sluggish pace. He can't save me. He can't even save himself.

He brushes the tears off my cheeks and brings his thumb to his face. He chuckles. "Real tears. This shit is amazing."

Anger rises in me so swiftly I almost slap his hand. He needs to be better. We can't be the people we were before, and he's never going to change.

With renewed determination, I yank open drawers, and I search for things to take. If I can't have him, I want anything that'll remind me of him—tokens to give our daughter someday that might mean something.

"Oh, this shit is good. If Ellie was here, she'd take one too." Wyatt collapses back on the bed with a sigh.

"No, she wouldn't," I mumble under my breath. "That Ellie loved you too damned much for her own good. But not anymore. Not anymore." Tears clog my throat, and I have to stop speaking.

I stuff my purse with photos, trinkets, things I left behind. Knowing him, he'll think he threw them out or burned them. His impulse control is terrible when he's wasted.

When I have everything I want, I stand in the doorway of the bedroom. My chest is caving in on itself. Even though I understand he's no good for me, the urge to crawl into the bed with him, let myself drown the same way he's drowning, is so tempting. For the first time, his claim of not wanting to feel whatever emotions drove him to addiction makes sense to me. I don't want to feel this way anymore either.

But I won't lose myself in the bottom of a pill bottle, in a glass of lean, or in a fingertip of coke. We'd never forgive each other if I slid into this world with him and sacrificed our child. She'd be the victim of our reckless love.

"Wyatt," I call out into the room. Silence greets me. Maybe Calshae is right. He has a right to know, but he doesn't deserve a place in her life. Not like this. "We had a baby. I named her Haven. I hope you're well enough to meet her someday." I turn my back on him and walk past Blanca doing cocaine in the living room and straight out the door. A shudder threatens to blow me apart.

Home. Hold it together until you get home.

I stop at the hut to ask Kyle to keep my visit a secret, even from Wyatt, and then I take the next plane back to the island.

Instead of going to my house, I go to my mom's office at the medical clinic. With a deep breath, I knock on her door.

"Come in." She glances up from her desk when I enter. "Ellie! What a nice surprise. Did you bring Haven?"

At the sight of her, I press a hand to my chest, a sob lodged in my throat. Wyatt, lying in bed, too out of it to realize I was there, flashes in my mind. He'll never get help. But I have to.

"What's happened? What's wrong?" She circles her desk and envelops me in a hug.

"Help me." I force the words out with a sob. "There's something wrong with me. I need help."

ELLIE

Present Day

I tuck my breasts into my teeny-tiny bikini and hope that nipple-gate doesn't happen on top of baby-gate. Or, I guess, child-gate? Although my breasts might take the focus off Haven. My brain is fried, and I haven't even stepped into the glare of the sun, the glare of the cameras. Wyatt's right. They'll be there whether I see them or not. We'd better be good enough actors to make our relationship seem authentic.

I make my way to the water, where Wyatt and Haven are laughing and screaming. Listening to her high-pitched voice paired with his deeper tone is like hearing music for the first time. I want to stand and soak in the sound, imagine every note. For a moment, concealed by the trees, I close my eyes, take a deep breath, and allow myself to pretend this life is normal.

Wyatt's baritone laugh reverberates around the cove below. My heart swells. His laugh, his genuine one, wakes up my body. I press my palm to my chest and rub, like the memories are a spot I can scrub out, as if the ache will disappear with enough effort.

Ten years of repressed feelings. They won't go away—nothing and no one makes me feel this way except the man himself.

When I step onto the rocky shore, he spots me and swims over. He rises out of the water, ripe for the cameras to catch every ripple of muscle, every rivulet down his chest. He scoops me up, and I laugh as he tosses me into the deeper water. I emerge to Haven's giggles.

"He's been doing that to me too, Mom. It's so fun. He can throw me so far."

I stroke my way to the shallows. Wyatt takes Haven, counts her off, and throws her out again. He does make it look easy. He wades to me while she plays in the water, a school of fish looping around her ankles. With his arm around my waist, he guides me to his side. Bending his head, he whispers, "Relax. You're better than this."

Under my lashes, I glance up at him, and he sucks in a sharp breath. Rising on my toes, I brush my lips against his cheek. "Better?" I let our bodies slide together.

"Almost." He tugs me flush against him. His blue-green eyes darken, and he places his hands on either side of my face. He kisses my forehead and then my cheek. His attention lingers on my face, the way it once did when we were telling each other secrets in bed. The moment sings with a new kind of tension, and it's got nothing to do with anger.

When Haven swims closer, he releases me so quickly I'd have stumbled if we were on land. The water saves me from looking like too much of a fool.

"Again?" he asks her, grinning.

"And again, and again, and again." Haven's smile matches his. "This is so fun."

He picks her up, and the muscles in his back ripple. After he's released her, he says to me over his shoulder, "Haven said something about a tube?"

"Oh." I'm startled out of my thoughts about his thick muscles, and his toned back. He's so good with our daughter—a natural, as though the years without him never happened. My mind is going to places, to memories it has no business journeying to. "I'll get it."

He takes my wrist, drawing me close again so his lips graze my ear. "Let me get it. If I seem familiar with where things are, anyone watching will think I've been here a lot."

"Right." I stare at his chest, afraid to make eye contact. He'll realize what I've been thinking. Reading me, when he was sober enough, was second nature.

"Ellie." His voice dips low, the tone weakening my knees.

My name from his lips has always sounded so much better than from anyone else. Unable to resist, I glance up, and my heart lodges in my throat. I long to rise onto my toes, press my lips to his, see if the chemistry is still there. It is. Has to be. Parts of me have already ignited at the mere thought of his exploratory hands.

A knowing smirk quirks up one corner of his lips. "Where's the tube?"

"In the little storage shed, on the far corner of the cliff face." My voice hasn't sounded turned on like that without me doing it on purpose in years. *I could rip his clothes off right here.* My eyes half flutter when he dips his head into my neck.

"Got it," he murmurs against the sensitive skin. A shiver plays the most fantastic notes along my spine. I clutch his impressive biceps to keep myself upright. The skin-to-skin contact is delicious.

"Again?" Haven calls out, just before she goes under and comes up next to us. Her reappearance snaps me into reality.

I step back from Wyatt as though I've been stung. He yanks at his swim shorts, which are mostly concealed by the water. I'm not the only one with my engine revving, nowhere to go. He winks at me as he turns to Haven. "What about this tube?"

"Oh yeah." Haven jumps around. "The anchor is really heavy, though."

"Too heavy for me?"

Haven turns to me for confirmation. "I'm sure Wyatt will be fine." Nikki and I always cart out the anchor for the giant tube together, but I doubt Wyatt will have the same trouble. He just came off filming a superhero movie, and if his Instagram pictures are anything to go by, he lifted a lot more weight than the anchor in preparation for the role. I spent far too many nights scrolling through those pictures.

Haven and Wyatt wade to the shed and then make short work of digging out the tube and inflating it. Wyatt lets Haven drag the tube through the water to me. He follows with the anchor cradled in his arms.

"Too heavy?" I call out.

He chuckles and changes his grip to hoist it over his head.

"Guess not." Every time his arms flex, my heart pumps heat into areas of my body that haven't felt this way in ten years. I take a deep breath. *Get a grip, Ellie.* Lust. That's all this is. Supercharged lust. He doesn't even like me right now. But these last few days, when I stare at myself in the mirror, there's a change in me.

I'm awake. The hibernation is over.

For another hour, we jump on and off the tube, float in the ocean, flirt, laugh, pretend. The easiness isn't an act for me. I've almost convinced myself we've always been this way when Haven starts to shiver. She's so petite the cold hits her hard. The sun has disappeared behind some clouds. Wyatt wraps her in a towel and carries her up to the house with me trailing behind.

When the door to the outside closes, the chill follows us in.

Haven and Wyatt spend the rest of the day ignoring me unless Haven wants to know where something is, when a particular experience happened, or how old she was when she did something. Sometimes I catch Wyatt observing me, but I'm terrible at deciphering his thoughtful moods. Ideas are bubbling below his surface, but I have no idea what they are.

Nikki comes into the kitchen as I'm putting items away after Wyatt's complicated snack. "He's better with her than I expected." Nikki takes a seat at the island.

"He is." I can't dispute that. Parenting is hard, sometimes really hard, but he's taken to it with ease.

"What are you going to do?"

"What do you mean?" I stop cleaning, cloth in hand.

"He leaves tomorrow." She checks her phone.

I straighten when Wyatt comes into the kitchen. He grabs a glass and gets water from the fridge without speaking and then disappears out the door.

"Has he said anything to you since you came up from the beach?" Nikki asks, eyebrows raised at the frosty air that entered the room with Wyatt.

"Does 'do you want any?' count? He was making lunch at the time."

"The only person he should be mad at right now is himself. You gave him a choice, and he chose wrong."

"Bit of a false choice when I don't tell him everything, though, isn't it?" I say.

"You did go back. He doesn't remember." Nikki runs her hands along the granite island. "Says a lot."

"I'm not throwing that in his face. I knew he wouldn't remember. Again, it's not a real choice when he doesn't understand what's happening."

"You're being too easy on him."

"I'm trying to be fair. Telling him when I knew he wouldn't remember wasn't the right thing to do. Made me feel better at the time, but it wasn't the right thing to do." Wyatt and I know each other too well for either of us to accept one visit when he was wasted as being a genuine effort to offer him a choice.

"Fine. I want you to close your eyes and think about how things might have been if you'd stayed. Tell me about that." Nikki leans back.

"So many things. Too many things." I hold up a finger. "And not all of them bad, Nikki. You see him now. He's great with her.

With very few exceptions, he treated me like the most precious person in the world." He cherished me, and despite the fame and the women, and everything else that could have doomed us, I trusted him. He never gave me reason to doubt.

"Getting back together with him when he's been in your life less than a week is a mistake."

"He's so angry with me right now, he doesn't want me. He might never want to be with me again." My voice catches, and I swallow my anxiety.

"What if he does? What if he tells you he wants it all with you?"

"I don't know. I don't know what I'd do." Other than Anna's presence in his life, I trust him. He's not the man he was. But I don't trust her or her habits. I really don't trust the drug addicts and pushers she likely hangs around with. Maybe Wyatt doesn't knowingly let her use in the house, but it doesn't mean she isn't hiding needles, powder, or pills where kids can find them. I left Wyatt to keep Haven away from the drug abuse, the violence, the unpredictability of an addict. Letting him take our daughter into a situation where those things exist nullifies the ten years I stayed away.

"He leaves tomorrow. What's the plan for tonight?"

"I'll drive him back to his hotel after dinner, when Haven's in bed. I don't want to talk about any custody or visitation things with her around. Sometimes we say things that aren't always . . . kind."

"You're having those discussions when you take him back to his hotel?"

"I have to. We're out of time." I'd prefer not to get lawyers involved if we can be adults about this. I rub my face. "Haven can't be around Anna. It's a hard line for me."

"Not sure how you stop that."

"If Wyatt takes me to court . . ." I can't finish my thought.

"It'll get nasty," Nikki agrees and rises to stand beside the island. "He's led a very public, very messy life."

"I'm not sure I can do that to him or Haven—drag him through the mud."

"Maybe you won't have to. You say he's changed. I guess we'll see if that's true." Nikki walks out of the kitchen and back into the living room.

Every time my thoughts drift to Anna, I'm not sure how we'll ever solve our custody problem—if she can't stay away from drugs, and he won't abandon her, we're at an impasse.

He's on the back of my bike, and we're taking the alternate route off my property. The path is too narrow for a car. When I first bought this place, I paid to have this tiny road carved out as an escape route from the paparazzi in case they came calling. They never did, but I've kept it cleared in case. Now they are camped out in droves by the security hut. I checked with Jerome before taking the secret exit.

Wyatt's dinner reminded me he can make delicious food with very few ingredients. Haven helped him in the kitchen, learning alongside him as he talked about flavors, cuts of meat, spices, ways to cook things, and anything else she asked. My heart melted like butter in a pan. His patience was limitless.

When he put her to bed, I stood outside the door, listening as he read her stories and answered her questions. I rushed back down the hall when I heard him getting up to leave.

The rhythm of my life with him is something I could get used to. I have no idea how he's feeling. He hasn't said two words to me on the ride back. Not about the path, not about Haven, not about custody arrangements. Nothing.

When we left the house, I texted Calshae, and she suggested the employee entrance. The fewest paparazzi were there, and she could use her workers as an excuse to move people along without raising suspicion. We're arriving at shift change.

Calshae holds open the door as we squeeze through. "I had anyone turned away from staying here who was obviously a member of the press," Calshae says as soon as we're in the door. "But my employees aren't detectives. There could be people here who work for gossip outlets who slipped through the cracks."

I nod and glance at Wyatt. His jaw is tight, but he nods too. Out of the corner of his eye, he looks at me. "Are you coming up?"

"We should talk." Worry eats at me, a worm in an apple. After the quiet stage, the next is the vindictive one, though I was never on the receiving end. He's already called lawyers. Going up to his room might lead to another fight. There's not much choice, with him leaving tomorrow. Determining a way forward over the phone gives us too much room for misunderstandings.

He takes my hand and the small action, so deeply familiar, gives me hope. He offers a gentle squeeze when our fingers intertwine, once a silent form of reassurance. Maybe we won't fight. Heat floods my cheeks. Calshae gives me a sly look but this isn't what she thinks.

When we get to his room, he drops my hand the minute we're in the door. He sits in one of the chairs by the desk, hands clasped across his middle.

I perch on the edge of the bed, waiting. Starting with the lawyer seems confrontational, but I don't want to hide what I've learned either.

"I just keep getting angrier." He runs a hand down his face. "It's like an endless spiral of rage. I don't know when I'll get to the bottom, but I'm not there yet."

"Do you want to talk about it?"

"About why I'm angry?"

"No, I understand why you're angry," I say. "But if you want to talk about anything . . ."

Wyatt's shoulders fall. "There are so many things. The firsts with Haven. All of them—gone."

"There are still some left. Lots of them."

"Don't. Okay? I don't want to fight with you. I don't." He shakes his head. "I'll say shit I don't mean. Or that I mean right now, but won't mean later. I don't want to hurt you, but I'm also not sure how to move forward."

I scooch back onto the bed, drawing my knees to my chest. The answers don't exist in me either. There's no clear path to get past what we've both done to each other.

He examines me for a while before he speaks again. "You used to sit like that when we lived together. Do you realize that? If we got in a fight and you were in the wrong, you'd curl up into this little ball." He stands and shoves his hands in his pockets. "I know that about you. I notice so many things. The last few days, I'm remembering more and more. Weird, right? I come after you because I love you and then spend these last few days *remembering* why I love you."

Tears prick at my eyes. Seeing him again has been like that for me. Except I've spent years denying my feelings existed. Embracing them wasn't an option. I have no idea if it is now either. His back is to me like he can't stand to look at me.

"Everything about Haven's nine years bothers me. All of it." He goes to the curtain on the sliding door, drawn tight, and twists it back, peeking out. Turning, arms crossed, he stares at me. "The other thing that makes me angry, irrationally angry"—he chuckles and runs a hand through his hair, as though he knows I'm going to think he's lost his mind—"is that I didn't get to see you pregnant with my kid, with Haven." He comes to me and takes my hand, tugging me to my feet.

"I had terrible cravings for the strangest combinations," I whisper. "Some things you might be glad you missed."

"I'm not so sure." He presses his hand against my stomach. "I think I would have loved it all. God knows I loved you." The raw need in his voice hits me straight in the chest, piercing my heart.

"Wyatt," I breathe out. The heat from his hand burns through me. I itch to shift his palm a little lower. My thoughts from earlier today are tiny fires threatening to become an inferno.

"All day, I've been looking at you, wondering what it might have been like if I'd gone to rehab like you asked, if I'd stayed that day instead of leaving, if I wasn't so fucking out of it when you came back." His Adam's apple bobs. "I'm sorry about everything I said during that fight, Ellie."

Going back to either of those days doesn't help us now. Without realizing it, we've shifted closer, so close that breathing makes our bodies touch. Every exhale skims us together. My heart wants to escape my chest and brush up against him. My eyes flutter closed, lost in a haze of sensations that have nothing to do with thinking. Wyatt's breath stirs my hair next to my ear. I long for the press of his body against mine, for the length of him to fill me, to be sure he's mine again. I'd give anything to have him mine again.

"Not unless you say yes." Wyatt's mouth is close enough to my ear his lips graze my earlobe, and I suppress a moan.

Fireworks go off in my brain, leaving behind a haze of memories. Every time he's whispered in my ear in a crowded room, under the glare of lights, beneath the cover of darkness, bursts to the surface. I don't want to think anymore. I don't want to argue anymore. I want to feel.

"Yes," I whisper, eyes closed.

"Look at me." His voice is gruff, one hand cupping my cheek.

Opening my eyes, I see my desire reflected on his face. So familiar. If I say the word again, there'll be no turning back. If I think about what saying yes means, I won't speak the word. "Yes."

His hands sink into my hair, and his lips rush to meet mine. I wrap my arms around him, everything so natural I can switch off my brain, go on instinct. In one swift movement, he lifts my shirt over my head, my hair tumbling around my shoulders. Both hands come back to my hair, and he deepens the kiss. His lips are firm but soft, and his tongue tangles with mine.

I slide my hands up his muscular chest, taking his shirt with me. Our lips break contact only long enough for his shirt to pass his head. His kisses are hungry, demanding, as though we can rewind ten years in one night. Maybe we can.

My shorts pool at my feet. I step out of them while Wyatt trails his mouth down my neck. Nibbling my earlobe, he returns to my lips while I push his shorts off him. My hands slide into the waistband of his boxer briefs, grazing his ass and coming around to cup his manhood.

He groans into my mouth. "Ellie." A rasp. The way my name used to sound on his lips before he came, as though he couldn't control himself, as though he'd never loved anyone more.

Desire swells in me. Hearing him say my name like that causes my knees to weaken. This wildfire of emotion is the standard he set, and I don't understand how I was ever with anyone else after. Our chemistry burns through me. He scoops me up, laying me back on the bed. Trailing his hand down my body, he follows with his mouth. When he gets to my stomach, he pauses, his palm skimming across my middle. "No trace," he whispers, his voice full of awe and sadness.

An ache blooms in my chest. My job, my life, depended on there being no sign I was ever pregnant. He doesn't wait for a response, just continues to drop lingering kisses along the edge of my panties. His lips skim my inner thighs before he removes my panties in one swift action. Shifting his body to the side, he comes back to my lips while his fingers circle my sensitive spot, working magic on my most intimate parts. In the years we were together, he took pleasure in learning every way to take me over the edge—quickly, slowly, and every increment in between. I moan into his mouth, slick with need, headed along the path of no return.

"Not yet. Not without me," he says.

I arch my back, then he takes each breast into his mouth, sucking and licking the nipples. When his teeth graze them, I gasp, and he chuckles.

"Say it," Wyatt murmurs into my neck. "Tell me, Ellie."

"I want you." I bite his earlobe and scrape my nails along his shoulders. "Please, Wyatt."

His lips return to mine as he positions himself between my legs. Cupping my ass with one hand, he pushes into me, filling me. I wrap my legs around his waist, keeping him tight. Both his arms come up underneath me, cradling me as he rocks into me. The full body contact is delicious and sends a flood of sensations through me.

"I love you, Ellie," he murmurs before he kisses me, long and deep.

Our mouths barely break contact, and he shifts to rub me the way I need to climax. I missed him. I missed this. No one makes me come alive like he does. The way we move together, the tenderness and love of being cradled in his arms. There's nothing like being with him.

"Ellie." His voice is strained.

"Yes," I say, breathless. "A little more. Yes." I moan. "God, Wyatt, yes."

He pushes into me harder, the contact sending me over the edge, crying out his name in a haze of ecstasy. He chases my orgasm with his own and then kisses me tenderly.

Rolling to the side, he tucks me against his chest. He wraps both of his arms around me, and he presses his lips to the top of my head. "I've missed you." His chin rests on my crown.

"Me too." The truth is so much easier to admit than I expected. I have missed this version of him, which I got so often when we first started dating and less often as he spiraled out of control. Maybe we can carve out happiness together.

Exhausted, lulled into a sense of security by the soft thud of Wyatt's rhythmic heartbeat, my eyes drift shut.

Hours later when I wake up, Wyatt has me secured to his chest, his arm a weight across my middle. His steady breathing is near my ear and stirs my hair. I shouldn't stay any longer. Haven will get the wrong idea if she realizes I slept here, and I'm not sure what the right idea is yet. We didn't talk. Still, hope fills my chest. I shift Wyatt's arm, even though I long to stay.

"Where are you going?" Wyatt mumbles into my neck.

"Bathroom." Another shiver flows down my spine and across my body. I'll never understand how he can make me want so much with so little. Fingers crossed he falls back to sleep. I don't want to fight, and he won't be happy with me sneaking out, even if it's for the best right now.

He releases me, and I tiptoe to the bathroom, collecting my clothes as I go. I dress and then stare at myself in the mirror.

What am I doing? I grab a tissue and brush away the mascara that's smudged under my eyes. Balling it up, I toss it toward the garbage, and I catch sight of a familiar bottle. I crouch to examine the trash can. My heart kicks at the realization of what's stashed inside the white plastic bag. There are fifteen or more minibar bottles, empty.

He lied to me.

I suck in a sharp breath. Anger rises in me, but tears leak out. Removing each bottle from the garbage, I line them up on the counter. From my purse on the floor, I find a pen and a scrap of paper. With tears blurring my vision, I scribble a note and leave it propped against the bottles.

How could you? What else have you lied about?

I risk one last glance at him before leaving the room. His sleeping form almost undoes me, but the row of bottles I laid out mocks me. He made me believe he had his addictions kicked, or at least under control. He fooled me. There's nothing controlled about that much alcohol. A headache builds behind my eyes. I embrace the anger and frustration because my other option is heartbreak. We were so close.

Twenty in total. He's still drinking.

When I leave his room, the door closes behind me with a click.

WYATT

PRESENT DAY

"Ellie," I murmur. For the first time in years, her name on my lips as I wake up is a comfort. I reach out an arm to secure her warmth against me again. Instead, I'm met with a cold mattress. With a frown, I rub the heels of my hands into my eyes and sit up.

"Ellie?" I squint into the semi-light sneaking through the curtain. She must be here somewhere. Please, let her be somewhere. Anywhere but gone.

The curtains to the balcony are still shut, so I check the bathroom first and freeze. "Shit!"

Shit. Shit. Shit. Shit.

My shorts are on the floor, and I fish out my phone from the pocket. No messages from her. I hit redial on Calshae's number and rub my forehead. *This is not good. You fucked up, Wyatt.*

"Need a ride?" The buzz of the hotel in the background almost drowns out her voice.

"Yes." I yank out clothes from my packed bag and tug them on while keeping the phone to my ear. "To Ellie's."

"Wyatt, you'll miss your flight if I take you to Ellie's. What happened?"

I check the clock on the bedside table and realize she's right. I'll be lucky if I make my flight as it is. Being with Ellie last night made me forget anything else existed. I didn't set an alarm. Tanvi won't ever agree to watch Jamal again if I don't show.

"Fuck." I grab the tips of my hair. "I'll be down in a minute."

With my dirty clothes from the floor tucked into my bag, I practice deep breathing. I sweep the room for anything I might have left behind and try to keep a level head.

Maybe it's not that bad. Maybe she'll be reasonable.

A piece of paper is propped against the bottles in the bathroom. In giant letters, she's scrawled: *How could you? What else have you lied about?*

Reasonable is out the window.

Each bottle represents my weakness, and I throw them at the shower wall. A few are glass and shatter on impact. The sharp sound is satisfying, but the tang of alcohol fills the room again, reminding me I'm an idiot.

A fucking mess. I drag my hands down my face. Tommy, my manager, has probably been earning his money this week. I scroll through my recent calls.

"I need the name of whatever family lawyer you turned up," I say as soon as he answers.

"Hello to you too, Wyatt. Why would you want that? Your little family promotion parade yesterday was gold. TMZ has taken the bait. They're running with their version of reality. You, Ellie, Haven—a secret family for years, everyone was duped."

"I fucked up." I sink into the desk chair. My leg bounces. I need a run. Or to go box. Something physical. The flight home will kill my nerves.

Silence greets me on the other end of the line. "What'd you do?"

"I was drinking," I admit. Even saying the truth out loud is a betrayal. So stupid. I was so close to getting everything I wanted. "There's no way in hell Ellie's going to let me near Haven now."

"Who knows?" Tommy is in damage-control mode. He's scrambling for a pen and paper, I'm sure.

"No one. The hotel owner's daughter, who is also Ellie's friend, thinks I poured them down the drain. I had myself half convinced I did."

"Hmm . . ." Tommy taps the pen on the table. "She believed you?"

"Yeah, I think so." *I hope so.*

"Bluff. Have her confirm to Ellie you weren't drinking, that you poured them down the drain. Come back at her hard, full of confidence."

"With what?" Adding more lies to the mix seems like a bad idea, but if I'm honest, I'll take any chance I have with Ellie and with Haven. She won't believe I can control this, that alcohol doesn't spiral into drug use.

"You and Ellie have been getting along?"

If this morning hadn't happened, I would have said we'd been getting along *very* well. Even before last night, there'd been an ease between us, as though we both remembered how good it could be if we let ourselves go there. That ease will be gone now. I lean forward in the chair, resting my elbow on my knee, letting my head fall into my hand.

"They're still after a costar for your next movie."

"Seriously, Tommy?" She won't agree to be anywhere near me. I'll have to fight dirty to see Haven after this morning.

"It's not a terrible idea. The publicity will be huge."

"Which she'll hate." Tommy is used to me, someone who loves the press. Ellie has never been a fame whore like that.

"You can insist Haven comes to set. Prove to Ellie you can stay clean and sober. You can do that, can't you, Wyatt? Be sober?"

"I wasn't drunk. A couple drinks. I didn't know Haven was my kid. Ellie dropped me off, and I started to pour them out. Most of them went down the drain. That's the truth."

There's a knock on the hotel door.

"Not sure how much the truth matters anymore, Wyatt, my boy. You're gonna have to spin this like you've never spun anything before. Your drug- and alcohol-filled exploits haven't exactly been discreet."

"I realize that." I cross to check the peephole. "I gotta go." I hang up and swing the door open in one movement.

"We're not going to make it." Calshae enters the room before I invite her in. "Were you drinking? Smells like alcohol in here. Please tell me you and Ellie didn't get drunk last night and sleep together."

I raise my eyebrows, at a loss for words.

"Oh, Lord." She whistles. "Which part of that is true?"

"We were not drinking last night. But I did throw empty minibar bottles at the shower wall."

"Why?"

"Ellie found them in the trash after I fell asleep last night. Then she left." The reality of how stupid I was keeps slamming into me. She was here, and we were on the cusp of something, something good. We won't recover from this. I can feel it in my bones. She'll keep me away from her, from Haven, and I'll have to fight tooth and nail for the bare minimum.

"Can you reschedule your flight?" She grabs my carry-on suitcase and deposits it by the door.

"I need to get to LA for Jamal." My phone is heavy in my hand. Tanvi will understand if I call, just as long as Anna's still on her bender and not trying to break down her door. "When's the next flight out?"

"Three hours." She checks her watch for confirmation. "I'll have enough time to take you to Ellie's, for you two to hash it out real quick, then to the airport. The hashing part will need to be *unbelievably* quick." Her dark eyes are sad when they meet mine. "Maybe you shoulda let me have someone clean your room."

Of course, that might mean I'd have someone selling "Wyatt Burgess on a Bender" stories to the press. Not quite true. Truer than I'd like.

"How many bottles were there?" She peeks into the bathroom and retreats.

"All of them." I don't mention the phone call to the front desk to order more in a moment of weakness. Luckily, she doesn't spend long enough in the bathroom to count the bottles lying around. The number of unbroken plastic ones screw my story right away. "Would you . . ." I clear my throat, gathering my nerve. "Would you consider telling Ellie you never saw me drinking, never smelled any alcohol on me?"

"That's true." Calshae gives me a rueful smile. "It's just . . . I can't say for sure that you *weren't* drinking. I know you told me you poured them down the drain." She eyes me. "I'll bet you've learned a thing or two about how to cover your tracks over the years?" Her voice rises at the end.

I've brought my A-game to this conversation. My facial expression is going to match these words. I will not crack. She needs to be in my corner or Ellie will never let me near my daughter again. "I understand what's at stake. I was not drinking." If she checks my room bill, she'll catch my lie.

"But you still drink?"

"Not anymore."

"Poor Ellie." Calshae chuckles. "How is she ever certain you're telling the truth? Your ability to sidestep a direct question is astounding."

"Will you help me or not?" I sigh.

"I'll help you. You want to be better, but you're not there yet. You can keep your foot in the door. But you're going to need a crowbar for Ellie to let you in after this."

If a crowbar is what I need, I'll find one. No matter what it takes, I'm wedging myself into Haven's life, and Ellie's too.

"I'll meet you downstairs." She picks up my bag. "We're going in the secret entrance to Ellie's place?"

"Yes. Can you get in touch with her security?" I'm already dialing Yasmeen, my travel agent, to get on a new flight.

"Yeah, I can do that." Calshae shoves the suitcase out the door.

I turn away from her while I fill in Yasmeen, and then call Tanvi and tell her my flight's been delayed. She could check my lie, but she won't. No matter how things go with Ellie, I'll be in LA today. She tries to talk about Haven, but I brush her off as kindly as I can, saying we can chat about my daughter over tea in person.

To get to Ellie's house, Calshae takes us on a long detour to lose the paps trying to follow us. The ride gives me too much time to ponder the depths of Ellie's anger. I lied. I'm going to keep lying. But I'm done drinking. That certainty needs to beat like a drum in my head when I talk to Ellie. I must convince her I'm clean and *sober*.

Dipping into the path, Calshae glances behind her before accelerating along the tight route. Parking in front of the side entrance, she peers behind us again. "Do you want me to come in?"

"Yes," I say, gruffly. "I need you to tell her what we agreed."

Climbing out of the car, she knocks on the side door.

Nikki answers, a weary expression on her face. "Haven's here, Wyatt. Ellie's barely holding it together. You were *drinking*?"

Each of her phrases is a bullet to my gut. "I wasn't drinking. Ellie doesn't understand. I need to talk to her."

Nikki glances over her shoulder and then whispers to me, "Based on how Ellie's acting, I can guess what happened between you two last night."

"She misunderstood." That part I believe. She sees a few minibar bottles as a sign of my addictions. A weakness, maybe. But alcohol is not a problem. I'm not downing a bottle of Jim Beam every night.

"I bet you've never lied to her about something like this before." Nikki raises one eyebrow.

I hate how she's gotten to the root of Ellie's anger. Whether I'm telling the truth or lying doesn't matter. Ellie will believe whatever she wants to believe because she thinks she understands how I operate. Those empty bottles are not indicative of who I am now, and I won't let her turn me into someone I'm not.

When we come through the kitchen and into the living room, Ellie rises from the couch, and her tear-streaked face is a knife to my heart. My gut clenches. I did this. After telling her she wouldn't be sad with me anymore, I've ripped her heart out.

"Ellie." I shove my hands in my pockets to keep from sweeping her up, comforting her.

"No." Holding up a hand to ward me off, she pressed her other one into her chest. "You've been drinking. You promised me you were clean." Her voice catches. "There's nothing you can say right now. Nothing."

Beside me, Calshae's intake of breath is audible in the room. "I never saw him drinking, never smelled alcohol on him. He poured those bottles down the drain in a fit of rage."

"Did you see him do that?" Ellie crosses her arms.

"Yes." Calshae doesn't look at me, doesn't elaborate.

Ellie's jaw is tight, and she comes around the couch. Her brown eyes scan my face, searching for the truth. It's buried deep. All she'll find is my lying confidence. She comes almost toe-to-toe with me. She turns to Calshae. "I don't believe you." Then she stares at me. "I don't believe you either."

"You're wrong not to trust me." Confidence oozes out of me. Whatever I have to say or do, I'm going all-in today. She's not shutting me out.

"Supervised visits, that's what you can have." She whirls to leave my side.

"Perfect. That'll be great during our joint filming schedule." The words are out before I can reconsider. Ah, well. Maybe Tommy was on to something. At least this way, she'll be forced to spend time with me, and I will not screw up again. I understand the stakes now. I didn't when I let the liquid roll down my throat, warm my stomach, soothe my rage. If I'd been aware of what I was risking, I wouldn't have allowed myself the luxury of a few drinks.

"I'll be at the car. Watch your time." Calshae ducks out of the room to the kitchen.

Good instincts. A fight is brewing.

"I have my own commitments." Ellie scoffs. "Just because Kathleen Kirkton flaked out doesn't mean I step in. Any movie with the two of us would be a media circus."

"Fine." I swallow my anxiety, and I raise the stakes. "I'll take you to court. There's a lawyer lined up."

She glances at Nikki. There's no surprise between them. Eve-lyn must have told her. Her mother has been giving everyone's secrets away. Nikki rises from the couch and disappears down the hall. Is she going to monitor Haven or giving us privacy?

"Court wouldn't go well for you."

"Who knows? I'll take my chances."

"Haven," Ellie says. "She doesn't deserve to be dragged through a messy court battle."

"You don't believe I haven't been drinking. Fine. I have a promotional tour for *Sixty Seconds to Live*—it's not long. Then I should start work on the Kirkton project if we have a new lead. Step in for her. Give me a chance to prove I'm not the man you think I am."

"You couldn't stop drinking for a week. Why would I tie myself to you for months?"

"We're already tied for years. Her name is Haven."

She lifts her hair and lets it fall and then gathers it up again, placing it over one shoulder. With her arms crossed, she bites her lip. "Why this project?"

"Why not a movie project? We'll both have a few weeks to cool off. Then we have a few months to work together. During our free time, we can figure out this family thing."

"This 'family thing'?"

I don't like her mocking tone, but I'm also not letting this opportunity go. I'm close to winning her over. She doesn't completely hate the idea, though I'm surprised. "You, me, and Haven."

"I'm off the table. There will be no relationship between you and me. We're not anything. Co-parents. We're not a family."

Her words slice through me. I came here for her, but with Haven in the picture, a life I never knew I could have stretches out in front of me. But it doesn't include supervised visits or never being with Ellie again. After last night, I want it all.

"We could be a family. I know you've felt it too. It's possible."

"You're lying to me. Not a doubt in my mind." She points her finger at my chest. A deep shuddering breath only partially conceals the sob rising into her throat, leaking into her voice. "And it breaks my heart that I let myself believe you were better than this last night."

The sob escapes her now, and I draw her into my arms. She comes willingly, and my shirt absorbs her tears while my heart breaks with hers. One stupid fucking mistake, and it's all crashing down around me.

"I'll prove you wrong," I murmur into her hair. "Do the movie. I'll prove you wrong."

"We'll never be anything again." Ellie pushes away from me, sniffing and wiping her tears.

There's so much conviction in her voice that anger rises in me. One mistake, one I didn't realize had this much weight, shouldn't have the power to undo the progress we've made this week.

"Tell me last night meant nothing," I say.

Ellie steps toward me, fury vibrating off her. "It meant *everything* to me." Her voice fills with agony. "And then I found twenty minibar bottles in your garbage." She points her finger at me again. "Tell me the truth. Did you drink them?"

"No," I fire back. "I'm not drinking."

Her shoulders drop, and the fight goes out of her. "I'll do the movie. But I'm doing it for your relationship with Haven. That lie—the one you just told me—it cost you us. I can't trust you."

If I told her the truth now, the consequences are laid out before me. Supervised visits, court battles, more lost time. She's giving me the movie. Months of time. I can win her over. Show her that whether or not I was drinking here, she can trust me. I'm not returning to my old habits.

A text pops up on my phone from Calshae. I need to go, or I'll miss this flight too. "I have to go," I say. "I need to get home to Jamal."

"Have your manager contact mine with the details. We don't need to talk."

"We have a daughter." I throw up my hands. "You're not denying me access to her."

"I'll figure out a way for you to speak to her that doesn't involve me." She glares at me.

My instinct is to dig in and keep fighting, but the longer I press her, the worse what little is left of our relationship will get. If I leave now, maybe we can salvage something. We both need time to cool down. "Make sure you do." In frustration, I run my hands through my hair before passing her on my way to the side door.

"Did you get what you wanted?" Calshae asks when I climb in beside her.

"Not yet," I say. "But I'm one step closer."

ELLIE

Present Day

The section of Algonquin Park in Northern Ontario that the film scout pinpointed for our movie's location is full of evergreens and a lot of snow. If I had to be on a set with my nine-year-old for the next three months, I would have picked almost anywhere else. Perhaps I should have asked Wyatt or my manager more questions. Other than negotiating an exorbitant amount of money for my participation, I didn't care about much else. He wanted me here, and agreeing was what was best for Haven's relationship with him.

Our trailer, by Hollywood standards, isn't lavish. I asked for something kid-friendly, which seems to have been translated into an interior covered in shades of lemon and pink. There are two bedrooms, plus a bathroom, a kitchenette, and multiple sitting rooms.

"When is Dad getting here?" Haven picks up the throw pillows on our trailer's couch, examines them, and puts them back. She's spoken to Wyatt every day since he left the island.

"Call and ask him." We saw him briefly earlier today when we arrived, but he's been on set for the last couple of hours prepping with James, the director.

I've given in and gotten Haven her own phone so I don't have to be the intermediary between her and Wyatt. Terrible parenting. Hearing Wyatt's voice drifting down the line reminds me too much of what I want to forget.

Setting down my purse and the backpack filled with Haven's school supplies, I close my eyes. We haven't talked in any detail since he left the island. I haven't kept Haven from him, but I've kept myself as far away as possible. What he's said, what he hasn't admitted, echo in the distance between us.

"Knock, knock." Wyatt peers in the door. "Your tutor-nanny is in my trailer."

Of course she is. "Did Stacy get lost?" I hope my tone hides how much seeing him again turns my insides to mush. His dark hair, his light eyes, his tall, toned body. The memory of what that body can do to mine rises to the surface.

"I ran into her in the parking lot." Wyatt grins as Haven tackles him in a side hug. "Needed to meet whoever was going to be looking after my daughter." He starts at my feet and travels up my body. "Wanna come meet her, Haven? She seems nice." Once we make eye contact, his eyes never waver from mine.

"Should I bring my stuff?" Haven points to her backpack and the winter jacket I bought for this trip.

"Might as well." He shifts his attention to her. "You can make my trailer study central. It'll be nice to hang out with you." She leaves him to grab her things and then he slings his arm around her petite shoulders when she returns to his side.

The two of them have grown so close, so quickly that it rattles me. I shouldn't be surprised. Haven's wanted her father in her life since she understood he existed, and so many things about her have reminded me of him.

They leave together, the door clicking closed behind them. I sink into the couch. Flopping back, I let the tension ease out of me. Managing three months of being on edge and queasy with anxiety will be my undoing. To make matters a tiny bit worse, this movie is being hailed as the return of the cinematic rom-com. Wyatt and I have to pretend to be funny and romantic together when we're neither. *Oh, joy.*

There's a knock on the door. I yell for them to come in without moving. Wyatt clears his throat, and I bolt up. "Oh." I smooth my clothes. "I didn't realize it was you. Where's Haven?"

"The tutor-nanny is doing the nanny bit. Stacy wants to get to know Haven before the production schedule starts later today."

"I guess we have the same call time." I stand. "Did you want something?"

"I wanted to talk to you without Haven around." He unzips his heavy jacket.

When he eases it off his shoulders, my heart rate skyrockets. I could so easily walk over and help him. Let my hands slide along his arms, across his chest, lead him to the bedroom.

"About what?" I ask.

"I saw you and some guy went to a charity thing together a few weeks ago." He slides into a seat at the table.

I shrug and wait for whatever he'll throw at me. The guy is an old friend, but Wyatt wouldn't know that. When I asked him to attend the fundraiser with me, he didn't realize I was asking to spite Wyatt, but I understood the effect the pictures would have. We're not getting back together—not if he's drinking and definitely not if he's lying about it. A little buffer, something to throw Wyatt off, is useful.

"I'm capable of dating other people."

"Any other man is second choice." His jaw tics. "How'll they feel when they realize that?"

The trailer becomes claustrophobic. He's coming for me whether I've tried to create a smokescreen or not. I should have known. When he truly wants something, very little can hold him back. Another reason his "just a few drinks" terrifies me. I've seen where that slippery slope leads, and I'm not letting him drag me or our daughter down it.

"I don't see why any other man would realize that. It's not true. Your drinking took you out of the running. You're Haven's father, but otherwise you don't have a place in my life." I wander to the far end of the trailer. Space. I need space.

"I'm carving myself back in. I didn't do what you think I did." Confidence cascades off him.

"You drank. You told me you were done with the drugs and the drinking. Then one of those nights—maybe even the night you found out about Haven—you let the urges get the best of you."

"I never had the same problem with alcohol that I did with drugs."

"Yeah, it's perfectly normal for people to have Jim Beam in water bottles. From there it becomes smoothies laced with codeine. Just one sip, right? Something to take the edge off." I hold his eye contact in challenge. "You did it all the time." I cross my arms. "If you can't last one week without drinking, you have a problem."

"People drink alcohol socially, after a long day, as stress relief. I wouldn't say any of those people have a problem." He rubs at a spot on the small table.

"You're right. Sometimes, after a long day on set, I love a glass of wine. Hell, maybe even a whole bottle. But I never disguise my drinking. I don't pour wine into a flask and hide it on set to drink between takes." For three years, I bore witness to every trick. If he's drinking, the word *moderation* doesn't exist.

"I don't do any of that anymore." Wyatt clasps his hands, and his expression is steady. "I'm not doing that."

"But you're still drinking." My education in the things Wyatt doesn't say runs deep. He's being evasive. Not a lie. Not the truth.

"Not anymore."

"When was the last time you drank?"

"I don't remember."

I chuckle. He'll recall the next one. "When was the last time you took a pill?"

"December, two years ago. Around Christmas. It was . . . Anna was . . . and I couldn't stand seeing Jamal crying like that."

Wyatt winces. "That was my last relapse. I've been good ever since."

"You've memorized that, but you don't have a clue when you took your last drink?"

His jaw hardens. I've caught him. If he digs in, I'll never believe another word he says. He stands up and crosses the trailer. "I'm not drinking. You want a Breathalyzer installed? You want me to breathe in your face every day? You want to follow me around? I'll do it to prove I'm sober."

He's so close that his body heat warms me. I glance up at him and then I put my hands on either side of his face.

"All I've ever wanted from you, Wyatt, is the truth. The ugly or the beautiful." Rising onto my toes, I hug him tight. "Tell me the truth, please. I want to trust you. I need to trust you."

He tugs me flush against him but doesn't say anything, just breathes me in, his lips pressed in my hair.

Haven bursts in the door and stops short when she sees us. "Mom, Dad's trailer is about five times nicer than ours."

He draws away, but his hand seeks mine and squeezes.

"He always has better riders than me." My senses are still tuned to Wyatt, to his smell, to his body heat, to the sensation of being pressed against him.

"That trailer is nothing," he says. "Sometimes I get a three-story one."

"Like a house?" Haven gapes.

"How is Stacy?" I interrupt. Haven doesn't need the details on Wyatt's sixty-five-page riders. When he and Isaac used to make them up, they sometimes got ridiculous. The person tasked with making sure he had only blue M&M's, perfectly round, earned their money. He and Isaac held them up to the lights in the trailer, laughing at their roundness, their blueness.

"Nice, I guess," Haven says. "Do I have to do my schoolwork? Can't this trip be a vacation?"

"No." Wyatt and I answer at the same time. I glance at him and smile a little. At least we're in agreement on the importance of school.

"Is my real school going to care?" Haven puts her hands on her hips. Her bulky jacket is almost comical on her small frame.

"Your mom agreed to let you come if you could stay on track. It's not negotiable, Short Stuff."

"What were you guys doing in here?" Haven huffs and flops onto the closest couch.

"Talking." Wyatt drops my hand and shoves his into the pocket of his jeans.

"Sounds boring." Haven picks up the TV remote.

"I'm going back to my trailer." Wyatt ruffles her hair on the way past. "You want to come play some games? I asked for gaming consoles, an iPad, a few other things I thought you might like."

Her face lights up. "Yes!" She turns to me. "I mean, can I?"

"He's your dad. You don't have to ask my permission unless it goes against something I've already said no to." I try to catch Wyatt's attention, hoping he heard that too. She'll play us off each other if she can. In the past, she's tried her luck with me and Nikki.

Haven disappears out the door ahead of him.

"Wyatt." His name is a last plea before he closes the trailer door. *Be honest.*

He stills and then turns. "I'm not giving you a reason to limit my time with her."

"That's not why I'm asking."

"I'm sober. I'm not drinking. That's the truth. Anything else doesn't matter."

"It matters to me," I say. "We can't build anything on lies."

"We're not building something while you're tossing other people between us like they matter. They don't. You need to be honest with yourself. What we've got, you're not finding that with someone else. Neither am I." Wyatt's posture is strung tight.

In ten years, neither of us has really moved on. Being dragged back into anything remotely close to the chaotic lifestyle we lived or balancing on the knife's edge of tipping back into it won't work for me. Every time I look at him, twenty minibar bottles lined up on a counter flash across my vision. If that's controlled, I don't want to see out of control. Until he tells me the truth about his drinking, until he can acknowledge there's an issue there, we're stuck as we are.

"I would never stop you from seeing her."

"You already did, Ellie. For nine years. I'm not giving you a reason to do it again." With that, he shuts the trailer door behind him.

WYATT

Present Day

We're halfway through filming and the frost between us hasn't thawed. Haven's amazing, but parenting is fucking hard. The first time she threw a temper tantrum, I was sure aliens had invaded her body. Her attitude changed on a dime. All these years, Ellie has dealt with her mood swings by herself. Well, she had her family but still, it's incredible. *Alone.*

Hair and makeup are retouching us before we do another take. The movie scenes are shot out of order, which is normal. This is the first take on one of two endings for the film. In this one, Ellie's supposed to run toward me, and I sweep her up into my arms and kiss her. I offered to rehearse this moment several times, but she turned me down.

The three of us have spent a lot of time together over the last six weeks. Anytime I try to see Ellie without Haven, she finds a reason to evade me. Phone calls, meetings, people visiting, conveniently timed. Her crafty scheduling would be unbelievable if she hadn't spent ten years avoiding me with expert precision. In another life, Ellie commanded an army.

James, the director, is grumbling orders, and the crew duck away, out of the shot. Ellie is framed in the natural sunlight, and she's surrounded by an ethereal glow. Takes me back ten years. Life should be that easy—get the right lighting, everything else falls into place. James calls out a few minor adjustments to the person in wardrobe who is fixing Ellie's coat. Winter scenes aren't as much fun as I remember. It's absolutely freezing.

A frown creases James's face, and with difficulty, he gets off his chair and ambles to Ellie. They engage in a back-and-forth discussion that has Ellie shooting me a worried look over his shoulder. I'm tempted to leave my mark to see what's being debated. Just as I'm about to go, she gives James a pained expression and nods.

When James walks away from her, she calls out, "Can you tell Wyatt, please?"

He turns on his heel and strides to her faster than I expected. His wide, thick back is to me. What he's saying isn't audible, but his stiff posture sets me off. Ellie and I might not be getting along, but there's no way I'm letting him treat her with any sort of disrespect.

I leave my mark and approach them. "What's going on?"

"Minor change." James half turns to me.

"If Ellie doesn't like it, it's not minor." I'm taller than him, and I have no problem using my size for intimidation if he's harassing Ellie.

"Sell it, Ellie." James gives her a warning glance before turning around. "You're being paid to make me believe."

"Are you okay?" What the hell is he getting her to do?

"It's fine." Glancing up at me, she says, "And I'm sorry for what's coming next. I—I tried to talk him out of it."

"Come on, Wyatt," James calls, back at his seat now. "I don't want to lose the light."

The light is excellent, so I'm going to let whatever he said to Ellie drop for now. I give him the finger, and I stalk back to my mark. With a roll of my shoulders, I try to relax and remember the point of the scene. Easy. I'm in love with Ellie's character. She runs up to me, one line, one kiss, done. I can do this. Whatever note he gave her, I can improv. Wouldn't be the first time a director tried to get an authentic reaction by doing something underhanded.

As soon as James calls action, a light flips on in Ellie. Her expression becomes one I used to see when she looked at me. She sprints to me and I catch her, swinging her around, and her legs circle my waist. We laugh, and I drink her in. I want to live in this moment, this false happiness. Doesn't matter if she's pretending. I'm not, and I smooth back her hair. "You came. Wasn't sure you'd come."

For a beat, she stares at me. Deep in her dark depths, the light dims a fraction. Her features soften before she says, "I love you. There's nowhere else I'd want to be."

My sharp intake of breath stills everyone on set. Three extra words seize my heart. The quiet is eerie. Fuck it. They don't get this moment. It's mine. Blocking everyone out, I secure Ellie tighter, and our lips collide without hesitation. She kisses me like a woman in love—slowly, deeply, a kiss full of promise, a kiss that doesn't end when a director calls cut. My heart beats a staccato, afraid to believe, wanting so badly to believe. I don't want this moment to be fake.

"Cut," James calls, laughing. "Yes!"

Ellie draws away, and we make eye contact before her focus slides over my shoulder. Bulky winter clothes or not, she must realize the effect our kiss has had. She slides along my body, and I keep her pressed tight. I want her to notice, to peer up at me again.

James claps us both on the back and whistles. "I knew you two had chemistry, but that's the first time I've seen it combust on the screen. Whatever happened there needs to happen more." Turning, he laughs and then shouts, "Fire. They were on fire!"

Ellie glances at me, a small smirk on her face. "Not the only thing on fire."

"What can I say?" I grin and when she shifts back, I adjust my pants. "You have a way with words."

"James said . . . I don't want to mislead—" Her eyes are filled with uncertainty.

"I get it." Grabbing her hand, I link our fingers. "But if that take ends up on the cutting room floor, I'm stealing it."

"All right, let's go again," James calls out. "Everyone reset."

For the rest of the afternoon, Ellie tells me she loves me over and over. There may be a special place in hell for James, our director. Listening to her say the words and knowing she doesn't want to mean them is torturous. But kissing her over and over is worth the agony. By the time we break for dinner, my engine has been revving on high. I need an ice bath. And a stiff drink. One of those I can do, the other I cannot.

When I get to my trailer, Haven and Stacy are bundling themselves up in winter clothes. "What are you two up to?" I take off my coat. We have two hours before the lighting is right for the next shot.

"One of the crew mentioned there was a dogsled demonstration at the park entrance tonight. I was hoping to take Haven. Ellie said it was okay . . ." Stacy bites her lip.

She's fallen into a habit of checking with both of us before committing to anything. Ellie and I were in a giant pissing contest when the shoot first started. We're mostly beyond that now. "If Ellie said it was fine, then I guess it is," I say. "Haven, you want to go?"

"I like dogs. Mom says she travels too much for us to get one. Aunt Nikki doesn't want to take care of it."

"Jamal loves dogs too. Maybe I'll get one for my place." Slowing my schedule has been on my mind. I could spend time getting to know my daughter, and I could help Anna stay on the right track.

"Really?" Haven squeals.

"Yeah, we can talk about it. I'm not saying right away, but I can make a dog work."

A knock sounds on my trailer door, and I call for them to come in. Ellie enters and focuses on Haven. "I was hoping to catch you before you left." She envelops Haven in a hug. Her lips press to the top of Haven's head, and she closes her eyes. Calshae was right. Ellie's a good mother. Responsive and caring. Everything Anna and I never had as kids. And what Anna still can't give her son.

"Dad said we could get a dog." Haven's voice is an octave higher than normal.

"Did he?" Ellie's expression is unreadable. She unzips her heavy winter coat but keeps it on. She must plan on avoiding me some more once Haven leaves.

"I said we could talk about getting a dog." I wish Ellie would acknowledge me. After the day we've had, I want us to be closer, even if that closeness is artificial.

"We need to get going." Stacy checks the clock on the wall. "One of the crew said the start of the show was the best."

"Okay." Ellie steps back, giving Haven space.

Haven grabs me into a hug before embracing her mom one last time on the way out the door. Ellie watches them go, ignoring me. Once they're gone, I expect her to leave, but she doesn't.

Slowly, the trailer grows thick with a tension I recognize too well. Today was a challenge for her too. The realization gives me a jolt of confidence.

"You okay?" I set my phone on the kitchenette table.

Ellie glances at me over her shoulder. "I should go." But she doesn't move.

The slant of her shoulders, the way she looks back tells me she doesn't want to leave. I close the distance between us, and I run a hand along her side, letting it linger on her hip. "Something you need, Ellie?" I murmur into her ear.

Her breathing is ragged. She turns into my arms without saying anything, and my lips meet hers, hot and hungry. I lift her up, and she wraps her legs around my waist. With my hands cupping her ass, I press her against the wall of the trailer. She sheds her jacket with a few quick movements, tossing it to the side.

I'd resigned myself to blue balls after eight hours of foreplay. If she'll let this happen, I'm going for it, even if we have unresolved issues. My dick is so hard it's aching.

On the kitchen table, my phone rings, shrill and insistent. Ellie's fingers grip the hem of my shirt, and she tugs it over my head. Her soft hands glide along my chest, and the noises she's making are going to undo me.

Her shirt is gone, and I'm unsnapping her bra when my phone starts again.

The only time it rings back-to-back is when there's bad news. I draw Ellie closer, deepening the kiss. Maybe if I pretend my phone won't ring a third time, it won't. Ellie snaps the button on my jeans, and my phone bursts to life.

"Important?" Ellie murmurs against my lips.

"Not as important as you." My hand massages her inner thigh. She still has her jeans on, but her bra hangs off her, ready to fall to the floor.

When my phone kicks off for the fourth time, I sigh, easing Ellie's legs to the floor. I snatch it off the table. "What?" Irritation and frustration make the word more of a growl than anything coherent.

"Sorry, sir. Anna's taken off again. I've got Jamal here. He was asking for you. I've called Tanvi, but you like to be in the loop." Kyle fires the information off in a rat-a-tat-tat.

Even from this far away, he reads my mood. I run a hand down my face. A burst of swear words almost escapes. Trust Anna to run out on her son while I'm in another country. When I'm there and able to talk her out of leaving, she's somewhat stable. Once I'm on a shoot or a promotional tour, the question of Anna leaving is never *if* but *when*, and then the next uncertainty is how long it'll take her to return.

"Uncle Wyatt?" Jamal's voice is small across the phone line.

"Yeah, buddy. I'm gonna come get you. I'll be there tomorrow." My anger circles and drains. None of this is his fault. "You go to Grandma Tanvi's till I get there, okay?"

"Okay." Jamal's high-pitched voice causes an ache in my chest.

How does Anna leave him? Then I remember I wanted a drink today, and there have been a lot of days in the last few months when taking a Perc or oxy or mixing a glass of lean have crossed my mind. I relapsed so many times before I got it right. Kicking drugs is not easy. When I hang up, Ellie's dressed.

"Anna, again?" She grimaces.

"Yeah."

"I'm going to my trailer. You probably need to talk to James." She zips her coat.

"Ellie."

"It's probably for the best. Sleeping together wouldn't have meant anything. We'd still be in the same place we are right now."

"We don't have to be." I tuck my phone into my pocket.

"No? You're going to be honest about your drinking?"

"I am being honest." Since I left the island, I haven't touched a drop. I might have had a drink today, though, if she wasn't here; I'm not sure. I grab my shirt off the floor and slip it over my head. She's still creating too many artificial roadblocks for us. Maybe she doesn't trust me, but I don't trust her either. "I wasn't drinking. How many times do I need to say those words before you believe me?"

She sighs. "Good luck getting Jamal. I guess my tutor-nanny will be working overtime?"

"*Our* tutor-nanny," I say, an edge to my voice. Even now, she's cutting me out as though I'm not part of these decisions.

She slams the trailer door behind her.

ELLIE

PRESENT DAY

Haven chases after a giggling Jamal, their feet slapping the tiled floor of Wyatt's kitchenette as they race through. Jamal's high-pitched, delighted laughter makes me smile. Having a playmate has been good for Haven, and having another buffer between me and Wyatt is a bonus. According to Wyatt, Anna will show up. In the last two weeks, there's been no sign of her.

"Are you okay to watch them?" I ask Stacy, who is prepping some crafts for them in the next room. "I need to pop over to my trailer for a few minutes."

"Sure," Stacy says. "When is Wyatt done?"

"Not sure." I throw on my coat, hat, and mitts. The walk is short, but the cold is bitter and the frigid wind biting. "They're running behind." I check my watch. My hair and makeup slot is coming up soon. "It's going to be a late night."

"Your sister arrives today?" Stacy lays out some more pom-poms, Popsicle sticks, and other crafty things.

"Tonight, yeah." I swing open the door. "I'll be back."

Once I'm in my trailer, I shed my layers as fast as I can. My place is warmer than Wyatt's. He must find mine tiny and stifling compared to his. Must be why we're at his more often than here. A thin sheen of sweat breaks out on my forehead. Stress is taking its toll on my body. No temperature regulation, and I'm queasy.

On cue, my stomach rolls at the thought of making out with Wyatt again in front of a gaggle of crew members. A perfectly terrible night. Nikki will be here, so there's zero chance of a repeat performance up against the wall of a trailer when shooting is done.

The kettle is boiling for tea when there's a knock on the trailer door. Wyatt pokes his head in. "The kids here?" Without waiting for a reply, he steps in.

"No, they're in yours. Haven says our trailer is no fun." I pour the boiling water into a cup. I stare at the tea bag floating to the surface before raising the cup toward Wyatt, questioning. Inviting him to be here without the kids is a no-no. But we've been getting along so well, it's hard to remember he can't be trusted.

"Sure." An easy grin spreads across his face. "I take it Stacy is with them?"

I shoot him an annoyed look. This parenting thing isn't new to me, and I've never been the irresponsible one. The kids move between the trailers with ease, but they're always supervised. With a spoon, I mix milk and sugar into his tea.

"Thanks for being so good with Jamal." Wyatt slides into the bench seat of my kitchen table.

"Whatever I might think about your sister, her behavior and these circumstances aren't his fault. He's a great kid. Happy. Listens pretty well. Cuddly." At night, if I'm around, Jamal presses his tiny face into the crook of my neck as I rock him and sing. He loves it. He might not be the only one. I place a hand to my lower abdomen. "She really has no idea who the father is?"

Wyatt shrugs and takes his cup of tea from me. "Says she doesn't, but I'm not so sure. I've never pressed her on it." He sighs. "But I might ask again. Probably should." He takes a sip of his tea and winces.

"More milk?" I bring the container over and pour another dollop into his cup.

"Thanks." The barest hint of a smile touches his lips. "You remembered."

"Some people are hard to forget." I return the milk to the fridge, trying not to dwell on what I've said. Shouldn't have, even if it's true. Wyatt's focus burns a hole in my back. "What makes you think Anna knows who the father is?"

He takes a long gulp of his tea before speaking. "When she came off her last bender, we had a long talk about you, Haven, what it meant to me that I hadn't known about her for so long. How much I wish I'd had a choice."

"I can't keep apologizing for what I did, Wyatt. It takes us in circles." When I turn to face him, I rest my hip against the counter.

"I know." He nods, and there's no animosity in his expression. "I've been trying to remember what we said to each other the day you left. But it won't play. You didn't tell me about Haven, but I can't remember everything we said to each other. The next day I realized what an ass I'd been. The biggest ass. Bits and pieces of our fight came back. What I *can* remember, I shouldn't have said."

"It was a long time ago." My heart flutters.

"It was, but how I behaved that day changed everything. Would you have told me if I'd stayed?"

I bite my lip, searching for an honest answer. "Only if you agreed to try rehab. Whether you were successful wouldn't have mattered. I wanted you to try. To be sure you were capable of wanting what I wanted. What Haven and I needed."

"I've thought about it a lot, and there's no way to be sure what I would have done if you'd told me. Would I have gone? Even if I did, would one stint in rehab have been enough? You were always looking after me. Not sure it would have occurred to me you might need help sometimes too."

There's a knock on the trailer door, and the director's assistant pops his head in. "Ellie." He glances around until he spots me. "Oh, hey, Wyatt." He gives Wyatt the universal head tip. "Ellie, they need you in hair and makeup. We're trying to get back on schedule for the lighting tonight."

Wyatt and I were finally getting somewhere. I suppress a sigh and drain my tea. "Okay." From the couch, I gather my winter clothes. The door clicks closed, and the director's assistant is gone.

Wyatt appears beside me, swoops my hat off the couch, and sticks it on my head. When we make eye contact, his grin fades. One of his hands slides behind my neck. "A little practice before our scene tonight?" His voice rumbles through his chest, low, seductive.

Giving in would be so easy. If I didn't have to worry about Haven's safety and security, I'd have jumped into his arms long ago. I'd sacrifice my sanity, but I won't risk hers. "There are two things wedged between us. One is your drinking or your lying—one of those. The other is your sister's living situation."

"Then what? You'll be with me?" Wyatt's focus is locked on me. "You'll give me a chance?"

Someone has to relent or we'll never move forward. The last two weeks with Jamal here, we've been more like a family than I ever could have hoped for. We have a chance to change our future. Deep down, I believe we want the same things.

"If it wasn't for Haven, I would never have left you. Would have followed you to the ends of the earth. I loved you with everything I had in me. I would try again, see whether we can be good for each other. But I cannot do that if I'll be putting Haven in any danger because of your drinking or your sister's violence and addiction."

He presses his lips to my forehead. "You mean that?" he murmurs.

"If I don't leave soon, I'll be late." I frame his face with my hands. "I've been honest. You need to be honest too."

He searches my expression before stepping back and thrusting his hands into the pockets of his jeans. I close the door behind me, hoping he takes my words to heart.

Kissing Wyatt after telling him I have feelings is a slow torture unlike any other. The man can kiss. Soul deep, wet-my-panties kinds of kisses. My very first love scene was with him, and it was eye-opening. We had fun during those scenes.

After him, any of those types of scenes were professional or invasive or boring or too technical. None of them were fun, and while I wouldn't call tonight fun, it's been a neon reminder of how good we can be together. But by the time we're done for the night, I'm emotionally spent.

When I open the door to my trailer, I'm happy Haven is sleeping, and Nikki keeps such odd hours. She's wide awake, but I suspected she would be since we were texting back and forth between takes. There will be zero temptation to go to Wyatt's and follow through on those hours of foreplay. No matter how badly I want to.

"You look wiped." Nikki closes her laptop.

"Tell me about it. I don't know what's with me lately. I'm tired all the time. The last time I was this exhausted was when . . ." Realization dawns.

"Please tell me your sentence finishes with 'was when I had mono' and not 'was when I was pregnant.'"

"Let's pretend it's the first one, okay?" I grip the chair in front of me and ease around to fall into it.

"And if it's the second one?" Nikki winces.

I sink deeper into the chair. My winter clothes are still layered on, so I'm sweating for two reasons. "Please tell me I haven't done this again." Taking out my phone, I count the weeks to determine whether I'm crazy or if it's possible I'm pregnant. My body flashes hot and cold, hot and cold. We've been on set for two months. Wyatt and I were apart for almost a month before the shoot started.

"And?" she asks.

"Want to do me a favor and take a cab into town for a pregnancy test? Maybe, like, three or four of them?"

"Oh my God, Ellie. Are you serious?"

"I hope I'm not. Can you imagine?" I flop my head back against the chair.

"What a mess." Nikki grabs her coat off the rack and sighs.

"But I'm not pregnant." I rub my face. "I'm not. It's the stress of the last few months. Stress." My boobs are a bit tender. Pent-up sexual frustration, that's all. "Stress."

"Right." Nikki opens the trailer door. "I'll be back as quickly as I can."

While Nikki is gone, I pace in my trailer and drink water. I'm tempted to mention my situation to Wyatt. We've come to rely on each other the last few weeks. But telling him now is a bad idea. He'd get his hopes up. Might think my reasons for keeping us apart no longer matter. And they matter. They'll matter twice as much.

Nikki returns and drops a pharmacy bag and a jug of water on the table. "The package says it's best to do the test first thing in the morning."

"I'm doing it now." My bladder will explode soon with all the water I've been chugging. "I'll take another in the morning and then another tomorrow afternoon. I'll tell Wyatt if all three say I'm pregnant."

"How has Wyatt been since you've been here?" Nikki falls into a chair and puts her head in her hands.

Everything I ever wanted him to be. Realized he could be. Wyatt might not have been capable of being a genuine partner or parent before, but he's exceeded my expectations while we've been on set. I've been on the hunt for any of his old tells that he's been drinking or using, and there's been nothing. While I'm positive he drank on the island, I'm equally positive he's been dry here.

"Except for his sister and her situation, and the fact he still won't fess up about his drinking in Bermuda, everything has been so good. So good. We *could* be a family."

"Those two obstacles are big."

"Yeah, I know, and that's why we aren't together." The difference between how I raised Haven and how Jamal is shuffled around, desperate for a solid connection, has been laid bare. Wyatt might not say much, but I see the expression on his face when Jamal cuddles into me, clings onto me, cries for me. Children need stability and safety. Jamal is not getting either from Anna.

I protected Haven no matter the cost, and if I'm pregnant again, I'll do the same for this baby. I will not risk my children no matter how much I love Wyatt.

With a sigh, I snatch the bag off the table and then I disappear into the bathroom.

WYATT

PRESENT DAY

Ellie's avoiding me. Except for our scenes together earlier today, she's stuck to Nikki like glue. I don't get it. She admitted she's willing to try again under the right circumstances, and then she ignores me. Is this some sort of parry and retreat thing? She tells me what I need to do and then sits back waiting for me to do it? Someday, I'll figure women out. Today is not that day.

Maybe I should go to her trailer, admit I drank while I was on the island, but it wasn't much. Tell her I haven't touched a drop since I found out about Haven. I wouldn't dare risk my family. Alcohol, for me, has never been like drugs. The cravings don't hit me as hard. But I have no idea if those declarations are enough, or whether she'll use that confession against me at some point.

Jamal is napping. Haven is upstairs doing her schoolwork with Stacy. The only thing stopping me is Nikki. She doesn't like me. She's made that clear. Eating crow while she looks on isn't on the top of my list.

My phone buzzes in my pocket. An automated alert from the credit card company. I've purchased a plane ticket to Ottawa on United Airlines. Not a surprise. I was expecting this notification. Anna's coming for Jamal. Without missing a beat, I dial Camila and ask her to get on a flight as soon as she can. If Anna arrives here without a buffer, she'll be explosive. When she comes out of her spiral long enough to realize she's abandoned her son again, she's a bear. And not the soft, cuddly kind.

I tell Stacy I'm leaving, and after throwing on my winter clothes, I aim for the head of security. Rick needs a warning that Anna's coming—and to keep her away from Ellie and Haven at any cost.

"Rick!" I call, and I jog to the small crowd gathered around him. He's talking to a group of uniformed officers and private security agents.

"Wyatt." Rick raises a hand to the group and half turns to me, cutting his conversation short. "Everything okay?"

"I need a word."

He steps away from the other men and women to follow me. "A security concern?" Rick asks when we're out of earshot.

"My sister, Anna." Flicking through my camera roll on my phone, I find a photo and turn the screen toward him. "Don't let her on set, in my trailer, around Ellie or Haven, anywhere near Jamal, unless I'm present. I can't stress this enough."

"Send me that photo, and I'll push it out to the team to get everyone on the same page." He scratches the back of his neck with a gloved hand. "Violent?"

"Sometimes. Mostly with people she knows." I scroll through my photos, looking for the most recent ones of decent quality.

"Sounds pleasant." Rick grimaces. "Is this a just-in-case thing or do you have information?"

"She's purchased a plane ticket. I'm guessing she'll be here tonight or first thing in the morning, depending on her connections."

"Got it." Rick's phone pings with the photos I sent.

The rest of the day passes in a blur. Anna's imminent arrival is a constant distraction. I miss marks, flub lines, and we have to do more takes than normal. Ellie shoots me concerned glances but doesn't ask. She isn't behaving like herself either.

Something is in the air.

Maybe she regrets saying she'd give us a second chance. I need to buck up and talk to her, whether or not Nikki is in the trailer.

When I finally work up the nerve to knock on her trailer door, it's late. Lights are on, so I know she's awake. Or maybe it's Nikki. Either way, I have to try.

"Ellie's busy right now." Nikki cocks her head to the side.

"I'll wait." I step up. Nikki lets me in, but she doesn't give me much space. "Showering?" There are noises coming from the bathroom.

"Uh," Nikki says. "A bath, maybe? I'll go check." She walks to the bathroom at the back of the trailer and knocks. "Wyatt's here. You want me to leave?"

Ellie's reply is muffled, but Nikki collects her computer and gathers her things.

"Nikki, can I talk to you for a minute?" Might as well meet her dislike of me head-on. Whether Ellie and I can work things out doesn't change her role in Haven's life.

She raises her eyebrows as she shoves an arm into her coat and picks up her gloves.

"I wanted to thank you for the help you've given Ellie over the years. The role that you've taken on in Haven's life—I realize you don't like me, that you told Ellie to leave me back then. I get it. I get why."

"You've got the wrong end of things there." Nikki chuckles and gives me a rueful smile. "I was on your side when Ellie was pregnant. I couldn't understand why Ellie'd want to leave you. Her love for you was so clear, and if I'm honest, how much you loved her was obvious too. It was everywhere you looked, shining out of the two of you. Then she left. I grew up, and I saw the truth. How reckless you were, consumed by fame. I got it, then—why she couldn't stay."

"That was me. I'll own that. I was that guy." I shove my hands into my pockets. "More than anyone else, I loved your sister, and yet not quite as much as I should have. Not that I loved the drugs more, but I had myself convinced I needed them. Couldn't function without them. Now"—I nod my head toward the bathroom—"now I can say with absolute certainty there isn't anything I wouldn't give up for Ellie."

"Except the truth?"

"Touché, Nikki." I tip my head. "It's why I'm here. No more bullshit. We've got to trust each other to do right by one another."

She searches my face for a long beat. "I want Ellie to be happy. The happiest I've ever seen her was with you. I don't understand your relationship, knowing what I know now, but there's a light in her when you're around, and no one else seems able to turn it on." She frowns. "If you hurt her or Haven, I'll hire a hitman. I'm not kidding."

"I'll help pay for it."

"Do you truly believe you're better?" Nikki zips her coat. "That you'll always be better?"

"Truthfully? I won't ever be better." The gum in my pocket rattles. "The minute I convince myself I'm fixed, I take risks and chances I shouldn't. So for the rest of my life, I'm an addict. Each morning when I wake up, I choose Haven. I choose Ellie. I don't choose the bottom of a bottle of pills or alcohol."

"You seem sincere." Nikki's pale eyes are serious.

"I am. I've never meant anything more."

"Why is it so cold here?" She tugs her hat onto her head and glances at me one last time before smiling.

"Canada, eh?" I use a thick Canadian accent. "The movie's supposed to be set around Christmas . . . I guess that means there has to be snow."

"Next time you make my sister do a movie with you, can it be in a better location?"

"I like it here." That's actually true. The only drawback is the layers Ellie wears. *Layers.* A valid point. Maybe a beach next time.

"Let me know when I can come back." Nikki closes the door behind her.

The couch calls to me and I sink into it with a sigh. When Ellie emerges from the bathroom, her face is devoid of color. With a frown, I get up and close the distance between us. "Are you okay? Are you sick? I'll talk to James and get things rearranged if you're ill."

"You going to hold my hair back if I throw up?" Ellie's dark eyes connect with mine. Her lips quirk up.

"All day long if that's what you need." I envelop her in a hug. "I'll talk to him and come back."

She wraps her arms around me and sighs. When I try to leave, she tightens her embrace. Her face is buried in my chest. My hands rise on her back as she sucks in a deep breath.

"There's something I need to tell you, Wyatt."

"I gotta talk to you too."

Both of our phones buzz in unison on the kitchen table. Ellie glances up at me and lets me go to cross the room. If it's possible, she gets paler. "Anna's on set?" She throws on her jacket. "She's in your trailer. Nikki sent an SOS for help."

"Holy fuck." I grab my coat.

Ellie clatters out the door, and I leave my coat undone, running past her. There's no way I'm letting Ellie in there before me. *Well, Rick. You did a shitty-ass job on security.*

I burst through the door to find Anna storming around the trailer, screaming for Jamal. His wails come from his bedroom upstairs, but she's too out of it to notice the stairs to the next floor. Nikki and Stacy trail behind her, asking her to calm down, take a seat, wait for me.

"Anna." None of them realize I've entered.

"Where's Jamal?" She turns wide eyes to me. "He should be at your house. Why is he here? Why'd you bring him *here*?"

"Anna." I keep my hands up, my voice measured. I scan the area to make sure she isn't near anything she could use to do serious damage to me or anyone else. "You left him, and I went to get him. We've done all of *this* before."

"You calling me a bad mother? Are you saying I do this all the time? I love my kid." She raises her face to the ceiling. "Jamal! Jamal, baby. Come to Mommy."

"I don't think he should see you like this." Ellie's measured voice causes me to whirl around.

Anna's eyes narrow. "You broke my brother. Broke him. How has he possibly forgiven you?"

"We're working on forgiving each other." Ellie stares at Anna. "That's what family does."

"Not my family." Bitterness seeps out of her. "Isn't that right, Wyatt? We just take and take and take from each other. You're not taking my kid anymore. When I leave here, we're going to go somewhere far away. You'll never see Jamal again."

My heart thump-thumps at the suggestion. She's repeatedly made this threat. So far, she hasn't followed through. She encouraged me to go after Ellie, but Anna's never had to face the notion of Ellie as more important than her and Jamal. Haven tipped the scales. An unspoken truth. Anna is family, but so is Haven, and by extension, as my daughter's mother, so is Ellie. Even if I didn't love her, that's the truth.

"Mom," Haven calls for Ellie from the hallway.

My breath stalls. "Go back to bed, Haven," I call out.

There's terror in the depths of Ellie's eyes when she looks at me. I shift so Anna can't get down the hall without going through me first. My sister wouldn't hurt Haven on purpose, but I'm not gambling with my daughter's safety. Anna is capable of scaring grown-ups. Seeing what she can be like when she's high at the tender age of nine might be too much to bear.

"Mom!" Haven says with a touch of panic.

"I'm here, honey," Ellie says. "Do what your dad says, okay?"

"That's her?" Anna tips her head in the direction of the hall-way. A sheen of sweat coats her forehead. "She'd probably like to meet her aunt, right? Haven, Aunt Anna is here. I'd love to meet you, sweet girl."

Haven comes out of the darkness of the hallway and into the light. My heart contracts so hard I worry it'll stop. She inherited my stubborn streak.

"Haven." My tone is a warning to her, to Anna.

"You look sick." She stares at Anna, curiosity and fear mixing on her face.

Anna probably hasn't showered in weeks, and her eyes are wild. I scan the room again for weapons. From looking at her, she could be on a high or a low. Hard to believe I'm out of practice.

"You're like your mother." Anna turns her hateful expression toward Ellie. "Full of judgment."

"She's nine." Ellie's tone is sharp. "And she's right. You look awful."

"Mommy." Jamal comes around the corner of the stairs, wiping his bleary, sleepy eyes. I scoop him into my arms, and he tucks his head under my chin, snuggling in. He reaches out for Ellie and calls her name.

"She's not his mother!" Anna storms over to me, yanking Jamal from my arms. Jamal wails, trying to scramble back. This isn't the first time he's been in this position, hungry for stability and torn from it.

"Anna." I offer Jamal my hand as he cries and screams. "Can we talk about this in the morning, please? You're scaring Jamal. You're not thinking clearly." I glance at Ellie, and I'm about to take a chance. I don't want Anna in here while people are sleeping. "You can have Ellie's trailer to yourself. In the morning, we'll talk about Jamal, about you, about getting both of you back to LA. Okay?"

"Her trailer?" Anna eyes Ellie. "Queen Ellie is okay with that?"

"Yeah." Ellie scrapes her hair into a loose ponytail and lets it fall. Her expression isn't happy, but she'll understand why I've suggested it. The local hotels are full with the crew for the movie. Giving her the other trailer is the best, safest option for everyone. "I need to get a few things before you go over. Wyatt?" She nods toward Haven.

"Yeah. I got it." I'm still a barrier between Anna and Haven. My daughter's tiny form is rooted to the hallway entrance. No matter what I have to do, Anna won't be allowed to touch her.

Nikki follows Ellie out, probably to get her things as well. Anna steals from me, from stores, from anyone she can. She wouldn't hesitate to take items from Ellie or Ellie's family.

Jamal's wails have turned into whimpers, but he's still straining toward me. His desire to escape Anna hurts my heart. Would this have been my life if Ellie had told me about Haven, and I hadn't gotten clean? There were times I was this far gone, this out of my head. An overwhelming urge to apologize to Haven draws me to her. I wrap my arm around her shoulders and tug her into my side.

Ellie and Nikki return with small suitcases clutched in their hands. "It's all yours, Anna," Ellie says.

Anna heads toward the trailer door, Jamal still in her arms.

"Jamal should stay here." I drop my arm from Haven. "His things are here. He's used to being here."

"He needs to be with his mom." She sniffs.

God, she's a mess. Not sure how anyone looked me in the eye when I was this bad. "Tomorrow. As soon as you wake up, come knock. It's late. He needs his sleep. You know what he gets like." Appealing to her motherly instincts is a gamble.

Reluctantly, she passes Jamal to me. She gives him a kiss, but he tries to get away, clawing at my shoulders.

"It'll be better in the morning," I say. Not always. Maybe Camila will be here by then.

Anna runs a hand through her stringy, greasy, midnight-colored hair. She sniffs and grabs a small bag by the door. When she leaves the trailer, the cold winter air rushes in. She isn't wearing a coat. I shake my head. High as a kite. She must not be able to feel the bitter wind at all.

"I'm sorry," I say to everyone in the room. Stacy hasn't said a word the entire time I've been here. She must be shell-shocked.

"That's Jamal's mom?" Her voice is little more than a whisper. "How's he turning out okay? That was awful."

I cradle Jamal closer to my chest. His life isn't easy with her constant mood swings, periods of absence, and drug use.

"I kept thinking she was going to attack one of us. She stormed in here with no warning," Nikki says.

Rick is getting his ass handed to him in the morning. Unacceptable. I click the locks into place on the trailer. "Nikki, you can take the other bedroom upstairs next to Stacy, okay?"

"On it." Nikki rises from leaning against the armrest and heads for the stairs. She glances at Ellie before she leaves.

"We need to talk, Wyatt," Ellie whispers.

"I know. Yeah, I get that." My eyes are closed, and I'm envisioning what she'll say after seeing Anna's behavior. This wasn't *that* bad. Could have been worse. Not a sentiment that'll comfort Ellie. "I'll take Jamal back to his room, okay?"

"I'll meet you in the living room?" She loops her arm over Haven's shoulders to take her to bed.

She'll have to sleep with me as my trailer's officially out of rooms. Haven's single bed would be too tight for both of them to get a good night's rest. I nod my agreement and head upstairs with Jamal.

ELLIE

Present Day

Wyatt's heavy footfalls as he comes down the stairs wake me up. I straighten and run my hands through my hair.

At the entrance to the main living room, he takes me in. "You're exhausted. And you weren't well to begin with. I'm so sorry, Ellie." When he reaches me, he scoops me into his arms and carries me into his room. He drags back the covers and slides me under as though I weigh nothing.

"Did you still want to talk?" He perches on the edge of the bed beside me.

"I need to talk to you." I yawn. "About a lot of stuff." My eyes are heavy, but I can't fall asleep until we talk. "Are you sleeping here too?"

"I want to." He scans my face before staring at the door. "I'm sorry about Anna."

"How she behaves isn't your fault. But I wish Haven hadn't seen her like that. She had a lot of questions. I said you and I would answer them sometime tomorrow. I don't have all the answers." Remembering the evening wakes me up. Anna's wild eyes. A chill slithers along my spine.

"Me neither. Jamal is such a great kid. I worry she'll destroy him."

There's an opening, but I'm afraid to plunge in. This solution has been on my mind for weeks, but I wasn't sure it was my place to suggest it. "What about getting custody? Giving him the stability and love he needs?"

"Anna loves him." He clenches his hands together.

Her love is toxic, at least right now. Whatever she has to hit to turn her life around, she hasn't hit it yet. Her son is paying the highest price.

Wyatt sighs and stands, taking off his shirt in one swift movement. His muscles ripple, and I long to run my hand down his chest. I want to hear the sound of his heart beating under my ear again.

Before he drops his pants, he raises his eyebrows in silent question. My sleep attire is the tiniest pair of shorts and a tank top. When I nod, he lets his pants drop to the floor with a sly grin. I can't help smiling back, wishing things between us could be this easy all the time.

Once he's in bed, his hand lands on my hip. I scooch backward a tiny fraction, and that's enough of an invitation. He rolls onto his back and draws me into his body so my head can rest on his chest.

"There's something I need to tell you, Ellie. Is it okay if I go first?" Wyatt's voice rumbles through his chest. "You had something you wanted to say too?"

"Yes." Given what we just saw with Anna, I'm even more nervous about telling him.

He takes a deep breath, holds it for a beat, and then releases it. "I was drinking on the island."

Surprise floods me, and relief chases it. *Finally.* "When? How much?" *Twenty bottles.*

"I'm going to trust you." He kisses the top of my head. "God, I'm so worried you're going to use this against me." The words are murmured into my hair. Silence hangs in the room for a moment before Wyatt takes another deep breath. "Of the twenty bottles, I'm not sure how many I drank. Most of them went down the drain, then I ordered more and drank them. Whatever I drank, it wasn't enough to be drunk."

"When?" I slide my hand across his chest. My heart is beating erratically, but his is slow, steady. He's telling the truth.

"The night I found out about Haven. The story wasn't out yet. You dropped me off, and I was raging. So angry because you were keeping us apart, keeping something from me. The frustration was too much. Big emotions trigger me."

"I came to see you that night when the story broke," I whisper, thinking back to the room. If there'd been the sharp tang of alcohol on his breath or in the air, I'd have noticed. Or maybe not. Too much swirled in my brain, and if I should have noticed he'd been drinking, I didn't.

"Yeah, you did. So you know I wasn't drunk. Hell, Ellie, you didn't even notice. The smell is why the balcony door was open." He traces patterns on my back.

My mind ticks through this information. When Wyatt and I were together, alcohol went hand in hand with drugs. To me, they're inseparable. "When you came to the island, you were hoping we'd get back together, right?"

"Yes." He tenses under me, his hand stilling.

"Is that still what you want? After everything?"

"It's the only thing I've wanted for years. That fight is the biggest regret of my life. I was too afraid to go after you. But I'm not afraid anymore. I'll burn my life down to keep you and Haven."

"Would you do an alcohol treatment program? The length doesn't matter—thirty days, sixty days, whatever." Maybe he's fine and doesn't need it. But maybe he's still not being honest about his dependence. If we're traveling this route together, I need to be sure. In the future, if I ask him to get help, I must be certain he'll do it.

He tightens his grip on me and kisses the top of my head again. He's still tracing idle patterns on my back in silence. Under my ear, his heart races.

"Wyatt?" I lift my head. A shot of anxiety goes through me that he won't agree, and I'll be back to where I was ten years ago.

"Okay, Ellie. I'll readjust my schedule, and I'll go." He stares down at me and then he hauls me up his body, so our lips are mere inches apart. "What does this mean? Are you saying we can try again?"

"There are still some things to be worked out." My practical side can't give in just yet. "Anna, Jamal, where we'd live . . . They're not small things."

He rolls us so I'm pressed into the mattress with him above. "Sounds like a yes." His lips dip into my neck.

"I haven't told you what I need to tell you." My voice shakes.

"What's wrong?" He raises his head, his brow creased. "Isn't this the part where we get to be happy?"

"I think, maybe, hopefully, really happy." *Deep breath, Ellie.* "I'm pregnant."

Wyatt, still above me, scans me for any sign of teasing. "You're . . . pregnant?" His expression is tortured. "How do I ask this without sounding like a complete and utter asshole? Either way—I don't care. We can figure it out. Okay?"

I laugh and raise myself off the pillow to place a quick kiss on his lips. "That's very comforting. But the baby is yours. The baby could *only* be yours."

His shoulders collapse, and he closes his eyes. "Oh, thank God." His eyes pop back open. "Not that I wouldn't have loved *any* child who was half of you."

I giggle and bring his mouth to mine. "I thought you might be upset with me."

He shakes his head, and he kisses me again. "Never. Never. Shit, I should have remembered protection too. I'm sorry, but I'm not sorry." His hand eases between us to touch my stomach. "A baby?"

"A baby." The joy I've been too afraid to experience surges through me. On top of that is a sense of relief. He's getting help for his drinking, he's open to talking about Anna's situation, and he hasn't freaked out about the pregnancy.

He slips a hand under my thin cotton tank top. He pushes the covers off us, and very gently, he kisses a line along the top of my shorts. "My child." There's so much reverence in his voice. Tears spring to my eyes.

"Wyatt." I thread my fingers through his hair. We have to discuss what we're doing about Anna.

As though something's just occurred, he stills. "If you weren't pregnant"—his lips whisper across my stomach—"would we still be trying again?"

I frame his face to force him to make eye contact. "You think the baby is the only reason I'm agreeing to try to have another relationship with you?" My thumb grazes his rough stubble.

"Who knows, Ellie? Even when I'm *doing* the right thing, it *feels* like the wrong thing."

Many people have told Wyatt they loved him and then betrayed him. Given his job and his status in the industry, I saw this when we were together, and gained a mild distrust of everyone, just like he had. We never knew who was going to sell us out next. We clung to each other more times than we blew apart. Lifeboats in the chaos, tied to each other for safety.

Leaving LA and Wyatt meant I left most of the chaos behind, but Wyatt didn't. He drifted on the currents of those stormy seas for years, abandoned. I'm amazed he survived. Looking at him now, I realize what I've denied for weeks, months . . . years. *I love him*. He won my heart years ago, maybe even that first night in the limo. I tried to give pieces of it to other people. Those fragments were never mine to give. When I left him, I got to keep half my heart, and I named that piece Haven, but the other half? He's had it. It's always been here, in his arms, in his eyes, in the light inside me when he's around.

A familiar tide rises in my chest, the one I've been running from for ten years. There's no more running. The swell pushes up, breaking the dam I constructed. I'm free, unguarded, whole.

"I love you, Wyatt. I've never stopped loving you. I knew if I saw you, I wouldn't be able to tear myself away. The reason I couldn't see you wasn't just because of Haven; it was me, too. I loved you too much to leave you again."

The crease in Wyatt's brow melts when he realizes my answer to "why now?" is to give him my heart, even though he's had it all along. His lips meld with mine, deepening the kiss, seeking more. Our bodies are pressed so closely together I think I hear his heart beating. But it's mine—wild, erratic, alive.

He works his way from my lips to my neck and then nips at my ear. He whispers, "I love you, Ellie. Forever. Always. Nothing's ever coming between us again."

I sigh, wrapping my arms around his back, and I let myself get swept away by the current of our love.

WYATT

PRESENT DAY

The full moon shines inside the trailer, illuminating Ellie while we chat. I've never seen anything as beautiful as Ellie's face as she speaks to me, really opens up, for the first time in ten years. We've been winding our way through the lost years for most of the night. God, I was a fool to let her go. Never again. *Never* again. Doesn't matter what I have to do.

"Wyatt." She presses her face into my shoulder.

"Still here." I kiss the top of her head. Inhaling her shampoo, I want to smother her with love. If my heart was this full the first time around, the drugs must have dulled it. A damn tragedy in itself. I get Ellie. I get Haven. A fresh start with our new baby, and a chance to be a present, involved father right from the beginning.

"I should warn you about something, or ask you to . . ." She purses her lips and seems to be searching for her words. "Watch out for me." She rotates to stare at the ceiling.

"What's that mean?" I prop my head on my hand.

"When I had Haven, I got sick. Kinda scary-sick." She glances at me. "My mom told me the same thing may never happen again, but if it does . . ."

"What happened?" I lace our fingers together. Ellie was sick enough to scare herself and her mother last time, and I wasn't there to help her, to protect her.

"Postpartum depression. Quite bad." She mirrors my pose, her head in her hand. She focuses on our intertwined fingers. "I hope I never feel that way again. It was terrible. I thought I was the worst mother ever. My mom says postpartum is common and nothing to be ashamed of, but it leveled me. I've never felt that low—didn't realize those feelings existed. A maze I couldn't find my way out of."

When we were together, she was the rock, the tough one. In any crisis, she was the person I looked to, the one I leaned on. That I wasn't there for her when she needed it most makes my chest ache.

"Is that why you came to see me in LA after Haven was born?"

She's quiet for so long I'm not sure she's going to answer. "I was mixed up, and I needed you to be someone you weren't capable of being."

"I can be that person now. You won't be alone." I tip her chin so she's forced to look at me. "I won't let you down."

"I believe you." Tears pool in her eyes and she gives a curt nod.

On the bedside table, my alarm buzzes. I hit the snooze before glancing out the window. The sun hasn't come up yet. A damn early call time when I would give anything to stay in bed. I'm afraid to leave this room, with this bubble we've created over the last few hours. It's delicate, and anything could pop it and put me—*us*—right back where we were before.

"Wyatt." Her hand lands on my arm.

I turn and fold her into me. "Something else?" I squeeze her tight. If I'm a little late, no one will get too upset.

"Anna." She skims my shoulder with her lips. "I love you, and I want to be with you. For us to be a family. But the way she behaved yesterday . . . the way she is now, I don't want her around our kids." She presses her cheek against my bare chest. "I don't even want her around her own kid."

I rub my face with my free hand and draw Ellie against me. One of her legs settles over mine. "My situation with Anna is complicated."

"But that doesn't mean we do nothing. That poor kid. And Haven—she doesn't understand either."

"What are you suggesting?" Part of me has known for a long time where Anna and I were headed. I haven't been able to face that road.

"Custody. You and I go after custody of Jamal."

Having her here, talking about these things with her, is good and terrible. Anna's my baby sister. "Do you want to know why I haven't done anything yet?" She glances up at me, but she doesn't say anything. "Because Anna's rock bottom comes after she's lost him. To me, her rock bottom looks a lot like Isaac's spiral. I can't be responsible for someone's death again."

"Oh, Wyatt. What happened to Isaac wasn't your fault. There were things going on with him we couldn't understand because he didn't let us."

"But he lived with me. We were best friends from the time we were six until the day he died. If anyone should have known he was headed that way, it was me."

She feathers kisses meant to comfort across my skin, and her fingers graze my nipple. I cover her hand with mine, stilling her exploration. I can't concentrate when her hands roam my body. Sinking into her and forgetting the rest of the world exists is too tempting.

"I see the signs in Anna. If I take Jamal, she might end up dead."

"That's what you think?" Her hand flattens on my chest.

"There's a thin cord named Jamal keeping Anna from going too far. Without him, Anna won't have a reason to stop." Now that I'm clean and sober, I recognize the reasonable logic, but I understand how an addict thinks. The addict in me knows how Anna will respond. This isn't a leap.

Without Jamal, any reason she may have to get clean is gone. Pain and regret can so easily be buried under a pile of pills, hard drugs, and alcohol. I did the same with Kabir, with Isaac, and then I did it again when Ellie left. The spiral and I are well acquainted.

"What if you talk to her? Ask her to go to rehab or whatever else she needs to do?"

"You think we haven't had those conversations?"

Her shoulders rise and fall almost imperceptibly. "Maybe she didn't believe you meant it."

The day Ellie left me I didn't mean my threat. I didn't want her to leave. The cracks in my chest that were starting to seal over begin to re-open.

She squeezes me tight as though sensing the shift in my mood.

My alarm sounds again. Kissing the top of her head, I slide out of bed. At the edge, I sit for a minute with my back to her, feet pressed into the floor.

"Is Anna a deal breaker?" The trick will be to *tell* Anna I'm taking Jamal. The consequences of that conversation make my heart stutter. There's a light touch on my shoulder, but I don't look at her. I can't. There's nothing I won't give up to keep her, Haven, and this baby.

"My priority is our kids. I love you, and I'll probably love you until the day I die. That'll *never* change." Her hand withdraws from my back. "Our kids deserve to grow up happy and safe."

My skin tingles from her touch, and I don't want to leave this room. I can't face the idea of sending my sister to her grave.

Over my shoulder, I say, "I'll talk to Anna tonight. I've gotta work through how to do this. If I can stop her from hurting herself, I need to do that. You and the kids are my family, but so is she."

"If Nikki were in the same position, I'd move heaven and earth to save her. What can we do if she doesn't want the kind of help she needs?"

I need to make her want our help. Seems simple. Except I understand how impossible it is. Right about now, a little divine intervention would be amazing.

"I'll see you on set in a couple hours." Her smile is tired but genuine. "Right now, in this moment, I'm really happy."

"Me too." But there's a dark cloud swirling. No matter how I approach Anna, the outcome is clear. What I do next, I'll have to live with for the rest of my life.

ELLIE

Present Day

Before my own call time, there's a knock on Wyatt's trailer door. It's still early, and no one else is awake yet. Cautiously, I peer out the window.

Please don't let it be Anna.

A tall woman, bundled to the hilt, is outside, bouncing up and down on her toes, and her face is almost completely obscured by a scarf.

Nothing about her is familiar. After security let us down last night, I'm wary. "Who's there?"

"Camila Silva. Wyatt asked me to come. I'm an addiction specialist. Anna's here somewhere?"

I open the door and usher her out of the cold. As each layer is removed, I get a clearer picture of the woman who saved Wyatt from himself. She's older than I expected, but attractive with her shoulder-length dark hair, dark eyes, light brown skin, and muscular stature. She must work out a lot.

With the winter clothes gone, she thrusts out her hand. "Camila. It's nice to meet you in person, Ellie. I've heard so much about you."

Last night, Wyatt admitted Camila wasn't sure he should come after me. I'm a trigger. That part of the discussion hadn't been fun. My presence, my existence, might be harmful. No one wants to hear that.

"Nice to meet you too." I accept her hand. "He's told me a lot about you and how you single-handedly saved him."

"No." She gives a sharp shake of her head and purses her lips. "He's not giving himself enough credit. He saved himself. No one saves you when you're an addict. You have to *want* to save yourself more than you *want* the next drink, the next pill, the next whatever. The struggle never ends. Every day, he saves himself."

Scary and comforting. I threw a lot of money at the biggest addiction charity on the island, but I never asked a lot of questions. The answers weren't ones I wanted to hear when I didn't have Wyatt anymore. I am ready to hear now, and I need to pay attention.

"He's on set," I say. "Anna's in my trailer."

"And you're in Wyatt's trailer."

"Is that a problem?"

"No, I'm merely trying to determine what's going on. It's easier to work with people, to provide solutions, when I have the whole picture."

"He probably had you sign some sort of contract?" I take out a cup for tea, and I hold up the kettle to Camila. "Care for a cup?"

"Tea isn't strong enough if I'm dealing with Anna this morning. Coffee, if you have it, please." Camila crosses her arms. "And yes, we have a few ironclad, very expensive contracts protecting him from leaks. I'm very careful. As much as he trusts anyone, he trusts me."

"Good to know." I flick on the coffee maker. "Anna was a surprise. She's worse now than she was before. And we didn't get along then."

"He's been very good to his sister over the years. His patience with her is unending." Camila frowns, clearly holding something back.

"That might be coming to an end."

"You two are back together?" Camila sinks into the closest couch.

"We are." I sip my tea.

"And you're asking him to choose?" She squints at me, as though she can't fathom why I'd do that.

"I can't have Anna around Haven." My hand has fallen to my abdomen. "You understand what Anna is like—better than most. She showed up raging yesterday."

"Yes, she does that. She's *mostly* harmless, depending on what she's immersed herself in." She sits up straighter. "Wyatt would never agree to leave Jamal with her, so you've asked him to go after custody?"

"She's not good for Jamal." The trauma she's causing her son might take years to fix if we don't act soon.

Camila tips her head, leaning back on the couch again. She picks at the fur on her winter coat, which is piled in a heap beside her. Emotions flit across her face, and I almost smile. She does not have a poker face.

"You want to say something."

"Yep." Camila glances at me. "But he wouldn't be happy. It's a bit of a balancing act. When to hold your cards and when to play them."

"There's a lot going on between us right now. Our lives are complicated, but we want a relationship to work." I give her a long look. "I can handle Wyatt if you play those cards." I grip on to the counter behind me. Whatever she's withholding might be vital.

"You remember the contract you mentioned earlier? There are certain cards I *can't* play."

I take a deep breath. I don't have time for games and half-truths. In fifteen minutes, I need to be in hair and makeup. "Tell me. I won't tell him you told me. But I'll do something about it."

"My house is the collateral for talking about these things." Her dark brown eyes meet mine as she calculates whether to trust me. "Do you understand what I'm saying? I like having a home."

"He won't kick you out of your place." I can probably talk him out of that vindictive move if I absolutely must.

"The last time Wyatt asked Anna to give him Jamal, she told him she'd kill herself if he took her son. I don't think she was bluffing. He doesn't either. If he has to choose between you and Haven or his sister, he'll pick you. But at what cost?"

I chug my tea. He wasn't guessing last night; he knows what his sister will do. I'm not a monster. I don't want her to die.

"But the guilt he'll experience for the rest of his life for choosing you over her will break him. Quickly, slowly, somewhere in-between. Big feelings are hard for him. He already feels partially responsible for Isaac's death. Adding Anna's death—his little sister, Jamal's mother . . . He'll use again or the two of you will fall apart because you asked and he said yes." Camila comes to my side to pour her coffee.

"I'm not sure what to say." I stare into my empty teacup.

"For three years, I've listened to Wyatt tell me how much he loves you. You've let him in the door again. He'll do anything to stay there. Anything you ask."

"I don't want Anna to die. The picture you painted—that's not an outcome any of us wants."

"You deserved to understand. He'd never tell you."

He'd worry I wouldn't stay. We're in an impossible situation. "Was it hard?" I glance up. "For him to get clean?"

"Very." She shifts her coffee cup to her other hand. "A lot of trial and error."

"If I'd told him ten years ago when I was pregnant with Haven—do you think he would have gotten clean back then?"

"You don't pull any punches." Camila lets out a low whistle. "Did you ask him this question?"

"In a roundabout way, yeah."

"And?"

"He said it wasn't a fair question. But you're the expert. Maybe you can tell me."

"You want me to ease your conscience?"

"He's so good now. Such a *good* man." My voice grows thick, and I have to pause to collect myself. "He always was, but the addiction gripped him so hard. I've loved him so much for so long that I want to be sure I did the right thing."

"I can't answer with any sense of certainty. We'll never know." She runs her hand up and down my arm in a gesture of comfort. "People are unpredictable. You made a choice based on what you saw in him then." Sipping her coffee, she gives me a thoughtful look. "That's the thing about a choice. Once you make it, you can't ever go back to undo it. What's done is done."

I place my teacup in the sink, then I gather my hair up and let it fall over and over. "This choice with Anna and Jamal . . ."

"Is another one of those moments. It's a big one. A row of dominoes."

"I always hated that game."

Already I'm in over my head with Wyatt. Being with him is all-consuming. Since he left this morning, he's all I've thought about. Last night sparked something, and my feelings are burning down all my defenses. I want him, no matter the cost.

Nikki pads into the kitchen, yawning. "Don't you have to be there in five minutes?" She glances at the phone clutched in her hand and then spots Camila.

"Yeah, I do." I rub my cheeks, feeling emotionally drained yet again. Just when I thought I was on even ground, something else makes me wobble. "Nikki, this is Camila, Wyatt's addiction specialist. And Camila, Nikki is my sister."

"Nice to meet you," Nikki says and extends her hand for Camila to shake.

"Nikki, make sure Haven stays away from Anna today," I say.

"I'm with you there. She was scary last night." Nikki pats my shoulder. "Haven shouldn't be anywhere near her."

"She wouldn't hurt Haven on purpose." Camila grimaces.

"Maybe not. But Haven's not used to Anna. And we won't have a chance to talk until there's a break in filming this afternoon or maybe tonight," I say.

"As the ex-other-parent, I agree with Ellie." Nikki grabs a mug and fills it with coffee. "We keep Haven the hell away from Anna. She was unhinged."

"You said she's in your trailer?" Camila frowns and takes another drink of her coffee.

"She should be. It's not like we put a guard outside the door or anything." I grab my coat, hat, and mitts off the warming rack. "Security wasn't very useful last night."

"Noted," Camila says. "I'll go talk to her."

"Alone?" Nikki's voice fills with disbelief. "Nope. You need six Jedi masters with you."

"Nikki." I laugh as I tuck my hair into my hat.

"I'm not exaggerating . . ." Nikki starts the familiar phrase from our childhood.

"You're 'remembering big,'" I finish with a shake of my head. "Come get me if you need me." I open the door and head to work.

Wyatt and I have to talk. Camila is right. He'd never survive being the instrument of his sister's death, and I can't ask that of him.

WYATT

PRESENT DAY

James, the director, is a taskmaster. Normally, a day on set is an exercise in hurry up and wait. Lots of time to sit around and watch a clock turn over. Today, he's more organized and efficient than usual. He's annoying the shit out of me. I need mental space to decide what to say to Anna later tonight about Jamal.

"Cut, cut. Jesus, Wyatt. Get your fucking head in the game," James yells from his seat.

He'd better not get off his chair. The takes when he ambles over, he gives a close-talker lecture. His cocky attitude leads us to the cusp of a full-on brawl. Patience will not hold me back from hitting him today. My inner Zen is being stored up for later.

"There something you want to say to me?" I ball my hands up. Hitting him would help with these shitty feelings. Release them through my fists.

James ignores me. He must sense I'm not taking his shit today.

I check my watch and remember it's a prop. I curse under my breath. "Time?" I call out to anyone close enough to hear.

A crew member eating a bagel off to the side checks his phone. "Eight thirty."

Camila is here. Ellie is in hair and makeup. How do I split myself in three so I can check on them and still be in this scene? Anna's unpredictability makes me nervous. She shouldn't be near Haven today. Ellie's concerns echo through my brain. Of course, the situation isn't safe. I should have asked Kyle to fly with Camila. Then I'd feel like I was capable of being in two places at once, and he's good with my sister's mood swings. Almost better than me at talking her out of a rage.

"When are we moving on?" I call to James since he's ignoring me to talk to other people.

"Whenever you get your head out of your ass and nail the scene," James yells back before settling into his chair again. "Do you need me to give you a note or can you do your job today?"

Rage boils in me. I turn my back on him and suck in deep breaths. Today is not the day I blow it. *Calm.* I picture Ellie looking up at me, her face alight with a smile. Her dark eyes full of love for me. The anger leaves in a rush. *She loves me.* The rest of the world doesn't matter. "Let's get it done." I make a circling motion with my hand for everyone to reset.

I nail the next take so hard I consider pinning the cut to the director's forehead in triumph. He smirks, and I give him the finger. He's such an asshole. Instead of escalating our feud, he eases out of his chair to prep for Ellie's arrival on set.

Almost as though I willed it to happen, my lady love emerges out of the hair and makeup trailer. When she catches a glimpse of me, a grin breaks out on her face, lighting up my world. The tightness in my chest evaporates, and I can breathe again. Leaving the trailer this morning, I feared Ellie would talk herself out of *us* while I was gone. For ten years she's been doing it, and I understand better than anyone how hard old habits die. Today I've been so on edge I could embrace those habits like an old friend. A drink. One Perc. A fingertip of coke. Nothing drastic. Just *enough*. The gum in my pocket knocks against my leg like the pill bottle used to. That has to be my "enough." Taking out the packet, I pop a square into my mouth.

When Ellie reaches me, she wraps her arms around my middle and squeezes me tight. Her cheek presses into the down of my coat, and I nuzzle her neck. Her familiar scent is masked by foreign products, but below her ear, vanilla and flowers come alive. All I want to do is scoop her up, carry her back to the trailer, and pretend the rest of the world isn't here.

"Don't talk to Anna today, okay?" Ellie murmurs.

"What?" I draw back. "Did I hear you right?"

I'm tempted to sweep her hair out of her face, but she just spent an hour with the stylist. They'll murder me if I mess her up.

"You did. We should problem solve. Maybe there's another solution that doesn't involve taking Jamal from Anna." Ellie stares into the distance behind me. "She must love Jamal."

Hello, Divine Intervention.

I don't want to ask the next question, but I also don't want to be caught off guard later. "Are you sure?"

She nods, but there's no eye contact. "It's worth a try. See if we can help her."

"I love you, Ellie. You know that, right?"

"And I love you." Her expression brims with sadness. "I'm not sure there are enough words for how much I love you."

"This about-face on Anna can't be easy for you."

"Maybe if we put some effort into finding a solution, we can come up with something that'll work." She kisses me.

"Was Anna there by the time you left the trailer?"

"No. But I met Camila. I like her, actually. Makes sense how someone like her would have been good for you."

She's liked very few of the women I've associated with either before, during, or after our relationship. My high tolerance for women who weren't genuine irked her, but I grew up surrounded by those types of people. I understood them. They're easy to deal with.

Ellie mystified and intrigued me because her upbringing was so different from mine, but we got along so well. I only kept the women who came after Ellie around if they didn't remind me of her. None of them were Ellie, and I didn't want them to be.

"She's still good for me. It's why she's still in my life." Something occurs to me and I frown. "She didn't say anything to you, did she? Is that why you changed your mind about Anna?"

"I had time to consider what I'd asked for this morning before I left the trailer. I don't know Anna anymore. There might be other avenues." She's saying the right things, but each time she says them, she avoids looking me in the eye. Finally, when she glances up, her dark depths brim with tears.

"Hey." I bend to graze her forehead with mine. "Ellie . . ."

"I want you and the kids safe. If we can do that, then we can help Anna too."

"But you're crying." I kiss her forehead. "It doesn't seem like you're okay with your suggestion."

"I cried a lot last time I was pregnant too," she says. "I thought it was because of you." She shrugs. "Maybe I'm just a hormonal mess."

At the mention of the last time she was pregnant, I gather her closer. The whole experience will be different this time. If I have to watch her cry and give her tissues every day for the next six months, that's what I'll do.

"You'll tell me if your feelings become more than that, right? You asked me to watch out for you, but I can't do that if you're not telling me the truth."

"I don't want Anna to die." Her tears have left streaks down her face, ruining her makeup.

"Die?" Inside, my anger simmers. "So Camila did talk to you."

"Wyatt." Ellie frames my face with her hands when I go tense.

"She shouldn't have done that."

"Maybe not. But if you want honesty from me, then I need it from you too. When I asked you, instead of acting like you *thought* Anna might do something to herself, you should have been firm."

"I don't want to put my sister's choices on you. If you need Anna away from our family to feel safe, if you think Jamal's in danger being with her, I need to listen. And then I need to do something about it."

"If doing something leads to Anna's death, you'll never recover." Ellie grips my winter jacket in her fists.

I stare out at the snow-covered ground, and the evergreens surrounding today's location. Camila didn't hold back, apparently. "You can't decide that for me."

"So you'd be perfectly fine if she died?"

"No, of course not." Frustration leaks into my voice. "But I don't want to lose you." My voice breaks, and I clear my throat. We're building a family, and I'm not sacrificing her or our children for my sister and my nephew. We're surrounded by curious crew, and any second James is going to amble over here to put us to work. This isn't the right place for this conversation.

"And what I'm telling you is that you won't."

"I can't guarantee Anna will ever be clean." We might end up in the exact situation she didn't want: Haven exposed to an erratic addict.

"I understand."

"Do you?"

"Maybe not, but I'm trying. Don't talk to Anna until we have a chance to come up with some ideas. There has to be a way to make this work."

"All right, lovebirds, break time's over," James yells from across the set.

I grit my teeth.

She pats my arm. "This isn't the first time you've worked with him. You must have known." She nods toward James.

"The last time I worked with him, I wasn't sober or clean. Apparently, I liked him a lot better when I couldn't see his sharp edges." The phrase reminds me of Isaac, and a pang of sadness hits me. "I don't want Anna to end up like Isaac. But I can't fathom how to stop her."

"We'll figure it out." Ellie rubs my arm. "Together, okay?"

"I like the sound of that." I won't lose Ellie and our kids a second time, and I need to protect Jamal. But the other outcome is also true. If Anna killed herself and I had a part in leading her there, I'd never forgive myself. We all need to make it out alive.

ELLIE

PRESENT DAY

My feet ache. I'm exhausted, and every time I'm near Wyatt, I long to curl into him. Luckily, I can do that whenever I want. The one high point of our otherwise exhausting day is my proximity to him.

During our extended break, we checked on everyone in the trailers. Anna looked better after a shower and fresh clothes courtesy of Camila. She was on the floor playing with Jamal as though the day before hadn't happened. She was even civil to me. When we left, I felt better about trying to figure out a way forward together. Stable Anna wasn't that bad. Stacy, Nikki, and Camila were keeping a careful watch on the kids. Everyone was fine.

"She seemed good there, almost pleasant." Snow crunches under our feet on the way back to set. Wyatt grabs my hand and links our gloved fingers. My relationship with Wyatt has to work, and if Anna is part of the package, I have to find some bright spots.

"I used to be able to function pretty well some days too."

There were days when I would have sworn he was sober. When he dabbled in combinations he knew well, he managed himself with precision. I suppose Anna's the same.

"I don't want to worry about how we'll manage her or us." We're outside the hair and makeup trailer. "We'll figure it out."

Her ability to quit and her determination to get better—we have no power over that. I was powerless the day I asked Wyatt to quit too. In the end, the only thing I could do was leave. Neither of us wants to cut Anna out, but at some point, we might have to. I won't suggest that again until we've exhausted other avenues or until it's clear the kids won't be safe with her around. I rise on my toes to kiss him.

He tugs me closer, going for a second, deeper kiss. The fire that burns for him bursts to life. I want our break in filming back. An empty trailer. Him. Me. A lifetime will never be enough.

Kelly, one of the makeup artists, catcalls us from behind.

"Ignore her," Wyatt murmurs against my lips.

When other people join her, heat rises to my cheeks. Sometimes, it's easier pretending to be someone else. In character, it's routine to hide my real emotions. But right now, I'm pretty freaking glad to be Ellie Cooper. He breaks the kiss and gives Kelly an annoyed glance over my shoulder. "I'm making up for lost time here, Kel, and you're interrupting."

"Wyatt Burgess and Ellie Cooper, reunited. Myths and legends are made of this." There's laughter in her voice. "#TrueLoveReturns is trending on Twitter today. The two of you are the leads. #Wyllie."

My attention hasn't left Wyatt's face. I could stare at him all day, every day, for the rest of my life and never wish for a different view.

"*True Love Returns* is the name of this movie." He laughs.

"Just sayin'." Her sassy grin is visible out of the corner of my eye. She's flirting with him in front of me about his relationship with me. "The press is unreal."

Unease flutters in my stomach. I let my social media manager follow Wyatt across our social media platforms this morning. He followed me back. Perhaps that was a bad idea.

"It'll die down." He senses my mood and kisses my forehead. "It always does."

"I shouldn't have let my team follow you."

"Made me feel good to see those notifications roll in. Unfollow me now and people assume we're fighting or indecisive. Ride out the curiosity. It's been a while, but it'll fade. I promise."

Before this, I hadn't done anything gossip-column-worthy in several years. If we're forging a relationship, I'll have to get used to the attention again. Maybe it'll fade, but last time the extreme interest in my life didn't vanish until I left Wyatt and moved back home to Bermuda. My saving grace was my island hideaway where I was the only high-profile famous person, and it wasn't worth the cost for paparazzi to send their people there on the off chance they might see me. No one got a photo of me until long after Haven was born. The perks of having lots of family on the island to run my errands and shield me from curiosity. I could disappear then, but being back with Wyatt has tossed me right back into the center of the hurricane.

Reluctantly, I disentangle myself from him to walk to Kelly's trailer. My stomach squeezes at the way she watches him saunter away. Everything about him attracts attention—something else I'll have to get used to again. His magnetism makes him hard to resist in real life and when he's on a screen, big or small.

"So the rumors are true," Kelly says when I slide into the makeup chair to be touched up.

"It seems so." Someone who has such an interest in following social media trends gets few details.

"The press is loving this reunion. Secret child. Reunited lovers. I mean, the two of you, when you were together the first time, you owned Hollywood."

I laugh a little and suppress an eye roll. "It was fun then, for a while at least. Before most of this social media hoopla. Now I can't walk down the street without someone taking a video of me or asking for a photo."

"You don't like it?"

If it was once in a while, I might not mind. Back then a lot of our fans seemed to think that they owned us or that we owed them something other than the movies we made, the interviews we did, or the photospreads in magazines. They wanted to consume as much of us as they could. Paparazzi wanted the money a single controversial shot would get them, and they did anything to achieve it. Leaving the house meant being switched on. I haven't missed flipping that switch. "Would you?"

"I have no idea." Kelly rocks back on her heels and tips my face around. "I guess the attention might be a bit much. Personally, I wouldn't enjoy the bad photos."

"Ah, yes. The cellulite catches. 'Cause, you know, we aren't human."

"Was there a bit of a commotion last night? Wyatt tore hot Rick from security a new asshole this morning. Something about his sister coming on set? I thought they were close. Her kid's here, right?"

"Everything's fine." I keep my attitude breezy. She'd be the type to sell details.

"I've seen photos of his sister. She used to be so pretty." Kelly dabs my lips. "Pretty is too mild, maybe. Stunning. A lot like her brother." She winks at me in the mirror.

She hasn't been this chatty about Wyatt any other day. Annoyance tugs at me. Odd to have him back, mine again, and still have to share parts of him with everyone else.

"I bet he's also stunning in—" Kelly stops when the trailer door flies open, slamming against the wall.

Nikki appears in the entryway, her complexion ashen. My stomach drops to my feet. Something is very wrong. Nothing ruffles my sister. "It's—it's—" A sob spills out of her. "We called 9-1-1. They're on their way. It's Haven."

"What?" I tumble out of my chair and grab my coat. "What?" My brain stalls on Haven's name and 9-1-1.

"Come." Nikki latches onto my arm. "Wyatt—he's—he's on his way to the trailer."

Everything shuts down in my brain, and nothing makes sense while we run across the thick snow to the trailers. Wyatt sprints ahead of us. His presence, even from a distance, offers a strange reassurance. Whatever has happened can be fixed. Wyatt and I are creating a family. We're a family.

Nikki cries and runs. Occasionally, she whispers, "Oh, God," in a voice I've never heard from her.

I can't bring myself to ask. *Was it Anna? Will Haven be okay?*

Wyatt yanks open the door to my trailer, and I say, almost to myself, "Why's he going in there?"

"That's where Haven is." Nikki's voice catches on a sob. "Camila is with her."

"In my trailer?" When we left them, they were at Wyatt's. Anna stayed in my trailer last night. Irresponsible drug addict Anna stayed in my trailer. "Why? Why was Haven in our trailer?" My voice rises on a wail.

Nikki doesn't answer because we're at the door, and I'm throwing it open. Before me is a sight so haunting, it'll stay with me forever. Wyatt is doing CPR on Haven while Camila assists beside him.

"No," I whisper, clutching Nikki's arm. "No, no, no, no, no, no."

Wyatt glances up at me with unconcealed panic. He counts compressions. I rush to Haven's side, the one he's not on, kneel and grab her hand. It's warm, so warm. Warm means alive.

Nikki's sobs echo through the trailer.

My daughter is so pale, so still. The scene in the trailer is filtering through mud. I can't grasp what's before me. This isn't possible. I must be dreaming. We left here not even an hour ago, and everyone was fine. Haven was fine.

Wyatt pauses his compressions for Camila to breathe in Haven's mouth. "Anna—Narcan! Did you find it?" As soon as Camila backs off, Wyatt presses down on Haven's chest in a hard, fast rhythm.

Her little heart. Her poor little heart.

"El, Ellie," Wyatt says in between compressions.

My body is carved out, hollow. This can't be happening. A dream. I'm dreaming. No, a nightmare. For years, I dreamed of Wyatt coming. Then I dreamed this. My worst fear. The reason I couldn't stay.

His features are set in a look of determination. In between counts, he says, "We. Will. Save. Her."

"She's almost ten." I squeeze her tiny hand. "Her birthday's in a month. She's gonna be ten." Nikki's arm circles around my waist. She kneels beside me, and I notice a tiny rip in her jeans, just on her thigh. Sirens outside the trailer grow louder.

"The Narcan!" Camila calls to Anna, who is still in the bath-room banging around.

"I can't find it!" Anna's panicked voice catches on the last word.

Isaac, if you're out there: Don't let her die. I'm not ready to let her go yet. We need her here. We need her.

Isaac?

Isaac?

Are you there?

Something builds in my chest, rising, flooding, consuming. When the paramedics burst into the trailer, a guttural sob rips out of me.

WYATT

PRESENT DAY

The paramedics rush in and bark information to each other while they establish Haven's vitals. She has vitals. Weak, but there. God, I hope my CPR didn't hurt her.

Closing my eyes, I take a couple of deep breaths. When I open them, the female paramedic is staring at me.

"Accidental overdose," Camila says from beside me.

I missed the question.

Ellie was forced to step back from Haven. Nikki is holding her as she cries. I want to go to her, but this is my fault. My sister brought this here.

They inject Haven with Narcan and almost immediately her eyes fly open. She sits up, bewildered.

"Mom?"

Ellie's sharp cry of relief pierces my heart. She falls to her knees and envelops Haven in a hug, securing her tight.

"We need to get her to the hospital. She might need another dose," the male paramedic says, packing up in a rush. "Anyone know what she got into?"

"Anna!" I shout, turning on my heel.

"Fentanyl," Camila says. "Possibly cocaine. Maybe heroine. Anna doesn't know. She left everything strewn around the bathroom."

The female medic sighs, and they help Haven onto the stretcher. "We can take one of you." She checks between me and Ellie. She recognizes us.

"Me." Ellie clings onto Haven. "Me."

"I'll meet you there." She won't acknowledge me while she cries and grasps onto Haven. Her worst nightmare. The one thing she told me she needed above all else—keep our kids safe, and I couldn't fucking do it.

Once they're through the door, I follow them out of the trailer. At the ambulance, the paramedics slam the doors shut, but not before I catch a glimpse of Ellie's face. My heart beats double, triple time when the ambulance peels off the set and onto the road that'll take them to the hospital.

I don't even have a damned car.

Storming into the trailer, I stare at Camila and then at Nikki. "How the fuck did this happen?"

"Haven asked to come over here to get a doll. I didn't think anything of it. We let her go back and forth all the time before Anna. It never occurred to me Anna'd have littered the place with drugs." Nikki's voice trembles and her chin wobbles.

I turn to Camila. "What's your excuse?"

"I was mediating a session between Anna and Jamal. I didn't realize Nikki let Haven come here. Stacy was setting up a craft."

"Where is Stacy?" I ask.

"In your trailer with Jamal. Someone still had to take care of him when all hell broke loose." Camila uses her calm, collected voice that I usually find soothing.

The rage inside right now is astronomical. Haven could have died. The Narcan might not have worked if she'd been alone too long.

I drag my hands down my face. Finding a ride to the hospital is a priority. Ellie needs me, even if her face told me she doesn't want me. No matter what, Haven needs her dad. "You want to come, Nikki? I'll find us a ride to the hospital."

She nods. Her winter gear is hanging off her, hastily assembled from when she came to fetch us. There's an ominous silence from the bathroom. I couldn't care less how Anna's feeling. It better be guilt. Unbelievable guilt. And fear. She should be very afraid of me right now.

"Camila, you'll have to stay here to babysit Anna. She can't be anywhere near Ellie or Haven. Get Yasmeen to book the three of you flights back to LA."

"Wyatt." Anna's voice comes, tentative, from the doorway.

Without looking, I hold up a hand. Anger—sharp, fierce, enough to blow up this trailer— surges. "Save it. I don't want to hear anything from you. The sound of your voice right now makes me sick. Your irresponsible, selfish actions almost killed my daughter." I whirl to face her. "Ellie's pregnant. And because of you, because you can't think about anything other than getting high, I might have a second child I don't get to raise."

"She wouldn't do that," Anna whispers.

Nikki is silent. She knows Ellie as well as I do. The only thing Ellie told me she cared about was keeping me and her kids safe. Already, that's a bar I can't meet.

"Jamal and I will move out." Anna steps toward me.

"I can't talk to you right now. I can't. I'll say things, so many things." With my hand still raised to ward her off, I turn to Nikki. "Let's go. Ellie and my daughter need us." My voice cracks on the last sentence, and I clear my throat.

When we step out the trailer door, dickhead Rick from security is there. He should be fired by now. The backwoods of Ontario, Canada, must not have a lot of security options if he's still kicking around. "Mr. Burgess," he says. At least we're back to some level of formality. "I have a car waiting to take you to the hospital."

"Thanks." I jiggle the package of gum in my pocket. The car sits beside the trailer, and I go to the far side so Nikki can slide in right away.

Warmth presses in around me. I peel off layers while the car speeds away. There must be only one hospital because no one has asked where we're going.

Silence stretches between us. We're probably worrying about the same things, but different things too. *Haven.* My eyes ache, and I squeeze them closed at the thought of her inheriting my addictive personality. One taste was enough for me. Ellie will never get over the loss if one taste is all it takes for Haven. She can't turn out like me. I'll do anything.

"It's not your fault," Nikki whispers beside me.

"It's not yours either." Part of me blames her. Letting Haven into that trailer alone after Anna tore through was a mistake. But Ellie spent ten years shielding the people she loved from having to think about those things. Nikki isn't to blame. Maybe Anna. But maybe tonight goes all the way back to our parents. Anna and I never had much of a chance.

Ellie and the kids are better off without me. Haven has been safe for ten years. One small scar mars her forehead. Less than six months with me as her dad and she's at the hospital with an accidental overdose.

"Ellie did the right thing," I say into the quiet of the car.

"The right thing?" Nikki glances in my direction before looking away. "What do you mean?"

"Leaving me. She did the right thing for Haven when she left me."

"Maybe back then she did. But this, what happened today, isn't your fault."

"If Haven turns out like me." My voice cracks. Clearing my throat, I shake my head and run a hand down my face. Falling apart isn't an option.

"It was an accident, Wyatt."

Arguing with her is pointless. The truth sits between us, whether she wants to admit it or not. Ten years ago I wasn't good for Ellie, and I wasn't good enough for Haven.

"Ellie's not as strong as she seems," Nikki murmurs when the car pulls up to the emergency entrance of the hospital. "She's going to need you. Even if she thinks she doesn't."

"She deserves better than this, better than me." I open my door.

Nikki grabs my coat, stopping me from exiting the car. She takes a deep breath. "You're a good guy. I wasn't sure for a while, but I am now. What happened to Haven today isn't because you're a bad guy. You have this tremendous capacity to love and forgive the people who matter to you. Forgive yourself, Wyatt. Tonight isn't your fault." She releases my coat and steps out when the driver opens her door.

I sit for a minute, soaking in her words. The passenger door is propped open. Then I climb out of the car. Straightening my coat, I steel myself to be the man Ellie and Haven need and not the one I am. Her words bounce around my brain while we talk to the person at reception, when we walk to Haven's room, even as we stand outside her door.

I forgave Anna a lot over the years. That's on me. She squandered chance after chance. Each opportunity to cut her loose led me to this moment. Anna might have left the drugs lying around, but I'm the one who should have known better. I'm the reason Haven's in the hospital.

"You ready?" Nikki offers a tentative smile.

Thrusting my hands in my pockets, I square my shoulders. What I want, I'm not sure Ellie will let me have. I wouldn't blame her at all.

ELLIE

PRESENT DAY

The doctor finishes checking Haven and turns to me with a grimace. Her pen wags back and forth. "Hospital policy is to call the Children's Aid Society whenever a child overdoses—intentional or otherwise."

"Children's Aid Society?" My brain isn't functioning. Each breath Haven takes beside me is a gift, and I can't tear myself away.

"It's a child protection agency in Canada."

"But it was an accident." I stare at her, dumbfounded.

"Yes, but it still needs to be investigated." She scans her clipboard. "Her father has a history with drugs. They'll want to make sure she's safe."

"What did you say to me about Wyatt? Doctor . . . ?" I bristle.

"Boxton."

"Watching *TMZ* and *Entertainment Tonight* doesn't give you the right to judge him. *This* wasn't his fault. He's been clean and sober for almost three years."

Maybe it is his fault, at least a little. Had he taken custody of Jamal, done the hard things earlier, we might not be here right now.

"You don't know him." I grasp Haven's hand.

"Someone from CAS will be here soon. I wanted to make you aware."

"Is Dad in trouble?"

I shake my head. Maybe we're all in trouble, depending on what this agency decides. What's already happened can't be undone.

When Dr. Boxton reaches the door, she sidesteps Nikki and Wyatt. My heart pitter-patters in my chest at the sight of him. His broad shoulders, his dark messy hair, and his eyes, so haunted, twist my gut. The agony in his expression undoes me a hundred times. Any anger toward him seeps out of me. I can't blame him, not even a little. Instead of waiting for him to come to me, I close the distance between us and throw my arms around his waist, burying my face in his chest.

He draws me into a hug and squeezes me. His chin on the top of my head is soothing. "I'm so sorry," Wyatt whispers. "Is Haven okay?"

I nod, but I can't seem to find my voice. If I open my mouth, a sob might escape. Traumatic events and pregnancy don't go together.

"How are you doing, Short Stuff?" Wyatt asks over me.

"I feel weird."

Taking a step back from Wyatt, I keep my arm around his waist, and we go to Haven's bedside.

"I shouldn't have touched Aunt Anna's things." Her voice is little more than a whisper.

"Never touch Aunt Anna's things." Wyatt grips her small hand in his. "Ever again, okay? Aunt Anna has dangerous medicine."

I haven't had the courage or time to ask Haven how this happened. If Haven knew what she was doing, I'm not sure how I'll cope. The doctor was too concerned about taking blood, getting a toxicology report, and so forth to ask many questions.

"You moved Anna's things?" I ask. Wyatt brings a chair to her bedside.

She glances from me to her father. Her attempt to gauge how angry we'll be is needless; I'm more concerned with the truth. And that she's alive. I'm so grateful she's alive.

"Are you going to be mad?" A worried frown creases her brow.

"Probably." I brush a strand of hair off her forehead. "But you understand I love you, no matter what, always. I don't know what I'd do if anything ever happened to you." I choke out the last few words and tears trickle out again.

Wyatt tugs me into the chair beside him and keeps one hand clasped in mine while his other hand stays with Haven. "Sweetheart." His voice is gentle. "We're trying to figure out how we stop this from happening again. Okay?"

The answer is easy. Keep Anna away from our children, and that includes her own child. I stare at Wyatt and send a silent prayer to anyone listening that he never relapses. This Wyatt, holding my hand, guiding my daughter—my heart overflows with love for him. For the first time in a long time, clinging to him will get me out of this nightmare better than navigating this mess alone.

"I went to get my doll." Haven sniffs and takes a deep breath. "But then I had to go to the bathroom." She twists her hands together. "When I went in, there was stuff everywhere. Needles, pills, some powdery stuff. Mom doesn't like a mess. I tried to clean everything. I wiped the powder off the counter into the garbage. Then I didn't feel good."

She had to pick this time to worry about a mess. Haven's created lots of them with no concerns, and today she decides to be tidy.

"What'd you use to wipe the powder?" Wyatt's voice is soothing, understanding.

Haven holds up her hands. "I shouldn't have done that, right? Is that what happened?"

"No, you shouldn't have done that," Wyatt says.

Whatever she got into, he understands what it was. I'm afraid to ask. Ignorance might be bliss. "This makes sense to you?"

"With her hand?" Nikki pipes up from the other side of the bed. "This happened because she *touched* one of the drugs?"

"Unfortunately. Fentanyl is tricky." Wyatt squeezes my fingers, and someone knocks on the door.

We all turn to see a brown-skinned woman with long dark hair standing on the threshold, clutching an oversize purse. She's young, maybe younger than us. "I'm Priya Sidana." She comes toward the hospital bed. "From the Children's Aid Society. I was hoping to have a few moments alone with Haven to talk about what happened."

"She can't be questioned alone," I say. "She's nine." I stand, and Wyatt does too.

Priya glances over her shoulder, and Dr. Boxton enters behind her. "Dr. Boxton can act as the other adult in the room. The conversation is confidential."

Helplessness overwhelms me, and I check with Wyatt, needing some direction. We understand what happened, but I'm not sure how a stranger is going to interpret Haven's accident. Neglect? Wyatt's past might influence Priya. His drug use is the stuff of legends.

"I'll speak to you after." Priya gives us an encouraging smile.

Her sunny disposition isn't helping to ease my fear. Women in her job can turn that attitude on and off like a faucet. I shadowed a child protection worker for a movie. When they're called to a case, things can go downhill quickly.

"We'll be in the waiting room." Wyatt links his fingers with mine. He extends his arm to Nikki and draws her to his other side.

I take in their easy camaraderie, thankful they aren't blaming each other. I'm not sure I could handle any animosity between them. Before we leave the room, I stare at Haven, so tiny and pale in the bed. Her overdose was an accident. Wyatt and I were working. This woman, this stranger, can't fault us.

"It'll be okay," Wyatt whispers in my ear, and we head down the hall.

Nothing is okay right now. In the waiting room, we sit in a cloud of silence, the ticking clock above the door the only sound. Hearing that noise for any length of time will drive me insane. A dripping tap that can't be switched off.

"I'm going to call Mom and Dad." Nikki takes her phone out of her pocket. "Text me if you need me to come back right away."

I squeeze her hand on the way past. Wyatt gives her a curt nod and takes gum out of his pocket. He throws two pieces in his mouth. A now-familiar coping mechanism, but for some reason the action makes my heart drop. The way he does it reminds me of when he used to take pills. He puts his hand on my leg and leans back in the chair. His relaxed attitude is a front; the gum gave him away. But if I didn't know better, he'd appear unaffected.

Inside, I'm on the cusp of falling apart. We're in Canada, for God's sake. They can't take our kid from us. We don't even live here. "Why is it taking so long?"

"It's only been ten minutes." His eyes remain closed.

"Do you think she'll take Haven?"

"No."

"How can you be sure?"

"This isn't the first time I've dealt with people like Priya Sidana." He cracks open one eye and then the other.

"Jamal?"

"And me and Anna when we were kids. They came knocking. My parents said the right things. Appeared to understand they screwed up. Promised to be better. A situation, one of many, where it helps to be famous." He sandwiches my hand between his two bigger ones. "Trust me. I realize I've screwed up with Anna. This will *never* happen again."

"I'm not blaming you."

"You should. *I do.* If I'd done something more about Anna and Jamal, we might not be here."

Earlier I'd had the same thought, but I'm not laying his sister's choices at his feet. I run my free hand across his shoulders.

He kisses the back of my other hand, which is still clasped between his. "When I got to the trailer and saw Haven lying there, unconscious, my heart, Ellie. I thought it would fall out of my chest and die beside her. I've never been so scared in my life."

"Knock, knock," Priya says from the doorway. We turn to look at her. "I have a few questions for both of you and then I think I'll have everything I need."

Wyatt wraps one arm around my waist, his other hand in mine. "Have at it," he says.

Priya perches on one of the chairs across from us. The duct tape repairs on her plastic seat crunch as she settles. Scanning her notes, she then looks up at us, a nervous tilt to her mouth. Her pen is poised to start writing. "So, either of you can answer and then we'll go from there, okay?"

We both nod. Wyatt does most of the talking. He's never more charming than when he's trying to get out of something. Even when the pile of trouble he stumbles into isn't his, he has two methods of dealing with conflict: he'll either brawl his way out or turn on his razzle-dazzle star power. Sitting beside him,

I have a front-row seat; he's at full wattage. He anticipates each question, an answer at the ready. He said he's done this before with people like her, but I can't help wondering how many times. None of the questions trip him. He's smooth, confident, filled with the best answers. Was this how he learned to talk his way in or out of things? Was *this* his childhood?

"Well." Priya stands. "I'm satisfied you understand what happened here today. Haven's a very lucky girl. The outcome could have been much worse." She stuffs her papers into her bag and then hesitates. "I wish you both a lot of luck sorting out your sister, Mr. Burgess. Seems like you've turned your life around."

His grin is grave and bashful, as though her compliment means something. "Thank you, Priya. It's been a pleasure talking to someone who understands the struggles and the path to wellness."

Yeah, 'cause it's such a pleasure to be on the cusp of being called a bad parent. Probably better he did most of the talking in the last half hour. I may have gotten surly.

When she swishes out the door, Wyatt embraces me, and my cheek rests on his chest. "Let's go see Haven."

"Thank you." I stare up at him.

"Christ, Ellie. You don't have to thank me. I'm the reason we're here."

"You're not. I understand why you think that, but you're not. We have to make sure nothing like this ever happens again. To any of the kids."

He steps away from me and thrusts his hands in his pockets. The gum rattles around. He's focused on something over my head, not meeting my eyes. "Are you sure about me, about us? I wouldn't blame you if you've changed your mind."

"Wyatt, I'm pregnant with your baby." Although he doesn't say it, our past hangs in the air between us. Being pregnant didn't stop me the last time.

"No. I want to be with you. I want us to be a family." Tears pool, blurring my vision. He tugs me to him again. "But I need us all to be safe."

"Tell me what you want me to do, Ellie, and I'll do it."

And so I do.

WYATT

PRESENT DAY

The crew brought us a round table and put it in Ellie's trailer. It's a tight squeeze. Ellie or her manager should have insisted on a bigger trailer in her contract. God knows they would have given it.

The table set-up won't satisfy Camila. Cramped. Too tight. When the arrangement spells conflict, conflict comes. Wouldn't matter how spacious we made Ellie's trailer. Conflict is coming.

My focus strays to the spot where Haven's tiny body lay, half dead. Over and over, the scene flashes in my memory. Facing Anna in here isn't going to be fun, but being here is a good reminder of what's at stake.

No kids are allowed in Ellie's trailer because the powdered fentanyl Anna's been peddling could be anywhere. Camila had a cleaning crew scrub everything from top to bottom while we were at the hospital, but I'm not taking any chances.

The asshole in me wants to finish this conversation quickly. I'll say whatever the hell I want to say—no more holding back.

Her addiction almost killed my daughter. But the brother in me worries this might be the last conversation I have with my sister. Anna came out of the womb a fiery, directionless mess. Even still, I love her. We've had each other's backs, one way or another, for a long time now.

I text Camila to say that everything is set, and then I take a seat at the back of the round table. From here, I can see the door, but when Camila and Anna get here, it'll make storming out in a rage impossible. That may be for the best, depending on what Anna says. Seeing this conversation through is the only way I get the future I want, and the one Jamal deserves.

Camila knocks and then enters without waiting for a reply. Anna follows. They take off their winter gear before joining me at the table. My hands are clasped in front of me. They're at war over whether to strangle Anna or hug her.

My sister quakes as though she can't control her own body, and she pulls the sleeves of her shirt over her fingertips. Perched on a chair, she's ready to dart away at any moment.

"I'm so sorry," Anna whispers. "Can I—I want to talk to Ellie too. I need to tell her how sorry I am."

With my jaw clenched, I stare at my clasped hands. A "sorry" isn't going to cut it this time. There aren't enough words in the world to balance out what happened to Haven.

"Wyatt, do you need a minute?" Camila asks.

"I'm not playing around anymore, Anna." With a last squeeze of my hands, I release them.

"Never thought you were playing before." She sneaks a sideways glance at me.

"Really?" My anger is barely in check. "Come on. For three years now, we've been doing this dance. You screw up, and I clean up the mess."

"I don't do it on purpose," Anna says.

I bob my head in agreement. Spoken like an addict. The language is one I understand. "I think part of you didn't believe you needed to get clean once you came to live with me. I got clean enough for the both of us."

Anna breaks our eye contact and tugs on the sleeves of her shirt again.

"Anna," Camila prompts.

"Jamal was safe with you."

"Was he safe with you?"

"What do you want me to say? Do you want me to tell you I'm a shitty mom? Is that what you want to hear?"

Ah, there it is. That's the Anna I've been expecting. Her words are blistering with fire.

"Anna," Camila says again.

"What? He can speak to me however he wants, but I can't say anything back?"

"Yeah," I say. "That's exactly what's happening today. I'm not pussyfooting around you anymore. You—your addiction, your irresponsibility—almost got my daughter killed."

"I didn't mean for Haven to get hurt. It was an accident."

"It's always an accident with you, isn't it? You're never to blame for anything."

"Wyatt," Camila breathes out my name in a rush.

This conversation could so easily spiral out of control. Other times we've talked, I avoided anything confrontational. Pissing Anna off wasn't worth the consequences. I wanted Anna to stay. Jamal needed to live with me, and I couldn't take over full-time custody. He needed a mother, even if she wasn't a good one. The situation and my life are different now with Ellie, Haven, and the baby. For the first time, I can offer him the stability Anna can't.

"Look." Camila holds up her hands. "You both need to calm down. Wyatt, you mentioned you had a plan."

"I do," I say.

"A plan," Anna scoffs. "As if I don't understand what that is. You can't have him. I'll fight to the death for Jamal. To *my* death."

"At this point, I have to do what's right for my family and what's right for Jamal. I'm going to make you an offer. If you ask me, it's pretty fucking generous considering what happened. You can thank Ellie for it later. It's more than I would have offered without her input."

Camila places her hand on mine. She takes one of Anna's too, stilling her jiggling motion.

"Anna," Camila says. "Are you ready to listen?"

Anna glares at her and then turns her stare on me. "You can't have him. I don't care what you offer me."

A humorless chuckle escapes me. "It'll be the difference between staying in his life and not being there at all. It should be an easy choice."

She tries to pull her hand out from Camila's grasp but can't manage it without throwing a fit. Pursing her lips, she rolls her eyes.

"Go ahead, Wyatt," Camila says.

"Ellie and I are taking Jamal to Bermuda with us when filming is over."

Anna opens her mouth to protest, but Camila shoots her a look. "Listen to him," she says.

"Ellie would like you to come too. We think it would be good for you to get away from the negative influences you've had in LA. We'll get you a house or apartment within walking distance of us."

"You want me to go to the island?" Anna's eyes narrow.

"That's what I said."

"I'll live there with Jamal?"

"That's not quite what I said." I hold up a hand. "Jamal will live with us. You'll be able to visit him whenever you want, as long as you're clean and sober. No drugs in our house, *ever*. The kids are not able to visit you at your house, *ever*. Ellie's mother is starting a new treatment center. You'll go there until you're dried out. Clean and sober. You'll go there every time you relapse—without question or complaint."

"Treatment plans don't work." Anna shakes her head.

"They don't when you keep giving up, that's true." I shrug. "I'm proof they *can* work."

"That was with Camila, though—"

"And clearly her methods haven't been successful for you. So what worked for me isn't going to work for you. Instead of ignoring the problem, we'll have to try something else." I take a deep breath. "I'm not giving up on you, Anna." Taking her hand from Camila's, I clasp both of Anna's hands in mine. "I'm not giving up on you." The brother in me is straining at the seams to save her.

"I don't think I'm worth saving," she whispers. "You're wasting your time. Everyone would be better off." There are tears in her eyes.

"Never." Standing up, I yank her into a hug, and I squeeze her tight. "Never. I'm never giving up on you. We're not better off without you. Jamal should know you, the real you." My voice is gruff when I say, "I love you, Anna. You're my sister. But I'm not propping you up anymore. I'm going to push you to get better. You're gonna hate me sometimes. We'll probably say terrible things to each other because I'm not backing off this time. Jamal deserves to have you, the best you, in his life, however long that takes."

"I don't want to lose my son." Anna sobs into my chest. "I can't lose him."

"You don't have to. We're not taking him. We'll look after him, give him stability, love him. When you're ready, when you're healthy, and you're good for him, he can come home to you."

She sobs into my chest, and I hold her tight. My heart aches. Three years ago, when she turned up with Jamal on my doorstep with Tanvi, I wasn't any better than her. We were lucky Jamal never bothered with our drugs. It helped that by the time he was walking, I decided one of us had to be clean and sober. Anna couldn't hold it together, so I had to.

"I'm not sure I can do this." Her words are garbled.

"One day at a time," I murmur into her hair. "We're all just going to take it one day at a time."

"I think this is a good direction, Anna." Over my sister's head, Camila winks at me. "It's a fresh start in a new place."

Anna sniffs and wipes her nose with the heel of her hand as she steps back from me. I pass her the tissue box off the table.

"Ellie hates me," Anna says. "I know she does."

Ellie doesn't like Anna when she's been using, but I don't think Ellie has ever met sober Anna. "When you let the person I know you can be shine through, she'll love you too. I know she will."

"Why would Ellie agree to this? You'd have done anything to keep her and to keep your family."

I sink back into my chair, and Anna does the same. "She loves me, Anna, and I love you," I say in a rusty voice. Saying those words out loud to someone else is cathartic somehow, like they're finally true. "She understands what it's like to be a mom, to love a child. She doesn't want to take that from you."

"I'm not a good mom." Her voice catches, and another sob threatens to escape. "But I do love him. I really do."

"I know you do. I never doubted that." I touch her shoulder.

Doubt isn't the right word for how I've felt watching her let Jamal down over and over. I wanted her love to be greater than her cravings, but she could never seem to get there.

"You're going with Camila to LA to pack up. Camila will escort you to Bermuda, where Evelyn, Ellie's mother, will be waiting. Together, you'll go to the treatment center, and you'll check yourself in. Once the movie finishes filming, we'll head back and have a place waiting for you to move into once you're released. Ellie and I are taking some time off work. We're sticking close to home. Help you. Get Jamal settled." A small smile escapes me. "Have the baby."

"You're happy." She scans my face and twists the tissue in her hand.

"I had a lot of regrets for a lot of years." I lean back in my chair, calm washing over me. "Never thought I'd get here—with Ellie, with kids, with everything somehow falling into place. So yeah, I'm going to soak in my stroke of luck. I'm going to let myself be happy. 'Cause not every day is going to be great. But right now, in this moment, I can't imagine wanting anything more than what I've got."

"I hope I can get better, see this through, stop feeling like I'm chasing happiness." Anna's voice is quiet, and she stares at the tissue she's holding.

Without an ounce of hesitation, I loop my arm around her shoulders. "We'll do everything we can to get you there. I promise," I whisper.

ELLIE

Two years later

I click the trigger on the lighter again and try to keep the flame going long enough to light the candles on the cake. Haven and Jamal helped me bake and decorate it while the baby napped. A surprise for Wyatt, but we didn't quite get the mess cleaned up before he got home from his volunteer shift at the rehab clinic.

Finally, the last candle is lit, and I pick up the cake to carry it into the dining room. When I come through the door, Haven starts up the "Happy Birthday" song with Anna, Jamal, my parents, and Nikki. Wyatt's broad grin matches that of our baby, Cooper Isaac, who is perched in the high chair beside him.

My heart overflows. Cooper's little voice carries a tune just as well as his father's. We sing a lot in this house, and Cooper knows "Happy Birthday" by heart. We've gotten so lucky to create this life together.

Placing the cake in front of Wyatt, I lean over and whisper, "Happy birthday." I press a kiss to his temple, and he tugs me into his lap, one arm wrapped around me as he blows out the candles.

Anna gazes at her son with adoration. She's been clean for the last five months, and it's the longest stretch we've had. I'm happy to admit Wyatt was right. Sober, clean Anna is a delight, much like her brother. There's still fire in her, but she knows when to use it. The last five months have helped strengthen her relationship with Jamal too.

"This looks professional." Wyatt nods at Jamal and Haven. "I'm impressed."

"I know you could do better, Dad. Don't patronize us," Haven says. The joys of a twelve-year-old. There is no end.

"Just because I *could* do better doesn't mean yours isn't good," Wyatt says.

"Okay, then." I clap my hands and scramble out of his lap. "White or chocolate? We got fancy, and there are two cake flavors under there. Though I'm not sure which end is which, so that'll be an adventure."

My parents laugh, and Nikki shakes her head. While I'm getting plates and cutlery from the kitchen, Wyatt wanders in. His arms circle around my waist, and he draws me against him in a tight embrace. I'll never complain about the expanse of his solid chest behind me. We've become a real team in a way we couldn't be before. I don't have to look after him—we take care of each other.

"Thank you," he murmurs across the top of my head.

I stop what I'm doing and lean into him. There is so much joy in me, I could run a marathon or dance a jig in the middle of town. Not every day is this great, but the ones that are make all the hard days worth the turmoil we went through.

Turning in his arms, I tilt my head upward and our lips meet. He lifts me onto the counter in a fluid motion, as though I weigh nothing. A move familiar to us both from other moments, once we're sure the kids are sleeping.

"Wyatt," I say against his lips. "Anyone could walk in."

"Let them. I'm enjoying my present." He threads his hands through my hair and kisses me again. "I missed you today."

"You see me every day." I give him another peck.

"Soon I won't." He reaches around me to gather the plates from the cupboard.

In ten days, I'm leaving for my first movie shoot since Cooper was born. Wyatt's not sure when he wants to go back to work. Not until a script moves him enough that he needs to do it more than he needs to be with us, at least. I miss working, so the first half-decent script I read when I was ready got the green light from me.

"You'll be okay with the kids by yourself?" We've had this discussion many times.

"How hard can it be?" Wyatt winks.

"I guess we'll see." I laugh.

"It might mean I have to come visit you a lot." He helps me off the counter.

"Not going to complain about that." I count the silverware and get a good knife to cut the cake. "But Tanvi's coming to help you for, what, six weeks?"

"Yeah." He squeezes my waist. "She can't be away from her grandbabies for too long. You know what she's like."

Warmth spreads across my chest at the memory of introducing her to Haven. And when she found out we blessed Cooper with Isaac for his middle name, she bawled.

"So . . ." Wyatt taps his fingers on the counter. "Did you actually bake the cake?"

I give him a gentle shove and shoot him a glare of pretend annoyance. "It came from a mix in a box. How badly could we have screwed up?"

"Grin and bear it." A playful smile tugs at the corners of his lips. "Got it."

Setting down the cutlery, I wrap my arms around Wyatt's neck. "Wanna know what the secret ingredient is?" I purr into his ear.

"Probably not."

I laugh and kiss his cheek. "You're no fun." My closeness is getting to him, and my body heats in response. Taking advantage of our small window of privacy, I press myself a little tighter.

"You're a tease." He kisses me under my ear.

"The best kind." The people in the next room could disappear for a while, and I wouldn't mind one bit.

"Oi," Nikki yells from the dining room. "Is Wyatt in there cooking something else?"

"Just warming up my dessert," Wyatt calls back.

"Dad." Haven's voice drips with preteen annoyance. "That's disgusting."

Wyatt's eyes widen.

"Yeah," I say. "She got your joke."

"We're there already?"

"It goes quickly." I gather the plates off the counter. "We just have to remember to be grateful for what we have."

From behind me, as we exit the kitchen, Wyatt says, "Believe me, there is no man alive more grateful than me."

THE END

I hope you enjoyed the story. Bonus chapters and other exclusive content is available when you sign up for my newsletter: wendymillion.com

ACKNOWLEDGM

This book has been through a few different drafts, but I truly believe this one is the best. Deanna McFadden, I appreciated your guidance and patience as I molded Wyatt and Ellie's narrative into something I'm really proud to say I wrote. Thank you for all your help.

Thank you to the rest of the editing, typesetting, and cover creation team of Rebecca Sands, Rebecca Mills, Sarah Howden, Misha Dyer, and Ashley Santoro. It's been a pleasure to be part of the Wattpad Books team.

To all my Wattpad followers who have read and loved this story—thank you for taking a chance on me. It's been a joy to read your comments, see your votes, and receive your messages over the last few years. I hope, if you've read the story before, this version speaks to your heart in the same way. #Wyllieforever

Thanks to my dad and my husband, who are used to me dropping everything to read over edits. You're very patient when my body is here on Earth but my mind is off in another world with other people. I love you both so much.

Thanks to Brenda and Brian Lenzin, Gwen Doak, Al and Wanda Smith, Lynn and Larry Million, and my brother, Richard, and his wife, Lucie, who purchase my books with enthusiasm. It's a joy to be so supported.

A special thanks to my girls for their understanding when I'm sitting at the computer when they'd rather I was hanging out with them. I hope you're learning what it looks like to be passionate about something and to pursue your goals with your whole heart.

Thanks to my agent, Amy Brewer, for always looking out for my best interests. You're a gem.

Thank you to two other Wattpad writers who have navigated this writing experience with me and who I know I can always message for support. Avery Keelan and Cole Lepley—my writing world would be a lot less fun without you both.

I started this book on Wattpad back in 2017, after having been on the platform for less than a year. It's the book that helped me get my agent, the one my husband loves best, the one that earned me the coveted Watty Award, the one that spurred so many people to follow me, and the one that's landed me here, at Wattpad Books. I'll be forever grateful to this novel because it feels like the one that really made me believe I could write.

Also by Wendy Million

The Donaghey Brothers Series (Romantic Suspense)

Retribution

Resurrection

Redemption

Northern University Series (NA Sports Romance)

Saving Us

Fake Crown (straddles both Northern University and the Bellerive Royals)

With Wattpad Books (Second Chance Romance)

When Stars Fall
Miss Matched (coming 2023)
Novella (free with newsletter signup)

First Date Challenge
As W. MIllion – The Bellerive Royals Series
Fake Crown
Scarred Crown
Heavy Crown
Fallen Crown

ABOUT WENDY MILLION

Wendy Million is a Watty Award winner whose contemporary romances about strong women and troubled men have captivated her loyal readers. She is the author of the romantic suspense series *The Donaghey Brothers,* the NA sports romance *Saving Us,* and the contemporary second chance romance, *When Stars Fall*.

Writing as W. Million, she has the contemporary new adult royal romance series, the *Bellerive Royals*.

When not writing, Wendy enjoys spending time in or around the water. She lives in Ontario, Canada with two beautiful daughters, two cute pooches, and one handsome husband (who is grateful she doesn't need two of those).

www.ingramcontent.com/pod-product-compliance
Lightning Source LLC
Chambersburg PA
CBHW050848210726
48290CB00004B/1142